“Why do you hide from me?”
he said, his voice filled with torment.

She wasn’t hiding from him now. It was as if his rough touch, the rawness of his need, ripped open something inside of her and all the fear and uncertainty of the last few days, the desire she had tried so hard to suppress, broke free and flew out into the world.

She couldn’t think anymore, couldn’t remember; she could only feel. Feel what Aidan was doing to her, how he made all her senses flare into a burning life she didn’t even know existed. The fear was still there, hovering just at the edge of her consciousness like a black shadow, but she pushed it away.

Aidan’s mouth took hers, and as his tongue plunged inside she could taste the darkness in him, the lust, the primitive need that drove away everything else. She felt the hidden shadows of his soul that called out to hers.

They both hid from the world in their own ways. But now, for this one fleeting moment, they were free together.

Praise for Laurel McKee's

THE DAUGHTERS OF ERIN TRILOGY

Lady of Seduction

"As powerful and romantic as McKee's fans could desire. McKee shows readers she is a force to be reckoned with, an author who can turn a villain into a delicious hero. The action, romance, suspense, and intriguing historical details all add to readers' pleasure." —*RT Book Reviews*

"Book three in the Daughters of Erin Trilogy is riveting, exciting, and oh, so romantic... Readers will love this page-turner!" —RomRevToday.com

"5 stars! Had me hooked from the start... I absolutely loved this story." —SeducedbyaBook.com

"The third of this thrilling Irish series by Laurel McKee left me with no doubt that this series is truly a winner. McKee is able to spin an Irish tale like no other romance writer I have read before... [She] sweeps the reader away on a fantastical and romantic journey through old Ireland." —FreshFiction.com

"The story of Caroline and Grant's love is unexpected and romantic. Historical romance readers will devour it. Laurel McKee does a splendid job of continuing the series and will have readers coming back for more."

—NightOwlReviews.com

"A great concluding tale to the Daughters of Erin series... McKee writes spectacular love scenes for her characters in this novel that leave you breathless... [She] pens a lush and fabulous historical romance that will steal your heart and make you smile." —TheSeasonforRomance.com

"Stellar writing, a charismatic hero, and fearless heroine, an amazing blend of suspense, action, and romance, *Lady of Seduction* will entice, exasperate, and enchant readers without mercy... [The characters'] journeys have been unforgettable and their happily-ever-afters rewarding beyond expectations. As a devoted fan, I look forward to whatever stories come next. Laurel McKee books are automatic 'Must Buys.'"

—RomanceJunkiesReviews.com

"Fast-paced... an exciting thriller starring a courageous heroine and a man seeking redemption even if it means his life... Fans of the series will marvel at Laurel McKee's talent... Sub-genre fans will enjoy the entire well-written trilogy." —*Midwest Book Review*

Duchess of Sin

"4 Stars! Fascinating... readers will be eager to read the final story in McKee's trilogy." —*RT Book Reviews*

"For a thrilling, sensuous trip to old Ireland, don't miss *Duchess of Sin*... I recommend reading the first book, and I look forward to *Lady of Seduction*."

—RomRevToday.com

"A truly remarkable book that I could not turn away from... a one-of-a-kind read [with] a love to warm the heart and an adventure that never ends"

—FreshFiction.com

Countess of Scandal

"My kind of story!"

—Mary Balogh, *New York Times* bestselling author

"An unforgettable love story... captivating and poignant! Laurel McKee wields her pen with grace and magic."

—Lorraine Heath, *New York Times* bestselling author of *Midnight Pleasures with a Scoundrel*

"4 Stars! McKee sets the stage for a romantic adventure that captures the spirit of Ireland and a pair of star-crossed lovers to perfection." —*RT Book Reviews*

"I am completely hooked on this series already—and I was from nearly the first page of this book! Ms. McKee tells a masterful story of love, rebellion, and beneath it all, devotion to a land and people... Elizabeth and Will's emotional attachment, as well as the obvious physical chemistry they share, leaps from the page."

—RomanceReaderatHeart.com

"Ms. Laurel McKee's magical pen captivates you instantaneously! She has fashioned blistering, sensual, romantic scenes and a love story that will be forever etched in your mind." —TheRomanceReadersConnection.com

"Eliza's and Will's happy-ever-after, once reached, is both powerfully satisfying and forever engraved on the reader's mind and heart. Every word sings with unyielding intensity... Beautifully written, *Countess of Scandal* reads like a captivating love story of epic proportions. The ultimate page-turner." —RomanceJunkies.com

"A hero to steal your heart!"

—Elizabeth Boyle,
New York Times bestselling author

"An immensely satisfying and sophisticated blend of history and romance. I loved every gorgeous, breathtaking page!"

—Julianne MacLean, *USA Today* bestselling
author of *When a Stranger Loves Me*

"*Countess of Scandal* delivers on all fronts. The story raced along, zigging and zagging from Dublin to the countryside, from uneasy peace to all-out war. And the romance... very satisfying!" —MyShelf.com

"A vivid historical tale with breathtaking characters."

—Michelle Willingham, author of
Taming Her Irish Warrior

"Rich, vivid, and passionate."

—Nicola Cornick,
USA Today bestselling author of
The Undoing of a Lady

ALSO BY LAUREL McKEE

The Daughters of Erin

Countess of Scandal
Duchess of Sin
Lady of Seduction

One Naughty Night

LAUREL McKEE

FOREVER

NEW YORK BOSTON

Forever
Hachette Book Group
237 Park Avenue
New York, NY 10017

www.HachetteBookGroup.com

Printed in the United States of America

OPM

First Edition: June 2012
10 9 8 7 6 5 4 3 2 1

Forever is an imprint of Grand Central Publishing.
The Forever name and logo are trademarks of Hachette Book Group, Inc.

One Naughty Night

From Mary St. Claire Huntington's Diary

March 1665…

I have always thought my sister to be the romantic soul in our family. She is constantly devouring volumes of French poetry and wandering the woods sighing over their beautiful words of soul-deep love and flights of two hearts beating as one. She has always declared me a terrible bore, concerned only with prosaic, everyday reality! Concerned with running our father's house and trying to keep our family together amid the long war between king and parliament and all the troubles that followed.

I only ever laughed at her teasing. I was quite sure it was far better to be dull and content with everyday matters than to long for romantic dreams that can never be. But I was very wrong. Horribly, wonderfully wrong. For I have met him.

Prologue

London, 1841

It was a complete disaster.

Lily St. Claire ran down the red-carpeted stairs of the Majestic Theater and through the gilded, near-empty lobby. A few people lingered there on the velvet banquettes or at the mirrored bar, sipping champagne. But most were in their seats and their fine boxes, savoring her ruin.

The long, pleated silk and muslin skirts of her Juliet costume wrapped around her legs, and she stumbled. Even the costume seemed to be against her tonight. She snatched her skirts up in great handfuls, crushing the fine fabric, and kept running.

Lily burst out the doors and onto the marble steps that led to the theater. Earlier that evening, when her nervous hopes were still alive, carriages had deposited their owners at the foot of those same steps. Ladies in fur-trimmed cloaks and gentlemen in top hats had flowed up them, all of society come to see a new William St. Claire production.

"It is sure to be excellent," they said to each other. "His *As You Like It* last season was marvelous. A triumph!"

Her adopted father's Shakespeare productions were always a triumph, year after year, even in the crowded London theatrical scene. They paid for the Majestic and helped with all the St. Claires' many business operations, both respectable and not so much. But *As You Like It* had starred William's wife, Katherine St. Claire, a glittering star of the stage, in her farewell performance as Rosalind.

He had not been so careful in his casting of *Romeo and Juliet.*

"What a fool I was," Lily whispered. After her youthful life in the back alleys of London, she had thought she could never feel foolish again, especially over mere play-acting, but here she was. She hurried down the steps and around the side of the building, hoping to find a hiding place before the audience departed. They were all watching the farce that always followed the main play, but that would be over soon and everyone would be leaving the theater. She didn't want to hear their comments.

In his own gentle way, her father had told her that she was not yet ready for a lead role. "You learned so much as Bianca in *The Taming of the Shrew* last year, my dear," he said when she pressed him about Juliet. "Perhaps one more season would help prepare you..."

But no. Stubborn fool that she was, she had insisted that all her acting lessons, all her years of watching the St. Claires since they adopted her when she was nine, were enough. She was ready to be a real actress.

To be a real St. Claire.

But as soon as she stepped onto the stage, with the lights dazzling her eyes and the Renaissance velvet costume weighing her down, she froze. She could not remember her lines or her blocking, could not even remember her character's name. Only when the actress playing the nurse grabbed her hand hard and mumbled her first lines into her ear had she remembered.

After that she stumbled through the play like a numb, terrified fawn, the whole thing a horrifying blur. She didn't know how she ever made it to the end.

It was certainly not the most terrible thing that had ever happened to her, Lily thought as she kicked out at a pile of crates stacked by the wall. Pain shot through her toes. No, freezing up onstage was nothing to watching her mother die of opium addiction or starving and picking pockets on the streets of Whitechapel, as she had all her life before the St. Claires took her in. It wasn't like being caught by the wrong people at the wrong time.

But the St. Claires *had* saved her from all that, had raised her as their own, educated her, fed her, clothed her. Loved her. That made this failure even worse. It wasn't just *her* failure—it brought them down too.

The Majestic was her father's great dream. He had fought so hard for it and worked so much to make it a success. And she, with her foolish self-confidence and her stubbornness, had ruined its season opening.

Lily made her way through the maze of loading docks behind the theater, where scenery and crates of costumes were unloaded. Usually the stagehands hid there for a quick smoke or nip of gin, away from Katherine St. Claire's sharp eyes, but tonight the docks were deserted.

She dropped heavily onto a wooden bench, letting her skirts fall around her. She dragged her veiled cap from her head and shook out her heavy brown hair.

"I suppose I'll have to marry Harry Nichols now," she said, and shivered. Harry had been a most persistent suitor lately, and he was a prosperous one with his greengrocer stores and house in Piccadilly. He was also handsome enough in a florid way and well mannered.

But there was something in his eyes when he looked at her that she did not like.

"Now, that would be a shame," a deep, brandy-smooth voice said from the shadows.

Lily leaped from the bench and whirled around. It was so dark that at first she couldn't see anything at all. She could only hear the soft sound of breathing, the slight brush of fine wool fabric.

Her body grew tense and alert, every instinct from her childhood in the slums rushing back over her.

She had become weak in recent years, letting her guard down, not paying attention to every aspect of her surroundings. In Whitechapel, she would have been dead minutes ago.

"Who is there?" she called. Her hands curled into fists as she scanned the dock. "Show yourself!"

A man stepped from the shadows, his hands up, palms out. A lit cheroot was held between his lips, which curled in an infuriatingly amused smile. He didn't look like a Whitechapel creeper. He was tall and leanly muscled, dressed in a well-cut evening coat of dark blue wool and a cream-colored silk waistcoat. A simply tied crisp white cravat looped about his neck, skewered with a sapphire stickpin.

Lily stepped back to study him closer. He *was* handsome, she had to admit—almost absurdly so, as if he were a painting or a sculpture. His hair, a deep, glossy mahogany brown, swept back from his face in waves to tumble over his collar. His face was all sharp, aristocratic planes, with bladelike cheekbones, a straight nose, and a square jaw with the tiniest dimple set just above it. His eyes were very, very blue, almost glowing, set off by smooth olive skin and a shadow of dark whiskers along his jaw.

He didn't look like a criminal, lurking about to rob unsuspecting theatergoers. But Lily knew very well how appearances were deceptive. After all, didn't she appear to be a lady now—even if she was not a Shakespearean actress? In reality, deep down, she was still just that street urchin, daughter of a whore.

The man slowly plucked the cheroot from between his lips and held it between his thumb and forefinger as he exhaled a plume of smoke. It wreathed around his head, making him look like a demon emerging from hell. A handsome Mephistopheles sent to tempt her.

"Are you going to call for a constable to arrest me?" he asked.

"What are you doing here?" Lily demanded.

He held up the cheroot. "Just having a quick smoke. I don't much care for farces."

Or for pitifully bad productions of Shakespeare? She dared not ask. She watched as he dropped the cheroot and carefully extinguished it under his polished evening shoe.

"I'm not here to start a fire, I promise," he said with an enticing grin. "Or to accost young ladies fleeing from Verona."

"No," Lily said. A sudden weariness washed over her, as if the whole long, awful evening had caught up to her. She sat back down on the bench. "I don't suppose you are. And this is a good place to hide from farces."

"And from my mother," he said. "She *does* enjoy farces,

which may be why she's always trying to introduce me to blasted 'eligible females.' "

Lily had to laugh at the wry tone of his voice. She imagined "eligible females" chased him down wherever he went. She still wasn't sure about him—he was a stranger, after all, even if he was unearthly handsome. She knew better than to trust any man. But she was suddenly glad not to be alone.

He was as good a distraction as any.

She slid over on the bench in silent invitation, and he sat down next to her. He didn't touch her, but the bench was small, and he was close enough that she could feel the heat from his body. He smelled delicious, of some spicy cologne, expensive soap, and something wonderfully dark that was only him. She had to resist the urge to bury her head in his shoulder and just inhale him, as if he were a drug that could make her forget.

"So you have to marry too?" she said.

"Someday, I suppose." He took a small silver flask from inside his coat and unstoppered it before holding it out to her in silent invitation.

Lily cautiously sniffed it. Brandy, and very good stuff too. She took a long sip and handed it back. He also drank, and she watched in fascination as his strong throat moved above the cravat.

"But," he continued, "I am luckily not promised to this Harry Nichols, whoever he might be. The name alone sounds appalling."

Lily laughed. The warm smoothness of the brandy—and his close presence—seemed to be working its spell on her. "He's not so bad, I suppose. There are surely worse fates than to be Mrs. Nichols, queen of the greengrocers."

"But there must be better ones as well."

She thought of her wretched failure as an actress, her lack of skills in anything else except keeping accounts. She *was* rather good at numbers, but that held little appeal next to her glamorous brothers and sisters. "Not for me, I think."

He shrugged and put away the flask. "We all have to do what we must."

"Yes," Lily said. "And what do *you* do?"

"Not much at all," he answered with a laugh. "To the despair of my father. I left Oxford last year and have been adrift ever since."

"What does your father want you to do, then?"

"Go into the church or, failing that, the army. But he prefers the church, as he has a rather valuable living to bestow and it would get me out of the way."

Lily laughed at the image of this obviously rakish young man giving a sermon in black robes. His female parishioners would be wildly distracted, fainting in the aisle and cornering him in the vestibule. "You? A vicar?"

"Exactly so. You see, we have only just met, and you see the folly of such a scheme. My father is harder to persuade."

Lily shook her head. "The church is a most respectable profession."

"And as such, it deserves a respectable practitioner."

"And that isn't you?"

"Certainly not. I also have the chance to try my hand at some business in the West Indies, which would probably suit me much better."

His choices were the church or the tropics? Lily kicked at the hem of her costume as she thought about the suffocating expectations of other people, of the world at large. How they pressed in on all sides, no matter if you lived in a palace or a hovel.

"What would you do if you could do anything at all?" she asked.

He studied her closely, and for just a moment his careless, rakish demeanor fell away, and he looked older and far more serious. His blue eyes darkened.

"I would write plays, I suppose," he said.

Lily was surprised. She didn't know what she had expected him to say, but it wasn't that. "Write plays?"

His smile came back, like a mask dropping back into place. "You're astonished."

"Of course not. I completely understand anyone falling in love with the theater." She thought again of all her hopes for the stage—and the way they crashed down around her. "It just doesn't always love you back."

She suddenly felt a gentle touch on her hand and looked down to see his fingers against hers, his hand large and dark on her pale skin, his fingers long and elegant. She usually didn't like men touching her; it brought back the old, terrible memories. But with him, she didn't want to pull away at all.

"It was only your first night," he said. "I'm sure even Richard Burbage suffered stage fright at his debut. Who wouldn't when faced with Shakespeare? The next time will be very different."

Lily shook her head. Her cheeks burned to think that he, of all people, witnessed tonight's debacle. And now he tried to comfort her! "There won't be a next time, not for me. At least you will not have to speak your lines right there in front of everyone once you have written them."

"But I would have to give them into the hands of others and let them go," he said. "I'm not sure I have that much trust in me."

"I'm quite sure I wouldn't," Lily said. "It is very hard for me to trust at all."

"Yet you've talked to me, a stranger, tonight."

She smiled up at him. "You're rather easy to talk to. Maybe it's because you're a stranger."

"Odd. I was thinking the same about you... Juliet." He raised her hand to his lips and pressed a soft kiss to the back of her fingers.

His lips were warm, soft and hard at the same time, and their touch made a strange, sparkling haze drop over her. As she watched, fascinated, he turned her hand over in his and pressed an openmouthed kiss at the center of her palm. The tip of his tongue then touched the pulse that beat at her wrist, and she shivered.

Lily laid her other hand on his bent head and felt the rough silk of his hair under her touch. If she had to marry Harry Nichols, to spend her life in the real world of shops and streets and housework, didn't she deserve this one moment out of time? This one kiss with a sinfully handsome stranger who seemed to banish her fears with just a touch?

He took her in his arms and drew her close, until there was not even a particle of light between them. "Juliet," he whispered, and his mouth met hers in a hungry kiss.

Lily met him eagerly, holding tightly to his shoulders to keep from falling. His kiss made her feel just like that, as if she were tumbling through the night sky among the flashing stars.

His tongue pressed past her lips to touch and tangle

with hers. He tasted of brandy and mint, hot and delicious, and he was such a *good* kisser. Lily had never been kissed like this, never felt like this before. She curled her hands into the front of his coat and felt his heart pounding against her.

He groaned, a deep, echoing sound, and his lips slid from hers to press against the side of her neck. He kissed that soft, sensitive spot just below her ear, nipping it lightly with his teeth and then soothing it with the touch of his tongue. His breath brushed warmly over her skin.

"Lily!" someone called out, pulling her abruptly back down to the hard, cold earth. "Lily, are you out here?"

It was her mother, her voice filled with worry. And she was getting closer.

Lily tore herself out of the stranger's arms and leaped to her feet. She swayed dizzily, but when he reached out for her again, she stumbled back. "I...I have to go," she whispered.

He stood up beside her, not trying to touch her again. His blue eyes glowed in the shadows. "Where can I find you?" he said hoarsely.

She shook her head. He was a dream—and she had to wake up now. She whirled around and ran away from him, lifting her skirts to flee once again.

"Wait! Please," he called after her. But she didn't dare look back.

Chapter One

London, Three Years Later

"You see, Lily, it's the perfect place for sin."

Lily St. Claire Nichols leaned back on the seat of the open carriage as it came to a halt, staring up at the building from under the brim of her fashionable satin and net bonnet. It was a very handsome structure, to be sure, four stories elegantly built in the uniform white stone of Mayfair. Polished marble front steps led up to a glossy black-painted door, and there were lots of gleaming windows to reflect the pearl-gray London sky behind their discreet velvet draperies. It blended perfectly with its genteel neighbors.

But *sinful*? She had seen lots of places much better suited to that.

"If you say so, Dominic," she said with a laugh. "But I would have thought it the perfect place for drinking tea and playing the pianoforte."

"Ah, sister dear, as usual you have no imagination," Dominic said. As he leaped down from the carriage to the flagstone walkway, two passing young ladies paused to watch him, giggling and blushing under their fringed parasols.

Lily bit her lip to keep from laughing. It was always thus with Dominic—his golden, Apollo-like good looks, combined with the natural flamboyance of the St. Claires made it utterly impossible to look away from him. He always exuded energy and good cheer, a glow that drew people in, just as their famous parents and her siblings did. When the St. Claires were all together, they nearly obliterated the sun.

Where Lily, only an adopted St. Claire, contented herself with her brown hair, a sensible nature that kept her wilder siblings from too much trouble, and their reflected glory. Someone had to be a practical Athena to their Dionysian revels, to keep track of the accounts and organize their businesses. She liked keeping to the shadows, especially after her one disastrous moment in the theatrical sun three years ago.

She was done with the spotlight. Now she had a new task—to help her brother Dominic with his latest venture: a fashionable, luxurious gambling club right in the heart of Mayfair. It seemed a good plan. Aristocrats often had deep pockets and longed for decadent but discreet ways to empty them. The St. Claires were good at helping them with that task.

It seemed like a good place for Lily to start over too. Her husband had been dead for a year now. It was time to move on, to forget the past.

"Thanks to you, Dominic, I have plenty of imagination," she said as he helped her alight from the carriage. She looped her gloved hand through his arm and went with him up the gleaming steps. Despite her caution, she felt a bright spark of excitement deep inside. She had a good feeling about this place.

"It's a very pretty house in a fine neighborhood," she went on. "But how will anyone even know to come here and gamble their money away? It's not the most obvious."

"That's the very point! If we want to attract dukes and earls, we have to be discreet and very exclusive. They won't want the queen to know what they're up to." Dominic drew a shining brass key from inside his fine, blue wool coat. "We will have a small brass sign here on the door along with a demon's head knocker. 'The Devil's Fancy—Members Only.' And, of course, there will be a very strict and respectable butler to man the door."

"I'm glad you've thought of everything, even a dramatic name," Lily said, stepping inside. She blinked at the sudden, dark shadows after the bright day. "And where will these members, these dukes and earls, come from?"

"Nothing easier, Lily, as you well know. You're the one with the brain for accounting, after all. Our investors will drop hints among their friends. The word will spread through the ballrooms and the gentlemen's clubs. Everyone will want to join."

Lily untied her bonnet and swept it off to get a better look at the surroundings. She had to admit it was impressive. The foyer, with white and gold walls and elaborate wedding-cake plasterwork, soared upward to a domed ceiling painted with a fresco of a classical gods' feast against a bright, blue sky. A winding staircase with a fine wrought-iron balustrade led to the public rooms above, while just beyond she glimpsed a small room that could be the office of that stern butler.

She could picture liveried footmen greeting their guests

with glasses of champagne, could hear the rustle of lacy crinoline skirts, laughter, and chatter floating along those stairs. The whir of a roulette wheel, the clink of coins.

"You have investors, then?" she said. "Rich ones?"

"You always do get right to the point, don't you, Lily?"

Certainly she did. The stink of the streets, where she spent her childhood picking pockets and scrounging to survive until the St. Claires rescued her, was never far enough away. Even here in elegant Mayfair.

"Investors?" she said again.

"Of course, with Brendan's help." Their brother Brendan was magical with people—they could never say no to him. Odd, since he always seemed the strong, silent type, the sort of man no one could fathom. So different from Dominic. "Just a few so far, but very desirable ones. Viscount Brownville. Sir Archibald Overton. Lady Smythe. Even a duke's nephew, perhaps. Brendan was a bit secretive about that one."

"All those? How did Brendan reel them in?"

"They know a good investment when they see one." Dominic propped his booted foot on the lowest marble step, his handsome, smiling face suddenly darkening. "Maybe with one duke, we could lure Carston to invest here as well. Take a chunk of his ill-gotten gains."

The Duke of Carston. The Huntington family. It always came back to them. That high-in-the-instep ducal family always darkened every St. Claire moment of triumph. They hung over everything due to the old legend of the way they once ruined the St. Claires.

Lily gently laid her hand on Dominic's arm. She wasn't about to let Carston, or anyone, ruin this, her new beginning. "Show me the upstairs rooms."

He nodded and led her up the stairs, their footsteps echoing in the luxurious, empty space. Off the landing were three beautiful salons, shimmering with more white and gold. There were vast, elaborately carved marble fireplaces and tall windows draped in pale yellow brocade and velvet trimmed in heavy tassels and fringe.

"This can be the main gaming salon," Dominic said eagerly, his dark mood seemingly forgotten. "And over there a ballroom and a dining room."

Lily laughed. "Dining and dancing too?"

"Of course! A French chef, a fine orchestra..."

"It's a good thing we have rich investors, then."

"And we'll soon have more. Our investment will be returned many times over, Lily. You'll see." Dominic strode through the empty rooms, throwing back the draperies to let in the daylight. "I will order all the gaming supplies, but you must be in charge of hiring the staff and buying the furnishings. The most fashionable of everything."

Even as she calculated exactly how much "the most fashionable of everything" would cost, Lily couldn't deny that her brother's excitement was infectious. It would certainly be a splendid establishment. And with dukes and viscounts as their customers, leading the way for London's elite to come trooping to their doors, their fortune would be made.

Lily eased back one of the draperies to peer down at the street below. As she did so, she caught a glimpse of herself in the glass pane, a ghostly reflection of her pale face against the satin bow that tied her jacket collar. She sighed at the sight.

Despite her fine, blue velvet jacket and plaid silk skirt,

she was surely nothing out of the ordinary. A pigeon among the golden St. Claire peacocks, with brown hair and eyes, of middling height, and too thin for fashion.

"It's a good thing you can afford fine clothes," she murmured wryly. And that she had a stylish mother to help her choose them. Katherine St. Claire was known as one of the most fashionable women in London, and she loved advising her daughters. It helped Lily pretend, for a while at least, that she belonged here.

Lily unlatched the window and threw it open so she wouldn't have to look at herself any longer. The cool, fresh breeze of clean air, untainted by the smoke and muck of poorer neighborhoods, carried away the stale stuffiness of the salon. The prospect outside was as pretty as the one inside, with a green, shady park across the tidy street. Well-dressed people strolled there, ladies in crinolines and feathered bonnets on the arms of men in frock coats and gleaming silk hats, children with their hoops and wagons ushered by starchy black-clad nannies. Their laughter and bright clothes were like beacons in the gray day.

How pretty it all was, how fine and hopeful. How different from where she grew up on the streets of Whitechapel...

Suddenly a high, open carriage turned the corner and came flying down the street, scattering all the fine, placid people. It was painted bright yellow with green wheels and was pulled by a matched pair of bay horses. If the walkers were like beacons, this was like the entire sun. Lily leaned farther out the window to get a better view.

The carriage held only one passenger, the man who wielded the reins. He wore a brown velvet coat and brown wool trousers, a beautiful pearl-gray waistcoat, and a finely tied cravat—well cut and fashionable like his carriage but not too elaborate. He wore no hat, and she had a glimpse of his face and his glossy, dark brown hair as he passed.

"Oh, good heavens," she gasped. It was *him*—the man she met after her disastrous stage debut. It had been almost three years, but she had not forgotten a single detail of his face. She had thought never to see him again, sure he would appear to her only in her dreams.

Yet here he was, driving right past her. And he was even more handsome than she remembered, his face all elegant, sculpted angles, bronzed skin, and slashing dark brows. Surely his cheekbones alone could cut glass—or a woman's heart.

He looked up as he passed, laughing as if in deep sensual pleasure at his speed. His blue eyes, blue as the sea and sky, seemed to pierce through her even at such a distance. He raised one gloved hand to wave at her, his grin widening, and she drew back from the window as she tried to resist the urge to dive to the floor.

Her cheeks felt suddenly warm, and she pressed her palms against them. A sparkling excitement seemed to flutter deep inside her, and she wanted to giggle like some silly schoolgirl.

She had never been a schoolgirl of any sort, and she wasn't going to start now. Not even over the handsome god of her former dreams. Surely the disillusionment of her marriage had killed off any such foolishness?

"What do you see out there, Lily?" Dominic asked. He pushed past her to peer outside.

"Nothing at all," Lily said, cursing the silly breathlessness of her voice. "Just a pleasant morning."

Suddenly Dominic pounded his fist on the windowsill. His shoulders stiffened. "Damn it all! What is he doing here?"

"Who?" Lily leaned past him, wondering which blameless pedestrian had earned her brother's anger.

"Him, of course." Dominic gestured toward the yellow carriage, clattering away out of sight. "Don't you know him?"

A chill swept over Lily, driving away the last of her warm blush. Of course, it would be him Dominic hated. "No. Should I?"

"It's Lord Aidan Huntington," Dominic said, with what sounded suspiciously like a growl. "Son of the Duke of Carston."

"No! That can't be possible." Lily leaned out the window again, but he was gone from sight. She still saw him in her mind, though, that roguish smile, the glossy gleam of his hair. That sensual mouth she remembered kissing all too well.

How could her dream man be a Huntington, a member of that despised family? She felt numb and so cold, caught up in a dream turned nightmare.

"He's the duke's second son, and a greater rake you'll never find in London. He's nothing but trouble." Dominic pulled Lily back into the room and slammed the window shut. The glass rattled ominously.

"That's rich coming from you, Dominic," she said. "I thought *you* were the greatest rake in London. Just because he's a Huntington—"

Dominic caught her arm and gave her a little shake. "Just being a Huntington makes him trouble! They are all liars and cheats who care for nothing but their own lofty titles. They utterly ruined us once before—they would do it again without so much as a blink."

Lily had heard all this for years, ever since she became a St. Claire, and she surely hated anyone her family hated. The St. Claires did have good cause to despise the Huntingtons. But she also remembered the kindness in Aidan Huntington's eyes on that long-ago night, the sweet desire that rose up in her at his kiss. Could he truly be as black-souled as the rest of his family?

Of course he could. All men had the seeds of cruelty deep inside; she had learned that hard lesson over and over in her life. Even ones who hid behind a handsome face.

Maybe especially those.

Lily turned away from Dominic to rearrange the draperies. Now that her dream man was all too real, now that he had a name—and a hated name at that—she had to let him go. Harden her heart entirely even to his memory.

"We have far too much to do to involve ourselves in quarrels," Lily said, forcing herself to laugh. "Now, tell me more about these fashionable furnishings I must look for..."

Chapter Two

"I'm glad to see you haven't completely forgotten your duty to your family, Aidan," the Duke of Carston growled. He waved his walking stick menacingly at the hapless footmen who tried to help him maneuver his wheeled chair into the drawing room. "Your mother was sure you could never pull yourself away from your disreputable pursuits to visit us. We've been in town for a fortnight now."

"Perhaps if you'd let me know of your arrival, I might have ceased my disreputable pursuits and spared you an hour earlier," Aidan said lightly. He leaned lazily against the marble mantel, arms crossed over his chest as he watched his father being lifted onto a brocade settee. The servants fluttered about like a mad flock of crows bearing tea and blankets. The duke shooed them all away with his stick.

Aidan couldn't help but grin at the sight. *The old rascal.* Even riddled with gout, he terrorized everyone. No wonder Aidan and his brother stayed away whenever they could. The damnably hot months Aidan spent in the West Indies were bearable because it was very, very far away.

"If you were doing your duty and going about in good society, you would have known we were here," the duke said. "Your mother's friends say you refuse all their invitations."

"Because their balls and musicales and such are decidedly dull, Father, as you well know after years of enduring them. I have work to do."

"Work!" The duke gave a loud snort. "What sort of work d'you mean? Losing money at cards? Racing your blasted carriage? Chasing loose women?"

Aidan laughed. Yes, he did all of that on occasion—but he wasn't about to tell his father about his real work. As much as the duke disliked dissipation, he would hate Aidan's true passion even more. "A gentleman never tells, Father."

"Gentleman? Humph!" The duke sat back on his settee and waved at the chair across from him. "Sit down already. You're making my neck hurt staring up at you."

Aidan sat down, propping one booted foot on the low end table despite his father's fierce frown. His mother had recently redecorated in the new "Scottish" style, with tartan taffeta draperies at the windows, plaid-edged carpets, and gewgaws on every surface. Aidan had to be careful not to knock over any vases or statuettes.

"You're right enough that those parties are dull as tombs," the duke said. "But your mother wants you to go and meet her friends' daughters. She's been pining for grandchildren since you returned from the West Indies."

Aidan laughed. Was that what this official visit was all about? Settling down, begetting little Huntingtons? He wasn't ready for that yet, not by a mile. He was not yet thirty. And all those daughters, who paraded before him every time he dared show his face in a ballroom, were a lot of brainless gigglers trussed up in pink ruffles.

For an instant, another image flashed in his mind, of a different lady altogether. The woman who stood at the window of the house that was to let as he drove past. He had caught only a glimpse of her, a pale, heart-shaped face and shining brown hair. She was so still and serene-looking—until her white cheeks turned pink at his bold wave.

There was something so oddly familiar about her. He felt like he should know her, remember her, but the memory was just frustratingly out of reach. He only knew he had to find her again and discover who she was.

"Are you listening to me, Aidan?" his father barked.

Aidan glanced up to see his father sneakily pouring a tot of brandy into his tea. "Mother will be furious if she catches you with that. Didn't the doctor say no brandy?"

"We aren't talking about me, you impudent boy! We are talking about *you*, and your refusal to do your duty."

"You'll have to leave all that heir business to David. He's your firstborn, the future duke and all that. I don't care to marry yet."

"Your brother is worse than you are. He won't even leave the country, preferring instead to pretend to be a stable hand on his estate rather than behave properly. I have the two most ungrateful children in existence."

"Yes, yes," Aidan said impatiently. He had heard of his inadequacies and those of his elder brother for years. It was very boring now—especially when he needed to hunt down a certain lady. "We are wretched indeed."

"Well, I daresay you will change your mind soon enough when you meet the right girl. Just as I did when I met your mother. But that isn't the only reason I wanted to see you."

"Is it not? How astonishing. What else have I done wrong this week?"

The duke ignored him. "It's your mother's silly nephew William again. He's made a new investment and thinks I should look into it as well."

"Oh? What is it this time?" Aidan asked casually, swinging his booted feet. Bill was constantly getting into speculative schemes and trying to involve his family in them too. Aidan steered clear—they failed more often than not. "Canals? Ships on the India trade?"

"A gambling club. Something very much in your line, I should think."

Now that was a surprise. "A what, Father? Has Bill turned gamester on top of everything else?"

"I shouldn't think so. He's terrible at numbers, like everyone in your mother's family. He says this is strictly an investment."

"It sounds risky even for him. And especially for you."

"Not as risky as all that. It's to be an elegant, members-only sort of place, right around the corner from this street. All these brainless aristocrats will flock there and are sure to lose their money at such foolish things as faro."

"Right around the corner, eh?" Aidan said, his interest piqued. Perhaps it was the house with the dark-haired lady in the window? "And who is to be the proprietor of this elegant place?"

"A Mr. Dominic St. Claire. Surely you know of him, as you're always hanging about the theaters."

Aidan's interest rose. "I do know of the St. Claires. William St. Claire owns the Majestic Theater, and I heard Dominic St. Claire was a great Hamlet there only last month." Was the woman a St. Claire, then?

It was his lucky day.

"So what then, Father?" Aidan said, concealing his

interest. It would never do to arouse the duke's suspicions. "You want me to put my money into this club as well?"

"Certainly not! You can't afford to lose so much as a shilling. I just want you to inspect the place for me when it opens, see if it looks to be a good investment." The duke tried on a cajoling smile, always a bad sign. "I can't get out much with this damned chair, and I want to be sure of my money. It wouldn't hurt for you to meet some of the club's members either."

"Fine," Aidan said. As far as familial errands went, inspecting a gambling club seemed a fine one, enjoyable even. Especially if the St. Claires were involved.

The duke gave a satisfied smile. "Very good, m'boy. I knew you wouldn't let me down. Now, be sure and say hello to your mother before you leave. And not a word about any brandy."

Aidan managed to quickly escape the stuffy confines of Huntington House after fending off his mother's matchmaking hints and her attempts to lure him to a dinner party that night. He knew where he could find out more information on the St. Claires and their business concerns, and it wasn't in Mayfair. He made his way to the jumbled, narrow lanes around the theater district where the merchants and cafes catered to the theatrical set and any gossip could be had for the right coin.

Aidan spent a great deal of his time there.

He left his curricle and proceeded on foot, as it was futile to try and drive through the jostling crowds that filled the narrow streets. Shouts and shrieks of laughter blended with the yaps of ladies' lap dogs and the silvery ring of bells over shop doors. Aidan waved and smiled at the ladies' effusive greetings and their enthusiastic kisses on his cheek. Even away from the clamor of the theater doors, drama was never far.

Aidan bowed and smiled at a fluffy little blonde who giggled behind her fan at him, and turned toward the cafe that was his destination.

"Aidan!" he heard someone call as he reached for the door, and he turned to see his friend Lord Frederic Bassington hurrying toward him. A red-haired lady in a bright pink tippet held on to his arm as he pushed his way through the bustling crowd.

"Freddy," Aidan said, happy to see his friend and fellow theatergoer. "It's good to see you again. You haven't been in town much of late, I hear. But then neither have I."

Freddy smiled, but there was a strange shadow on his expression. It was most puzzling in a man usually so lighthearted. "I fear I've been busy."

"Care to go to the theater this week? I hear Mrs. Parker is appearing at Drury Lane, a few select performances only. She's a favorite of yours, I think? I need to make up for my time away from England."

"Quite so. I just haven't—"

"Freddy," the lady said, tugging impatiently at his arm.

"Oh, Aidan, I don't believe you've met my sister, Lady Christabelle," Freddy said. He looked surprised she was still there. "Christa, this is Lord Aidan Huntington, who is only recently back from the West Indies."

Lady Christabelle batted her eyes at him from beneath her flower-laden bonnet. "The Duke of Carston's son, of course. Freddy has told us an awful lot about you."

Aidan gave her a polite bow. "All Banbury tales, I fear, Lady Christabelle."

"Oh, no!" she protested. "He says only very good things, I assure you."

"Christa," Freddy said, "why don't you run ahead to the carriage and meet Mama there? I need a quick word with Lord Aidan."

She pouted, but left after another eye-bat and curtsy. Freddy, though, looked terribly solemn.

"I say, Aidan," he whispered after looking to be sure his sister was really gone. "I need your help."

"Of course, Freddy," Aidan answered in concern. This wasn't like his friend at all. "Anything. Do you need money?"

"No, no." Freddy shook his head. Even his red hair seemed faded. "At least I don't think so, not yet."

"What do you mean? I can't help you, my friend, if you don't tell me the problem."

Freddy bit his lip. "I...I can't say here. Meet me at the coffeehouse next week? Christa and Mama will be gone to Brighton by then."

"Of course. Just send me word of the time."

"You are a true friend, Aidan," Freddy said, looking a bit more relieved. He ran off after his sister, leaving Aidan alone. Freddy Bassington was one of his most lighthearted, uncomplicated friends, always good company, always ready to help him forget his own brooding. What trouble could he possibly be in?

Aidan turned back toward his errand, but his path was blocked by a woman just emerging from the music shop next door. A large, jostling, laughing group passed by and knocked against her. She tottered on the uneven cobblestones, her bonnet knocked askew over her eyes.

Aidan caught her before she could fall, his arms

coming around her waist before he could even think. She landed against his chest, soft and warm.

"Oh!" she said, laughing. Her gloved hands curled into his waistcoat to hold herself steady. "I do beg your pardon, sir. So clumsy of me."

"Not at all," Aidan said. He was rather intrigued by the bundle that had so suddenly tumbled into his arms. He held on to her as she found her balance. She wasn't very tall, her bonnet coming only to his shoulder, and her body felt slender and delicate under that softness. And she smelled like violets, as cool and sweet as a rainy spring day.

Intrigued by two women in one day—he *was* becoming a romantic.

But then she pushed her bonnet back into place and peeked up at him, and he saw it was only one woman after all. She was the same as his mystery lady in the window, and she had fallen right into his arms.

Her laughter faded away and her eyes, a sherry brown under thick black lashes, narrowed as she studied his face, and her brow furrowed a bit. A tiny dimple appeared in one pink-flushed cheek, and Aidan had the overwhelming urge to touch it. To kiss her just there and see if she tasted of sweet violets and an English springtime.

"It's very crowded here today. Collisions seem inevitable," he said near her ear. Dark ringlets curled there, soft against her skin.

"Indeed it is," she said uncertainly. "I was fortunate you were there to catch me."

"Not at all. The good fortune seems to be all mine today."

Her frown deepened, and she let go of his coat quickly,

as if she only just realized she held on to him. She took a step back, and Aidan felt cold where she had pressed against him.

He almost never felt this way about a woman, so very intrigued by just a glance, a touch. Who was she? What was it about her that drew him in like that? He couldn't let her go, not yet.

"Please, let me make amends for nearly knocking you over," he said.

Her frown flickered. "Amends?"

Aidan laughed, trying to put her at ease, making her stay with him. "Nothing too nefarious, I assure you. A cup of tea? This cafe is most respectable, I promise."

She glanced back over her shoulder, and for a moment, Aidan was afraid she might run from him. But then she gave him a little smile. A mere ghost of a smile over her pretty pink lips, but for the moment it was enough.

"Perhaps if you add a scone to that tea, I might be persuaded," she said.

"As many scones as you like," Aidan answered, and held out his arm to her. "And maybe emeralds or pearls? A fine carriage? A castle?"

She laughed out loud, a silvery, sweet sound Aidan feared he would do anything to hear again. She slid her gloved hand into the crook of his arm.

"Just the tea for now," she said as he led her into the cafe. "We'll see about the castle later."

Chapter Three

Lily settled herself at the tiny table in the corner and watched Aidan Huntington as he made his way to the counter to order. *Aidan Huntington*—she could hardly believe she was here with him after their long-ago encounter at the theater docks.

What was she thinking? She had vowed to harden her heart to him, to forget the memory of their kiss. She was just getting her life in order again; he was a distraction she did not need. He was a Huntington, for pity's sake.

But when he smiled at her, flirted with her, when she felt the hard strength of his body under her hand—somehow she simply could not turn away from him. She wanted him to smile at her again.

She was not the only woman who felt that way. Lily watched the crowd as he threaded his way through it, and every lady between the ages of five and eighty turned to study him under their lashes. They all blushed and looked away, only to peek at him again.

Just as Lily feared she was doing herself.

She busied herself with taking off her gloves and smoothing her jacket, but her attention kept drifting to him. Aidan. The slightly exotic, Celtic-sounding name suited him. He was tall and lean like some ancient warrior, with strong shoulders and snakelike hips and—her eyes slid lower—a taut backside in close-fitting trousers above long legs. His rich, glossy brown hair gleamed in the dim light of the cafe, and he shook it back from his brow as he peered over at her. For an instant, his face looked dark and intent, taut as a hawk about to dive onto its prey. His blue eyes, the most unearthly color she had ever seen, narrowed, and she stiffened in her seat. Then he smiled, that charming, careless grin that could capture any woman's complete attention, and something warm and melting touched Lily deep inside.

She didn't like that feeling at all, that sense that her moorings to the real world would snap and she'd drift up into the sky.

She turned away to pretend to study a menu on the wall. From the corner of her eye, she saw him lean his elbow on the high counter to order. He gave a smile to the waitress, and the girl giggled. Lily studied his profile, the sharply etched perfection of it, the way he casually brushed his hair back. She was accustomed to being around handsome men. The St. Claires were all very good-looking and garnered more than their share of female attention wherever they went. The actors they worked with were often the same. She hardly noticed such things now.

It was different with Aidan Huntington. She was all too aware of everything about him.

Don't be silly, she told herself. She twisted her soft kid gloves in her hands and forced herself to stay still. Aidan was no danger to her. Not here in this crowded place. Not if she didn't let him.

"You look very deep in thought," she heard him say. She glanced up to see him setting a tray of tea and scones on the table. He smiled at her but it was a different smile, quizzical, questioning. "And not very pleasant thoughts, I would wager."

Lily made herself smile in return and reached for the tea to pour. She welcomed the routine, the familiar motions, something to root her in the everyday. "I was just daydreaming, I fear. Organizing things in my mind."

"What sort of things?" he asked, watching her closely.

She peered across the table at him and tried to gauge whether he was merely being polite. But his blue eyes were focused only on her, waiting for her answer.

She passed him the cup of tea, and his fingers drifted over hers as he took it from her. His touch lingered a little longer than necessary, and she sighed at the warm feeling of his skin on hers, the strength of those elegant fingers. They were slightly rougher than she would expect from a gentleman.

She glanced down as he slid away and noticed ink stains on his fingers. She remembered his confession on that long-ago night at the Majestic, that he wanted to write plays. She wondered if he still harbored that dream or if being a duke's spoiled son took all of his time.

She wondered if he remembered that night at all.

She shook her head and tried to recall what he had asked her. "I am helping my brother with a new business venture," she said.

"Sounds promising," he answered. "What sort of business?"

Lily took a sip of her tea and studied him over the white rim of the cup. She almost answered him by name, before she recalled that they were supposed to be strangers. "I don't even know your name," she said.

He gave her that rakish grin again, and she saw the flash of a dimple low in his cheek. She had the strangest, strongest urge to press her fingertip there, to lean across the table and lick him, taste him, feel that tiny indentation on her tongue.

Lily sat back in her chair in shock. She never had such feelings about a man, such erotic urges. Not after seeing her mother's life in the brothel, the girls she knew on the streets, seeing where such things always led. She wrapped her hands tightly around her cup and looked away from him.

"Easy enough to remedy," he said. "I am Aidan Huntington, at your service. And you are..."

Lily touched the tip of her tongue to her suddenly dry lips and tried to ignore the way his gaze sharpened on that tiny gesture. "I am Lily Nichols."

"Nichols?" A frown flickered over his brow. "Why is that—Ah." He sat back in his chair and stared at her, studied her. As if this were the first time he saw her. "Juliet."

Despite the confusing swirl of emotions inside of her, Lily had to laugh at his thunderstruck expression. "I did wonder if you would remember. It was so long ago." And he had surely known so many women, so many intimate moments, between then and now.

"Not that long ago. I have been gone on family business to the West Indies since then." He leaned his forearms on the small table; he was so close she could smell him. The light touch of some expensive cologne, the dark scent of his skin. His stare was so intent on her face.

"So you married your greengrocer," he said quietly.

"Yes, I did. But he died last year."

"And you never went back on the stage."

Lily remembered too well the frozen terror of that night, humiliation that only burned away when he kissed her. "Never. Acting is not for me."

"I looked for you," he said. His hand slid over hers, a quick, soft gesture hidden under the folds of a napkin. "But the name in the program was a false one."

"Thankfully. One less embarrassment if no one knows who I really am. My sister took over the role after that."

"Isabel St. Claire is your sister? I have heard about her."

Lily gave a wry laugh. Of course he knew of Issy—everyone who saw her onstage fell in love with her red-gold hair, green eyes, and sweet manner. Any interest Aidan Huntington had in Lily would surely flee now. "My adoptive sister, yes."

She waited for him to ask her to introduce him to Issy, but he just frowned. His hand slid over hers again. His fingertip rubbed across the tiny band of skin where her wedding ring once rested.

"Lily," he said softly, as if to himself.

"Aidan," she whispered. She turned her hand palm up and let his fingers tangle with hers for the merest instant. She couldn't seem to help herself. He had her caught in some spell.

"There is so much I want to ask you," he said. He glanced over his shoulder at the crowded cafe. "But this doesn't seem to be the place. When can I see you again?"

Lily stared at him in surprise. "You would like to see me again?"

A rueful half-smile drifted over his lips. "You can tell

me to stay away, if that's what you want. I can't promise I will do it, but you can tell me to."

And that was exactly what she should do. But it was not what she wanted to do. Lily was suddenly weary of doing what she *should* do. She wanted to cease to be cautious for a moment, to be mischievous and seize life as her siblings did. Even as she knew it would not end well.

"My brother and I are opening an exclusive new club in Mayfair in a fortnight," she said. "If you will give me your direction, I can send you an invitation."

Aidan laughed, and his hand fell away. "There's no chance of anything a bit sooner, is there?"

Lily laughed, too, and shook her head. "I am too busy before then. It's not a long time to open a new business."

"I'll take what I can get, then. For now." His eyes held some hint of warning—he would not wait for very long.

Lily felt a shiver ripple over her skin at the threat and promise in his eyes. She didn't know what this was between them. The power of it both drew her in, like a moth to the fatal flame, and made her want to run. To never see him again, even as the thought of that was painful.

"Thank you for the tea," she said. "I should go now."

"Do you have your carriage here?"

Lily shook her head. "I took a hansom."

"Then let me drive you home."

She considered refusing. His dashing yellow curricle was so small; she wasn't sure how she would feel pressed close to him on the narrow seat. Her body against his.

But she found herself nodding. "Very well. Thank you. It's not far."

He took her arm in a light grasp as he led her out of the cafe and back onto the crowded street. He held her close, safe from the jostling, and drew her back toward the wider lanes outside the warren of shops and restaurants. He kept up a light stream of talk as they went, making her laugh at his jests, his observations of the people around them. She even found herself relaxing somewhat and let herself enjoy his touch on her arm, the protective closeness of his strong body.

But then they turned a corner, and she glimpsed a figure lounging against the brick wall across the street. A muscular figure with close-cropped black hair and clad in plaid trousers and leather coat and holding a stout, skull-headed walking stick.

Oh, Christ, that stick! It could not be.

Lily's whole body went stiff with a rush of raw fear. He was dead. She had heard he was, that he had died in Australia, and even the old nightmares had started to fade as the years went on and she never saw him again. This had to be an illusion. She was probably overly tired from working on the plans for the club.

She peered past Aidan's shoulder, back to the wall, but no one was there now.

Her skin still prickled with awareness, with the fear she had known all the time as a child, and she gave her head a hard shake. She had only imagined it. He was gone. He no longer had any power over her.

"Lily?" Aidan asked. "Are you well? You look so pale."

Lily jerked her attention away from the wall and back to Aidan's handsome face. He looked concerned, and his hand tightened on her arm. But the fear of the past, of that man, still held her in its cold, iron grip. She drew away from Aidan.

"I am quite well," she answered shortly, and walked away down the street.

Not real, not real, she told herself as Aidan fell back into step beside her. If only she could believe it.

Aidan leaned against his carriage door and watched Lily as she hurried up the back stairs to her house. She wouldn't let him leave her at the front door and walk her inside. She had insisted he drive her to the mews tucked behind the garden. And as he helped her down, he could swear she nervously scanned the windows to make sure no one was watching.

What was she hiding?

That hint of mystery, of intrigue, only made her more attractive to him. He had always loved a woman with secrets. It made it so much more fun to uncover them all, layer by layer.

Especially when the secrets came in as pretty a package as Lily St. Claire Nichols.

She paused by the door to glance back at him. She gave him a tentative smile, a little wave with her gloved hand. He barely had time to wave back before she whirled around and dashed into the house.

Aidan grinned as he flexed his fingers and remembered the brush of her skin against his just there, the rainy-violet scent that seemed to linger on his hand. He was a man who liked women, enjoyed their company, and he had known a great many of them in his life. If anyone knew exactly how many, it would be a scandal. Yet he had never felt anything quite like the sensation that shot through his hand when Lily touched him. The hot awareness that jolted straight to his manhood.

He glanced up at the windows, hoping for one more glimpse of her face, but the glass was blank. Aidan swung back up into the carriage and gathered the reins. Soon he was back on the crowded streets, turning toward his lodgings on Jermyn Street. But his thoughts were still on Lily St. Claire.

Usually he knew all too easily how to woo a lady, could see as soon as they met what would lure her in. With Lily St. Claire, he was baffled, thrown off his game. She was like no other woman he had ever met.

He drew up outside his lodging house and tossed the reins to a footman as he leaped to the ground. Soon enough he would get to see Lily again, when he went to her brother's gambling club—two birds with one stone.

And then he would start to slowly unravel the delicious mystery of Lily St. Claire.

Chapter Four

"I wish I could see the club when it opens. It's so unfair."

Lily laughed at the wistful sound of her sister Isabel's voice. She glanced at their reflection in the dressing table mirror as Issy lodged pins into Lily's upswept hair. "It will be very dull. Just work."

"Of course it won't be dull!" Isabel protested. "There will be music and dancing and handsome men. It will be fun, and I'm missing it as usual."

"You do have fun, Issy." Lily reached for her pot of rouge and carefully smoothed swaths of pink over her pale cheeks as Isabel finished her hair.

"I don't. I work at the theater and then I go home to sit by the fire all evening while everyone else goes out. I'm almost eighteen! James gets to go out far more than I do," Isabel said, referring to her twin brother.

Lily laughed. "Eighteen is not old enough to spend the evening at a gambling club."

"As if I would be in any danger. Not with you and Dominic and Brendan there."

"Maybe next year."

Isabel gave a pout and snapped off three red roses from

the bouquet on the table to wind them through Lily's hair. "Everyone always says next year."

Lily smiled at her, studying Isabel's loose fall of strawberry curls, her pretty oval face, the bright, angry glitter of her green eyes. Isabel was the baby of the St. Claire family, younger than James by a half hour, and they did rather shelter her too much. But Lily would never want sweet Issy to see what was really out there in the world beyond the circle of their family. She never wanted her to lose that shining innocence.

"It will be all work tonight," Lily said. "There will be time for fun when you go to the seaside next month. Aren't you looking forward to your holiday?"

"I do like the sea," Isabel admitted. "But I'm tired of children's holidays." She put the finishing touches on Lily's hair and smiled. "There, now, all done. What do you think?"

Lily twisted her head to the side to examine the elaborate creation of curls and waves, entwined with ribbons and the red roses. "Amazing, Issy. You have quite transformed this little brown wren."

Isabel laughed. "Hairdressing is one of my many talents. But I only gilded your beauty."

"And you are also the sweetest sister in the world." With her hair done and the kohl at her eyes and diamonds sparkling in her ears, she looked almost pretty.

Would Aidan think so when he saw her? Would he appear tonight at all? She had made sure he received an invitation, but that didn't mean he would come. It didn't mean she hadn't imagined the dark, intent look in his eyes when he helped her from the carriage. It had been many days since she saw him.

She shook her head. She was being a fool, mooning over a handsome man like that. He was a Huntington, her family's enemy, and a distraction she did not need. She had seen the way the women in the cafe looked at him. He could have any of them, pretty women who didn't carry the weight of their dirty past around with them like iron shackles.

Yet still she had taken the extra care with her appearance tonight. She had tried to cover up the nightmares and sleepless nights that had plagued her since she thought she saw *him* again.

"I am a very good sister," Isabel said with a laugh. "And don't ever forget it. I will expect a full account of the evening tomorrow. Now, let's get you into your gown. Which one did you decide on for tonight?"

An hour later, Lily stood in the main salon of the Devil's Fancy club, turning in a slow circle as she studied every detail. Soon, very soon, the doors would open, and their new venture would be open for business.

Everything had to be perfect.

She twitched the heavy draperies into place so they hung exactly straight and nudged a yellow-and-white-striped satin settee against the wall. The card tables were set up, lined with gilded French chairs also upholstered in yellow and white, and new paintings of cavorting cupids and pretty, plump-breasted goddesses hung on the silk-papered walls. Large arrangements of fresh flowers stood on marble stands, perfuming the air, and the soft amber glow of gaslight fell over everything. It all looked elegant, expensive, inviting.

Now all it needed was a crowd of guests, all happy and merrymaking, in the mood to cheerfully lose all their money.

Lily peeked into the dining room, where a lush buffet was laid out in all its tempting array and champagne fountains bubbled. In the ballroom, the orchestra tuned up in their alcove while the gleaming dance floor waited to be filled. Footmen were stationed at the doors, and the pretty girls who were to play banker stood at their faro tables. They all wore gleaming pink satin, soft, fluffy, and eye-catching.

Lily smoothed her full skirts. Unlike the girls, she wore a quiet, lavender-blue silk gown trimmed with white lace on the small, off-the-shoulder sleeves, simple and respectable. She knew her job, which was to fade into the shadows and let the club shine as she kept an eye on everything. Dominic would charm everyone and make sure they all had fun. It was what he did best.

She turned to watch Dominic and Brendan as they came into the room. Of course, everyone would be charmed by them—how could they not? Dominic so golden and laughing in his flamboyant, blue evening coat and striped cravat, Brendan dark and brooding in plain, stark black and white, the left side of his face crisscrossed with pale scars. Like her, Brendan took in every detail of the room, calculated every flaw, while Dominic clapped his hands. Her brothers were like the bright sun and the mysterious moon.

"Lily!" Dominic called, and hurried across the room to kiss her cheek. "Everything looks beautiful. You have worked wonders, as usual. But why the frown?"

Lily laughed and pulled away from him to smooth her

gown one more time before he could crumple it. "I'm only afraid no one will appear and our venture will fail before it begins. We've already spent our initial investment fund and then some. . . ."

Dominic shook his head and took her hands again to waltz her in wild circles around the salon, spinning her around and around until she couldn't quit laughing. Even solemn Brendan chuckled at the sight of their dance.

"Ridiculous!" Dominic shouted. "Everyone will be here. Haven't we been making the rounds of London for weeks, advertising our wares?"

"Ah, yes," Lily said breathlessly. She held tight to Dominic's shoulders as he spun her around. "Tearooms, assemblies, bookshops . . ."

"Coffeehouses, gentlemen's clubs, expensive brothels," Brendan added. He caught her out of Dominic's arms and swept her off her feet, swinging her in a circle.

"The talk among the *ton* is of nothing else but the Devil's Fancy now," Dominic said. "Everyone is dying for a glimpse of this place!"

"But after they have had that glimpse, will they come back?" Lily gasped. "Oh, do put me down, Brendan! You will ruin my hair, and Issy will kill you."

No sooner had Brendan set her back on her feet and she smoothed her hair than a carriage pulled up at their front steps, a fine equipage with a coronet emblazoned on its glossy black door. And Lily found it was silly to worry at all.

The elegant rooms were quickly filled to the walls with noisy merrymakers, their laughter and bright chatter tangling and flowing above the rattle of the roulette wheel and the clink of coins, the sound of dance music. Every chair was filled, jewels flashing in the light, silks and satins glinting. The scent of expensive French perfumes and powders blended with the flower arrangements in a dizzying mélange.

It made Lily's head spin. She made her slow way through the rooms, accepting greetings and compliments from the patrons, making sure all went well with the dancing and with the gaming at the faro tables, ensuring that the buffet and the champagne were well stocked. Her brothers had vanished in the crowd, and everyone seemed to be having a grand time.

Lily was finally able to find a corner for a moment and snapped open her fan to try and create a cooling breeze. Yes, things were going well indeed—but Aidan Huntington had not appeared.

She took a glass of champagne from a footman's tray and sipped at it as she scanned the salon again. It seemed even more crowded than just a few minutes ago, the laughter even louder and more reckless. She glimpsed Dominic standing at one of the faro tables, his arm around the waist of a red-haired lady in green taffeta. The woman whispered in his ear, and Dominic threw back his head and laughed.

Lily smiled and drained the last of her champagne. At least everyone was having a good time.

Then she glimpsed a group of newcomers in the doorway. She wasn't at all sure there was room for anyone else, but she pasted her most welcoming smile on her lips and stepped out of her corner.

Only to halt in her tracks when she realized who it was standing there. Aidan.

She watched him take in the room around him. He

wore plain, stylish evening clothes of black with touches of white, the only hint of color the sapphire pin at his cravat. His blue eyes were hooded, a half-smile on his face, and he gave away none of his thoughts or reactions as he looked around him. He seemed every inch the cool aristocrat.

From the corner of her eye, Lily saw Dominic's shoulders stiffen and saw him turn toward Brendan. Bloody hell, the last thing they needed here tonight was a St. Claire–Huntington fight! Not when business was going so well. Not when Aidan was here at last, after she had been trying not to think about him all evening.

She snatched up two glasses of champagne from a tray and made her way through the crowd to his side.

"Lord Aidan. Welcome to the Devil's Fancy," she said, smiling up at him as she held out one of the glasses. "I hope you have come here eager to enjoy yourself."

He turned to her, and his smile widened even as his eyes were still hooded and inscrutable, his thoughts hidden from her. He slid the glass from her hand, his bare fingers brushing over her kid glove. His other hand caught hers, turning it so he could raise it to his lips. His gaze met hers over their touch, and for an instant, Lily imagined his mouth lingering there, pressing to her vulnerable palm, the pounding pulse in her wrist. Tasting her...

But he let go of her and gave her another flash of his dimpled smile. He took a long sip of the champagne, and she watched his strong throat shift above his cravat.

"Mrs. Nichols," he said. "I did come here eager to see *you* again. I've thought of you often since our meeting, and you are just as lovely as I remember."

Lily laughed and turned away from the close scrutiny

of his otherworldly eyes to take a drink from her glass. The heat of the strong French champagne in her stomach gave her a shot of courage. She didn't want to admit how his lightly flirtatious words affected her—even to herself. She knew men too well to give in to this.

"And you are a charming flatterer, Lord Aidan," she said. She glanced around the room but could not see where her brothers had gone. That wasn't a good sign—she liked to know where they were at all times when a Huntington was around.

"Only an honest man, Mrs. Nichols." She felt the slide of his glance—the hot, bright blue of a summer sky—over her body, but he seemed to sense her tension. He examined the salon as he drank. "I have a cousin who is considering investing in this club."

Ah, business. Lily could easily talk business, even with Aidan Huntington's lean, hard body pressed so close to her in the crowd. "Do you?"

"Sir William Meredith."

"I know him." William Meredith was a silly looby who often lost a great deal of money to her brothers at the gaming tables, but she wasn't one to turn away investment funds. "Are you here to advise him on his investment, then?"

"Oh, I would be the last person anyone would turn to for advice on that, Mrs. Nichols."

What *would* he give advice on? Charming women? Walking so easily into any room as if he owned it? Belonged there? She couldn't help envying him that. She was never sure she belonged anywhere. "Well, as you can see, his investment would be a wise one. We seem to have a great success on our hands." Lily caught a glimpse of blue from the corner of her eye and turned to see Dominic and his lady friend across the room.

"Indeed you do," he said, still with that inscrutable smile on his face. "But it is early yet."

"And fashion is fickle. Is that what you're saying, Lord Aidan? That is true enough. But my family and I know how to adapt to fashion." Some impulse made her brush her hand against his under the cover of a fold of her skirt. "We know what people want."

Aidan laughed, a deep, rich sound that seemed to ripple through her body. He turned his hand along hers, sliding his fingers over hers. "And how to give it to them?"

Lily shrugged and moved away from him. She felt so strange tonight, not her careful, wary self. She handed their empty glasses to a footman and slid her hand into the crook of Aidan's arm. "We all must live somehow, Lord Aidan. Come, let me show you our establishment. You'll see what a fine investment it is."

She gave Dominic a hard, warning look, telling him silently to back off, not to ruin tonight. He spun around and disappeared with his redhead, and Lily led Aidan into the crowd. He went with her willingly enough, their bodies pressed together in the crush. She could feel the flex and strain of his muscles under her touch, his body so hard under the soft, expensive wool of his coat. If she turned her head, she could rest her forehead against his chest and the brocade of his waistcoat. She could inhale deeply of his clean scent, dark male skin and expensive cologne, starched linen and wool. She could wrap her arms around him...

"You see we offer something for everyone," she said, her voice unsteady. "Faro, roulette, loo, piquet, whist.

And if one does not care for cards, there is supper, dancing. Quiet parlors for conversation."

He looked down at her, and she could feel the warm brush of his breath over her hair. "Quiet conversation, eh?"

She glanced up at him. He no longer smiled, just watched her steadily, closely. As if he waited to see what she would do next.

Somehow that quiet, steady waiting was more frightening than any aggressive threats.

Lily shook her head. She suddenly felt too warm, almost faint. The crowd, so welcome because it was necessary to the success of the business, seemed to press in on her with all their perfumed heat. She had been drinking champagne on an empty stomach—that was all. It had nothing to do with the nearness of Aidan Huntington.

She swayed, her head swirling, and his arm came around her waist.

"Too much champagne," she whispered.

Aidan chuckled, and his arm tightened. "Perhaps we should find one of those quiet parlors for a moment."

That was the last thing she should be doing with him; Lily knew that very well. But the room swayed again, and his arm seemed to be all that held her steady. She nodded. "For a moment."

She led him out of the crowded salon, his arm still around her as they left the cacophony of the revelers behind, and silence slowly enfolded them. They made their way up a narrow flight of stairs to the third floor, their way lit by a few hissing wall sconces that flickered over the white walls.

She could hear only their footsteps on the wooden

risers and the rustle of her silk skirts and net petticoats. The soft sound of his breath. The silence was almost deafening after the roar of the party.

The corridor at the top of the stairs was for storage and offices, not meant for public view. Lily led Aidan to the darkest end of the hall and slowly opened the last door there.

It was her own private sanctuary, her office where she could be alone and attend to business without the constant interruptions she always found at home. No one was allowed here, not even her brothers. Yet here she was with Aidan.

She ushered him in and lit a lamp on the desk as he leaned back against the door. The soft glow illuminated the old desk and shabby leather chair, the chaise piled high with pillows in the corner, the small fireplace. It also showed her books, on the shelves lining the walls, stacked on the floor, piled on the windowsill. Her treasures.

She watched Aidan's face as he took it all in. If he could truly read her secrets with those beautiful eyes, Lily thought, then she might as well have opened her heart for him to look at rather than bring him here. This was *her* room, her secret place, the shelter of a street girl who had spent much of her childhood illiterate and ignorant and now craved all the wonders books could give her.

Why would she show it to him at all? But he had once said he wrote plays; perhaps he would understand her need for escape. For new realities.

"What is this place?" Aidan said quietly.

Lily leaned her palms on the cool, scarred surface of her desk and took a deep breath. "It's my office."

He pushed himself away from the door and moved to

one of the shelves with a quiet, catlike grace. "Sophocles, Plato, Milton, Byron. Shakespeare, of course," he said, running the tip of his finger over the worn leather bindings. "You have quite an extensive library, Lily."

"I must be a bluestocking, then," she said lightly. But she had to swallow hard against the imagined vision of that caressing touch tracing the curve of her bare back, the swell of her backside. "I could not be an actress, so I read plays instead. That is all."

Aidan shook his head. He turned away from the books, his body close to hers in the small space, and he reached out to touch her just as she had imagined. He traced the spiral of one of her loose curls where it lay against her neck, one long, slow caress that made her shiver. "You seem to be a lady of many talents."

Lily could hardly breathe. Her skin tingled wherever he touched, a rippling, sparkling ribbon of feeling right into her core. She only wanted him to touch her again, wanted to explore this some more. She braced herself against the bookshelf to hold herself upright and reached up to catch his hand in hers. She held it tightly as she stared up into his eyes and tried to read his thoughts there. But his eyes were still veiled to her as he stared at their joined hands. He slowly twined his fingers with hers.

"Whatever my talents might be," she whispered, "I'm sure they're nothing to yours, Aidan."

"Oh, I'm utterly useless. Just ask my family," he answered roughly. His blue-sky stare slid from their hands to the lacy edge of her bodice, along the pale swell of her breasts. His avid gaze felt like a physical touch, hot and needful.

Lily couldn't stop herself. She went up on tiptoe to

frame his face in her palms, tracing the sharp line of his cheekbones, the wings of his brows. She gently used her fingertips to urge his eyes to close, and when they did, she kissed him.

She had never craved a kiss so much. Aidan tasted of champagne and mint, of that deep, masculine darkness that was only him. She traced the tip of her tongue over the softness of his sensual lower lip, craving more. Craving all of him.

With a groan, his mouth opened under hers, and his arms came hard around her body, lifting her against him. His tongue pressed past her open lips to touch and tangle with hers.

It wasn't a soft, tentative kiss, a gentle seeking. Aidan devoured her, his lips and tongue and teeth seeking out every part of her, claiming her, possessing her. And she *wanted* it, wanted more. It was as if his taste intoxicated her, and something white-hot exploded inside of her. She felt him press her back tightly against the shelf, bracing her there as he lifted her higher against his body.

Her skirts fell back in a ruffled froth as she wrapped her legs tightly around his lean hips and let herself fall completely into his hungry kiss. She shoved his coat away from his shoulders and dug her nails into his linen-covered back.

"Lily," he groaned. His lips tore away from hers, and she cried out in protest, only to moan as his mouth trailed down the arch of her neck, his tongue tasting her skin. He licked and nipped at her, until her head fell back, and her fingers drifted into the waves of his hair to hold him to her. He bit down hard on the sensitive spot between her neck and shoulder.

"Aidan!" she cried, and her hips arched into him. Through the silk of her underthings and the wool of his trousers, she could feel his iron-hard erection. Wetness slid down her inner thigh, proof of how much she wanted him. How much they wanted each other.

She spread her legs wider and dug her heels into his taut buttocks. She let herself rock against him, her tight heat sliding over his hardness.

"Damn it all, you are killing me," he growled, and Lily laughed at the deep, hoarse sound of his voice. At least she was not alone in this madness.

She closed her eyes tightly as his mouth trailed over the soft curve of her breast. He nudged the edge of her bodice out of his way until he could circle the tip of his tongue between her cleavage, on the bare, soft skin just above her corset. Her nipples tightened, and she wanted to feel his tongue on them, the heat of his mouth as he drew them in deep.

"Aidan, please," she whispered.

He held her between his body and the bookshelf, and one of his long, elegant hands slid down over her ribs and her corseted waist, grasping her skirts to pull them up even higher.

"What do you want, Lily?" he demanded, his mouth on her breast. "Do you want me to touch you? Kiss you?"

"Yes," she said.

He pulled hard on the silk of her bodice and the boned linen of her corset until her breast was bare. He bent his head to press hot, openmouthed kisses to the pale skin, soft and slow, circling teasingly toward her aching, erect nipple, then easing away until she tugged hard at his hair and cursed at him.

Aidan laughed roughly. "Such an unladylike mouth," he said, and took her nipple between his teeth to suckle it hard. In the same instant, his hand slid up between her legs, and his palm pressed against her through the damp silk of her drawers.

Lily cried out in a harsh voice she didn't even recognize as her own. She had never felt this way before, drowning in so much pleasure she couldn't remember anything but this moment.

"So hot and wet," he said, and he sounded as if he were in pain, as if he would snap at any instant. "Damn it, Lily, I want to put my mouth between your legs and see if you taste as sweet as you feel. I want to drive myself so deep into you, feel you tighten around me, pull me closer and closer until I don't know where I end and you begin. What kind of spell do you have over me?"

Lily frantically shook her head. *He* was the one who had cast a spell over her. All she could see were those images in her mind: Aidan kneeling between her legs as he licked her, Aidan plunging into her as she wrapped her legs around his waist. Her head arched back, her eyes closed in pleasure as he drove into her again and again.

Aidan sprawled facedown across her bed as she stood over him with a riding crop…

That last image, so vivid and explicit in her mind, was like a burst of cold water over her burning lust. Her eyes flew open, and her hands tightened convulsively in his hair.

No! She was not like her mother. She wouldn't be, couldn't be.

Yet here she was in her office, her body open around Aidan Huntington as he drove her mad with his kisses, his words. She *was* under some spell. He had unleashed something deep inside of her she had fought for years to forget. She couldn't let it free now. Couldn't let it destroy her again.

Aidan seemed to sense something was wrong. His hand slid to her knee, and he looked up at her. His eyes burned in the shadows. It made her shiver, and she closed her eyes tightly against the sight.

"Lily, what's wrong?" he said. "Did I hurt you? I'm so sorry I forgot..."

She shook her head. She kept her eyes shut as he slowly lowered her to her feet, and her skirts tumbled back into place. He hadn't hurt her—he had given her more pleasure in a physical act than she had ever thought possible, but she was shaking as if she stood in a winter storm. She turned away and pressed her hands to her burning cheeks.

"I've been gone from the club too long," she said.

"Of course. Let me escort you back downstairs."

Lily smoothed her hair back into its pins and tugged her bodice over her shoulders. She caught a glimpse of her reflection in the window glass and saw to her surprise that she looked almost like she had before. If no one looked too closely at her overly bright eyes and swollen mouth.

She touched the spot on her neck where he had caught her with his teeth and hoped fervently there was no mark. Her brothers would know at once what had happened, and she didn't want a quarrel on top of everything else. Her emotions were in enough of a swirling turmoil.

She drew in a deep breath and slowly turned to see Aidan still standing half in the shadows. His hair was tousled over his brow, and he was retying his cravat as he watched her. He frowned as if he was as strangely affected by what had happened between them as she was.

Lily almost laughed at the thought. This sort of thing probably happened to Aidan every day. Probably he only wondered why she had stopped him before he gave her all of what she so clearly wanted.

"I'm sorry, Lily," he said. "I don't usually get quite so...uncontrolled."

Lily shook her head. "There is nothing for you to be sorry for, Aidan. We kissed. That's all."

Kissed—and so much more. She had wanted so much more, wanted him inside of her, thrusting deep until she could feel him in her very core. But that would be so foolish. She opened the door and slid out into the corridor. Aidan followed behind her, close to her but not saying anything. As they made their way down the hall, the noise of the party grew louder and louder, the lights brighter. On the landing outside the salon, she turned to him with a smile she hoped looked cool and calm, not as shaky and unreal as she felt.

"I should probably go in alone," she said.

Aidan slowly nodded, that frown flickering over his face again. "When can I see you again?"

It was the same question he asked her when they left the cafe, and again it was not what she expected. He wanted to see her again? Him, the handsome son of a rich duke? It was astonishing.

But did she want to see him again? She feared she did, far more than was good for her. She knew she should push him away now, once and for all, but she simply found it impossible. "Write to me soon," she said. Later, in the light of day, faced with a letter instead of his warm, living, all-too-attractive presence, she would be able to think rationally.

She started to turn away, but he caught her hand and raised it to his lips for a quick kiss, his mouth hot through her glove. "You won't escape me that easily, Lily," he whispered. Then he let her go, and she dashed into the salon.

"Mrs. Nichols!" a breathless footman cried. "There is something in the ballroom that requires your attention right away…."

Lily spent the rest of the night seeing to one small crisis after another as their patrons got drunker and rowdier, and between rescues, she avoided her brothers and tried to forget what she had done with Aidan.

But his voice kept whispering in her mind, deep, rough, and alluring: *"You won't escape me…"*

Chapter Five

Aidan slowly tapped the end of his pencil against the warped edge of the coffeehouse table. He frowned down at the scribbled lines in his notebook and crossed out a few words before scratching in others.

He was vaguely aware of the room around him, the murmur of low voices, the smell of rich coffee and the tang of pipe smoke, the serving girl's interested glances at his corner table, and the fact that Freddy Bassington was late for their meeting. But he was far away from it. He was deep in the action of the scene he was writing, the words and images rushing into his mind, tumbling over each other. It had been this way ever since he saw Lily St. Claire at the Devil's Fancy. The inspiration was right there at his fingertips, because of her.

Lily. Aidan closed his eyes and rubbed at the bridge of his nose. Had it really been a week since their encounter? It felt like a year. At night, he could close his eyes and see her face, so pale in the moonlight, her lips parted as she gasped his name. He could feel her soft skin under his hands, taste her nipple in his mouth, so sweet. Her legs tight around his hips as she arched into him. He could feel the wet heat of her even through their clothes, and hot lust urged him to tear the cloth away and thrust into her.

He had gone to his favorite brothel one night, looking for release, for something to make him forget Lily. Mrs. Bronson ran a luxurious house with the most beautiful and skilled of girls, and she always seemed to have what he wanted. But even the blond, buxom Swenson twins could not distract him. He didn't need their ample charms. He needed Lily's dark slenderness, her mysteriousness, her wariness that drove him to want to uncover all of her secrets.

So, like a callow schoolboy, he went home and came into his own hand while he imagined it was Lily's mouth.

Aidan laughed at himself and threw his pencil to the table. He was acting like a fool, a boy with his first infatuation. He knew she was attracted to him; he could see it in her eyes and feel it in her kiss. He should go to her, give her no chance to think, make her his and get her out of his mind.

Yet something held him back. He remembered the flash of fear when she turned away from him that night, the delicate wariness that made him think of an exotic bird, fluttering away from a predator that swooped down from the sky. She would run from him if he wasn't careful. He had to play the game just right, to chase and chase hard when he wasn't accustomed to pursuing. One minute, Lily seemed confident and sophisticated, and the next frightened.

So he had sent flowers, violets like her perfume, and brief notes. He was a patient man when the reward was great enough. He could take the time to make his plans.

If only he could get his manhood to be patient too. It wanted Lily, and it wanted her now.

Aidan smiled ruefully and closed his notebook. He just had to pour his urges into his writing right now. The new play was going well, especially now he had his inspiration for the heroine.

The bell over the door rang as someone stepped into the coffeehouse. Aidan glanced up and saw it was Freddy at last. He slipped the notebook into his coat pocket and waved his friend over.

The impression he had had the last time he ran into Freddy—that his friend was in some kind of turmoil—was even stronger now. Freddy Bassington was the most lighthearted of Aidan's friends, the kindest and most generous if not the most intelligent. Freddy always laughingly proclaimed himself to be "thick as a plank."

But today his red hair stood on end, and his freckles were dark on chalk-white skin. He needed a shave, and his cravat was tied crookedly.

"Blimey, Freddy," Aidan said, pushing a chair back for his friend. "You look as if you need something stronger than coffee."

Freddy shook his head and dropped heavily into his seat. "My head hurts enough already."

Aidan gestured to the serving girl for more coffee. As she brought it over, he leaned his forearms on the table and studied Freddy in concern. "What is happening, Freddy? I know you said you don't need money, but if you do..."

Freddy gulped down the strong brew and shook his head. "I don't. At least not yet. Not until I know what she'll do."

She. "Ah." Aidan sat back in his chair and almost laughed. Of course it was a woman who had Freddy tied up in knots. It always was. Wasn't he going crazy himself, all because of Lily St. Claire? "And who is she, then? A friend of your sister who refused your proposal? An opera dancer who sent back your gifts?"

"Nothing like that." Freddy finished his coffee and took a deep breath. He seemed a little steadier and gave Aidan a sheepish smile. "She's not a society debutante *or* a whore. I... well, I thought I was in love with her."

"Thought you were?"

"She... well, damn it all, she's not like any other woman I've ever met." Freddy shook his head again. "I misread things with her. I'm always doing that."

Aidan knew the feeling well. His attempts to read Lily were obviously going nowhere. Maybe hearing someone else's romantic woes would make him feel better. "Where did you meet her?"

"I went to a dinner at the Majestic Theater a few months ago, when you were in the West Indies."

"The Majestic? You met her there?" Aidan sat up straight. The Majestic was the St. Claires' theater.

"I sat next to her. Mrs. Lily Nichols. She smiled at me, talked to me like I wasn't thick or dull. And she had such pretty dark eyes. I thought..."

He had thought she was different. Special. Aidan knew what Freddy had thought and felt when he looked at Lily St. Claire, because Aidan felt it himself. He wanted to be the one to discover her secrets, to delve behind the mystery. But he wasn't the only one.

"You wrote her letters?" Aidan asked tightly.

Freddy groaned and buried his face in his hands. "With poems and everything. I thought I could convince her to feel the same way I did, to see how much I cared for her. But she turned me away."

Aidan could envision it. Lily's dark eyes hardening, her face like marble as she pushed away what she didn't want to see. Her heart closed. "Did she laugh at you?" he asked, though he couldn't picture Lily laughing at anyone at all.

Freddy shook his head. "She tried to be kind, I think. She told me she intended never to marry again. But she kept my letters, and I don't know what she intends to do with them. You remember what happened to Arthur Collins, don't you?"

Aidan nodded brusquely. Arthur Collins was another old school friend of theirs, who was nearly ruined when his mistress took him to court in a breach of promise suit. She had used his letters begging her to marry him as evidence, even though those letters were obviously written when he was completely foxed. "Never say Mrs. Nichols is taking you to court."

"I don't know what she intends to do! She hasn't said anything. I'm just afraid of what my mother would say if she ever found out how foolish I've been."

Aidan studied his friend's gaunt face and his eyes so full of despair. "I will get the letters back for you, Freddy," he said gently.

Freddy almost sobbed in relief. "Would you, Aidan? I knew I could count on you. You always have such a way with ladies."

Aidan nodded. It was time for a trip to the theater.

Chapter Six

During Aidan's years in the West Indies, he had missed many things. The cool, soft rain of an English springtime. The brandy at his club. The conversation of his friends. But what he had missed most was the theater. Amateur theatricals in someone's drawing room or a touring company from New York, which was the fare available in the tropics, just wasn't the same as a real London theater.

He hadn't been in the Majestic since that night he first met Lily, and it hadn't changed. He focused his opera glasses on the stage and studied the elaborate gold and crimson velvet curtains, the frescoes above the proscenium that depicted the Muses. Gold boxes rose to either side, as elaborate as wedding cakes with their fashionable inhabitants in black evening suits and bright satin gowns. The excited sound of laughter and conversation hung in the perfume-scented air, along with the flutter of programs and the faint hiss of the gaslights.

There was nothing quite like a night at the theater, Aidan thought as he watched the audience file into the stalls below his box. The anticipation of escaping into another world, of living another life just for a few hours.

Those moments just before the curtain rose and a new world was revealed. It was this way every time he went to the theater; it was one of the things that kept drawing him back.

But tonight felt somehow different. Tonight he kept thinking about Lily and wondering if he would see her. Was she behind that curtain? He could picture her there backstage, the very image of cool efficiency as she had been at the Devil's Fancy, overseeing everything with her brown eyes. Her somber gown and sleek coiffure belying what was hidden inside of her, a fire that had nearly burned him when he dared to touch her. To kiss her.

To want her.

Aidan lowered his glass and frowned as he studied the laughing party in the box across the way. He *did* want Lily, with a raw passion that had caught him by surprise. It threatened to make him forget everything else but when he could see her again. But he had told Freddy he would find his blasted letters, and for that he needed a cool head.

He turned back to the stage and suddenly noticed a man standing in the shadows of the wings, watching him. Aidan couldn't make out his features, just the gleam of light-colored hair in the darkness and the intensity of his stare.

Such a glare seemed to speak of anger and brawls, but Aidan couldn't think of anyone he could have offended so deeply in the short time since he returned from the West Indies. Especially no one in the theater. It was unsettling, and he could feel his muscles tense as if he was prepared to fight.

But then the gaslights flickered, and the audience grew quiet in anticipation of the play beginning. Aidan glanced over to see the curtain sway, and when he turned back, the man in the wings was gone.

Aidan laughed ruefully. He was becoming infected with Freddy's paranoia, seeing danger where there was none. He needed to focus on his task, not on fighting imagined foes. And definitely *not* on alluring dark-haired women in gambling clubs...

"What is *he* doing here, the blighter?"

Lily could hear the barely leashed fury in Dominic's voice, but she was too busy lacing up one of the actress's gowns to turn around and look at him. "Who is here?" she murmured. She tied off the ribbons and sent the woman hurrying off to make her entrance. The first night of a play was always frantic; the last thing she needed was one of her brothers in a temper.

But Dominic didn't seem to be calming down. He paced to the end of the dressing room, the black cloak that was part of his costume swirling around him. "That Aidan Huntington, of course. First he's at the club and now here at the theater? What's his game?"

Aidan was here? Against Lily's will, her heart suddenly pounded, and her mouth went dry. Could he possibly be here to see her? Or was Dominic right and there was some darker purpose to him showing up everywhere so suddenly? Her old distrust of people always seemed to be there, simmering under the surface, but she couldn't imagine what nefarious reason Aidan could have for being here.

"Oh, Dominic," she said. She turned her back on his watchful stare and picked up a discarded costume. "He probably just wants to see the play. His mother sometimes comes here, doesn't she? Why do you suspect everyone of evil motives?"

"Not everyone—just a Huntington. The man just came back to London. Why would he want to hang about here?"

Lily dearly wanted to know that too. Why was he suddenly here, disrupting her peace of mind? Making her think about him far more than she should...

"Shouldn't you be getting ready for your entrance?" she said, carefully folding the costume. "You'll be off your game if you worry too much about who is in the audience."

Dominic gave a humorless laugh. "When have I ever been off my game onstage? But when the play is over..."

Lily spun around to face him, her arms crossed over her chest. "When it's over, you'll let him leave. The last thing we need at the beginning of a new season is you causing a scandal fighting a duke's son. You and Brendan both need to leave him alone."

Dominic's eyes narrowed. "What exactly is going on with you and Huntington, Lily?"

"Nothing! I barely know the man. I'm just trying to keep you from getting us all into trouble." A bell rang in the corridor. "You need to get ready for your entrance."

Dominic gave a short nod. The door slammed behind him as he left, and Lily slumped down into a chair. Once Dominic had something in his mind, he wouldn't let it go. She just had to figure out a way to head him off.

But she also couldn't help but wonder why Aidan was really there. He said he liked the theater and wanted to write plays, which was reason enough, but could there be more?

Chapter Seven

"Anything interesting in the *Gazette* today, Lily my dear?" Katherine St. Claire asked as she poured more tea into Lily's breakfast cup.

Lily shook her head as she scanned the tiny newsprint columns and automatically ducked as Brendan tossed a bread roll at their younger brother James's head. Breakfast in the St. Claire house was always like an immature gentlemen's club. Brendan and Dominic didn't live at the St. Claire house any longer, but they always seemed to appear at meal times. "Just that the royal family are leaving for their new residence at Osborne House for the summer, after a trip to Coburg to see the prince consort's family. Wordsworth attended the Queen's Ball at Buckingham Palace. The prime minister will—"

"Oh, politics," Isabel moaned. "Is there anything duller? Especially first thing in the morning."

"Could you not talk so loudly, please, Issy?" Dominic groaned.

Lily studied him across the table. "You do look rather green this morning, Dominic. Long evening last night?"

Dominic winced. "You could say that."

Lily tried not to laugh, even when Katherine waved a plate of kippers under his nose and he went completely white.

"You should eat something, dear," their mother admonished. "It will do you good."

"Just coffee, thank you, Mama," he said tightly.

"Serves you right, you wanker, for going out and leaving me here," James groused.

"Language, James," Katherine said. "And you are probably too young to go wherever Dominic and Brendan went."

"Mama, I am almost eighteen!" James protested, but Lily knew how frighteningly adept he had become at sneaking out of the house. He was often gone somewhere where no one else knew.

"Oh, do read the society pages, Lily," Isabel interrupted her twin, buttering her toast as she cut him off. "I can't bear to listen to our brothers' nonsense another second."

Lily obligingly turned to the middle of the paper. She, too, could use the distraction of gossip, anything to keep her mind from spinning on one subject—Aidan Huntington.

It had been over a week since that night at the Devil's Fancy, and she hadn't yet seen him again. He had sent flowers twice, bouquets of violets, along with short notes in his dark, slashing handwriting, but that was all. She wasn't sure if she was relieved not to face him after what happened or disappointed. But thoughts of him caught her at the oddest moments. She would be working on accounts and see his teasing smile in her mind, that dimple set so incongruously in his chiseled cheeks. She would be riding in the park and smell his cologne.

And at night, in her dreams, she felt his kiss, his touch. Imagined him between her legs on her bed, drawing her feet over his shoulders as he plunged his talented tongue into her aching womanhood, again and again...

"Lily, whatever are you reading about there?" Isabel suddenly said, yanking Lily out of her heated daydreams. "Your cheeks are all pink. It must be something terribly scandalous."

Lily jerked her head up to find everyone at the table staring at her. Dominic looked pained, but Brendan's green eyes were narrowed in suspicion.

"Not at all. It's merely warm in here this morning," Lily said carefully. "I was reading an account of Lady Waldegrave's ball. I doubt she would let anything the least bit scandalous happen in her house."

"The old battle-ax," Dominic muttered. "Wonder what she would say if she knew what her nephew was up to at the Devil's Fancy last night?"

"Dominic, dear, I hope you are not getting into trouble at that club of yours already," Katherine cried. "Remember what happened last time, with the racetrack."

Lily sincerely hoped there was *not* trouble at the Devil's Fancy, not when they were all working so hard to make it a success. She glared at Dominic across the table, until he groaned and buried his face in his hands.

"Tell me about the ball, Lily, please!" Isabel begged. "Who wore what? Who danced with who? Were any engagements announced? Oh, I do wish we had been invited. I thought we surely would since we saw the Waldegraves at the assembly rooms last month."

"Issy, you're much too concerned with the doings of toffee-nosed snobs like the Waldegraves and the

Huntingtons," Brendan said. He snatched Dominic's kipper from his plate since it would obviously not get eaten there. "Who needs them?"

"I am not concerned about them," Isabel protested. "I just like gowns and parties. So ignore those philistines, Lily, and read to me about the fashions."

Lily laughed and bent her head over the paper. "Well, it seems Miss Perkins-Smythe wore white with yellow rosebuds, and Lady Angelina Anderson wore yellow with white rosebuds. The Countess of Salisbury wore a gown of eau de nil velvet and net from Paris, and Miss Chase was clad in pale pink silk with cherry satin trim and a corsage of white velvet roses. And she did become engaged to Lord Hernley, so there you are, Issy—all you could ask for."

"And what were the arrangements like?" their mother, the consummate hostess and decorator, asked.

Lily read aloud about the potted palms and swags of ferns and white hot-house roses, buffet tables laded with lobster patties and stuffed mushrooms, French wines and pink claret punch. Katherine and Isabel started criticizing the decor, and Lily read farther down the column about some of the other guests as she finished her tea. Many of the names she knew from the Devil's Fancy or the theater, families who held boxes at the Majestic. And no doubt many of their sons indulged in less respectable pursuits with her brothers, in brothels and music halls and such things.

It always seemed funny to her how the lives of the St. Claires ran parallel to, and sometimes bisected, those of these aristocrats. How they were so intertwined that one could not exist without the other, and yet they were still so vastly far apart. They saw titled aristocrats at the assembly rooms and theater parties and were sometimes even invited to their homes to be shown off as curiosities, but they were never truly friends.

Such as her and Aidan Huntington. *Lord* Aidan. The gulf between them was wide and dark, lined with jagged rocks and high walls. She could stand on the edge and look across at him, call to him, but she could not cross.

Maybe he knew the chasm as well, and that was why he had not talked to her when he came to the theater.

Then she glimpsed his name toward the bottom of the page, in smudged black print. She closed her eyes and opened them again, sure she was imagining things since her thoughts were so intently on him. But it was still there: *Lord Aidan Huntington, younger son of the Duke of Carston*—Lily opened the page and read further—*was seen dancing with the beauteous Lady HL, daughter of the Earl of D and the diamond of the season. Is a betrothal in the air? Will two of England's oldest families be momentously united? And will Lord A's elder brother be next? He has not been seen in London for many a month…*

Lady HL. Lily flipped the paper closed and reached for her tea. It had to be Lady Henrietta Lindley. Of course he would be linked with the "diamond" daughter of an earl. She would expect no less. But still the thought stung, the vision of him dancing with a white-clad deb. Kissing her, touching her, telling her all the things he wanted to do with her, as he had with Lily in her office. The chasm didn't seem so wide between them then.

Her cup clattered in its saucer.

"Lily?" Isabel said. "Was there something disturbing in the paper after all?"

"Not at all," Lily answered in a strangled voice as she dabbed at the spot of tea on the tablecloth.

"Let me see," Dominic said, and snatched the paper away from her before she could protest. He flipped through the pages until he came to the one she had been reading.

He scanned the gossip columns until suddenly he scowled, and his eyes became darker than the hungover shadows on his face.

"Lord Aidan Huntington," Dominic said, and threw the paper back at her. "Does it upset you that he's practically betrothed, then, Lily? Were his attentions at the club last week not enough? Or when he appeared at the theater?"

"Don't be stupid, Dominic," she cried, and threw the paper right back at his head. It bounced off and scattered on the rug. "He was hardly paying me attentions last week, and he did not even talk to me at the theater. I was showing him the club, as he said his cousin was an investor. *You* would have tossed him out and caused a scene on our first night in business. At least I know how to control myself."

"Control yourself?" Dominic thundered. "You disappeared with him for an hour!"

"An hour?" Brendan said, his scowl matching Dominic's. "What were you doing with him, Lily?"

Lily felt her face turn uncomfortably warm, and she turned away to fuss with her napkin as Isabel looked on, wide-eyed, and James smirked. "That's hardly any of your business, is it? I am a grown woman, a widow. And where did you and that red-haired hussy Louisa Carstairs go off to, Dominic?"

"Damn it all, Lily!" Dominic burst out.

"Language, Dominic," Katherine said, quelling their argument with the sound of her quiet voice. "I won't have such talk at my table."

"Sorry, Mama," Dominic muttered.

Katherine tapped her fingers on the table and examined Lily thoughtfully. "Aidan Huntington? The son of the Duke of Carston? He was at your club?"

"And being very attentive to Lily," Dominic said.

"No more than he would have been to any other hostess," said Lily.

"Was he the one who sent the flowers?" Katherine asked.

"He sent flowers?" Dominic exploded, only to sit back at a look from his mother.

"Violets," said Isabel. "They were beautiful. Oh, Lily, was it him? Is he as handsome as they say? Did he dance with you at the club?" Isabel cared nothing at all for the past between the St. Claires and the Huntingtons—she was too young and romantic, and too softhearted.

Lily sighed. "Yes, he is good-looking. But handsome is as handsome does, and they also say he is quite the rake. I would be a fool to get involved with him." She glared at Dominic and Brendan. "Not the least of which because my hotheaded brothers would cause a scandal by dueling with him."

Isabel rolled her eyes. "I think it sounds romantic."

"Romantic to let Lily be taken advantage of again? Just as she was with Nichols?" Dominic said.

"I can take care of myself," Lily answered. "And you have better things to worry about. Don't you have a rehearsal today?"

"Yes, boys, your father has been at the Majestic for an hour already," Katherine said. "I think we have exhausted the topic."

"Shall we go riding in the park today, Lily?" Isabel asked. "I've been stuck here at home too long. I need to see people who are not my bossy brothers."

Lily nodded, still distracted by the quarrel and by Aidan and Lady HL and violet bouquets. "After I finish going over the accounts. I could use the exercise myself."

"I will go with you," said James, but Katherine shook her head.

"Your sisters will be fine on their own today," Katherine said. "I need your help with something later. And, Dominic dear, who exactly is this Louisa Carstairs?"

Lily pressed her hand to her mouth to keep from laughing at the chagrined look on Dominic's face and quickly made her escape from the breakfast room.

Rotten Row was crowded by the time Lily made her way there with Isabel, the graveled pathways crowded with riders and sleek carriages all jostling for prime space to see and be seen. It was an unseasonably warm day, the sky a pale, sunny blue, and everyone wanted to be outside enjoying the exercise. And the gossip.

Lily guided her horse smoothly into the slow parade, Isabel close behind her. The lane was a tangle of dark riding habits like her own forest-green one, of sleek horses and shining carriages, of lacy parasols and feathered bonnets. She glimpsed the famous courtesan Therese La Paiva from Paris, in her trademark skintight red habit and surrounded by black-coated men, as well as countesses and marchionesses and baronesses.

Everyone mingled at the high hour on Rotten Row. Even Queen Victoria sometimes appeared there in her carriage, though there was no sign of her today.

Lily studied everyone through the net veil of her riding hat, automatically scanning to see who was there, who talked to who, who snubbed who, who wore what. When she was a child, this would have been a prime spot for a con, a shivering dodge or the fake wedding band scheme. Now, though, observing everything around her was just good business.

And she was not looking for Aidan. She was *not*.

Isabel drew in next to her as they rode along slowly by the rail. "Dominic and Brendan aren't here now, Lily," she said. "You can tell me all about Lord Aidan Huntington."

Lily shook her head. "There is nothing to tell, Issy. I've met him once or twice. He was interested in the club, that's all, and was at the play last night."

"Mmm-hmm. Then why do you blush when I say his name to you?"

"I do not. It's merely a warm day," Lily protested.

"Not that warm. My friend Annabelle, the one in the chorus at the Majestic, says he is amazingly handsome. All the girls pray to see him in the green room at the theater, but he never is."

"I'm surprised to hear it. Gossip says he's a rogue of the first order."

"Maybe the gossip is wrong. They also have a lot to say about the St. Claires, don't they? And most of it is untrue."

Lily gave Isabel a startled glance. "What do you mean?"

Isabel laughed. "You all can't protect me from everything, you know. Besides, who cares what the tittle-tattle says? I want to hear about Lord Aidan. Was he really the one who sent you the violets?"

"Yes," Lily said reluctantly.

"I wouldn't think he'd send bouquets to every lady he meets 'once or twice.' "

"I am not sure why he sent them," Lily said quietly. She wished she *did* know what Aidan wanted from her and what she wanted from him.

"Because you're pretty, of course. And smart and loyal and brave. He would be a fool not to send you flowers."

It was Lily's turn to laugh. "You are my sister; of course you would say that. Society would see it very differently."

"Oh, pooh. Who needs society anyway? They're all so boring—Dominic is quite right about that." Isabel grinned at Lily. "But Lord Aidan doesn't sound boring. He sounds like a dashing character in a play."

"No," Lily murmured. "Boring is the last thing he is."

"You need more excitement, Lily. All you've done since Mr. Nichols died is work. And don't listen to our stuffy old brothers either. They don't know any more than society does."

"When did you get so wise, Issy?" Lily said with a laugh.

Isabel shrugged. "I learned it from you, I suppose. What else is an elder sister for?"

Lily smiled, but she wasn't at all sure excitement was what she needed. Not the kind of excitement Aidan offered, the kind that turned her body and her emotions upside down. They turned at the end of the lane and started back in the other direction, moving into the flow of the crowd again.

"Oh, look, Lily," Isabel exclaimed, pointing with her riding crop. "Isn't that that Bassington character who was chasing after you a few months ago?"

Lily sighed and looked to where Isabel pointed. It was indeed Freddy Bassington; she could see the sunlight on his unruly red hair. She had heard he had gone off to the country and had hoped it was true. She had certainly hoped he would go away once she refused to give back his letters. Those rambling missives, full of ardent declarations and bad poetry, were her guarantee he would keep his distance.

"I'm afraid so," Lily said. "That is quite the last time I am kind to some eager puppy I find myself seated next to at a dinner party."

Isabel giggled. "He did send you massive bouquets there for a while. The whole house smelled of lilies. But I must say I prefer those violets Lord Aidan sent. They suit you better."

Lily preferred them as well, but she wouldn't ever say so aloud. She didn't want to hear any more of Isabel's opinions on her romantic life. What pitifully little there was of it.

"Shall we ride back the other way?" Isabel asked. "Maybe he hasn't seen you yet."

"An excellent suggestion, Issy. But I fear it's too late." Bassington had turned his head in their direction, and his face went as red as his hair. He had definitely seen her.

Lily gave him a cool, polite nod and tried to edge her horse into the concealment of the crowd. Then she caught a glimpse of the man beside Freddy, and a gasp escaped her lips before she could catch it.

Aidan. It was Aidan who rode with Freddy Bassington.

His face was shadowed under the brim of his hat, but it was undoubtedly him with that austere, elegant profile. He wore a brown riding coat, plain and sharply tailored over his muscled shoulders and lean back, his hair curling over the velvet collar.

Lily felt her stomach clench under the tightness of her corset, and she pressed her palm to it. The handle of her riding crop bit into her skin, the pain holding her steady. What was Aidan doing with Freddy Bassington? Were they friends? Confidants?

That hardly made sense to her. The charming, easy-going Aidan and poor, bumbling Freddy, friends? But she knew both men enjoyed the theater, and strange bonds were formed at places like Eton and Oxford. Or maybe Freddy relied on Aidan to bring him confidence, and Freddy amused Aidan. Aidan did seem to like to be amused, as if life were one long party.

Lily frowned as she thought of that. Her brothers were the same way. Life was an amusement, one long swirl of dancing and drinking and playing cards, chasing women, and smoking opium. They took the theater seriously because out of all the other St. Claire business concerns, that was their very heart. To act, to create. Everything else they did—the music halls and gaming den—were all to support the work that went on at the Majestic.

So, yes, she did understand the bonds that could be formed at the theater. The beauty and profound truth of the plays was what mattered, and to keep it alive, to bring it to the audience, they needed the money for sets, costumes, and the best actors and playwrights. So they went out into the world, the "scandalous" St. Claires, objects of derision, shock, speculation, and desire among "respectable" society, but it did not matter. For one day, everyone they met would want something very much, and they would have to go to the St. Claires to get it. And they would pay a price for it.

Lily closed her eyes and thought of the old tales about her adopted family, the tales that showed just how wrong a Huntington was for a St. Claire. The St. Claires had once been a fine gentry family in their own right. Respected, revered almost, by the people they cared for on their estate. Not the wealthiest of families, nor the most influential. But they worked hard for their comfortable lives as a close-knit country family.

Until King Charles I came riding through St. Claire Abbey during his civil war, exhausted, hungry, wounded, barely kept upright by the battle-weary courtiers who were with him. They stayed a mere two days, resting and readying to flee onward. Young Mary St. Claire, barely more than a child, watched all the chaos with wide eyes. She had never seen wounds or death, had never seen despair and weakness in her sheltered life. It shocked her into silence.

But there was one young man, John Huntington, only a few years older than Mary, who served as standard-bearer to the king. The legend had it that they looked at each other across the tumult of a house preparing for war, and they were lost. They would never be parted again. That was the blessing and curse of the St. Claires, the depth of their passions.

But when they married amid the glitter of Charles II's court as lovers and spouses, things did not end well for poor Mary St. Claire. And her suffering still filled the family with rage toward the careless, cruel Huntingtons...

"Lily? What's wrong?" Isabel said, and Lily felt her sister's hand on her arm. "You looked so far away just now, and you were so distracted at breakfast. Are you ill?"

Lily tore herself away from brooding on the past and made herself smile at Isabel. She couldn't see where Freddy Bassington was now, or Aidan either. Maybe she had just imagined seeing Aidan with Freddy. "I was just daydreaming."

"It must have been an unpleasant dream. You were frowning so fiercely."

"Must be a headache coming on. The sun is so bright today."

Isabel peered doubtfully up into the sky. "Perhaps. Maybe we should go home now. I've had enough of these gawking crowds anyway."

Lily nodded, and they turned their horses toward the gates of the park. The sun was slowly sinking toward the horizon now, the trees casting larger shadows, and the knots of horses and carriages were thinner. Everyone had to go home to change for the night's revels, balls, theaters, suppers, or more disreputable pursuits.

Lily was still distracted by her thoughts and didn't see the man on horseback until she was nearly beside him.

"Mrs. Nichols," he said, and she looked up, startled by the familiar, rough, dark sound of that voice. The voice she had been hearing in her dreams.

Her fingers tightened on the handle of her crop as she stared at Aidan. He tipped his hat to her and nodded, all politeness. But his smile—she hadn't seen such a smile on his lips before. She had seen him roguish, teasing, coaxing. She had let the golden heat of his smile wash over her, carry her away.

This smile looked thin, almost cynical, and it didn't meet his blue eyes. His gaze swept over her, quick and assessing. Lily felt suddenly cold despite the lingering warmth of the evening.

"Lord Aidan," she said. "Such a surprise to see you here."

"Is it?" he replied, and she still had that strange sense of something off, something not right. Something just beyond the edge of what she could see and understand.

She didn't like that feeling at all. Her whole life depended on observing and knowing what went on around her, how to respond to every situation, how to control it. But Aidan was closed to her.

"I hope you've enjoyed your ride," he said.

Lily nodded shortly, very aware of Isabel watching her and of Aidan's narrowed eyes and that faint, knowing smile. "Though I would prefer a *real* gallop across a country field, not just this sedate walk." A hard ride that would whip her hair free of its pins and clear her mind of all her confused thoughts. Thoughts *he* had put into her calm, quiet life.

"Not much chance of that in London, I fear, Mrs. Nichols," he said. "I would not have taken you for a woman who seeks out danger, though."

"Oh, she is a bruising rider!" Isabel piped up. "She even leaves our brothers in the dust when they dare to race her, much to their chagrin."

Aidan's glance flickered to Isabel, and his smile transformed to that charming, white flash Lily remembered. "Is that so? How very interesting. I must remember to place my wager on her, if the chance ever arises."

Lily swallowed hard. "Where are my manners? Lord

Aidan, may I present my sister, Miss Isabel St. Claire. Issy, this is Lord Aidan Huntington."

Isabel laughed and held out her hand for him to bow over between their horses. "Oh, I have certainly heard of you, Lord Aidan! I'm very happy to meet you at last."

"Have you really, Miss St. Claire?" Aidan said, his smile widening. "I am not sure if I should be flattered or frightened."

"Oh, I've heard only good things," Isabel said. She glanced at Lily from the corner of her eye. "The violets you sent to the house were lovely."

"Thank you." Aidan looked at Lily again, with that speculative glint in his eyes that she did not trust. His eyes slowly slid over her body in the close-fitting habit, until she shivered as if he caressed her with his hands.

She wanted to turn and run—or slash at his too-handsome face with her crop. She wrapped the reins tighter around her fist and held her ground. She wasn't about to let one man's changeable temper frighten her away.

Aidan leaned toward Isabel and said confidingly, "If only your sister liked my flowers just as much. I'm afraid my offering displeased her."

Isabel's eyes went wide. "Not at all! Violets are her favorite flowers. She kept them in her own sitting room, and she never does that when someone sends her flowers."

"Indeed?" Aidan's smile drifted over her again. "And does she receive many flowers from admirers?"

"Oh, I think she—" Isabel began, only to freeze when Lily reached over and grasped her arm. Lily wanted to scream at her sister to stop talking, to catch Isabel's reins and pull them both out of the park as fast as they could go.

But she just gave a tight smile and said, "Isabel, I do believe we are expected at home soon."

"No, we—" Isabel turned to Lily and gasped. "Oh, yes. Yes, of course."

"I do thank you for the flowers, Lord Aidan," Lily ground out, not quite meeting his eyes. "Isabel is right. They are lovely, and it was most courteous of you to send them."

Aidan leaned toward her and said in a low, dark voice only she could hear, "Oh, I did not send them to be *courteous*, Lily. I sent them in hopes you would remember those moments in your office every time you looked at them. Remember what we did together…"

Lily reared back from him, startling her horse, who shifted restively under her. "We do need to be going now."

"Then allow me to escort you home," Aidan said.

"That won't be necessary, thank you," Lily said. What if Dominic or Brendan were at the house and saw a Huntington bringing their sisters home? Her head throbbed at the thought.

Isabel shot her a frown, and Lily's head ached even more at the thought of how her sister would interrogate her once they were alone.

"At least let me see you to the gates, then," Aidan said easily. "I wouldn't want two ladies trampled in the exodus from the fashionable hour."

Lily couldn't see much danger of that. The crowds were much sparser now, and they had the pathway nearly to themselves for the moment. But she couldn't see a way to escape without being blatantly rude. She nodded and said, "Thank you, Lord Aidan." And they turned their horses toward the main gates of the park.

Aidan and Isabel chatted easily about the theater, Aidan complimenting Isabel on her performance as Juliet and Isabel complaining it was the last time her parents would let her take a lead role until she was older.

Lily half listened to them, murmuring polite replies when they asked her a question, but she kept thinking of Aidan's strange smile, the look in his eyes when he studied her. What had happened between them since the last time she saw him? What had hardened that look in his eyes?

Then she remembered that he was with Freddy Bassington earlier. Lily almost groaned aloud. *Freddy!* If Aidan was his friend... Oh, damn it all, what would Freddy have told him? What did Aidan think about her now? That she was a flirt, who rejected men's affections and then kept their letters for nefarious purposes? Better that than the truth, though.

Everyone always thought they knew things about her, when they didn't know her at all. She couldn't let them.

They reached the gates of the park with Isabel still chattering. Lily thought she saw escape at hand, but then she was distracted by the sight of a young child standing on the pavement just beyond the gilded gates. The girl was thin and pale, dressed in a ragged, much-mended gray dress and knitted shawl and a grubby cap over her tangled hair. She held a basket full of packets of matches tied to her waist, with a handful of them held out to passersby.

"Matches! Penny per dozen," she cried out. Everyone ignored her as they rushed by out of the park.

Lily's heart ached at the sight of the child. How often had *she* been that girl when she was young? How many days had she spent hungry and terrified she wouldn't have enough money to take to Beaumont at the end of the day?

She started to climb down from her horse in order to give the girl what money she had, when suddenly a man in a fine coat and silk hat brushed by the child. It was the merest touch, but her matches fell from her hand and scattered on the walkway. The girl sent up a loud wail, and Lily knew what was going on. The child was a Lucifer-dropper.

Lily remembered the scheme very well, for she had tried it once or twice herself. A child selling matches would suddenly duck in front of a passing well-dressed gentleman and drop her matches and then start crying and fussing as if he had pushed her. Usually a crowd would start to gather to see what the noise was about, and the man would pay off the child just to stop her from making a scene.

But this man was having none of that. He grabbed the girl by the arm, making her cry out in unfeigned pain. “I’m not listening to any of your lies!” he said. “You street rats have done this to me once too often. I’m calling the constables this time.”

“Oh, no, sir! Please,” the girl sobbed. “I didn’t do nothin’, I swear.”

The man gave her a hard shake, and Lily swung down off her horse. Isabel called her name, but she was hardly aware of what she was doing. She only knew she had to stop what was happening to that child.

She pushed her way through the crowd that had predictably begun to gather and shoved the man away from the girl.

He was so startled by her sudden interference that he fell back a step, and the girl’s wails faltered. He swung around toward Lily, and she saw that his bearded face was bright red, his eyes blazing with fury.

"What is the meaning of this?" he shouted.

But Lily was just as angry as he was, and she stood her ground. "Apologize to her for your unacceptable behavior," she said. Her voice was steady and cold even though her hands were shaking.

"I should do *what*?" the man choked out.

"You are behaving like a brute on a public walkway, sir, and to a child at that," Lily said. "Someone should call the constables on *you*."

"I don't have to take this nonsense," the man said. He suddenly shoved the child away and strode off into the park. The girl landed hard on the pavement and whimpered, a more fearful sound than her loud wails.

Lily dropped to her knees beside her and reached for the child's scraped, dirty hand. "Are you all right, my dear?" she whispered. The girl yanked away from her. "No, it's all right now, I promise."

The feral glow in the child's eyes as she glared past the tangles of her hair made Lily want to cry. She tried to smile reassuringly, to ask the child her name, but suddenly she was pushed out of the way and a woman swept the girl up in her arms.

Lily sat back on her heels and looked up to see a thin, gray-faced woman. She also glared down at Lily as she clutched at the weeping girl.

"You leave her alone! All of you," the woman cried. Before Lily could stop her, she whirled around, and the two of them disappeared. The crowd, sensing there was nothing more to see in this impromptu little scene, dispersed.

But Lily couldn't move from where she knelt. She stared numbly at the spot where the child had been, at the scattered matches. She let out a sob.

"Shhh, Lily, it's all right," Aidan whispered in her ear.

Slowly, slowly, his soft words pierced through the buzzing in her head, and she became aware that he held her hands. She had stripped off her gloves when she knelt by the child, and he rubbed at her cold, bare fingers.

Lily shook her head and raised her gaze from their joined hands to meet his eyes. They watched her face carefully, the blue so dark it almost looked black. She couldn't tell what he was thinking at all, but she remembered his cynical smile when they first met in the park, the way he seemed to know something, some secret, about her. And she had just behaved appallingly in front of him. The girl's plight had catapulted her back into a past she would never want anyone to know, least of all him.

She tried to pull away from him, but he held on to her. "I'm quite all right," she said, and tried to laugh. "So silly of me to overreact like that."

"You did not overreact," he answered. "Anyone with a heart would have been angry."

"But no one else made a scene, did they?" No one else here at the fine park gates knew what it felt like to be bruised and hungry, to know there was no place to run. She tugged harder at his hands, feeling a hot bubble of panic rise up in her when he wouldn't let her go. He looked at her searchingly, as if he wanted to see what she hid in her locked-away soul.

But she couldn't let him see. She could *never* let him see.

"Please, Aidan, I'm fine now!" she cried. "You can let me go."

"Lily, you almost fainted. Even now you look as if you just saw a ghost."

"I did," she whispered.

He let her go then, but only to put his arm around her shoulder. He seemed to have forgotten they stood on a public pavement, but Lily remembered. She eased away from him and rubbed her hands over her arms. Where was Isabel?

"Please, let me see you home," Aidan said.

Lily shook her head. Finally, to her relief, she saw Isabel making her way toward them on the lane, leading Lily's horse by the bridle.

"Thank you, Lord Aidan, but there's no need," Lily said. "I see my sister now."

Before he could argue, she brushed off her sister's cries of concern and swung up into the saddle. "Good day, Lord Aidan," she said.

He stayed her with one hand on her saddle. Lily stared down at his long, elegant fingers against the brown leather, so powerful in their very stillness. So alluring. That panic to get away choked her again, and she wanted to bring her crop down on his hand, to make him ache as she did.

"You can run now, Lily," he said quietly. "But not forever."

Then he let her go and stepped back. Lily tugged at the reins and guided her horse as fast as she dared to the end of the road, Isabel scrambling to keep up with her. Lily could sense that her sister practically vibrated with the force of the questions she wanted to ask, but Isabel stayed silent as they rode home.

And Lily could swear she felt the burning force of Aidan's blue gaze on her skin long after she knew he was out of sight. She forced herself not to look back at him.

Aidan slowly drew the small pair of black leather gloves across his palm. He had found them on the ground where

Lily had knelt beside the child, and he had put them in his coat pocket to give back to her, but in the rush he forgot.

The smell of her violet perfume drifted from the crushed folds, and he closed his eyes to inhale deeply.

Damn Lily St. Claire. Why did she get under his skin like that? Invading his senses until she was all he thought about.

She was a puzzle, a mystery, and it was true he could never resist a challenge. Every time he thought he had seen who she was—a lonely widow he wanted in his bed, a temptress who held on to men's love letters to torment them—she changed completely. She slipped out of his grasp, leaving him more baffled than ever.

Leaving him still wanting her. And he wanted more than her body for a few diverting nights. He wanted her secrets, her smiles.

Aidan frowned as he stared at the patch of pavement where she had knelt by the ragged child. He had been angry with her for what she had done with Freddy, playing with his heart while keeping his letters. He had been ready to confront her, to do whatever he had to do to get those damned letters back, to give her a taste of her own malice.

But then he saw her face as she looked at that child, the raw torment in her brown eyes. For a moment, her cool mask fell away, and he saw a world of pain behind it. He remembered the burning longing he had seen all too briefly when he kissed her in her office; it seemed a part of that same complex, tormented world she tried to hide away. She said she was no actress, but Aidan thought she was the finest actress he had ever seen.

What would he see in her eyes if he had her in his bed,

her body under his as he slowly made her come apart? What would she do then? Would he hold the real Lily at last?

Aidan shook his head and muttered an oath as he reached for his horse's reins and leaped into the saddle. Lily was becoming a distraction he didn't need, almost an obsession. It was because she still hid from him, ran from him, and the chase had his temper up. Once he held her, knew her, the fire would fade, and he would see she was like all other women.

And Aidan liked all women too much to settle for just one for very long. He liked his life just as it was.

He turned the horse toward home and resisted the strange urge to ride past Lily's house. He would let her run for now. But soon, very soon, he would go after her, and she couldn't hide from him forever.

"So there you are."

Lily whirled away from the mirror in the foyer, gasping at the sudden sound of a voice. Isabel had gone upstairs, and Lily thought she was alone for a moment. Her heart pounded as Dominic stepped out of the evening shadows that stretched over the polished parquet floor.

"You scared me," she said breathlessly. "I thought everyone was at the theater."

Dominic held up a stack of papers as he studied her carefully, frowning. Lily always hated it when he turned serious. "Father forgot these. Did you enjoy your ride?"

"Very much." Lily turned back to the mirror to finish unpinning her hat. The eyes that stared back at her in the glass glittered too brightly, and her cheeks were slashed with red. She looked and felt feverish, shaking with old memories and new, frightening feelings for Aidan.

When he had held her after the child was snatched away, she had wanted to cling to him, losing herself in the clean heat and strength of him. In that flashing moment, she had *needed* him, and she didn't like that feeling at all.

"You're back late," Dominic said.

"The park was very crowded today," Lily answered. She wished he would go away and quit looking at her like that. She had had enough today of people trying to peer into her soul. She needed to be alone, to rebuild the walls of her careful defenses. To forget.

"I'm sorry, Lily," Dominic said suddenly.

Surprised, Lily raised her gaze to meet his in the glass. Dominic so rarely apologized. "For what?"

"For pestering you about Aidan bloody Huntington. You were quite right—it's none of my business."

"No, it's not." Lily slowly put her hat down on the pier table under the mirror. "But you seemed so deeply opposed to me even talking to him. Why be sorry now?"

Dominic scowled. "I had a talk with Brendan."

"Oh? And what did the two of you decide about my life?" she asked wryly.

"Know thy enemy."

She blinked. "What?"

"Perhaps it would be a good thing for one of us to be friends with a Huntington."

"Oh, would it now?" She whirled around toward Dominic, trying to resist the urge to hit him with her hat. It had been a long, trying day, and she was sick of people trying to use her. "Well, Dominic St. Claire, I am not your spy."

He held up his hand. "That is not what I meant—"

"Oh? Then pray tell, what did you mean? Because that is exactly what it sounded like. To spy on the Huntingtons through Lord Aidan."

"We just want to know what they're planning. They've caused the St. Claires enough grief already."

"That was long in the past! And perhaps you want to cause them a bit of grief now?" Lily lifted the heavy hem of her habit and hurried up the stairs. Her head was pounding in earnest now, and she was tired. Tired of men and their schemes, tired of her own emotions tying her up in knots.

"Well, you and Brendan go and do your worst to the Huntingtons—get yourselves killed in duels, cast out of society—and see if I care," she called over the balustrade. "I won't be your spy."

"Lily, please." The soft tone of Dominic's voice stopped her foot on the next step. Her confident, laughing brother never sounded like that.

She peered down at him as he came to stand just below her.

"I'm sorry," he said again. "I shouldn't have said anything tonight, not when you're tired. I didn't mean it that way. It's just... Damn it, Lily, it's the Huntingtons."

"And we are the St. Claires. I know," Lily answered quietly. No two families could be further apart. None could hate each other more. And she could not forget that no matter what else he was, Aidan was a Huntington.

"We'll talk more of this later, Dominic," she said, and continued up the stairs toward the empty darkness of her room.

Chapter Eight

Lily slowly wandered around the edge of the main salon of the Devil's Fancy, watching the people gathered around the card tables. It was not as crowded as the night they had opened. She had heard that Queen Victoria was in attendance at the Italian opera tonight before she left for Coburg, and most of society would be gathered there to curry her favor. But they still had quite a crowd at the club, people who were becoming regulars, who would prefer the thrill of winning and losing on the turn of a card to staring at the young queen and her stern German husband.

Lily rubbed her lace-gloved hands over her bare arms as she listened to the laughter and chatter and the clack of the roulette wheel spinning. She saw it all and took it all in, but she didn't feel as if she were really there. She felt like she had been wandering in this strange half-waking state ever since the incident at the park yesterday.

Her nightmares of the past and Dominic's hints that she should spy on the Huntingtons, it was all tangled up in her mind. She worked to pull her usual calm coolness around her, tried to lose herself in account books and the club, but it all hovered there at the edge of her thoughts.

She noticed Brendan staring at her from across the room, and she made herself smile at him. He didn't smile back, but he gave her a nod before looking down at the cards in his hand. In the rosy-amber glow of the gaslight, the tracery of scars on his left cheek was softened and his brushed-back sweep of black hair gleamed. He was fashionably dressed in his usual black-and-white evening attire, yet still there was that air of barely leashed rawness about him, something dark and primitive and angry.

Brendan was the brother Lily understood the least, for he always stood slightly apart from the rest of the world. He never told anyone how he got those scars, what had happened to him when he disappeared several years ago and returned with his gorgeous face marred. And Lily never dared ask.

But his hatred of the Huntingtons had seemed even hotter after that. Lily would rather talk to Dominic about the Huntingtons than Brendan, if she had to talk about them at all. She couldn't even imagine what Brendan would want her to do as their spy.

She strolled slowly to the other side of the room, making sure everything was going smoothly and all their patrons seemed happy. The steady flow of champagne always seemed to lessen the sting of losing, and she made a note to order more from the vintner.

"Mrs. Nichols," a footman said at her shoulder. "A gentleman wishes to see you in your office."

"My office?" she said sharply. No one was to go in there without her; everyone knew that.

The footman flushed and shuffled his feet. "I am sorry, Mrs. Nichols, but he was quite insistent. You did say we should never upset the patrons."

Lily sighed and shook her head. These arrogant aristocrats, pushing their way in everywhere! God save her from them and their demands.

And from one "arrogant aristocrat" in particular, she added as she thought of Aidan's blue eyes and his smile.

"Very well, I will see to them. But from now on, fetch me *before* they are shown to my office." She hurried from the salon and up the stairs, intent on ejecting whoever it was from her room. And if they protested, so much the better; somehow she was itching for a fight tonight.

She pushed open the office door and strode across the threshold, only to freeze. It was not just some drunken patron who waited for her. It was Aidan.

He stood next to the bookshelf behind her desk, lazily studying the titles there with his hands on his lean hips. He turned to smile at her, his teeth flashing white in the dimness of the room. There was only one lamp lit on the desk, and he stood just beyond its light. Yet she knew without a doubt it was him. No one else was that tall, that elegantly powerful, like some jungle cat just waiting to coil its strong muscles and pounce. He seemed to fill up her whole room, possess it, just by standing there.

"Good evening, Lily," he said.

Lily closed the door behind her and leaned back on it. "What are you doing in here?"

"I wanted to see you."

"Then you should have come to the salon. I've been there all evening."

"I wanted to see you alone," he said bluntly. "And I came to return these."

He laid something on the desk, and she saw it was her riding gloves, lost in the confusion at the park. His fingers slid over the leather, and she braced her hands harder on the door.

"You could have just sent them to me," she said.

Aidan shook his head, and in a sudden flash of movement, he was across the room and pressed against her.

Lily gasped at the sensation of his hard body sliding over hers, and she tried to whirl away. But he held her in place, his prisoner, with his palms to the door above her head, his knee between her thighs. He didn't even touch her, not skin to skin, but his heat wrapped all around her and held her faster than any chains.

"Fuck it all, Lily," he growled, and she startled at the sound of the crudeness in his brandy-smooth voice. "Do you know how crazy you make me?"

"Aidan..." She couldn't stop shaking. She pressed her palms to his chest, trying to push him away, to escape. Somehow instead she found herself twisting her fingers into the slippery coolness of his satin waistcoat and tugging him closer. The lace of her gloves rasped over the smoothness, and she could feel the ripple of his muscles underneath. The pounding of his heart echoed her own.

He lowered his face into the curve of her shoulder, and she felt his open mouth on her neck. His warm breath on her skin, the scrape of his teeth. She made *him* crazy? She felt ready to be sent to Bedlam just from his touch.

He bit down lightly, and she cried out. Her hands convulsed on his waistcoat, twisting it tighter.

"Why can't I stay away from you?" he whispered as his open mouth slid over her ear, pressing a kiss to the pulse pounding at her temple. One of his hands slid into her hair, his fingers combing through the strands to scatter her pins and combs until it tumbled over her shoulders.

His caress tightened, and he pulled her hair back, the tug of it just on the dark border between pain and pleasure, until her throat was bared to him.

"Why do you hide from me?" he said, his voice filled with torment. He closed his teeth on the vulnerable hollow of her throat, and Lily arched her body into his.

She wasn't hiding from him now. It was as if his rough touch, the rawness of his need, ripped open something inside of her, and all the fear and uncertainty of the last few days, the desire she had tried so hard to suppress, broke free and flew out into the world.

She couldn't think anymore, couldn't remember; she could only feel. Feel what Aidan was doing to her, how he made all her senses flare into a burning life she didn't even know existed. The fear was still there, but she pushed it away.

Aidan's mouth took hers, and as his tongue plunged inside, she could taste the darkness of him, the lust, the primitive need that drove away everything else. She felt the hidden shadows of his soul that called out to hers.

They both hid from the world in their own ways. But now, for this one fleeting moment, they were free together.

Not breaking their hungry kiss, Aidan pulled her heavy silk skirts up to her waist, the soft fabric and stiff net of her petticoats foaming around them. She wrapped her arms around his neck and held on to him tightly.

"Why do women wear so damned many clothes?" he muttered against her lips.

Lily gasped when his fingers suddenly closed on the soft muslin of her drawers and ripped them apart at the seam.

He pinched the soft curve at the top of her thigh, and the sensation of pain/pleasure shot through her core. She arched her hips into him, her bare sex rubbing at his erection behind his trousers. It slid over the sensitive little bundle of nerves inside her, making her clench, but it wasn't nearly enough.

Still holding her against him with one hand, Aidan slid the other between her legs as he kissed her shoulder, the curve of her breast. Her nipple puckered and pebbled, aching as it pressed to her corset.

"Aidan," she cried as he slid one long finger into her damp folds. He pressed deeper with a delicious burning friction, exploring her, stretching her, until he could press in another finger. His thumb brushed over that spot, and she almost sobbed with pleasure.

"So tight," he whispered. He moved slowly in and out of her, the same rhythm as his tongue against hers, brushing against her most sensitive spot again and again until she moaned.

She threaded her fingers through his hair and moved with his touch. The pleasure built inside of her, flickering from his fingers inside of her until it spread over her whole body. The floor seemed to tilt, the walls moving.

Startled, Lily tore her mouth from his and eased her head back. It wasn't the room that was moving; it was her. Aidan had swung her around, both his hands under her legs as he spun her toward the chaise by the wall. He lowered her onto the cushions as his teeth closed over her soft earlobe, tugging at her cameo drop earring.

"You have too many clothes," she said, and let her head fall back for his mouth. She shoved his coat off his shoulders and tugged at the folds of his cravat until it unwound from his neck. She wanted to see him, touch him. Feel his body against hers as it had been in her dream.

Aidan unfastened his waistcoat and shirt, never taking his mouth from her skin. He groaned against her shoulder when she slid her fingers between the loose linen folds and caressed his bare chest.

His skin was smooth and hot, damp with sweat, satin stretched taut over iron muscles. He felt so *good*, so perfect under her hands. Her fingertips traced over his ribs, down a long, thin scar that marred his perfect skin, over his ridged abdomen. He was no soft, idle nobleman.

She swept her hand along the band of his trousers, over the hard angle of his hip until she could cup his erection beneath the fabric. She wrapped her fingers around him and swept them down to its base. He seemed to grow even harder under her touch, and his hips thrust against her.

"Minx," he growled.

Lily laughed, but her laughter faded when he knelt between her legs and reached for her hands. Before she could tell what he meant to do, he pressed them to the wall and wound his cravat around her wrists in a tight loop. He pulled on the silk, and she was bound, her body arched up into his.

"Aidan, no," she whispered. She felt all her control slipping away, falling into his hands, and fear and desire tangled up in her.

He slid one finger under the silk bonds as if to test their tightness. "Does it hurt, Lily?"

She shook her head. It didn't hurt, not physically. But being vulnerable to his desires, his domination—it awakened something in her she wasn't sure she wanted.

A slow, feral smile spread over his lips, and he leaned down to kiss her again. As he held his hand over her bound wrists, his tongue swept into her mouth, tangling with hers, scraping over her teeth, making every part of her his.

Under his kiss, the fear faded, leaving only a hot haze of lust. His mouth trailed away from hers, over her cheek, her arched throat, the curve of her shoulder. The flat of his tongue circled her breast, dipped between her cleavage. As he tugged down her bodice to take her nipple deep into his mouth, suckling it hard, he pulled her skirts up higher and pressed his palm to her mound.

Tied as she was, Lily could do nothing but submit to his touch, to feel every sensation, every touch and kiss. He seemed to be all around her, all she knew.

Her nipple slid from his mouth, and she opened her eyes to see him kneel back at the edge of the chaise. He pressed his hands to the inside of her thighs, just above the ribbon garters of her stockings, and gently urged her farther apart with her knees drawn up. She couldn't see him past the froth of her skirts, but she could definitely *feel* him. He laid her flat on the chaise, the linen of his shirt abrading her soft skin, and then she felt the tip of his tongue trace her damp seam, one long, wet sweep as he tasted her.

"Aidan!" Lily twisted in her bonds but she couldn't get free. She had seen this done so many times; she had seen everything growing up in the brothel. But no one had ever done it to her. It was shocking in its intimacy, somehow more intimate than any kind of intercourse. Shocking, and so, so pleasurable.

She tried to jerk away from him but his hands tightened on her thighs, holding her open to him. "Do I have to tie your ankles as well?" he said, and blew a soft, hot breath against her. Then she felt his tongue on her again, driving through her folds, deep into her.

He groaned with pleasure, and Lily squeezed her eyes closed. There in the darkness, she felt every lick, every scrape of his teeth, driving her higher, higher. When he slid his finger into her, tracing his nail over that one spot, she cried out and leaped into that swirling abyss of climax. He caught her between his teeth, tugging at her, and she fell even harder.

She sobbed as his mouth trailed away from her, and he kissed the quivering skin of her thigh. She could feel the taut tension of his body against her, the desperation of his touch as he hooked his fingers behind the curve of her knee.

"Lily, Lily," he said hoarsely. "God, the way you taste... I have to fuck you now."

"Yes," she gasped. "Yes."

His hand tightened on her leg, and he flipped her over onto her stomach with her skirts caught around her. She pressed her bound hands to the curved back of the chaise and closed her eyes as he raised her up on her knees. She heard the harsh rasp of his breath, the pounding, erratic rhythm of her heart, the scrape of wool fabric as he pushed down his trousers and lowered his body over hers.

His arms were braced on either side of her, his chest pressed to the arch of her back, and she felt his hair brush over her skin as he kissed the nape of her neck. Then he pressed the tip of his penis against her, rocking back and forth as he found his angle and slid inside her.

She was so wet with need that he plunged all the way to the hilt, balls-deep in her, and she cried out at the fullness, the slight burning. It had been so, so long, and never like this. Her head dropped down between her arms, pressed to the chaise as she felt him with her. Part of her.

He went very still, and his lips swept over her shoulder. "All right, Lily?" he said hoarsely, and she nodded.

Better than all right, it felt too good. Too right. That fear hovered near her again, spreading its dark wings.

But there was no time for it to catch her. Aidan drew back and thrust into her again, driving away everything but the feeling of their joining. She arched back into him, meeting him thrust for thrust until they found their rhythm together. He moved faster, harder, and she felt his sweat on her back, heard the sound of skin meeting skin, and it drove her need higher.

"Lily!" he shouted amid a torrent of dark curses. His palm landed hard on her bare buttock, and the bite of it sent her soaring into another climax.

"Again," she gasped, and cried out when his open hand landed hard on her skin.

He suddenly pulled out of her, and she felt him press his hand over himself as he came. She felt the heat of it as some of the liquid landed on her naked thigh, and it made her shudder.

She collapsed to the chaise, her cheek pressed to the cool leather. She struggled to breathe again, trying to pull herself back down to earth. She felt as if she floated somewhere outside herself, weightless, numb. Free.

Aidan fell to the chaise beside her, his chest moving hard with the force of his breath. He gently kissed her shoulder and reached around her to untie her hands. She moaned at the sting of the blood rushing back to her fingertips.

He smoothed his palm over the tangled fall of her hair, a slow caress over her neck and shoulders and back before he wrapped the long strands around his wrist. They lay there like that for long minutes, close in the silence, the dreamy aftermath of pleasure.

But all too soon, Lily became aware of other things. Of the cool air on her bare backside, the press of the chaise on her cheek, the muffled clatter of traffic from the street below. The man whose body lay against hers.

Aidan Huntington's body. Aidan, who had just had sex with her, bound her hands, slapped her ass, and made her go mad from it all. Made all her defenses come tumbling down.

She pushed herself up to sit on the edge of the chaise and tugged her gown over her shoulders and down along her shaking legs. Her hair unwrapped from his wrist, but she felt him catch a fold of her skirt between his fingers. He rubbed the crumpled silk.

"Why do you dress so somberly?" he said, his voice rough. He held up the fabric to let the fading lamplight fall on its dark purple color.

"Because I am a widow," she answered, and snatched her skirt out of his hand. She heard him roll to his back, and she looked over her shoulder to see that he lay there with his hands clasped lazily under his head, watching her with hooded eyes. As if he had all night to ponder her mysteries.

"For more than a year now," he said. "You're too young to stay in purples and dark blues."

"I like my clothes." They let her fade into the scenery. Hide from everyone.

Except this man. He wouldn't let her hide from him at all.

He grinned up at her, his dimple flashing. Just like that, he went from dominant lover to careless rogue.

He caught her around her waist and drew her down on top of him. He took her lips in a lingering kiss. Unlike their frantic, lustful embraces of earlier, this kiss was slow, seeking. He traced the tip of his tongue along her swollen lower lip before he drew back to look into her eyes.

"Well, I like you *out* of your clothes better," he said.

She couldn't help herself. She laid her hand on his cheek and let her fingertips trace over his sharp cheekbone and the line of his nose, the ridge of his brow. She outlined his sensual mouth, the mouth that had driven her to such heights of madness. He was such a good-looking man, almost godlike with his skin gilded in the lamplight. Had they really just come together?

"We never did quite get around to losing the clothes, did we?" she murmured.

He caught her hand in his and pressed his lips to the soft center of her palm. He slipped the tip of her finger into his mouth and gently nipped at it. "Next time," he said.

Next time? "Aidan..."

He shook his head and tightened his hold on her hand so she could not turn away.

"Come with me to the theater tomorrow, Lily," he said.

"I go to the theater every day," she answered, still bemused that he wanted to see her again. That she wanted to see him again. She couldn't stay away from him, even as she remembered that strange smile he gave her when they met in the park and a warning bell rang faintly in her mind.

"Not like this one. Please, Lily. Don't say no. Come with me, just this once."

Lily laughed ruefully. "Very well. Just this once, Aidan, though I fear I'm sure to regret it."

Aidan grinned and kissed her hand again. "I won't let you regret it. Meet me in your back garden again. And for pity's sake, woman, wear some color. There's no need to be the respectable widow where we're going."

Lily nodded and watched as he gathered his discarded coat and waistcoat from the floor. He straightened his clothes and his hair, which was tousled from her fingers. She smoothed her own gown before she led him to the back stairs that would take him to the street out of sight of her brothers.

He kissed her hand one more time, whispered, "Tomorrow," and then he was gone.

Bemused and dizzy, Lily made her way back to her office and locked the door behind her. The small room felt stuffy and warm, the air filled with the heady scent of sex and skin, of Aidan's cologne mingled with her own violet perfume. It made her remember all too clearly what they had done together, his mouth and tongue on her, her body bound and stretched beneath his, that dark need.

She hurried over to open the window and let some of the cool night air in. A fog was rolling in off the Thames, thick and damp, gray with the smell of coal fires and the tang of the river. Through the clouds, she just glimpsed a flash of bright yellow as Aidan's carriage drove away from the club. She stared after him until he was gone, and then she crossed her arms tightly at her waist and turned back to the room.

The lamp was sputtering low. One of its fading beams fell on her gloves laid out on the desk where Aidan had left them. She placed her hand over them gently, stroking her fingertips over the smooth leather.

Then she noticed that one of the desk drawers was

slightly ajar. She was always so very careful to keep them tightly closed. She slid it open to examine the contents, the papers neatly filed, the account book, the stack of creamy stationery engraved with her initials. It all seemed to be in order, not moved as if someone had been rifling through them.

Lily rubbed wearily at her eyes. "And now you are becoming delusional," she whispered.

She should go home now, find her own bed, sleep—and decide whether or not she should really go to the theater with Aidan Huntington.

Aidan bounded up the stairs to his lodgings, feeling lighter than he had in a very long time. Lily had agreed to go out with him, and strangely enough, just being with her made him feel as if the world were somehow new again. That life was taking some strange, fresh direction. He couldn't wait to see what would happen next, what new facet she would reveal.

He unlocked his door and slipped inside. The only light in the room came from the window, and in the shadows, he almost didn't see the mail scattered across the carpet where the postman had thrust it under the door. On top of the pile was a letter addressed to Aidan in Freddy Bassington's messy handwriting.

At the sight of it, some of Aidan's high spirits dimmed, but there was no escaping from the letter. He knelt down to pick it up and broke the wax seal.

It was a short missive, with none of Freddy's usual enthusiasms. He demanded to know if Aidan had made any progress retrieving his letters or if he had discovered anything of Lily St. Claire's intentions. The penciled words were hastily scrawled, smeared, full of desperation.

Aidan couldn't tell his friend he had discovered nothing of his letters—though he *had* learned much about their possessor lately. And he intended to discover more very soon.

He went to his desk and stuffed the note into a drawer. There would be time to figure out all he needed to know about Lily St. Claire. . . .

Chapter Nine

"You were quite right," Lily said. "This is nothing like the Majestic."

Aidan laughed as he watched her study their surroundings, her face solemn as she took in every detail. He hadn't been sure he should bring her here. It wasn't the usual place he brought a woman. A society miss would faint dead away at the scandal, and a courtesan or an opera dancer wanted fine suppers in expensive hotel restaurants. But he had taken a chance on Lily, on the depths he glimpsed behind her serious, dark eyes.

On the sense of adventure he found with her in bed, much to his surprise.

He slid his arm around her shoulders and drew her closer, just to feel the brush of her body against his. The smell of violets lingered in her hair, and he leaned his head down to inhale the sweet scent, the warmth of her skin.

Damn it, you are a fool tonight, he thought. Finding excuses to touch her, to smell her hair. He hadn't been so lustful since he was a boy. He needed to back away, to keep control.

"I haven't been to a place like this in years," she said.

"Do you like it?"

Lily glanced up at him, a faint smile on her lips. Her eyes were so dark in the dim, smoky room, so opaque and cool. He could hardly believe this was the same woman who had let him tie her up and spank her bottom, who came apart in his arms.

"I don't know yet," she said.

"Well, let's get something to drink while you decide." Aidan slipped his arm lower around her waist and led her into the crowded room.

While his friend Nick's place didn't have the grandeur of the Majestic, it was not exactly a penny gaff either. It was spacious, carved out of an old, abandoned dissenters' chapel, with plenty of tables and chairs and a dance floor. A large wooden stage was built at the far end of the room, with benches for the audience lined up in front of it.

Along the adjacent wall was the bar, its long wooden surface full of the scars and nicks of hundreds of patrons. The cloudy mirror behind it reflected the crowd of workmen in rough wool, shopkeepers in their black coats, and girls from the shops and factories in their cheap, colorful finery out for an evening of fun. Nick mostly kept out the rougher sorts.

Aidan led Lily around the edge of the crowded dance floor to a place at the end of the bar. He caught a glimpse of the two of them in the mirror. She had done as he asked and left her solemn silks and satins behind, but even in a simple rose-pink muslin skirt and pink-and-white striped bodice, her hair drawn back to a plain knot at the nape of her neck, she stood out. She looked like a fresh summer flower. A very serious flower. She studied her surroundings so carefully, as if she would be tested on them later.

Aidan frowned as it suddenly struck him that he didn't actually know much about Lily St. Clair at all. He knew she wasn't one of the St. Claire offspring but adopted from somewhere; she had been married to some frightfully respectable-sounding greengrocer; and Freddy had been in love with her, and she took advantage of that love.

And he definitely knew the way her soft, slender body felt against his own, the way she cried out his name. His body knew hers, craved hers.

That was more than he usually knew about his women. But he wanted to know more. He would know more.

He gestured to the barkeep, an intimidating-looking hulk with a shaved, scarred head and beefy arms in his rolled-up shirtsleeves. The man grinned widely, revealing broken teeth as he turned toward them.

"Aidan, my man!" he shouted. "Haven't seen you here in an age. Come to see the show, have you?"

"You know him?" Lily whispered.

"An old friend," Aidan answered. If he wanted to know Lily, he had to let her see him. At least a little bit. He had learned long ago never to reveal his very deepest heart.

"I've been busy, Robbie," Aidan said, reaching over the bar to shake Robbie's hand. "But I can't stay away forever."

"You've been missed. Molly and Annie won't stop asking about you." Robbie's curious gaze slid over Lily. "Looks like they'll just have to keep waiting. Who's the pretty lady?"

"Robbie, this is Lily. Lily, Robbie here was the most famous prizefighter between here and Edinburgh."

"Really? That sounds impressive," Lily said with a smile.

Aidan thought her voice suddenly sounded different, the accent softer, rougher at the edges.

"Retired now," Robbie answered. He reached for Lily's hand and raised it gallantly to his lips, making her laugh. "Always happy to meet a friend of Aidan's. Where has the old rascal been keeping you?"

Lily gave Aidan a sidelong glance. "I think it's more, what is he hiding *here*?"

Robbie roared. "Oh, love, the tales I could tell you. Later, after I feed and water this sorry lot. What'll it be? Ale? It's good stuff, none of that watered-down swill you'll find at Aikan's place across the street."

"Two ales, Robbie," Aidan said. "And no telling tales to my girl. I'm trying to impress her."

Lily just smiled and turned to lean against the bar to watch the dancers. Musicians hidden up in the old choir loft played a lively polka, and the couples swirled and stomped around in a kaleidoscope of color and noise. When Robbie put a large beaker of dark ale before her, she reached for it and took a long swallow.

"He's right," she said. "It's not watered-down swill."

Aidan laughed and drank down his own ale as he watched the room with her. Oh, this *was* dangerous—he feared he could actually like her. Enjoy spending time with her, talking to her, even with their clothes on. Was this how poor, pitiful Freddy felt when he wrote her those wretched letters? Was he, Aidan, getting to be pitiful as well?

"How does a duke's son come to find a place like this?" she asked. "How does he get to be friends with ex-prize-fighters and girls named Molly and Annie?"

Aidan shrugged. "If I only had friends my parents approved of, I would be wretchedly bored. I met Nick, who owns this place, at one of Robbie's last bouts. Nick was planning to open a music hall and needed writers to create new vignettes."

"You write plays for him?"

"When I have time."

"And will I get to see your work, then?"

"Not tonight," he said. "I haven't been able to write for some time." Not until he met her and the ideas came back to him.

Lily shook her head and took another drink of her ale. "You are a strange man, Aidan. I don't think I've ever met anyone like you."

"If you think I'm strange, you should meet my brother David. He's the heir, and yet he lives like a hermit. Makes my father crazy." Aidan finished his own drink and watched Lily closely. She seemed just as comfortable here, drinking cheap ale and watching shopgirls dance, as she had been sipping champagne at the Devil's Fancy. "And you are rather unusual yourself."

Her smile turned wry. "You have no idea."

He put down his empty beaker and wrapped his arm around her to pull her closer to him. She gasped in surprise at his sudden move and braced her hands against his chest. He kissed her hair, feeling the soft strands under his lips, the twist of her body under his hands. Just like that, he felt his groin tighten.

"I want to know, Lily," he whispered. "I want to know everything about you."

She shook her head, but he felt her body relax into his, her palms flatten onto his chest. Her fingers stroked him through his thin linen shirt and wool vest, and he almost groaned.

"Believe me, Aidan, you don't," she said.

"It's all right, Lily. You don't have to tell me everything right now." He reached for one of her hands and raised it to his lips. He slowly, gently, kissed every fingertip until he sucked the tip of her index finger between his teeth and bit down. Her breath hissed in her throat, and he smiled at the sexy little sound. He wasn't the only one affected. "I can wait until I have you tied up again, in my own bed this time."

Lily snatched her hand away and turned her back to him. "You'll be waiting until doomsday, then, Aidan Huntington."

He certainly hoped it wasn't nearly that long. He wasn't sure he could wait past tonight. He laughed and reached out to run his hands lightly over her shoulders. She stiffened but didn't pull away. "I've told you before, Lily—I'm a patient man. In the meantime, will you at least dance with me?"

She glanced toward the dance floor, which seemed even more crowded now. The chairs were all filled, with the overflowing crowd lined up along the walls to watch the dancers. "Very well," she said slowly. "One dance."

One dance. It was a start.

Lily laughed helplessly as Aidan twirled her around in the dance. The room, so packed with people and filled with the warm, damp smells of ale, cheap perfume, and wool and cotton, swirled in a blurry, bright haze. All she could do was twine her arms around his neck and hold on.

The dance wasn't like the decorous waltzes and mazurkas in the ballroom of the Devil's Fancy, or the stately pavanes she had once learned for *Romeo and Juliet.* There seemed no pattern to the steps, only instinctive movement to the pounding beat of the music and the turns of the other dancers around them. Aidan understood how to move with the crowd, how to turn and spin her in a series of quick, graceful steps that awakened an answering instinct in her.

She hadn't danced in so long, she realized as Aidan spun her out and back into his arms, smiling down at her. Not since she danced with her husband at the assembly rooms, and that was never like this. Harry would move her woodenly around in one waltz before going off to play cards with his business associates and leaving her with their dull wives. This seemed to be more than dancing, more than learned steps in a set pattern. She and Aidan moved together perfectly. Just like when they had sex and their bodies knew the rhythm of each other.

Lily had never enjoyed a dance so much.

Another couple bumped into them, making her stumble even closer against Aidan. She laughed and held on tighter to his neck.

"All right?" he said against her ear.

She nodded. He lifted her off her feet and twirled her to the edge of the floor where the crowd was a bit thinner.

"Having fun?" he asked.

Lily tilted back her head to smile up at him. He watched her with hooded eyes, a half-smile on his lips.

"Very much," she said. "I haven't been dancing in years. You're very good at this."

His smile deepened, revealing that enticing little crease

in his cheek. "Oh, I have many hidden talents, Lily. If you're nice to me, I just might show them to you."

She bit her lip as she remembered the "hidden talents" he had already shown her. If they got any more intense, they would surely make her faint away. "Perhaps I have a few secret talents of my own."

Aidan laughed and lifted her higher in his arms. "I have no doubt of that at all. You show me yours and I'll show you mine?"

Suddenly a hard arm closed around Lily's waist from behind and yanked her away from Aidan. Shocked, cold fear washed over her, numbing her. Instinct took over, the instincts of a child of the streets, and she lashed out with her fist at the same time she drove her foot back between her captor's legs.

He tilted his hips back just in time, but her fist connected with a bristled jaw with a crack. She was suddenly dropped to the floor, and she scrambled back, ready to fight.

She whirled around to see a tall, broad-shouldered man, striking and almost sinister-looking with long black hair and green eyes, wearing a black leather waistcoat over his white linen shirt. He laughed as he rubbed at his bruised jaw, and to Lily's surprise, Aidan also laughed as he wrapped his arm around her shoulders and drew her back to his side.

"Please don't frighten my lady, Nick," Aidan said. "I'll never be able to persuade her to go out with me again."

"I didn't know you'd brought a hellcat to my place," the black-haired man said ruefully in a musical Irish accent. "They're usually a bit more... amenable."

Lily frowned between them. "You know this man?" she asked Aidan. Her body still hummed, ready to fight.

"Lily, meet Nick Riley, owner of this fair establishment," Aidan said. "And a barbarian who has no idea how to treat a lady."

"They don't show up here very often, and never with a rascal like you, Aidan." The man gave her a low bow and offered his hand. "Forgive me, miss—Lily, is it?"

Lily studied his hand for a long, suspicious moment before she lightly laid her fingers on his palm. "Mr. Riley. I suppose I can forgive you if you forgive me."

Nick laughed and raised her hand to his lips. His kiss lingered, until Aidan pulled her closer to his side and Nick laughed even louder. "Where did you get such a mean right hook, Miss Lily?" Nick asked.

Lily glanced up at Aidan. "One of my hidden talents."

"Remind me never to provoke your temper, then," Aidan said.

"Any more than you already have?" Lily teased. She found herself relaxing again, her fighting instinct slowly ebbing away.

"Don't remind me," Aidan said wryly.

"Come, have a drink on the house," Nick said. He led them back to the bar and signaled to Robbie. "Let me apologize properly. Tell me, Miss Lily, where did the villain find you? And are there any more like you there?"

Lily laughed and sipped at her ale. She couldn't help but like Nick, despite the fact that she had just tried to break his jaw. He had an easy charm laid over a hard, careful watchfulness that reminded her of Aidan. Perhaps that was why a duke's son was friends with an Irish bar owner.

"I do have a sister, but she is not much like me, and she is very carefully guarded by our very large brothers," she said. "I doubt charming villains like you and Aidan could get anywhere near her."

Nick grinned at her, his green eyes sparkling. Oh yes, she would make sure a man like him never got near Isabel. "I do like a challenge. And at least I am a *charming* villain now. I go up in your estimation."

"Careful, my friend," Aidan said. "Remember the lady is taken."

Lily scowled at him. *Taken* indeed. She was no man's to claim; she never would be again. But somehow Aidan's flash of possessiveness gave her a primitive satisfaction.

"I'm no poacher, no matter how tempting the hunting might be," Nick said. "Tell me, Aidan, did you see Mrs. Neil's show at the Lyceum last week?"

The two men went on to talk about the local music hall programs, and Lily sipped at her ale as she studied the crowd in the mirror. The alcohol had been flowing, and everyone was even louder now, the dance steps wilder, faster, as the musicians raced to catch up. She tapped her foot against the bar rail, enjoying the music and the merriment.

Suddenly she caught a reflection at the edge of the room. A figure slightly apart from the others in the smoky shadows. It was a man, tall, almost painfully thin, dressed in a long, black coat. His face was concealed by a brimmed cap tugged low. And he leaned on a walking stick with a pale skull's head handle.

"No," Lily whispered. Her cup fell from her hands to land on the bar with a loud thud. Drops of ale spilled across the scarred wood and onto her hand.

She didn't even notice as Robbie caught the cup before it could roll onto the floor and as Aidan cupped her arm in his hand and said something to her. She could see only that stick, that horribly grinning death's head. She had seen that stick recently, on the day Aidan took her to the cafe and she glimpsed a man outside on the street.

Before that, she hadn't seen it, feared it, in years. Why would it be here now?

She twisted around to peer over her shoulder, frantically scanning the crowd. She couldn't see the man in black now; it was as if he had just vanished into thin air. Was she just imagining him? Was something summoning up the past in her mind, a past she had thought dead and buried?

Was she going mad?

"Lily?" Aidan said, his hand tightening on her arm. His voice pierced the cloud of her fear, and she looked up at him.

He gave her a bemused smile, and she tried to focus on that, on the fact that she was here, with him. The past was gone. This was the present moment, her life now.

Yet the past did not feel banished. It felt too close, too vivid, always ready to swoop in and tear away the thin facade of civility she had worked so hard to build around herself. Lily, the no-surname daughter of a whore, always lurked behind Lily St. Claire Nichols with her fine clothes and jewelry. And she didn't want Aidan to see that.

She smiled at him. "I'm so sorry. I must be getting tired. So clumsy of me."

"Do you want to leave?" he asked. "I can take you home."

Suddenly there was a commotion from the other side of the room, a burst of screams and shouts, breaking glass. A brawl was forming, quickly becoming out of control.

"Excuse me," Nick said tightly, and he plunged into the crowd. Everyone was suddenly tumbling over each other, rushing to see what the fight was about. Robbie reached under the bar and came up with a cricket bat. Lily was sure she didn't want to see what he could do with that.

"Come on," Aidan said, and took her hand to draw her toward the doors.

She followed him, but the fight had escalated very quickly and their exit was blocked.

Suddenly a burly man careened toward them out of the swirling melee, and Aidan shoved him away. The man's fist caught Aidan hard on the jaw and sent his head snapping back. He looked stunned for an instant, but then he lithely sprang back to his feet and landed a hard punch of his own, right to the man's thick neck. The man bellowed with rage and came at Aidan, swinging wildly.

"Stay back there!" Aidan shouted at her. Then he leaped onto his opponent.

Lily pressed herself against the nearest wall, staring at Aidan in astonishment. She had never imagined a duke's son, or anyone, could fight like that. She had seen brawls all the time when she was a child, but those were vicious, animal-like things, quick and brutal. Aidan was just as effective, but he moved with a smooth, effortless grace, dodging, blocking, his feet sliding over the floor as his fists shot out in a sudden, unexpected blur.

His attacker grew more and more furious as Aidan evaded him. His blows were more unfocused, and Aidan finally drove him to his knees with a powerful right hook that took the larger man to the floor.

Aidan shook out his fist and grabbed Lily's hand. "Come on!"

"Where did you learn to fight like that?" she cried.

"West Indies," he said shortly as he pulled her through a break in the crowd. He pushed her roughly up onto a table. "Stay there!" he ordered. "Don't move until I come for you. I'll find a way out of here."

"Aidan!" she cried, but as she reached for him, he plunged back into the brawl. He was swallowed up in the tangle of arms and legs, screams and shouts of obscenities. People were suddenly crashing into her on all sides, jostling her violently.

Lily wanted to shout out a curse or two herself. The shock of the sudden fight was wearing off, leaving the half-remembered exhilaration of the brawl. Once she had seen and run from such things nearly every night, but she had begun to forget the rush of violence, the terrible urge to flee.

But she couldn't flee. There were too many people between her and the door. She strained to glimpse Aidan but couldn't see him. She saw Nick by the bar, bashing some man's head into the wood.

Lily reached down for a chair that leaned against her table perch. A few good, hard cracks broke off the leg. The next time a stumbling man reeled into her, she swung her makeshift club into his shoulders and drove him back.

She almost laughed at the primal satisfaction of landing a blow. When someone else tried to grab her, she hit him too. She pushed her loosened hair back from her face and spun around to swing again and again, keeping everyone away from her little island.

"Miss Lily, behind you!" she heard Robbie shout. She whirled around to swing yet again, but the chair leg was wrenched out of her hands so hard that she felt the painful reverberation all the way into her shoulder. Something hard and solid caught her at the back of her knees, and she fell off the table with a cry of panic.

She would have hit the floor, but bony, unyielding arms closed around her waist and dragged her to the edge of the room. The stench of acrid sweat, wet wool, and cheap whiskey overwhelmed her and created the sensation of smothering and drowning.

She kicked out frantically through her skirts, flailing against her captor. She was suddenly shoved up against the wall, the breath knocked out of her lungs. Her scream strangled in her throat when a calloused hand pressed to her windpipe.

"Well, well, Lily," he said, his voice harsh with the accents of her childhood. The accents of Whitechapel and St. Giles. "You're quite the lady now, ain't you? Done better for yourself than your mum done, eh?"

Oh, dear heaven, *no*. No, it couldn't be, couldn't be. Lily frantically tried to twist away, but those fingers on her throat held her fast. She managed to wrench herself around and drive her elbow into his ribs, pushing back a few steps. He let her go, and she glimpsed his face in a ray of light. It was a face she knew in her nightmares, older, etched with deeper lines, with sunken dark blue eyes.

He gave her a terrible smile and a salute with his death's head stick. Then he was gone.

Lily was shaking so hard she couldn't stand. She slid down the wall until she fell to the floor, her hands pressed to her stomach. Sickening nausea rose up in her, choking her as if he still held her.

She had to kill him. Find him and kill him.

"Lily!" she heard Aidan shout. She looked up to see

him kneeling beside her. He had lost his coat, and his shirt was torn. A deep gash on his brow dripped blood onto his handsome face. "Are you hurt?"

Lily shook her head. She tried to reach up, to touch his face, but her hands were shaking too much. "No, but you are."

"It's nothing," he said with that careless smile of his. "A scratch. But you don't look well."

She felt cold and insubstantial, like a ghost, a shadow. Someone who no longer existed. But she couldn't tell him what had happened, what she saw. She just shook her head again.

"You have to see to your wound," she said. "You wouldn't want to ruin your pretty face."

"You like my looks, then?" he said. He slid his arm around her waist and helped her to her feet. When she stumbled, he picked her up and carried her.

The fight had died down for the most part. People slumped on the floor or argued by the bar amid the remains of splintered chairs and broken glass. Nick was nowhere to be seen.

As Aidan carried her out of the building and into the chilly night, Lily glimpsed some constables running toward the doors with their sticks at the ready. *Too late*, Lily thought. Aidan turned toward the opposite side of the street, and as he walked, she could feel the quiet stillness soak into her. The foggy night closed around them, and she felt calmer.

Perhaps it was all a dream after all, she thought. An illusion born of the fight. Tiredness seeped through her.

"Where are we going?" she asked as Aidan hailed a passing hansom.

"Just rest right now," he answered. "I'm sorry I got you involved in all that, Lily. Let me take care of you now."

She nodded wearily and let her head drop onto his shoulder. She let herself hold on to him and to the illusion that she was not alone. That her life, her life as a respectable widow, as a St. Claire, had not changed.

But if "Handsome" Tom Beaumont was still alive and back in London, everything had changed.

Chapter Ten

Aidan closed his eyes and felt Lily's soft fingers flutter over his face gently as she washed away the blood. The silence in his sitting room was so complete that he could hear the soft whisper of every movement she made, her breath, the rustle of her skirt. He could smell ale and dust, the coppery tang of drying blood, but underneath it all was the sweetness of her violet perfume.

He should never have taken her there tonight. She was a lady, and despite her cool wariness, he could sense the vulnerability she tried to hide. He should have protected her.

"You should send for a doctor to stitch this up," she said quietly.

Aidan felt the touch of linen on his skin as she wound a bandage around his brow. He opened his eyes and looked up into her face.

The lamp was behind her, and its light cast a glow on her loose hair, turning the dark brown strands honey-gold. It looked like a halo, as if she were a saint in some Renaissance painting or a character in a tragic play, serene in the face of danger. But he remembered her raw, shaking fear in the barroom.

"I've had worse," he said. "It will mend without stitches."

A faint smile touched her lips. "That scar on your chest? Where did you get it?" She tied off the end of the bandage and shifted to step back, but Aidan wound his arms around her waist and held her close to him. Her pretty dress was torn and dirty, and he closed his eyes to rest his head just below the softness of her breasts and the boning of her corset.

At first she stiffened, but then he heard her sigh, and her hands threaded through his hair to hold him against her.

"What if I told you I got that scar in battle, defending a maiden's honor?" he said. "Would your heart soften to me then?"

Lily gave a wry laugh. "My heart is too soft where you are concerned already."

Really? A bolt of foolish hope shot through Aidan. He didn't want her heart, shouldn't want it—he needed only her body, her company, for a time.

Her fingertips skimmed lightly over the nape of his neck. "But you didn't get it defending a maiden's honor, did you?"

"Oh, in a way I did, though she was no maiden. She was a prostitute in the West Indies. It was in a fight much like the one tonight, but my opponent drew his knife before I could."

She stiffened in his arms, and her fingers went still. "You carry a knife?"

"Sometimes." He wrapped his leg around her calf, pressing it close so she could feel the blade strapped close to his skin. "It's a damned handy thing to have at times."

He felt her turn her head. She didn't move away but she

did go very still in his arms. "You go to a lot of places like that, know a lot of *people* like that."

"I enjoy a wide variety of acquaintances, yes. But I promise you, Lily, such things don't usually happen at Nick's place. He runs a secure establishment; he'll be utterly furious someone caused trouble tonight. I would never have taken you someplace I didn't think was safe."

"Oh, Aidan. Believe me, I've seen far worse."

Aidan tilted back his head to look up into her face. For an instant, she was open to him, and he saw a myriad of emotions written on her pretty face—fear, sadness, anger. Her brown eyes were so black and deep, an endless, swirling pool filled with pain. Then she gave him a gentle smile and laid her palm against his cheek.

"When I was younger, I had little choice in my companions," she said. "But you do—you are a duke's son. How did you come to know music hall people, ex-pugilists, Irish bar owners..."

"Pickpockets and whores?" Aidan said. Her eyes narrowed, and he laughed. "Oh, yes, I know those too."

"How? Why?"

"It's a long tale, and what it comes down to is merely curiosity, I suppose. I've always wanted to know about people, about life, all sorts of life. About what makes us human, what makes us all do the sometimes insane things we do."

She traced a soft, fluttering touch over his cheekbones, the arch of his brows, and he closed his eyes to feel her caress. "Curiosity can be a very dangerous thing," she said.

Aidan laughed. "Don't I know it. You saw what happened tonight."

"Most men in your position have no curiosity at all about other people. They think everyone else is merely there to serve them, to revolve around them in their own little world."

"Perhaps that is because that's how everyone treats them? They see nothing different, and they come to think that *is* the world, the whole of it."

"Is that how your father is?"

Aidan shook his head, frowning. "My father certainly enjoys his share of high privilege. He was not a good father, but I have to admit he is a good duke. He takes on the responsibilities as well as the privileges, and he has never been one to shirk his duty. The respectability of the family name is everything to him."

"But what of the family itself?"

"Producing sons was something my parents saw as their first duty, and they did it with admirable alacrity. My brother and I were born in the first four years of their marriage, even though the daughters that followed hardly lived to draw their first breaths." Aidan opened his eyes to see her staring down at him with her dark, dark eyes. "But our nurse used to say we were changeling children, left in the nursery by fairies when they stole away the duke's true offspring. Neither David nor I have ever really belonged there."

"You sound so matter-of-fact about it all."

Aidan shrugged. Truthfully he never thought much about his life; he just lived it. He had long ago accepted who he was, even though his father could not. He had never said these things aloud to anyone before, until now. Until Lily. "That is just how it is, right or wrong. My family must put up with me, and I with them. We rub along well enough. After all, I am not the heir. Thank God." Though sometimes he had disquieting thoughts about his brother abandoning his duties, leaving Aidan to take them up. That would be a disaster.

"I don't understand you, Aidan Huntington." Lily tried to move away again, but he wouldn't let her. He closed his hands on her waist and drew her down onto his lap.

"We are quite a pair, then, Lily St. Claire, for you are a complete mystery to me."

She wriggled against him as if she would fly away, his panicked bird. Her movements made his manhood stir and harden, lust suddenly hot in his belly, and he pressed himself up against her through her skirts. She went still.

"I'm quite dull," she whispered. "There is no mystery in me to decipher."

Aidan nudged her hair away from her neck and laid his lips to the soft, vulnerable spot below her ear. She smelled so warm and sweet there, and he closed his teeth lightly on her skin. He wanted to devour her, to fall into her and be lost. To make her reveal herself to him.

She gasped, and her head fell back as if in surrender. A surge of triumph rushed through him. At least he had her in this.

He tangled his hand in her hair and pulled her down to cover her mouth with his. He swept his tongue past her parted lips, claiming her, marking her.

Lily met his kiss with a need of her own. He could taste it, feel it in her body against his—she wanted to lose herself in their passion as much as he did. He had never felt such raw hunger for a woman before.

She wrapped her arms around his neck as her tongue slid over his. He felt her turn until she straddled his lap, her legs braced on either side of his hips.

Aidan reached down to grasp the hem of her skirt and

pull it up until he could touch her warm skin through the thin linen of her drawers. It wasn't nearly enough; he was hungry for the feel of her bare against him. He ripped at the fabric until he could slide his palm over the heat of her naked thigh.

Her neck arched back, and she cried out at the sound of the tearing fabric. "Aidan! You already owe me new underthings."

He traced his open mouth down her throat and laughed. "Go to any modiste you like, order whatever you want, and send me the bills. I'll happily pay for anything. Black satin corsets, embroidered stockings, lace petticoats..."

"Just so you can tear them off me again?"

"And again and again." He bit at the curve of her shoulder and pushed her short sleeve out of his way. He wanted to taste every inch of her. Even now his penis grew harder as he remembered the taste of her arousal in his mouth. The way her soft womanhood closed around him and drew him deeper and deeper until he lost himself in her.

His fingers deftly slid beneath her bodice and her stiff corset to the yielding softness of her breast. He pinched her nipple lightly and laughed at the curse that burst past her lips.

"Just take me now, Aidan," she whispered hoarsely. "Make me forget. Make it all just go away."

Make what go away? A hint of cold disquiet pierced Aidan's lust. He braced his hand on the back of the chair to peer up at her. Her cheeks were flushed a dark pink, her eyes glittering with desire—and with something else. Something frantic and violent, tinged with fear.

She had looked just like that when he found her slumped by the barroom wall. Like a wild creature caught in a cage, desperate to get out. She had also looked like that with the little girl in the park. Flashes that came through her somber armor. He would happily make her forget, over and over, all night, but he wanted to know what scared her like that.

She reached between them to unfasten his shirt and push it off his shoulders. Her palms skimmed over his shoulders and down his bared chest, exploring every inch of him with her hands and her eyes.

"Lily...," he groaned.

"I've never seen you without your clothes," she murmured. "How can a man be so beautiful like this? So perfect, like a Greek statue in a gallery."

"Believe me, I am no statue," he moaned as she smoothed a caress over his ridged abdomen, just above the band of his trousers. His cock surged against the confinement of the wool placket.

Lily braced one hand in the center of his chest and slid the other one lower until her fingers cupped him through the fabric. She bent her head to kiss him at the base of his throat, and her tongue caught the drop of sweat there just as she wrapped her fingers around him and slid them down, hard.

"Lily," he growled, but she only touched him again. She seemed to know exactly what she was doing, where to touch to drive him out of his mind, how rough he liked it.

His whole body was braced in the chair, his mind spinning out of control while she unfastened his trousers until his naked manhood was in her hand.

"Mmm, beautiful," she purred. Her thumb pressed the throbbing vein on his underside, and she stroked him from base to crown and back down again. "And so, so hard."

"Hard for you." Aidan had to force himself not to throw her to the floor and thrust into her, to make her just as crazy as he was.

She swept a soft, tickling touch over his balls, and then he felt her slender fingertip slide lower to press on the opening to his ass. A hot bolt of sensation shot through him and his whole body arched up on the chair as he shouted her name.

Her hand moved from his chest to wind around his neck as she held on to him and stared down at him with her night-dark eyes. Her other hand, though, stayed where it was, her fingertip so lightly circling and teasing. The nerves along that tight ring of muscle seemed to vibrate at her touch.

"Haven't you ever been touched there?" she asked.

"Not by you," he said roughly.

"Hmm. Have you ever been with a man?"

Aidan prided himself on his unshockability. He had seen too much, done too much, knew too many people to be surprised by anything. But Lily had surprised him with her dark, daring words.

"No," he said shortly.

She shook her head and lowered her mouth to his shoulder, sliding the edge of her teeth over his skin. Her hand slid away to lightly cup his buttock. "Never mind. It doesn't matter what either of us has done before, not tonight. Tonight this is all there is."

That sounded good to Aidan. Just him and Lily and sex, everything else closed away and lost in the gathering fog outside. He pulled her lips down to his for a hungry kiss as he spread her legs wider over his lap and arched his hips up into hers.

Lily took his cock in her soft hand and pressed his damp tip to her womanhood. As she braced her knees to the chair and slid down, he thrust up through her wet, tight folds until he was seated fully inside of her, all her tight heat surrounding him and drawing him deeper and deeper. He *was* lost in her. He couldn't tell where she ended and he began.

"Aidan," she moaned. She held on to his shoulders, and he felt her nails bite into his skin. The edge of pain just drove his need higher, hotter.

As he watched through the white-tinged haze of lust, Lily's head fell back, and her hair spilled in a loose, tangled fall to her waist. Her eyes were tightly closed, and for a moment they just hung there, suspended in that instant of joining.

Then she rose up slowly on her knees, and her body dragged along his whole length, so tight and wet, so hot, he groaned at the sensation. He felt that familiar tingling at the base of his spine and knew he wouldn't last long. He needed to slow things down, draw them out. Pleasure her until he did make her forget.

But Lily didn't seem to want slow. She slid her body back down onto his until their hips were pressed together. Her nails scored his back, raking down the groove of his spine.

"Fuck me, Aidan," she whispered. "I need you to. Just like in my office."

"I never want to disappoint a lady," he managed to rasp. He wrapped his arms tightly around her waist and swung them both down to the floor. Still joined, Aidan laid her on his hearth rug on her hands and knees, facing away from him. He thrust into her, hard, and she moaned his name.

He wondered for an instant why she didn't want to look

at him as he took her, why she wanted it this way, but then she pushed her bottom back, driving him in deeper, and he couldn't think at all. He could only let the familiar fog of lust close over him and drive him toward his climax.

"Harder," she whispered, and he was happy to oblige. He thrust again and again, each time harder, deeper, until he knew he had found that one secret spot inside her, the one that made her scream his name. He slid against it, over and over, until he felt her convulse around him.

She threw her head back, her whole body as taut as a drawn bowstring. Aidan tangled his hand in her hair again and held on as he drove himself into her until he knew he was about to come. He pulled out of her just at the last second, and he shouted with the force of his release. It was as if all the violence and energy, the lust and need, of the night flew out of him.

He collapsed to the floor next to Lily and covered his face with his arm as he struggled to breathe and to think. Lily lay flat on her stomach beside him, her breath uneven, her body shaking as hard as his. As if they lay together in the eye of a terrible, inescapable storm.

Slowly, when the spinning of the room had eased, Aidan slid his arm away and turned his head to look at her. She lay on her side now and studied him through the tangle of her hair.

She said nothing and neither did he. There could be no words, nothing to put aside whatever upheaval had happened tonight. Something had shifted between the bar fight and their lovemaking. Something had moved between them, and he couldn't even begin to fathom what it was. He was too exhausted and beginning to feel the bruises of the fight.

"You're bleeding again," Lily said quietly. She reached out and brushed her finger over the bandage. "You should be in bed."

Aidan caught her hand in his and kissed it. "Only if you join me there. I believe after our encounter in your office, I promised you the next time would be in my bed. I fear we didn't quite get there."

A ghost of a smile fluttered over her lips. "Almost."

Aidan pushed himself to his feet. Yes, he could definitely feel the bruises now. He would be a right old mess in the morning. He held his hand out to Lily. "Come with me. I think we both need to sleep on a soft bed for a while."

She slowly sat up, staring uncertainly at his hand. "I should get home. I can't be caught coming in looking like this."

But Aidan found he didn't want to lose her just yet. Something in him, some part he didn't understand, wanted to keep her close for a little while longer. "Just for an hour or two, and then I will take you home. It's a long time until dawn."

Finally she nodded and took his hand. Aidan led her through the doorway into his bedchamber. The gaslight from the street outside cast shadows over the carved bed, making an undulating, inviting haven of the piled-up quilts and pillows. It was a small room, plainly decorated and furnished with old, unfashionable pieces from his family's country home attics, but he usually didn't bring women here. It was his own space, a place for escape, for writing and thinking. A place where he was only Aidan, not the son of the Duke of Carston.

But Lily seemed to belong there, a quiet, watchful

presence that didn't mar the peace. He pulled back the bedclothes and drew her down beside him onto the soft sheets. She still wore her disheveled dress, and the fabric rubbed over his bare chest as she slid into the angle of his body. He wrapped his arm around her shoulders, and she rested her head against him with a sigh.

Slowly, slowly, she relaxed until at last he felt her arm slide over his waist. They just lay there together, still and silent.

Aidan wound her hair around his wrist, combing the tangles from the long strands with his fingers. She traced a light pattern over the skin of his chest. It was a gentle, soothing touch, a connection in the darkness.

And it was much too intimate, too close. Aidan knew he should take her home now, push her away, but he couldn't move. It felt too good to have her next to him. Tomorrow would be soon enough to move away.

The back of his hand rested on the soft, vulnerable nape of her neck. "Tell me why you were so frightened tonight," he said quietly.

Lily stiffened against him, but he tightened his fingers in her hair and held her still. "Anyone would be frightened in the middle of a fight," she said.

"Of course. Yet there was more than that. I saw you earlier, when I put you up on that table. You fought like a Valkyrie. But when I found you at the end, you were almost paralyzed. You can talk to me, Lily. You can tell me what happened, tell me how I can make it up to you." Aidan knew even as he said the words and asked her to let him in that he was only digging himself deeper into a place he did not want and could not have. A place of real intimacy and understanding. A place where he could truly see a woman and let her see him. But that romantic notion was something that could only be found in plays.

Still he asked her that. Still he lay there with her, his body wrapped around hers.

She was so taut against him, and he saw her again as a delicate, trapped bird, her wings spreading to take flight and disappear.

"I don't want to talk, Aidan," she said. "It's late, and I'm tired."

She sat up with one hand on his chest and slid her other hand softly over his face. She made him close his eyes and then leaned over to press her lips against his.

"Just sleep now, my warrior," she whispered. "And tomorrow you will see that you don't really want to know anything about me at all."

Aidan felt himself falling down into a dreamless sleep, her hand caressing him. And when he awoke with the sun on his face and his head pounding, she was gone.

Chapter Eleven

"You seem distracted today, Lily my dear."

Lily glanced up from her account book and rubbed at the bridge of her nose as she smiled at her mother. Katherine St. Claire was arranging a large vase of roses at a table by the drawing room window. It was a dismal, gray day, the fog rolling down the London streets to banish the sun they had enjoyed for the last two days, and the dampness seemed to have seeped into the cheerful pale yellow room.

Two days had passed since she had seen Aidan. Two days since she had slipped from his bed in the predawn light, stealing one last glance at his gorgeous face as he slept.

The sight of him in his bed, his muscled torso glowing a pale gold on the white sheets, his hair tousled, had lingered in her mind every time she closed her eyes. She felt his hands on her, heard the murmur of his voice, saw the flash of his smile. She remembered how they had talked, how tempted she had been to confide in him. So, yes, she was a bit distracted today.

"I suppose I'm just tired," she answered.

Katherine looked at Lily over the red flowers, a worried frown on her brow. She looked like a bright flash of summer in the gloomy day, with her pale blue dress and her hair the same red-gold as Isabel's, only lightly touched with threads of silver. The frown seemed foreign on her pretty face, yet it had been there too often lately when she looked at her children.

"You've been working too hard, Lily," she said. "You do the accounts for that club and the theater, and who knows what else Dominic and Brendan drop on you. You should let someone else help. Hire a secretary."

Lily laughed. "I doubt we would want a secretary, an outsider, to pry into our accounts."

"Then your brothers should help more." A wry, affectionate smile touched Katherine's lips. "My dear William is brilliant at many things, but the practicalities of numbers is not one of them."

Lily shook her head. Her father was often off on flights of fancy, deeply into a play or a piece of music, or off talking to people. "I like doing the accounts. That is not what's making me tired."

"We wouldn't be where we are if not for you, Lily," Katherine said. "We wouldn't be so secure financially. You have been a blessing to us, and if we ask too much of you..."

"You have been *my* blessing, Mama," Lily protested. "I'm only happy there is something I can do for you. I would be dead now if not for you and Father. Or worse—I would be like my mother."

"No, my dear! No, you must not say that." Katherine hurried over to Lily's side, dropping onto the satin slipper chair by the desk to take Lily's hand. "You are strong and clever. You would have found a way to save yourself even if we hadn't come along when we did. But I am thankful every day that we did."

Lily smiled at her mother. Katherine held so tightly to Lily's hand that her rings bit into the skin, but she didn't care. Her mother's soft touch, the rosy smell of her perfume, was always a comfort. "I'm thankful as well."

Katherine nodded. They never spoke of that day so long ago, when Lily had been caught trying to pick William St. Claire's pocket as he and Katherine walked past in the Covent Garden crowd. Rather than box her ears or shout for a constable, rather than leaving her to Tom Beaumont for another beating or worse, Katherine had knelt beside her and stared deeply into her eyes. She had smiled at Lily and spoken softly, until Lily let William lift her in his arms and carry her away.

When Beaumont tried to get her back, William's men gave him a thrashing, and she never saw him again. Her life of dirty streets, hunger, crime, and beatings was over. Instead there were lessons with a governess in a clean, cozy nursery, with new brothers and a sister, pretty clothes, the theater, books.

She heard that Beaumont was transported to Australia soon after. Until now. Until he held her against that barroom wall and smiled that terrible smile.

Lily pressed her other hand to her eyes and tried to swallow back the cold nausea that rose up in her throat. She couldn't worry her mother with Beaumont. It was her own problem, her own past, and she would find a way to take care of it. But how she hated Tom Beaumont for what he had done! Such burning, violent hatred she had thought—hoped—was long banished from her life.

"Lily, something *is* wrong," Katherine said. "Is it that man? The one who sent you violets?"

Lily sat up straight and pulled her hand away from her mother's. "Why would you say that?"

Katherine laughed. "Because you haven't said anything about him. Whenever you turn all quiet and cautious like that, I know something is amiss."

"He is just someone I met once or twice. We…talked a bit."

"And he sent you flowers after talking?"

Lily shrugged. She tried to be casual, careless, but she didn't meet Katherine's watchful green eyes. Aidan was her secret, just as the return of Beaumont was. She couldn't let her family know she was actually seeing a Huntington. They would explode with fury. Except Isabel, sweet, romantic Isabel, who she knew would keep her secret.

Lily owed the St. Claires far too much to do anything to hurt them.

"Come, my dear, sit with me on the settee. I'll ring for some tea," Katherine said, letting the subject of secret admirers drop for the moment.

Lily glanced back at the open book on her desk. "I should finish these…"

"Later. It's teatime. And I want to ask your advice about something."

Lily nodded and went to settle herself on the settee as Katherine rang the bellpull. It had begun to rain, cold, hard droplets that battered against the window glass and made Lily shiver. Her mood felt just as gray, and even her mother seemed affected as she sat next to Lily. Her beautiful oval face, so much like Isabel's, was creased with some secret worry.

"What is it, Mama?" Lily asked, her concern growing. Had she been so preoccupied with her own troubles that she had missed something going on in her family? "Are you ill? Is it Father?"

Katherine shook her head. "Oh, no, we are perfectly well. It is James I'm worried about."

"James?" Lily said, her mind racing. She thought back over the last few weeks and realized that it was true—James had not been his usual lighthearted self. She saw him only at breakfast and in quick snatches in passing, as he didn't seem to be home very much, and when he was, he seemed quiet and brooding. Even Isabel had appeared a bit worried about her twin.

Lily almost cursed aloud. How had she not noticed before? "What is wrong with him?"

"He won't talk to me. He is gone so much, and he won't say where. Not that that should be anything unusual—he is a man now, and his brothers at that age never wanted to tell their mother what they were about either. But he won't even talk to Isabel, and they have shared everything since they were born. I think she is rather hurt by that."

"What of his friends?"

"There were the young men he knew at school, but he never mentions them now. He won't go with us to the theater or the assembly rooms, and he shows no interest at all when your father tries to involve him in the productions at the Majestic." A blush touched Katherine's cheeks as she added, "I do think Dominic and Brendan tried to take him to…to a place they know for gentlemen, but I don't know how that went."

She paused when the maids came in with the tea trays. Lily's thoughts turned.

"I can ask around, Mama, discreetly try to find out if he's been seen in any of the usual places," she said when they were alone again. "I could speak to him myself, but he wouldn't tell me anything he wouldn't tell you."

Katherine nodded as she poured the tea. She seemed a little steadier now that she had shared her worries. "Thank you, my dear. I'm sure it's just a phase of some sort, and soon enough he will settle into some kind of interest. But I do worry about my children. I can't help it, even though you are all grown now."

Over the gold rim of her cup, Lily met the steady, painted gaze of Mary St. Claire in her portrait. The image of the woman who had married a Huntington hung over the marble fireplace where she could be a reminder to the St. Claires never to trust the Huntingtons or people like them. Never to trust in love.

She thought of the often-told tale of Mary St. Claire, how she was the most beautiful woman at King Charles's decadent court, pursued by every man, including the king. But she would have only John Huntington, the man she had loved since she was a girl, the man who swore he loved her in return. He made her his wife, his duchess, and carried her away to live in his castle.

Yet something went terribly wrong in their romantic paradise, something so dark and secret no one knew what it was. John cast Mary out, claiming she had been unfaithful, and went on to use his wealth and influence to ruin her whole family. The St. Claires went from respectable country gentry to bankrupted outcasts and eventually a motley collection of theater owners, slum landlords, and gamesters. Mary died of a broken heart, while John remarried and perpetuated his ducal line.

And no St. Claire could love a Huntington again.

"What really happened to you, Mary?" Lily whispered as she rubbed at her aching temple. Mary just smiled back, so sweet and sad.

"Are you quite all right, Lily dear?" she heard her mother ask.

"I'm fine," Lily answered. "Just a touch of a headache. I think I'll just go and lie down for a while before I go to the club tonight."

"A very good idea. These late nights can't be good for you, though I confess I had more than a few late nights myself when I was your age," Katherine said with a laugh. Lily and her siblings always wondered how her parents had met, but they never told the story. Had it been a part of those "late nights"? "You have been working much too hard lately."

Lily kissed her mother's cheek and made her way up to her chamber, only to find one of the maids waiting for her there.

"This came for you while you were having tea, Mrs. Nichols," the maid said as she laid a white box bound with red ribbons on the bed.

Lily studied it suspiciously, as if the harmless-looking cardboard might come to life and snap at her. There had been too many unpleasant surprises lately. "Delivered from who?"

"The messenger didn't say. Will you need help dressing later, Mrs. Nichols?"

"Yes, thank you."

As soon as the maid left, Lily carefully slid the ribbon off the box and reached for the lid. She noticed a small label emblazoned on the white and red lettering that proclaimed it came from an exclusive French modiste. Curious, she tucked back the layers of tissue to reveal a silken, violet-scented cloud of pastel-colored underthings.

"Oh my," Lily sighed. She lifted out pair after pair of featherlight drawers, pale pink, sky blue, butter yellow, and pure white, all with matching chemises and pairs of stockings tucked into satin bags. They were trimmed with the finest lace and gossamer ribbons, lovelier than anything she had in her wardrobe.

At the bottom of the box was a folded note, and Lily's heart pounded as she reached for it. She already knew who had sent it, and the sight of the bold, spiky black lettering, the same writing she had seen on the notes that came with the violet bouquets, confirmed it.

With abject apologies, the note said. *I hope these replacements are adequate for what I so carelessly destroyed. If so, come riding with me tomorrow. I promise to take you somewhere the horses can really run, no staid park pathways. Aidan.*

Lily laid the note back down on the bed and stared at it as she rubbed a fold of pink silk between her fingers. Against her will, she found herself smiling.

If this was what Mary St. Claire had felt for her Huntington scoundrel so long ago, well surely the poor lady never stood a chance. And Lily feared that neither did she.

Chapter Twelve

"What is this place?" Lily asked. She drew in her horse at the crest of a hill and stared down at the vista that opened before her. It was beautiful, a rolling, pale green meadow that seemed to go on for miles, all empty and fresh and real under the gray sky. So different from the crowded London streets she saw every day.

She took a deep breath and let the clean, cool air fill her lungs. They had not ridden too far today, just over London Bridge and past Greenwich to where the old villages that surrounded London gave way to farms and dairies. Yet it felt like a different world.

Aidan drew his horse in beside hers and studied the land from under the shadowed brim of his hat. "I told you I would bring you someplace where you could run. Do you like it?"

"It's beautiful. I forget there's a world beyond the city sometimes." Lily's horse shifted restlessly beneath her, and she tightened her hold on the reins. "But will we be caught trespassing?"

Aidan laughed. "Not at all. This land belongs to my father, though he never comes here."

"This is your family's?" she said in surprise. She studied the meadow again, the way the grassy slopes rose to the crest of another hill. In the distance, she glimpsed the redbrick chimneys of a house.

"If this was mine, I would never leave," she said. "It's so quiet and peaceful."

He laughed again. Aidan seemed to be in a good mood today, lighthearted, and he made Lily feel the same. "Well, we can't have that, can we? Come, I'll race you to the top of that hill." He took off at a gallop, leaving Lily to chase him.

Their horses' hooves pounded the earth as they raced, fleet-footed and light, and the wind tore at the veil of Lily's hat. It caught her laughter and carried it away, and she felt her heart rise with the speed and movement.

It had been so long since she really got to ride! To feel the power of her horse beneath her, controlled by her light touch on the reins. To feel the wind on her skin, the sky stretched above her, and to know she was free. That nothing could hold her down.

She knew it was all an illusion, that too many things held her tied with unbreakable bonds and she couldn't outrun them. But in that moment, racing across a country meadow with Aidan, they didn't matter. Only the fleeting movement and the sound of his laughter mattered.

She leaned down low over her horse's neck and urged it faster and faster until at last she pulled ahead of Aidan. They soared over a ditch and turned to thunder up the hill, almost neck and neck. Lily managed to beat him by mere inches. She threw back her head and shouted with triumph.

"I wish I could accuse you of cheating," Aidan said,

laughter thick in his voice. "But I fear you beat me quite fairly. Where did you learn to ride like that?"

Lily twisted in her saddle to smile at him. He had lost his hat in the wild race, and his hair was tousled over his brow, gleaming in the gray light, and his blue eyes glittered.

Her stomach suddenly twisted with nervousness. He was really so outrageously good-looking. He was handsome in evening dress at the Devil's Fancy, but here he looked like a Celtic god in the midst of the elements, so free and powerful. *Oh, I am in trouble.*

She turned away from him to pat her horse's neck. "I never even got on a horse until I was twelve, and my parents decided we should all learn to ride. I was completely terrified at first; the horse seemed so huge and unpredictable. But as soon as I sat in the saddle, it felt...right."

"You're a natural-born rider, then."

"I do enjoy it. I just don't get to ride very often, and a sedate walk in the park doesn't count. But you must have been riding since birth."

"Very nearly. I think my father gave us ponies for our first birthdays. But my brother is the real equestrian."

Lily laughed. "If he's better than you, then he must be a centaur."

"Up to a rematch, then? I'm sure I'll beat you this time."

She tossed him a challenging smile. "Care to make a wager, Lord Aidan?"

"Prepare to lose, Miss St. Claire."

They took off again, laughing, their horses flying as they leaped over fallen logs and dashed between the stands of trees. Lily suddenly realized something startling—she was having *fun*. She never had fun, never laughed out of sheer enjoyment, never forgot her family duties, her past, her work. Right now there was only Aidan.

And it was Aidan who gave her that gift.

They drew up at a wrought-iron garden gate just as the first fat, cold raindrop hit Lily's neck. She tilted back her head to stare up into the slate-gray sky, still laughing.

"I declare that a draw," Aidan said.

"Only because you don't want to admit you lost the wager."

"Perhaps we should go discuss it inside before we get drenched," he said.

"Dren—" Before Lily could even get the word out, the heavens opened and rain poured down on them.

Aidan caught her horse's bridle and led her into an empty stable just beyond the trees. Once the horses were settled, he took her hand in his, and they ran laughing through the rain. They stumbled up the stone steps of the country house and through a door into an empty, echoing foyer.

Lily dragged her wet hat from her hair and dropped it to the stone floor as she stared around her. A curving staircase with an elaborately carved balustrade swept up until it vanished beyond the domed ceiling, where a fresco of a blue sky looked down at them. Open doors to either side revealed more half-empty rooms, the few pieces of furniture draped in pale canvas like ghosts.

"What is this place?" she whispered, as if she were afraid to awaken those ghosts.

"A hunting lodge," Aidan answered. He ran his hands through his hair to slick the damp strands back from his face. His hair was almost black with rain, and without its softening frame, his face looked austere, sculpted.

"At least it used to be a hunting lodge," he added. "I don't think it has been used since my grandparents' time. The woods that housed the game are mostly gone."

Lily strolled slowly across the cold foyer to study the empty niches on the wall that had once held statues and objets d'art. Her boots clicked on the hard floor. "But you come here?"

"Sometimes," Aidan said, a wary note in his voice. "It's close to London but far enough away to be private. My brother sometimes comes here as well. It's as near to town as he wants to get."

Lily rested her hand on the curved end of the balustrade and stared into the shadows of the upper floors. Despite the deep silence of the house, the emptiness, she could sense the lingering memories of old parties and merriment. "If I had a house like this, I would never leave it."

She heard the slow, deliberate tap of Aidan's footsteps as he crossed the foyer to stand right behind her. The heat of his body made her shiver.

He laid his hand lightly on her waist. "Come see the rest of it," he said.

Lily nodded, and he led her up the stairs. They passed sitting rooms and small, intimate dining rooms, window nooks enclosed with heavy draperies, small spaces made just for intimate conversation. She could see why this house had been built—for pleasure. But why had it stood empty and silent for so long? Why was it alone except for Aidan's and his brother's fleeting visits?

She paused to study a painting hung on the corridor wall. This seemed to be the only picture left in the house, and it was a very pretty one, a scene of a forest picnic party. Judging from the elaborate, lacy clothes and the curled hairstyles, long on both the men and women, it was a Restoration-era party. Shadows and sunlight dappled over the gathering, illuminating their conversations and flirtations.

Lily wondered if Mary St. Claire was one of the painted figures smiling up into a swain's eyes with no fear of what was to come. Had Mary walked through these very halls, arm in arm with her husband? Lily shivered and wrapped her arms around herself. The riding crop in her hand pressed hard to the corseted curve of her waist.

"You're cold," Aidan said. "Come, let's find you something to wrap up in, and I'll build a fire."

"*You* can build a fire?" Lily teased, trying to push away that disquiet, the feeling that ghosts lingered in the house.

"Like you, I have hidden talents. I've learned many things out of necessity." He led her into one of the bedchambers that opened off the corridor. It wasn't a big room, but it was comfortable and cozy, with large windows looking down at the overgrown, windswept gardens. An old-fashioned four-poster bed was hung with faded red curtains and spread with an old, embroidered coverlet. It was the only furniture except for a carved clothes chest and two straight-backed chairs by the fireplace, with a pile of wood in between them.

Aidan stripped off his sodden coat and waistcoat and knelt by the grate to arrange the firewood.

Lily watched him, mesmerized. His damp shirt clung to his back and shoulders, outlining every shift of his muscles. He had a beautiful body, so elegant and yet so strong. So talented too; she couldn't help but remember how that body felt as it moved over hers, driving her mindless with pleasure.

She turned away and laid her crop and gloves on the chest to unfasten the tiny buttons that ran down the front of her riding habit. The soft, fine wool was damp, clinging to the buttons, and her fingers were cold. That, plus the knowledge that Aidan was half dressed only a few feet from her, made her fumble with the fastenings.

"Let me help," he said, and she spun around to find that he stood right behind her. A fire now crackled and grew in the fireplace, and he had removed his shirt to reveal the taut, glistening expanse of pale gold skin and the width of his shoulders.

How was he not pale and flabby, like most men of his idle station? she wondered vaguely. He looked almost unreal, a god of sensuality who came to Earth to lead mortal women astray.

But then, he was *not* idle. He rode; he fought in barroom brawls.

Her gaze drifted down to the thin, white scar low on his chest, and then even lower to the hard erection in his trousers, the curve of his backside as he half turned to trace a light touch over her shoulder.

He leaned closer to nuzzle his lips over her temple. "Let me help you," he said again, his voice low, dark, and so seductive.

Lily let her arms fall to her sides and closed her eyes. She felt his hands at the high collar of her bodice, and his long fingers nimbly slid the rest of the buttons free of their loops. The cold air, tinged with the smoky warmth of the fire, curled over her skin as he peeled away the habit.

She slid her arms out of the tight sleeves and let it drop to her feet. His breath hissed between his teeth, and she opened her eyes to see him staring intently at her bared body, his blue eyes midnight-dark. His long lashes cast shadows on his cheeks, and his hair fell over his brow, making him look almost boyish but also so dark, a dramatic contrast.

"You wore the purple," he said.

Lily smiled. She had thought of him that morning as she chose those underthings out of all the lovely pieces he had sent her, pale lavender silk trimmed with gossamer ivory ribbons, so soft on her skin. "You have superb taste, for a man. Do you like it?"

In answer, he gave a hoarse groan and seized her by the waist to drag her closer. He pressed his open mouth to the side of her neck, his teeth scraping lightly over her skin. He kissed her jaw, her cheek, before he slid his hands up to frame her face as his dark, hooded eyes studied her. His thumbs skimmed over her mouth, and she sucked the tip of one of them between her lips.

His face tightened, drawn taut over his high, sharp cheekbones as his attention focused on her mouth. It made the hard, hot knot of desire inside her tighten until she couldn't breathe. She felt wild, free—powerful.

The laughter of their wild ride was still in her, and she spun away from him with a giggle. She *never* giggled—it was only another sign of the unreality of this afternoon, with Aidan in this strange, empty house. She was not herself.

Or maybe she was. Maybe she was a part of herself she had denied for too long.

Aidan reached out for her, but she slid away with a laugh. She picked up her crumpled habit and laid it on top of the chest. As she smoothed the damp folds, she saw her riding crop there where she had left it.

She ran her fingers lightly over the smooth ivory handle and felt something seize inside of her, some confused tangle of memory and desire.

"My mother, my real mother, was a whore in a 'French' house, where they specialized in flagellation," she said, her voice strangely calm and steady. She hadn't said such a thing aloud in many years, not since she first went to live with the St. Claires and told Katherine her whole, sad tale. Her birth mother was only a distant memory now, an image of a beautiful face, a tragic fate.

A memory that suddenly seemed too close. Lily felt like she could shut her eyes and see the red wallpaper, smell the sweet sickness of opium, musky-rose French perfume, and sex. And hear the crack of the whip and the cries of forbidden pleasure.

Aidan had gone very still behind her. She could feel his tense watchfulness, but he didn't move away. He didn't recoil from her in disgust. "Was she?" he said quietly.

"Oh, yes. She was the most sought-after woman in Madame Josephine's house. She was actually French, you see, and very beautiful. She had black hair and such dark eyes, but very pale skin. Like a ghost. And she was a marvel with a whip. She knew exactly where to land the lash, how hard, how long. And she knew what dirty things to say in that lovely French accent." Lily picked up the crop and ran her hand down its length. "She was perfect at it."

"And what happened to her?"

"The opium got her in the end. She couldn't stay away from it." Lily slashed the crop neatly through the air, and her wrist remembered that little flick at the end. She turned around to look at Aidan, who watched her intently. "Have you ever been to a place like Madame Josephine's, Aidan?"

His eyes narrowed, and she laughed. "Of course you have," she said. "You have been everywhere. You know what it's like, then. What happens there."

"It's not entirely to my taste," he said quietly.

"No? You probably didn't get the right girl, then. Most of them aren't as skilled as my mother. Or maybe you liked to be the one wielding the whip? They can do that too. Whatever the customer desires."

Aidan didn't answer, and Lily slowly nodded. Yes, he would like to be the one in control, directing the scene, bringing a woman up to that exquisite border between pleasure and pain. It made her shiver to imagine it. But her mother had known the flip side of that power, and she had taught it to Lily. Her one perverted legacy to her daughter.

She reached out and traced the leather tip of the crop over his bare shoulder. She felt the ripple of the powerful muscle under his skin, but otherwise he didn't move. That feeling of power grew in her, and she realized that she had felt helpless for so very long. Too long.

With Aidan, she felt free.

"After my mother died," she said, tracing the crop in a light pattern over his chest, "Madame Josephine wanted me to take her place. I was very young, but some men like that, and my mother had been teaching me. I didn't want my mother's way of life, her end, and I ran away. But I do remember some things."

She stepped closer to him, one slow movement after another, until her body leaned into his. She could feel all his coiled, primitive strength, could smell the salt and rain on his hot skin. His nostrils flared as he looked down at her.

She slid her arms around his back and grasped both ends of the crop with her hands as she used it to pull him even closer to her. She pressed it hard to the underside of his buttocks.

"Do you want to see what I remember?" she whispered.

"Lily," he growled. "You make me crazy."

He made her crazy, too, made her feel like a different person, made her remember dark, sensual delights, and made her crave them. Made her want to please him, draw him into that world with her. She gave him a smile and let go of the end of the crop. She lightly hit him on the back of his thigh. She was deeply gratified when his erection hardened even more against her and his breath grew harsher.

"I wouldn't do this with anyone but you, Aidan," she said.

"And I wouldn't let anyone but you do it, Lily. I'm completely insane when I'm with you." He eased back from her and watched her as he reached down for the fastenings of his trousers. His eyes never left her as he kicked off his boots and clothing until he stood before her completely, gloriously naked.

Lily studied him greedily, every inch of his body, the gleaming, muscled chest with its light arrow of curling brown hair, the lean hips, and long, powerful legs. His erect penis.

He really was the beauty of a classical statue come to hot, hard life. She ached to touch him, taste him.

Aidan grinned at her as if he could read her thoughts, the arrogant man. Then slowly, deliberately, he turned to face the bed. He braced his palms flat on the edge of the mattress and leaned over, baring the hard length of his back and his tight buttocks to her. The firelight glinted on his skin.

"You *have* done this before," Lily murmured.

He gave her a smoldering glance over his shoulder. "I told you I'm a curious man."

"And one with many talents." Still wearing her boots and her beautiful new underthings, Lily moved closer to him. She studied every tempting inch of him and couldn't believe he was here with her now. Offering himself to her like that.

But she half feared that she would be the one truly possessed. The one who fell into madness when this was over.

She reached out and laid her hand on the back of his neck. His hair, the strands curling damply, brushed over her fingers like a soft caress. He stayed very still under her touch, and she slid slowly down his back and over the sharp angle of his hip, reveling in the leashed power of him. She slid one fingertip over the curve of his backside and smiled as he growled curses.

"Show me, Lily," he demanded. "Now. Show me what you learned so well."

She stepped away from him and drew back her arm. She let all the old instincts, the old memories come back, and flicked out with her wrist. The crop landed low, just at the top of his thigh, with the lightest of kisses. His buttocks tightened, and she moved again and again, harder and harder, the strokes carefully, artfully placed.

"Lily!" he shouted, and a shudder coursed through his body. But then he braced his hands more firmly against the bed and went very still. "Again."

She lowered the crop again, the faint whistling sound of it through the air soft and deafening at the same time.

His very stillness was powerful, the harsh sound of his breath making her want him. She was so wet now beneath her fine underclothes, shaking with the force of desire, and she wondered what would happen when his power was unleashed.

Faint welts appeared on his glistening, sweat-damp skin, and she could smell the musk of his arousal and her own, blending in the warm air like the rarest of perfumes. She tossed the crop aside and wrapped her arms around his waist as she kissed the marks on his skin.

Her tongue slid along them, one after another, as she tasted him. She slid her fingertips over his hard abdomen and down the length of his erection. It jerked against her touch, and Aidan gave a raw groan as she stroked him. The skin there was tight and hot, and so, so hard. She gathered the drop of moisture at its tip with her fingers and touched him again, a long, slow slide.

"Oh, God, Lily, yes. Just like that," he said, and she hardly recognized his rough voice. His body arched up, and she sensed he was on the edge of losing control.

And *she* had done that to him. No one else.

She could feel her own control slipping away, could feel herself falling down into the dark abyss of passionate need. He rolled onto his back on the bed, and his hands closed roughly on her arms to pull her down on top of him as his mouth claimed hers. His kiss was so deep, so hot, his tongue thrusting against hers to take her. His hands skimmed over her shoulders, her back, rough through the thin silk.

She melted into him. All she could do was brace her hands against his shoulders and hold on as he kissed her, his tongue stroking deep.

Suddenly he pushed her away. He rose up and held

her by the waist until he sat on the edge of the bed with her standing between his legs. Dazed, she watched as he jerked at the lacings of her corset. His hands were so deft and sure as he worked, and she remembered how many women he must have done this to before.

His eyes burned with that raw blue fire as he looked up at her, the fire she had come to know meant he wanted her. Her corset fell away, and she sucked in a deep breath.

"Take off the rest of your clothes," he said, and lay back on the bed to watch her. He lounged against the piled-up pillows, his arms behind his head, so lazy, so in control. He had taken the power from her just like that, with no effort at all.

So he wanted a show, did he? She could give him one. It was yet another thing she had learned from her mother and the other girls at Madame Josephine's.

But she doubted any of them, in their opium-addled minds, had ever felt like she did now. So warm and melting, so filled with the sparkling heat of desire. So right in this moment, with this man. She knew that would fade as soon as they were apart, and she remembered who he was, who she was. Remembered how wrong these feelings were. Right now, though, she just wanted him, and she wanted him to want her.

She stepped back from the bed and gave him a teasing smile as she let her gaze wander down his body, spread so alluringly across the bed. Oh, yes, he *did* want her, if that iron-hard erection springing from the thatch of dark hair between his legs was any indication.

He wrapped his long fingers around himself and stroked lazily, making Lily shudder when she thought of how it felt to have *her* hand there.

"Do it, Lily," he said, his voice full of a quiet, steady determination. She had to obey.

She turned around and loosened her hair to toss it over one shoulder as she slowly reached down and grasped the hem of her chemise. She let the whisper-soft fabric glide over her skin one inch at a time. She drew it over her head and let it fall to the floor with her corset before she untied the ribbons at the waist of her drawers.

She took off her boots and slid the drawers over her hips and legs until she stood there in only her white silk stockings. She heard Aidan groan and peeked over her shoulder to see the lust in his eyes.

"Enough," he said, staring at her through those glowing eyes. "Come to the bed, Lily."

"Are you sure?" she answered. She turned to face him and let her hand slide down her body, over her breasts, her aching nipples, her trembling stomach. Her fingers drifted over her damp mound.

Suddenly Aidan lunged up from the bed and seized her by the waist to drag her down onto the mattress. Lily laughed as they landed hard in the middle of the feather bed and sank down into the soft velvet counterpane. His body came down over hers, his hips pressed hard between her spread thighs, and he bent his head to lick and bite at her neck. Her laughter faded, and she wrapped her arms around his shoulders, her legs around his waist.

"God, you're beautiful, Lily," he whispered against her shoulder. "So beautiful. How do you do this to me?"

"What do I do to you?" she gasped. He moved down her body, his tongue circling the softness of her breast before tracing a hot, wet pattern around her navel.

"You make me completely mindless," he said, biting

lightly at the curve of her hip. "I can't think of anything except you, the way you look, the way you smell. The sound you make when I do this…"

She cried out when she felt his tongue drive into her and taste her deeply.

He wrapped his hands around her thighs and spread her wider. "Yes, just like that, Lily. Tell me how much you like this." He draped her legs over his shoulders and pressed a gentle, openmouthed kiss to the top of her slit as one finger slid into her.

Lily bit her lip and turned her head to the side. She closed her eyes and reached down to wind her hands into his hair. Oh, she did like this, and he was so very, very good at it. She felt his hair brush against the sensitive skin of her thigh as he sucked that tiny, hot bundle of nerves between his teeth.

He slid another finger into her, and she cried out again. She could feel the heat growing deep in her core, spreading through her. Sparkling white lights glimmered behind her closed eyes, blue and green, popping like fireworks on a royal birthday.

"Aidan!" she screamed as she exploded, her hands pulling at his hair. Before she could even start to come down, his mouth slid away from her. He kissed the inside of her trembling leg and knelt up on the bed.

Lily's eyes fluttered open, and she looked up to find him watching her with glittering eyes. He slowly wiped the back of his hand over his damp lips.

"Do you want me, Lily?" he said, and she had never heard him sound quite like that, so dark.

She swallowed hard and nodded. She did want him, with a terrible desperation she had never known before.

She lay back on the bed and spread her legs wider in invitation.

He came down over her and kissed her, his mouth hard on hers, his tongue rough and deep, stealing away any thought and leaving only sensation. She felt his hard penis against her stomach, and she wrapped her arms around him to feel his sweat-damp skin under her fingers. His muscles bunched and shifted under her caress, all supple power, and she could taste herself on his lips. Everything went hot and blurry around her, and she was falling deeper and deeper into him.

He seemed to feel the same way. With a deep groan, he pushed himself back from her and braced his palms on the bed at either side of her head.

"I have to see you this time," he said. "Have to watch your face."

Lily nodded. This was the only way her husband had wanted to claim his marital rights, her vulnerable under his portly body as he lifted her nightgown and drove into her. Mercifully, he was always quick because the smothering feeling of being so overpowered made her want to scream in panic. She had never let anyone else take her like this, only from behind or her on top.

But now, with Aidan, it felt so very different. She didn't feel as if she were drowning. She felt... safe. Surrounded by his warmth and strength.

He tightened his hips and moved into her in one strong thrust, sliding deep.

"Aidan," she whispered.

"Lily, Lily," he answered, her name like a supplication, a prayer, on his lips. He slowly, so slowly, pulled out and then thrust back in, to the hilt.

She wrapped her legs around his waist again and tangled her fingers in his hair as he kissed her, wet and rough. He fell to his forearms above her and wrapped all around her. He moved faster, deeper, their bodies sliding against each other in a hot, sweaty friction.

"More, please. Please," she begged, and he thrust harder and harder. He reached down between them with one hand and rubbed over that sensitive little spot, circling it with his fingertip until she exploded again.

And suddenly he went still inside her. His head arched back, and she opened her eyes to see the muscles of his throat go tense, his eyes tightly closed. He shouted out her name, and she dug her hands into his taut backside as he clenched.

"Fuck it all, Lily," he groaned, and fell to the bed beside her.

His head rested on her stomach as he shuddered in the aftermath of his climax, their legs tangled together amid the rumpled wreckage of the bed. Lily stroked his damp hair back from his brow, one gentle, rhythmic caress after another until she felt him relax. His deep, even breath told her he had fallen asleep.

She was almost into that dark oblivion herself when she realized Aidan had climaxed inside her—without a sheath.

Aidan held Lily against his shoulder as she slept, listening to the soft, uneven sound of her breath. She had been restless when she first fell down into sleep, tossing and turning, her brow creased as if she were haunted by disturbing visions in her sleep. But as he gently stroked her hair, whispering soothing words in her ear, she slowly grew quiet.

The fire in the grate burned low now, the light flickering over her bare skin in red and black patterns. He traced a soft caress over her shoulder with his fingertip and buried his face in the loose waves of her hair to inhale her scent of violets and rain. It was intoxicating, and it made him want to drown in her, in this mysterious, complex, amazing woman.

Something had been freed inside of her tonight, something he sensed she had held tightly down in her soul for a long time. But she released it when he gave himself over to her, let her feel her power, and the look on her face had moved something in his own soul. He had always been adventurous in bed, ready to try almost anything just to see how it made him feel, but he had never experienced anything like the sudden connection with Lily St. Claire. Anything like what he felt as he moved inside her and looked into her eyes.

Aidan wrapped a long strand of her hair around his fist as she murmured in her sleep. He didn't *want* to feel that connection. It was deeper, darker than anything he had ever imagined outside his writing, something he had always imagined was for other people, not for him. It made him want to shout at her, push her away, hurt her.

And it made him want to never let her go. To tie her down here to this bed so she couldn't get away.

He pushed himself onto his side and propped up on his elbow so he could look down into her sleeping face. His backside gave a twinge as he moved, reminding him of what they had done earlier. Her hair spread out over the pillows, a shining dark river. He smoothed a swath of it back from her brow, and her frown eased under his touch.

Aidan feathered a light touch over the shadows that lay against her cheek, the soft curve of her lower lip. Asleep, she looked so young, so vulnerable and open to him. When she was awake, she was always so guarded and careful. When they had sex, it was like being swept away in a storm. Here, in this quiet moment, it was just the two of them in their own still, perfect world.

He leaned down to press a soft kiss against her shoulder. She even tasted like rain, so sweet and clean. He traced his tongue over the soft swell of her breasts above the line of the sheet she had wrapped around herself. She stirred beneath him, and he felt her fingertips trail through his hair.

"Aidan," she murmured.

"Shhh," he whispered against her. The moment felt so fragile and delicate, like an icicle in the sunshine, and he didn't want it to melt away. He had never felt like this before.

She wrapped her arms around his shoulders and held him close to her as he kissed her. He gently drew the sheet down and tossed it away so he could see her, her skin painted by the firelight. Her nipples were erect, dark pink from their rough lovemaking, so beautiful. It made him hard just to look at her, made him want her with a hot, urgent need all over again. That need never seemed to be satisfied.

There was a light pink pattern on her pale skin from the rasp of his beard, and he traced a soft kiss over it, trying to soothe the sting. She trembled, and her fingernails dug into his shoulders. He swept his tongue around the soft areola of her nipple, and only when she sobbed out his name did he suck her nipple deep into his mouth. He rolled it over his tongue and caressed her other breast with his fingertips, cupping its weight on his palm. She arched up into him.

Aidan trailed his hand slowly down her body, savoring every inch of her, feeling every curve and angle, every hollow. His mouth followed, tasting the rainy coolness of her skin, the curve of her waist, the flare of her hip, her slender thigh. He wanted to know, to memorize every part of Lily.

He trailed one finger along her womanhood and dipped into the wet, hot silk of her. He tapped the tiny, hard bundle of nerves at the top of her sex, and she let out a ragged sob.

"Aidan," she said brokenly, and her hands tangled in his hair again to draw him up along and over her body.

His mouth met hers, open and hungry, their tongues tangling. He felt her legs wrap around his hips and pull him even closer. He slid into her, thrusting slowly, steadily, until he was deep inside of her, their bodies pressed together, her soft breasts to his chest, her pelvis to his, their legs tangled.

He went very still and took her hands in his, their fingers entwined as he held them down against the bed. He rose up and stared into her eyes. She looked back at him, and for just an instant, they were completely open to each other. Completely bound to each other. It felt like the center of a whirling storm, a moment of perfect stillness amid the thunder and noise of the world.

Then Lily's eyes closed and her head fell back, snapping the still moment. Aidan moved against her, thrusting forward and sliding back, almost all the way out before he flexed his hips and moved deep again. Lily cried out as he slid against that one sensitive spot and he moved faster, deeper.

She still held on to his hands, and he pressed them above her head, leaving her open to him, her body stretched out beneath him. Her heels dug into his buttocks and urged him even closer. They moved together, the air growing heavy and humid around them, their cries and incoherent words blending and clashing.

Aidan threw back his head as he felt the familiar tight tingling gather at the base of his spine, felt his testicles draw up and tighten. His whole body grew taut with raw, pure pleasure, and he shouted out her name as he came, harder than he ever had before. For a moment, everything turned dark, and all he knew was the sound of her voice crying his name as she found her own pleasure.

He slowly sank down against her, his head on her breasts. He tried to catch his breath, to make his heart quit thundering in his chest. Their bodies were slick with sweat, and he felt her hands drift lightly over his back.

Slowly, he became aware of other things, the sound of rain hitting the window, the snap of sparks in the fire-place, the soft drift of her hair against his face.

He eased himself to her side so he wouldn't crush her, but he kept his arm wrapped around her waist. He couldn't seem to let her go.

She turned onto her side, her back to his chest, her hand curled around his arm. She let him hold her close as her body softened into sleep.

But Aidan couldn't find sleep for a very long time.

Chapter Thirteen

"...Don't you think, Aidan? Aidan?"

Aidan turned in his saddle, startled by the sound of his cousin Sophia's voice. The look in her eyes told him she had been chattering steadily as they rode through the park, but he hadn't heard her. His thoughts were far away, in that hunting lodge bedroom with Lily—again.

Damn it all, but he hadn't been able to get her out of his mind since he had left her at the mews behind her house that night. He had never had a sexual experience that felt like that before, a connection so intense. He had never wanted it.

He did not want it now.

He shook his head hard, as if that would clear it of the smell of her violet perfume, the sound of his name as she cried out to him. He hadn't been lying to her; he was a curious man and had visited a "French" brothel before. He had discovered it was not his usual sort of perversion. But when he saw the bright flash of pain in her eyes when she spoke of her mother, something in him wanted to do anything to take that hurt away.

But what they had done together had also released

something in *him*, some primal lust that had roared into fiery life and wouldn't let him go. And now it wouldn't be subdued.

It just wanted Lily.

"My, you really are distracted today," Sophia said with a laugh. She drew her horse to a halt beneath the shade of a tree, somewhat out of the flow of the fashionable traffic, and Aidan stopped beside her.

"I'm sorry, Soph," he answered. "I've been horribly inattentive. I don't mean to be, not to you." And he did not. Sophia was his favorite cousin, his uncle's only daughter. He knew she was a trial to her father, a beautiful young lady with glossy black hair and violet-blue eyes, spoiled since birth, who now cut a careless swath through society with suitors cast off on every side. She and Aidan had long been partners in family mischief.

"Poor Aidan, forced by your father to play nursemaid to your silly cousin when there are so many more fun things to be doing," Sophia said. She patted her horse's neck as she ignored the stares of the men who passed by.

"I never need to be forced to spend time with *you*. It's been far too long since I've seen you."

"Because Mama insisted on taking me sea-bathing at Weymouth." Sophia shuddered. "All those elderly people playing their penny-ante whist every night. I missed everything that was happening in London."

"It's been as dull as tombs here, I assure you."

"Has it?" She tilted her head to study him from under her veil. "It's never dull here for you, Aidan. Even all of Mama's senile friends were clucking about what a shocking rogue you are. And you've obviously been up to something while I was away. What is it? A woman? A new *affaire d'amour*?"

Aidan laughed. "Are you sure you're only nineteen, Soph? You've become quite shocking."

Sophia shrugged. "I'm a Huntington. We grow up before our time. And you can tell me. Is it an Italian opera singer? A voluptuous young widow?"

"None of the above," Aidan said shortly.

"No! Never say you have given in to your parents' demands and found a demure young miss to marry."

"Ah, Soph, you know me better than that. And I've been up to nothing out of the common way since you've been gone."

"But you are still distracted. Perhaps you've been working on your writing again?"

He had been writing, late at night when thoughts of Lily most plagued him. He put all his dark desires down on the page, though even that did not banish her.

"I've been working on something new," he said.

"Aidan, that's wonderful! I do wish you would let me read it."

He almost laughed again. His cousin was a bold girl, true, but she was still a girl, a young noblewoman who couldn't know every aspect of his life. She couldn't see his writing in the raw, burning, lustful stage it was in now. "Not yet. Perhaps one day you will see it on the stage."

"My heavens. Who is *that*?" she suddenly murmured, her head swiveling around.

Aidan frowned as he tried to see where she stared. Sophia was not usually so very still and attentive; she was always moving, always laughing, always so teasingly careless, just like Aidan. "Who?"

"That man there. On the white horse."

Then Aidan saw. It was Dominic St. Claire, Lily's

brother, who had glared at him so darkly that night at the Devil's Fancy. The sun gleamed on the man's uncovered golden hair, making him a sort of beacon amid the black carriages and dark riding habits. He laughed down at the women in the carriage he rode beside.

Aidan's gaze flickered down to see Lily looking up at her brother from under the brim of her green satin bonnet. She was actually smiling, at ease, her cheeks a happy pale pink. With her family, her usual caution was gone, and she looked happy. The darkness was banished.

Damn, he thought as his fist tightened on his reins. Why couldn't he make her that way? Make her smile that way?

But he knew very well why he couldn't. Because nothing was ever easy between them. Not even sex.

"That is one of those St. Claire actors your friends are always giggling over," he said. "Dominic St. Claire."

"Is it indeed? The sketches of him in the papers don't do him justice," Sophia said quietly.

Before Aidan knew what she was doing, she urged her horse in the direction of Dominic St. Claire. He hurried to follow her, suddenly wary of what Sophia might do. She was his cousin, after all, and too much like him for her own—or his—good.

Lily turned to say something to the older lady beside her and caught sight of him. Her smile faded, and she went very still. The other woman turned to see what Lily looked at, and he recognized Katherine St. Claire from her appearances on the stage. She went pale, and her lips tightened.

Dominic St. Claire only looked furious. Until he caught sight of Sophia. Men usually melted for her, but

Dominic's eyes narrowed. The white-hot anger almost radiated off his body.

Interesting, Aidan thought. The St. Claires did seem to know him—and they did not like him. Did they know of what had happened with him and Lily? Would Dominic St. Claire's seconds be calling on him in the morning, challenging him to a duel?

Aidan raised his hat and gave them a bland smile as he rode by their carriage. Dominic glared, and Lily gave him a small nod. He could read nothing in her eyes.

Sophia glanced back over her shoulder once they were well past. Her gaze lingered on Dominic. "My heavens, Aidan," she said. "I thought you said you didn't know the St. Claires."

"I don't." Except for one of them. Her he knew too well—and yet not as well as he wished.

"Well, they seem to know you. Whatever have you done to them? That angelic-looking Dominic looked as if he could kill you."

Aidan shrugged. He had no idea what he had done that they knew about. But he intended to find out. Soon.

Lily had run from him long enough.

"The nerve of that blasted Huntington," Lily heard Dominic say.

She rubbed at her suddenly throbbing head. "Oh, Dom. All he did was raise his hat to us."

"He shouldn't have even looked at you," Dominic said.

"There is no need to be rude, dear," their mother admonished. "We're in a public park. Just smile now."

Dominic fell silent, and Lily forced a smile to her

lips that felt more like a grimace. She hadn't expected to see Aidan today, and the sight of him had driven every thought out of her mind but what happened the last time she had seen him. But she couldn't talk to him or even let any emotion show on her face at all, since her family was there.

And Aidan wasn't alone either. She twisted around to glare over her shoulder at him. He was slowly riding away, the lady he was with leaning toward him as she said something. He laughed, his head thrown back.

The woman was very beautiful indeed, with glossy dark hair pinned in coils under her stylish veiled hat, and very white skin showed through her black dotted lace veil. She wasn't the blond, quiet Lady Henrietta. Was she another lady he was meant to be courting? Or perhaps an expensive courtesan?

I don't care, she thought fiercely. She had no claim on Aidan, just as he had none on her. He could certainly see whoever he liked. No matter what they did to each other in the bedchamber.

But she feared deep down inside that she did care. At least a little bit.

She half listened to her mother's chatter as they rode back to the house. But as Katherine and Isabel went ahead to the drawing room, Dominic caught her hand.

"What is that man to you, Lily?" he asked darkly.

Lily wrenched her hand away and turned to the mirror to take off her bonnet. "I don't know who you're talking about."

"You know very well I'm talking about Lord Aidan Huntington. You were talking to him that night at the Devil's Fancy, and then he showed up at the theater."

"I talked to many people at the club. And he was just being polite at the park." Lily glared at him in the mirror. "Don't tell me *you* weren't ogling the lady he was with either, Dominic St. Claire."

"I didn't even notice who he was with. I don't want to notice a Huntington at all." His voice turned gentle. "Lily, you're my sister, and I love you. I couldn't stand to see a blighter like Aidan Huntington hurt you."

Lily gave him a small, grudging smile. "I know, Dom, and I love you for it. But the last time I looked, I was a grown woman. A widow, even. I can look after myself well enough."

"I don't want to see you unhappy again, like you were with Nichols."

"I won't be." Aidan was nothing at all like Nichols had been, in any way. And she hardly thought he would marry her. "We should go and have some tea with Mama before she starts to fret."

"Yes," Dominic said. A footman was passing through the foyer, and Dominic stopped him to ask, "Is James with Mrs. St. Claire now?"

"No, Mr. St. Claire," the footman said with a bow. "He went out some time ago. He's not expected back this evening."

"Where the devil could he be this time? He's always gone these days," Dominic muttered. He strode toward the drawing room doors.

As Lily laid her gloves aside with her bonnet, the footman held out a folded note to her.

"This came for you while you were out, Mrs. Nichols," he said.

"Thank you." Lily turned the paper over in her hand,

studying it curiously. It was torn and stained, a cheap scrap with her name printed in penciled letters. It couldn't be from Aidan, and she felt an unwelcome flash of disappointment at the thought. Quickly followed by a flash of fear.

She ripped it open and read quickly, the ache in her throat growing with every word. *Meet me at the Lambeth market tonight if you want to see your brother. Your old friend, TB.*

Chapter Fourteen

It had been a long time since Lily had been there. Not just a matter of years, but something much deeper, something unseen. She had become a different person since the last time she went to the Lambeth night market. She had tried to forget it.

But now, as she made her way through the winding, narrow streets, she knew she had never really forgotten. That old Lily, the one who had once come here to try and steal a piece of bread or beg a shilling, had never left her. That Lily came out and shoved back hard when someone jostled her now.

She tugged her old knitted shawl tighter over her shoulders and caught a glimpse of herself in a dusty shop window. A cap covered her hair, and she wore a faded brown skirt and bodice she had bought from one of the maids. She looked pale against the muddy color, her face thin and strained. But she didn't look as on edge as she felt. She felt like she was about to shatter into a hundred pieces.

Tom Beaumont was really back. Her past had dropped down onto her with the crushing force of a cannon shot. And it was threatening to destroy her family.

Lily would never let that happen. She remembered what it was to fight, to scrabble in the dirt to protect what was hers. She could do it again. Beaumont would be sorry he ever saw her.

But she couldn't help the cold, icy knot of fear deep inside. It had taken hold the minute she saw Tom in the barroom brawl and remembered every painful thing he had ever done to her, and it was lodged there now, so hard, so overwhelming. She had never felt so very alone before, not even when her mother died and she ran away from Madame Josephine's.

But back then she didn't have so much to lose.

Beaumont had James, her beloved baby brother, but what he wanted was Lily. So she would go to him.

She tugged her shawl closer, even though she knew it wouldn't keep away the cold. Nothing could, not until James was safe and Tom Beaumont was gone. She pushed her way past a quarreling couple and into the market, scanning every face, every shadow, in search of Tom.

The Saturday night markets in Lambeth had come about as a chance for harried wives to buy a bit of food before their husbands drank up all the wages in dockside taverns. Sunday morning was too late. Now it had grown into dozens of stalls, rickety, open-sided structures lit with lamps and candles against the night. Cries of "Chestnuts all 'ot, a penny a score" and "Three a penny Yarmouth bloaters" rang out above the shouts of arguments and shrill haggling, the shrieks of children and the laughter of the rouge-cheeked prostitutes who strolled between the stalls.

The smells of the roasted chestnuts, buttered potatoes, cheap gin, and unwashed bodies hung heavy in the smoky air, caught above the close-packed crowd.

It wasn't the worst place Lily had ever been by any means, and the crowd of streetwalkers and dock laborers were far from the most desperate. But the lit-up stalls cast an ominous red glow over the faces.

Suddenly, Lily felt a tug at her skirt. She whirled around to see a grubby-faced little girl in a patched gray dress. She stared up at Lily with such old eyes, and Lily recognized her as the girl from the park.

"You Lily, then?" the girl said.

"Yes, I am."

"Come with me."

The girl turned and slipped into the crowd without looking back to see if Lily followed. She led her beyond the lights of the market into a narrower warren of alleyways, hemmed in by blank, dirty walls with lines of damp laundry hanging listlessly overhead. A few ghostly faces peered down from the windows, and Lily could hear the slurred sound of drunken arguments, the yowl of a cat, the slap of flesh on flesh.

She pressed her hand to the concealed pocket tied at her waist and felt the weight of her pistol there.

The girl stopped at a half-open doorway. "In there," she said, and held out her dirty hand. Lily dropped a coin into her grasp and then the girl was gone.

Lily peered into the building. It appeared to be a gin joint, a single large room with a rough plank bar and a few tables lit by one smoking lamp. Men and women lounged around, soft murmurs broken by barked demands for payment from the barkeep and whined pleas for one more glass.

As Lily stepped inside, the smell of unwashed bodies and the tang of spilled gin grew thicker, almost choking her. And underneath was something sweeter, headier, and more insidious—opium. It made her head swim, and she swallowed hard against the nausea.

"So you made it, did you, Lily?" she heard Tom say, and she turned to see him sitting by the wall, his chair tipped back so he could prop his scarred boots on the table. "I was startin' to worry."

Holding her hand over the gun, Lily slowly moved closer to him. She pushed away the old fear and reminded herself she was not a child now. This man had no power over her, not really.

But the sight of those burning dark eyes, so animalistic beneath heavy black brows, and the skull-topped stick that rested next to his boots on the table, made that ice inside of her tighten. And for some reason, she thought of Aidan, longed for Aidan. She wanted his quiet, deceptively powerful assurance at her side.

Pushing away that foolish desire, she stood in front of Tom. Aidan could never know about this, nor could her family. This was her battle to fight if she had any hope of beating Tom at his own game.

"Where is James?" she demanded.

"Now, Lily, is that any way to greet an old friend?" Tom said. He took a knife from his jacket pocket and slowly pared his nails as he smiled up at her. "It's been so long since we saw each other; we should catch up. And don't you worry about the St. Claire cub—he's upstairs now with one of my best girls."

"What do you want? Money?"

"I'm hurt, Lily m'love. We was so close once. Don't you remember?"

"Is that what you call it?" Lily said tightly, remembering

this man beating her. Locking her in a dark cupboard when she didn't bring him enough coin at the end of the day.

Once, before he was caught and transported, Tom had had one of the largest crime networks in the stews of London. Thievery, blackmail, prostitution, running dodges. Dozens of people like Lily under his power. Even now, with Tom marked by his years under the harsh Australian sun, Lily sensed that cruel power. She took a step back, and he slowly planted his boots on the floor. The skull grinned up at her.

"You was one of my best girls, Lily," he said. "Clever and quick-like. And look at you now. You landed on your feet right enough, without a thought for me after I took you in after your mum died. That's not very friendly, is it?"

"You kidnapped me off the streets when I ran away from Madame Josephine's."

"And gave you a place to live! You would've been a common street whore in no time. But I ain't here to quarrel about the past. I'm interested in the here and now. I hear you're friendly with a duke's fancy son, and I thought it was time you and me renewed our old acquaintance."

Lily stared at him, her whole body gone tense and watchful, like a forest animal about to attack or be attacked. "What do you want?" she said again.

"Just for you to be friendly-like to me, Lily, now that you've had such good fortune." Tom suddenly smiled, revealing cracked and broken teeth and the gleam of one gold incisor. "Your brother's friendly enough. He likes my girls, y'see. They give him what he needs."

"You stay away from him," Lily cried. "This is between you and me."

"That's just what I hoped you'd say. You've turned into

a pretty one, like your mum. You have her special skills now too?"

Lily shuddered at the tone of his voice, like a slimy slide over her skin. She wanted more than anything to pull out her gun and shoot him right here, right in his smirking, hideous face. But being seized in a cheap gin joint and going to prison for murder, hauled away to serve hard labor, would do no one any good. She had to stay calm.

And she remembered very well that she did still have a deft hand with a whip.

"Why don't you let me show you?" she said quietly. Right where she could snap his dick off with one flick...

Tom laughed. "I did miss you, Lily girl. We could do so much together. I'm going to rebuild my old network, find some new jobs here in London. You're just the one to help me."

"So it is money you want. How much?"

"What's money between friends? And I don't just want money."

"Then quit playing games. Tell me what it is you want exactly and let me take James home," she snapped.

A group of loud, laughing people suddenly fell through the door from the street, filling the cramped space with their noise. The gin-soaked stupor was broken.

One of the men, a large, burly monster smelling of pipe smoke, seized Lily by the waist and swung her around in the air. Startled, she kicked out at him, but he just laughed and pressed a wet kiss to her neck.

Lily yanked his hair hard and struggled to get free. Every old instinct she had suppressed for so long rushed to the surface, and she fought like a cornered alley cat. She twisted around and sank her teeth into his hand.

"Bloody bitch!" the man shouted. He dropped her hard to the floor and slapped her across the face. Her head snapped back, and she tasted the bitter tang of blood. It only made her more furious.

Above the roaring in her head, she vaguely heard shouts and screams and the shattering of glass. And she wondered how, after years of trying to live quietly and respectably, she had been in two bar fights in less than a month. But there was no time for thinking; she had to move on instinct now, and she had to move fast. She needed to find James and get out of there.

The enraged man lunged for her, but she was much smaller and quicker. She ducked down under a table, away from the tumbling bodies and crashing feet. She caught a bottle as it rolled off the table and smashed the end off to make a dagger of sorts.

The smell of stale, spilled liquor and rotten garbage was stronger there, tinged with blood. Lily swiped the back of her hand over her lip, and it came away smeared with red, but she knew she wasn't the worst off here. Already men were slumped against the walls, battered by the fight. She quickly scanned their slack faces, yet none belonged to Tom Beaumont.

He seemed to have vanished from the fray. She knew he wouldn't stay gone for long.

Suddenly she felt a fist close on her ankle and drag her from her meager shelter. She rolled over and brought up her other knee to try and ram her new captor in the groin, but he twisted away from her.

"What's a pretty morsel like you doin' here?" he said, and she felt a rough hand grope up her leg. She slung her bottle down on his greasy head, and when he collapsed to the floor, she kicked him out of the way and leaped to her feet. It was definitely time to get out of there.

She ran through the crowd, weaving her way past flying fists and falling bodies, until she found the narrow, dark staircase at the back of the room. She hurried up it, drawing out her pistol as she went.

It was much quieter there, the sound of the fight a muffled roar as she turned at the top landing and found herself facing a short corridor lined with closed doorways and filled with the scent of cheap perfume and opium smoke. Lily knew those were cramped cribs rented out to whores by the night or hour, a place where they could bring their customers—and possibly drug and rob them. No one here would want the trouble of a fight.

And James was here somewhere.

Lily hurried to the first door. The room was empty, as were the second and third. The fourth held two women and a naked man flung facedown across a small bed. The women looked at her from their kohl-rimmed eyes with no hint of surprise or interest, and the man was far too portly to be James, so she beat a hasty retreat.

James was in the fifth room, almost the last one along the corridor. As Lily pushed open the door, she glimpsed him sprawled out in a chair, his head arched back and his shirt open. A woman's dyed-red head bobbed energetically between his spread legs.

"Oh, I did *not* need to see that," Lily muttered, and spun away from the sight.

"Lily!" James shouted, and she heard the chair crash to the floor as he leaped to his feet. "What the hell are you doing here?"

"I charge extra for a threesome," the whore said sullenly.

Lily waited until she heard the rustle of fabric that told her James's trousers were up before she turned to face him. James was staring at her, fury and embarrassment written across his handsome face as he raked his hands through his light brown hair. The girl still knelt on the floor, her bodice tugged low to reveal rouged nipples.

"I think the gentleman might want to wait until another night for that particular extra," Lily said. "Considering I'm his sister."

The whore just shrugged. "Ain't nothing I haven't seen before. Are we gettin' on with this or not? I got lots of work to do tonight."

Lily crossed her arms over her waist, not looking away from James as he fastened his shirt. "I'm sure you've already been paid. The constables are probably already on their way, so you might want to get out of here."

"Constables!" the woman shrieked.

James groaned. "Lily, what have you done?"

"I have done nothing, except come here to get you and find myself in the middle of a fight. I suppose you've been far too occupied in here to notice what's going on downstairs," Lily said.

James's eyes widened, and he seemed to notice for the first time her bloody lip and torn dress. "Oh, God, Lily, I'm so sorry! What happened? How did you know I was here?"

Lily shook her head. "There's no time now. We need to get out of here." Before Tom found them. She turned to the woman, who had tugged up her dress and tied a shawl over her shoulders. "Do you know of a back way out of this place?"

"Follow me," she said, all brisk matter-of-factness now that she had earned her coin and had to avoid arrest.

Lily grabbed James's hand and pulled him with her as they followed the woman to the window at the end of the corridor. The whore climbed out onto an unsteady ladder that led down to the alleyway.

Lily pushed James out after her and tucked up her own skirts before she scrambled down the rungs. The whore was already gone before James even reached the bottom. He caught Lily around the waist and steadied her for the last few steps, and Lily couldn't resist throwing her arms around him for a quick, hard hug. He smelled of cheap ale and the whore's perfume, but he was *here.* She had him back, and they were safe.

Or almost safe. She heard a splintering crack of wood and shouts, and she whirled around to see that the fight was spilling out into the alley. A bottle flew over her head, only narrowly missing her before crashing into the wall and shattering.

"Come on!" James shouted, and dragged her into a run. They turned at the end of the lane and rushed on blindly, not knowing where they were going or what would be around the next corner. They just ran and ran until Lily was sure her lungs would burst.

This part of the city was like a maze, a squeezed-in rat's warren of close-packed old buildings and twisting alleys that ended in blank walls or hidden courtyards. Anyone could lose themselves here and be hidden forever. It was as far from clean, white Mayfair or the gilded splendors of the Majestic as anyone could get.

The people who lurked in the doorways or peered out the broken windows didn't stop them as they ran past; in fact, they didn't seem to notice them at all.

They careened around a corner, and Lily's foot slipped

into a hidden hole in the slippery dirt. Her ankle gave a painful wrench, and she cried out as she felt herself falling.

James spun around and caught her up in his arms. "Lily, what is it? Are you hurt?"

Spasms of pain shot up her leg from her ankle, and she cursed their bad luck. Just as they were about to make it away!

She held on to James's shoulder and tried to put her weight on her foot, but it buckled under her.

"I can carry you home," he said. Lily looked up at him and saw the concern written on his face. She had forgotten how very young he really was, so young and foolish. Her sweet brother.

Lily shook her head. "Too far. We need to find a safer street and hail a hackney, if one can even be found at this hour. Or..." She quickly studied their surroundings, trying to find something familiar. The lanes were a little wider now, a little cleaner. She glimpsed a grocer's sign she had seen before at the end of the street, and she knew where they could stop long enough to see to her ankle.

"Carry me just around the corner, James," she said. "I know of a place there."

James looked around suspiciously. His arms were tense as he lifted her up higher. "Are you sure?"

She gave a snorting laugh. "I'm not the one who landed us in that cheap gin joint, now, am I? Trust me. We'll be fine there, as long as no one followed us."

"How did you know where I was, Lily?" he said as he scooped her up in his arms and carried her where she pointed. "Do Mama and Father know?"

"Do they know the low company you have been keeping?

No, and they don't need to if you'll stay away from places like that from now on. As for how I found you..." A cold wave of weariness suddenly washed over her, and her head felt very heavy indeed. The sheer nerve that had carried her through the fight was ebbing away. She let her head drop to his shoulder. "That is a very long story."

They stopped in front of a locked door. The building was dark and silent, and Lily only hoped someone was there as she pounded on the door. She had no energy left to decide what to do next.

After several long moments, there was the scrape of a bar being drawn back, and the door opened. Robbie, the prize-fighter turned barkeep, help up a lamp as he peered out at them suspiciously. His eyes widened when he saw them.

"Miss Lily?" he said. "What's happened? Get in here at once!"

"How does that feel?"

Lily looked down at Nick's dark head as he pressed a hot, damp poultice to her swollen ankle. Robbie had vanished somewhere after he took them to this little sitting room behind the theater, and James sat across the room with the woman who came in with Nick. James was starting to look hungover, as well as embarrassed and angry. He watched Lily as if he had never seen her before.

She rested her head wearily on the back of the chair. She didn't blame him for looking at her like that—she didn't feel like herself tonight. She felt like a stranger, someone seen from a distance.

"Much better, thank you," she said. "It was kind of you to take us in, Nick."

He laughed as he wrapped a binding around the compress to hold it in place. "Nonsense. Things have been too quiet since the last time you were here. We needed a little excitement."

The pretty blonde he was with looked as if she certainly didn't agree, but she didn't say anything. Nick pushed himself to his feet and reached for a bottle on the table to pour everyone a dram of whiskey. The dark liquor was burning and bracing as it poured down her throat.

"So there was a fight at Jefferson's place, was there?" Nick said as he tossed back his own drink. "Serves the bugger right, with his watered-down gin. But how did you happen to be in such a place, Miss Lily? And all alone?"

Before Lily could answer, James said, "I'm afraid she went there to find me."

Nick's gaze narrowed on James. "Is that so? And who are you?"

"He's my brother," Lily said. "And it's all a bit more complicated than that."

"Interesting," Nick murmured.

Suddenly the door opened with a bang, and Aidan stood there. His blue eyes swept over the room, taking in the scene with one glance. He wore elegant black-and-white evening clothes, as if he had just left some society ball, but his cravat was loosened and his waistcoat unbuttoned. Perhaps wherever he was he had spent his time dancing with Lady Henrietta Lindley.

Lily knew she should be surprised to see him and angry that one more complication had been added to an already nightmarish evening. But she wasn't surprised at all, and a warm feeling of something that felt suspiciously like relief swept over her.

"Lily?" he said roughly. "What's happened? Robbie said you were hurt."

"I'm not," she answered. "I twisted my ankle, but it's much better now."

Aidan knelt down beside her chair and reached for her foot. He set it on his thigh, and his long fingers moved over it gently as if to assure himself she wasn't hurt. His other hand curled around her calf, warm and steady through her knitted stocking.

His touch might be gentle, but his voice held a touch of steel in its depths. "How did you get caught in a gin-joint raid?"

Lily straightened her shoulders back against the chair. "I went to find my brother."

"Your brother?"

"Er, I'm afraid that would be me," James said sheepishly. "I'm James St. Claire."

Aidan's eyes narrowed as he peered across the room at James in that cold, steely look Lily had come to be wary of. She reached down and grabbed his hand in hers.

"It's not his fault," she said quickly. "It was... someone else who lured him there. I only went to fetch him. I didn't know the place would be raided. I didn't know where else to go when we ran away, and Nick was kind enough to let us in. He didn't need to bother you, though." She glanced over his fine clothes again. "You must have been... busy. With family and society duties."

"I'd much rather be here," he answered. He looked up into her face, his eyes searching hers. "I want to know what really happened tonight, Lily. But I can see that you're very tired."

She nodded. Her head suddenly felt light, her whole

body aching with everything that had happened. "Yes, I am."

"Then I'll take you and your brother home. But you *will* tell me everything that happened. Very soon."

Lily slowly climbed up the wide stone steps into the almost-sacred hush of the British Museum as she closed her parasol. She blinked in the dim light after the bright glare of the day, and for an instant, the large, looming statues in the galleries to either side looked like lurking demons, waiting to leap out at her.

She rubbed at her eyes to try and will the pain of the headache away. She had barely slept at all after returning home from Nick's barroom, even though she had crawled into her bed and tried. The dreams kept plaguing her, haunting her, and there seemed nowhere to run. She was trapped by the past.

Then Aidan's note had come at breakfast, asking her to meet him here. She wanted to refuse, to forget the way he looked at her last night and his watchful silence as he took her home. It was a silence that told her he was only biding his time until she told him her secrets. So she had come here to face him.

The museum was quiet that day, a good place to share secrets. She could hear a few hushed murmurs echo off the marble and alabaster, could glimpse a few artists sketching and couples strolling together. Two children playing tag around a stone lion made the only real noise, until their nanny quickly subdued them. Lily hurried past them all, the heels of her kid boots clicking on the stone floor as she made her way to the Elgin Room.

She remembered her own days at the museum as a young girl, when their governess would bring all the St. Claire children there for a "history lesson." But the governess had really been more interested in meeting her suitor, and Lily and her siblings were left to their own devices. The boys always ran off to look at the mummies, while Isabel liked the gold Roman jewelry. Lily would seek out this room, longing to be alone in its quiet, elegant beauty. It seemed to her that here, surrounded by the pale marble and the scenes of ancient gods and heroes, so orderly, so perfect, nothing bad could ever happen.

She had loved those days when she was left alone in its cool hush and still came back there when she wanted to be quiet and think, away from the tumult of her family. It was a sanctuary in the midst of the noisy, dirty city.

Even after what had happened last night, after coming face-to-face with Tom Beaumont again, the beauty of the sculptures worked their soothing magic on her. As soon as she stepped through the doorway, she could feel it. She strolled over to the back wall where the long frieze depicting the procession of Athena's festival was mounted, tucked behind the massive bulk of statues of Theseus and a headless goddess draped in diaphanous robes.

There was no one else there for the moment, and Lily was alone. She stared up at the carved line of young women dressed in floating chitons and cloaks, all of them so poised and graceful as they carried their urns and libation bowls as offerings to the gods. The lighting was dim, but Lily could make out their serene expressions. They were where they were meant to be, doing the work they knew they had to do.

She glanced at the next wall, a more violent scene of

horses and soldiers in battle. The procession was how she wanted to feel, how she wanted life to be. But this battle was more the way things actually were.

She heard a footstep behind her and turned to see that Aidan had come into the gallery. He wore a dark coat and waistcoat, making him blend into the dim shadows, but his glossy brown hair gleamed. His face looked so solemn and austere as he took in the room, so still, as if he were one of those gods, come to walk among mortals for a time. He saw her there, half hidden behind the statue, and gave her a small bow before he moved slowly toward her.

Aidan even walked like a god, with a natural grace. She curled her gloved fingers hard over the ivory handle of her parasol and forced herself to stay still. To not flee.

"How are you today, Lily?" he asked quietly. He took her hand and pressed a kiss to her knuckles, as if he didn't notice their tension. As if they were in a ballroom someplace, and he had never saved her from a gin-joint raid.

"Quite well, thank you," she answered. "My ankle is a bit sore, but nothing that won't fade soon."

"I'm glad to hear it. And your brother?"

"Contrite. He has agreed to accompany my mother and sister on their seaside holiday and try to mend his ways. He is not a bad person; he is just... young."

Aidan nodded. "Sometimes young men just need a reminder that their actions can affect other people as well. People they care about."

"Do you need reminders of that?"

He grinned down at her. "Constantly, but I fear it never sticks. I'm a selfish bastard, remember?"

Lily bit her lip to keep from laughing. "I don't think you're supposed to use such language in the British Museum."

"Hmm." Aidan glanced up at a carving of Athena in her helmet and shield. "She *does* look rather stern, as if she would run me through with her spear if she took a dislike to me. She reminds me of you."

"Me?" Lily said, startled. "I am hardly so stern as that. And I am not at all goddess-like."

"Ah, but you are. A warrior goddess." There was a burst of laughter in the doorway, and Aidan looked over to the group who had just come in, breaking the precious hush with their merriment. He held out his arm to Lily. "Shall we walk? It's become rather crowded in here."

Lily nodded and slid her hand into the crook of his elbow. For a moment, she wondered if he knew those people, if they were society friends of his parents and what they would say if they saw Aidan with her. But then he led her into the next gallery, holding her up as if he knew her ankle was beginning to ache again, and she forgot everything but him and what had happened last night.

The gallery was a long, narrow room lined with a jumble of marble statues, a crowd of gods and goddesses and warriors, all staring down at the passage of mere humans with blank, disinterested eyes. The air was cool there, and no one else was around. Only those statues were there to listen to Lily's secrets.

Statues, and Aidan.

"Tell me what happened last night, Lily," he said quietly, and she knew the moment had come. "You said you went to save your brother from 'someone.' Who was it?"

Lily nodded. "I told you I ran away from Madame Josephine's after my mother died," she said. "I didn't know where to go, what to do. I only knew I didn't want to be what my mother was. I didn't want to do something, be something, where I had to numb myself with opium just to make it through the day. So I ended up like thousands of unwanted children, scrounging on the streets for a crust of bread and a warm place to sleep for the night."

She curled her hand harder on his arm and took a deep breath. "I was rather adept at picking pockets, but one night it was very cold and there was almost no one out and about. I didn't have the penny for a place in a padding-ken bed, and the landlady turned me away. I tried to sleep in a doorway. That's where Tom Beaumont found me."

She closed her eyes and shivered as she remembered that night, as if she felt the bite of the bitter cold wind again. "Tom had a great criminal empire. He ran pick-pocketing rings, prostitution rings, padding-kens, organized cons. He ruled by beatings and terror, even murder, but I didn't know all this at first. Perhaps you have heard of him?"

Aidan gave a tight nod. "I have heard tales."

"Yes. He's still famous among a certain sort of person. He's scarred now, but he wasn't as fearsome-looking then. They called him 'Handsome' Tom Beaumont, and for good reason. He spoke to me gently, coaxed me out of the doorway, and offered me food. All he needed in exchange was for me to crawl in through a small shop window and take a few things for him. If I had been caught, I could have been hanged, of course, but I was so desperate I didn't care. That was how it began.

"Tom had legions of people like me working for him. But I was rescued one day by the St. Claires when I tried to pick William's pocket outside the theater. I'm not sure what they saw in me, but they took me home with them and adopted me into their family. And soon after, Tom was arrested and transported to Australia. I thought I would never see him again, that that part of my life was finished. Until he showed up again."

"And lured your brother into his net."

"Yes. He wanted me to come to him, and he knew my family is the one thing I would always protect. He wants revenge on me, and I fear…I fear he won't stop until he has it. Or until I stop him."

They had come to the end of the gallery, and they stood there for a moment in silence. Lily didn't trust Aidan's perfect stillness or the way his eyes had turned dark, his face as hard as if it were carved from the same marble as those statues.

"Lily," he said with a terribly gentle smile. "I'm going to take you home now, and I want you to stay there until I send you word."

Lily tightened her hand on his arm. "Why? What are you going to do?"

"I'm going to help you, of course. You were quite right when you agreed with how selfish I am. It's past time I used some of my ill-gotten knowledge to help someone else. I know people who know how to find things, even things others prefer to keep hidden." A muscle flexed along his jaw, and his sensual lips tightened. "And I despise anyone who preys on the weak."

"I am not weak," Lily protested.

"No, you aren't." Aidan suddenly turned to her and reached up to frame her face in his palms. He traced his thumbs softly over her cheekbones as he looked into her eyes. "You are one of the strongest people I have ever met, the fiercest and the bravest. You don't deserve a piece of garbage like this giving you one moment of worry."

"Aidan," she choked out. She couldn't look away from his eyes, those eyes that seemed to pierce so deeply into her and see everything. She couldn't escape his words. "I won't let him hurt anyone I care about ever again."

"Neither will I." Aidan bent his head and lightly brushed his lips over hers. "Please, Lily. Let me help you. Let me do the right thing for once in my life."

Her throat felt so tight she could hardly breathe. This was the hardest thing she had ever done in her life. She felt that if she took this one step, gave this one thing to Aidan—her trust—nothing could ever be the same. She had never relied on anyone else like this before, not even her family. He said she was brave, but she felt utterly terrified.

"Lily?" he said.

She gave a jerky nod. "Very well."

He smiled and kissed her again. "Come on. Let me take you home."

Chapter Fifteen

Lily surveyed the main salon of the Devil's Fancy from the doorway of the dining room. It was the perfect scene, a sea of feathered and jeweled masks that flowed through the amber-lit rooms on a cloud of bright laughter and fashionable clothes.

A masked ball was a fine idea, a way to bring in potential new members with the promise of mystery and secret delights. And Dominic was always a master at setting a scene, even offstage. Lily examined the tapestries of red and amber that fluttered over the walls, the red silk drapes on the card tables, the faint, shimmering clouds of incense that perfumed the air. It looked like an exotic, expensive underworld.

But the smoke and the swirl of masks made her feel dizzy. She hadn't been sleeping well since the night she brought James home. Waiting for word from Aidan or for fresh threats from Tom. Trying to appear normal and cheerful for her family. It was all taking a toll on her.

Planning this party had helped. She threw herself into the preparations, ordering rare delicacies and exotic flowers and sending out the invitations. And now it all looked perfect.

She twisted the ebony handle of her fan between her hands as she watched the crowd. Dominic played cards with a mystery lady, a woman in black satin and lace that matched her sleekly coiled black hair. She leaned close to him, laughing as she studied the cards in her hand, and Dominic watched her with a small frown on his face as if he were bemused by her. Dominic was never bemused by a woman; he was always so firmly in control.

Lily almost smiled. It served her brother right to have a woman turn *him* around for once. He had been a growling bear ever since that day in the park when they saw Aidan. She wondered who the lady was.

Lily turned and made her way back into the dining room to make sure there was still plenty of lobster patties and pâté left. She plucked a shimmering red strawberry from the cornucopia of hothouse fruit and took a nibble of it. Sweet juice flowed over her tongue, and she smiled at its summery taste. She had almost forgotten what such simple little pleasures felt like.

"You look beautiful tonight," a man whispered darkly in her ear.

She whirled around and found herself staring up into Aidan's eyes behind a black silk mask. He didn't smile, but his eyes were a bright, merry blue. He reached for her hand and slowly tasted the strawberry on her fingertips, left bare by her lace mitts. She went very still at the touch of his lips.

"Thank you," she said.

"How have you been?" he asked. He let go of her hand to lightly trace her lace-trimmed sleeve over her shoulder.

"Well enough. James has gone off to the seaside for a few days with my mother and Isabel, so that is one less worry."

Aidan nodded. "He's young. Hopefully he's learned his lesson."

Lily stared up at him, studying the hard-set line of his jaw and the sensual curve of his lower lip. "Did you ever learn your lesson?"

He gave a bark of laughter. "Not well and never for long. But I sense that your brother is rather different. Do you have time to talk now?"

She glanced back through the doors to the salon. Everything seemed to be going smoothly there, everyone still having a good time. "Yes, for a while."

She led him to a hidden door in the wall just beyond the dining room. It concealed a winding staircase to the upper floors, and they made their way up to the dark silence of her office.

As Lily closed the door behind them, she tried not to think of what happened the last time she was alone here with Aidan. She went and stood behind the desk and carefully smoothed her burgundy satin skirts. Aidan pulled off his mask and ran his hand through his hair, but she kept the meager concealment of her feathers and pearl beads.

"Have you learned anything yet about Beaumont's whereabouts?" she asked.

"I am making progress. Your old friend certainly knows how to conceal himself well, but there are lots of people who won't yield even one iota of their territory to an interloper like him. He's been gone too long. I will find him."

Aidan's words weren't heated or angry but full of cool assurance. He sat down on the chaise, his long legs stretched casually in front of him as he leaned back on the cushions, a lazy jungle cat. She wondered once again how he managed to be the son of a duke; he seemed so easily at home wherever he went.

But she knew that his position gave him that calm, deadly assurance. That sense that no one could refuse him anything, and he knew it.

Not even Lily.

"You have many friends," she said. "Everywhere."

Aidan grinned at her. "So I do. And most of them owe me favors. They won't want Tom Beaumont getting his filthy boots under the table again. They'll tell me when they see him, and he won't get away for long. He won't bother anyone else in your family again."

Lily nodded. She knew he wouldn't; she would not let him. But it felt good to have an ally, no matter how unexpected, in the hard-eyed man in front of her.

"But then, I'm sure your family can take care of themselves," Aidan said thoughtfully. "I've been hearing their name a great deal of late among my more...colorful friends. They're owed more than a few favors themselves, from the slums all the way to the palace. Especially your brother Brendan, perhaps?"

Lily stiffened. "Brendan doesn't confide in me, especially about his business concerns. I doubt he confides in anyone at all."

"Yet you haven't asked for his help."

She sighed and slowly came around to sit beside him on the chaise. She suddenly felt weary, as if her legs didn't want to hold her up any longer. She untied her mask and let it fall to her lap. "He would help me, I know, and so would Dominic. They're certainly used to making problems go away when needed. But their methods can sometimes be less than subtle, and I don't want anyone to know about this. To know about..."

"Your past?" he said quietly.

Lily nodded and closed her eyes. She rubbed at the aching spot between her eyes.

"Lily." She felt the slide of his fingers over her chin, surprisingly soft and gentle as he turned her to face him. She opened her eyes to find him studying her intently, as if he tried to read her innermost thoughts and secret fears. "What happened in your life is nothing to be ashamed of. You should be proud. *You* were the victor in the end, never the victim. What you've done is quite extraordinary. *You* are extraordinary."

She gave a harsh laugh. She dared not believe his words, dared not trust the way they made her feel. That tiny, flaring spark of hope. "The daughter of a whore? A street thief and a beggar? I doubt anyone would agree with you."

"Your family would. Are you not a St. Claire?"

"Not a real one. A masquerade one." She held up the mask in her lap, studying the way the gaslight from beyond the window gleamed on the beads. "I don't belong with them, not really."

Aidan covered her hand with his, his fingers curling over hers on the soft feathers. "I don't belong with my family either. I never could be what they wanted. And if my brother were to decide to go against his duties, they would be stuck with me."

Lily slowly turned her head to study him. In the play of light and shadows, his handsome face looked sculpted and elegant, the sharp angles and smooth planes so perfect, his eyes so blue and so full of intelligence and the flash of a rare intuition. How could the Huntingtons *not* want what he was? She wanted it far too much. She could see how much he did not want to be duke, but she was sure he would be a good one.

"Your family chose you, Lily," he said. "And I know they care about you. They're as protective as a pride of lions whenever I come near you. I can tell they hate me."

Lily swallowed hard and let her hand fall away from his. She slid to the end of the chaise and he let her go. "It's just the old story. They are actors, you know. They believe very strongly in old battles and powerful vendettas."

Aidan leaned back on his palms and tilted his head as he studied her. "Old vendettas? That sounds promising. Tell me about it."

"You mean...you don't know?" Lily stared at him in astonishment. How could he not know? The hatred of the Huntingtons was such a part of the St. Claires' life, always there, always a part of what they did. It seemed inconceivable that it was one-sided.

But Aidan shrugged, and the look on his face was one of curiosity, not awareness or realization. And Lily suddenly felt so foolish. What his family had done to hers had driven the St. Claires to achieve all they had in the shadows of society. It had driven them onward for generations.

And the Huntingtons had just been leading their oblivious, privileged ducal lives.

Lily shook her head. "Well, there is a tale I have heard ever since I came to live with the St. Claires, and it goes something like this." She told him the story of that long-ago marriage of Mary St. Claire and John Huntington, how it all went horribly wrong. How Mary died of a broken heart and John ruined her St. Claire family, driving them to the fringes of society. How the St. Claires still bore their hatred of the Huntingtons today.

Lily finished her tale and found that the aching spot between her eyes had returned. She rubbed at it with her fingertips, almost surprised to find herself still in her office and not at some desolate castle, at the mercy of a ruthless lord.

She turned to Aidan to find that he watched her with narrowed eyes, his lips turned down in a slight frown. His long fingers curled tightly on the edge of the chaise, and she suddenly wondered if she was not at a Huntington's mercy after all.

"So your family hates mine because of what my ancestor did to yours?" he said quietly. "That is why your brother always looks as if he wants to bash my face in?"

Lily nodded. "The Huntingtons took away the St. Claires' place in the world, destroyed them."

Aidan gave a harsh laugh. "No wonder the St. Claires turned to the theater. It's like *Romeo and Juliet*. It's quite riveting. Why have I never heard this tale before?"

Anger suddenly burned through Lily. This was no game! This had eaten away at her family for years and years; her brothers truly hated him, and she knew she should hate him too. Especially if he was amused by it all, laughing at them. Acting on raw instinct, the instincts of a child of the streets, her hand flashed out to slap his grin away.

Aidan's fingers closed hard over her wrist and held her hand a mere inch from his face. A muscle tightened in his jaw as he stared up at her, and his eyes were as icy-blue as a winter's day.

"Don't do that again, Lily, unless you mean it," he said in a terribly quiet voice.

She tried to jerk away, but he used her own movement to tug her off balance and into his arms. His hands closed around her waist, and his mouth met hers in a bruising, hungry kiss, his tongue sweeping over hers as she moaned into him.

And just like that, her anger exploded into passion, and she only wanted to be closer and closer to him, to crawl into him and let him be part of her. Yes, she was sure this was how Mary St. Claire felt about John Huntington, how he was able to keep his power over her. This burning, terrible desire. It had destroyed Mary in the end, left her life in ashes, and Lily was afraid it could do the same to her. But still she held on to him and let him pull her deeper into the abyss.

She drove her fingers into his hair and let the soft strands wrap around her as he kissed her. He tasted of wine, of the strawberries from her lips, of anger and lust.

"God, Lily," he groaned as his mouth tore away from hers. He caught her earlobe between his teeth and nipped it lightly before he kissed the side of her neck. His breath was hot on her skin. "How do you do this to me?"

Lily shook her head, and something in her reveled in his words. In the knowledge that he wanted her as much as she wanted him, even if they fought against it. She pushed her palms against his chest until he lay back on the chaise.

He stared up at her, his chest heaving with the force of his breath as she knelt between his legs. She didn't look away from him, didn't say anything; she just slid her hands slowly down his body. She could feel the shift and stretch of his hard muscles beneath her touch, and she let her eyes drift closed to imagine what he looked like under that fine wool and linen. How he looked when all that aristocratic civility was stripped away and there was only him. The graceful power of his naked body.

She opened her eyes and unfastened his trousers to peel them away from his hips. His buttocks clenched, and he arched up into her touch. He was already as hard as iron, his penis springing free from the fabric confines as she stroked one long, caressing touch down its length and up again.

"Lily," he said, his voice a low growl.

She smiled at him and fell down amid the cloud of her skirts to run her tongue over him. His whole body went still, and he lifted his hand as if he would push her away. But when she delicately licked his crown, he fell back with a moan.

He tasted clean and salty, and she could smell the light musk of his arousal. It made her feel dizzy, his need driving hers even higher. Slowly, slowly, she slid her mouth over him to take him even deeper inside of her. He brushed the back of her throat, and she drew back again, sucking him between her teeth.

"Fuck, Lily," he said, and she felt his hand twine around the back of her neck. She slid her fingers beneath the edge of his shirt to feel the ripple of his abdomen. She scraped her nails over his warm skin, and he jerked against her.

She flicked her tongue over him and felt the throbbing vein just under the velvet-taut skin. She moved her mouth up and down, slow and then faster, until he pushed harder against her tongue, sliding in and out. He was so close to his climax, she could feel it, and it made the core of her womanhood clench.

He cried out, a harsh, hoarse shout, and pulled himself out of her mouth. Dizzy, she felt him spin her down to the chaise beneath him. His hands were rough as he pushed up her skirts and tore open her silk drawers. Everything was hot and desperate, and Lily needed his body inside hers as she had never needed anything before.

But as he leaned down for a kiss, his lips on hers were shockingly gentle, his tongue a slow slide against hers as his fingers curled around her bare hip. She wrapped her legs around his waist and arched up into him as he had with her.

He touched his open mouth to the delicate curve of her collarbone, the merest light kiss. Lily shuddered. Somehow that one small, fragile touch made her feel as if she would shatter into a thousand pieces.

"Hold on to me," he said against her, and she looped her arms around his neck as he slid up to kiss the shell of her ear.

He sat up, and the shift of their bodies together made his penis slide into her, all the way to the hilt until their hips were pressed against each other, their bodies as close as they could get. So close it was as if they were no longer two people at all. Her legs trembled as they wrapped tighter around him.

"Lily," he whispered, and he started to move.

Her hips rolled in one long, smooth movement, and he slid out and in again, a delicious friction that brought him even deeper with each slow thrust.

Lily moaned as her head fell back, and she held on to him as he moved faster. That hot spiral of pleasure began to uncoil deep inside her as his thrusts grew harder, rougher. She felt his fingers dig into her hips, almost bruising, and it made her cry out as her lust burst into flame. Her hands slid into his hair and pulled hard.

"Come for me, Lily," he said hoarsely. "Let me feel it on me, over me."

"Then take me harder, Aidan." *Make me yours.* The words rang through her mind even as she feared they were already too true.

His teeth fastened at the soft curve between her neck and shoulder, and his hips pistoned up into her. And just like that, she did shatter, like a dam breaking inside of her and letting all her walled-up emotions run free. She drove herself down hard onto him as she cried out, and it was as if she could feel every inch of him joined with her, part of her.

His teeth bit down harder, and she felt his body go rigid against hers with his climax. Her fingers pulled at his hair, and she let all thought go, let herself drown in him and be lost.

She fell back onto the chaise, his arms around her easing her down. Through her dazed, dreamy haze, she felt him collapse beside her. She could feel his harsh breath against her shoulder, and somehow the fabric of their clothes sliding together, clinging and tangling, seemed even more intimate than naked skin. How very desperate they had been for each other, how fast lust had overpowered them.

What was it about this man that did such terrible things to her?

Lily turned her head away and bit down on her lip to keep from sobbing.

Aidan smoothed his hand gently over Lily's hair as he watched her sleep. It was not an easy sleep; her brow was creased with a frown, and she shifted restlessly in his arms. But she grew still at his touch.

If only he could be still too. Already he could feel himself getting hard again, his body craving hers. He hadn't come up here with the intention of having sex, but once they were alone in the darkness, once he touched her, kissed her, the need to have her overwhelmed everything else. When Lily was near him, all he could see, all he wanted, was her. She made him feel like a mere Neanderthal, dragging his woman back to his cave by her hair to drive himself into her again and again.

Even when he did that, it wasn't enough. It was never enough.

Aidan shifted on the chaise and held her as she murmured in her sleep. He knew they couldn't stay there long; even now he could hear the masquerade ball growing louder downstairs. But Lily had looked so tired and weary. He wanted to hold her for a few more minutes and let her rest, even if *his* body was on fire with lust.

He studied her in the glow of gaslight coming from outside the window. Her face was as pale and still as marble as she slept, and her dark hair fell in loose curls over her neck. Her gown fell away from her shoulders, the shadowed hollows of her throat and collarbone making her look so fragile.

What was it about her that had such a hold on him? Aidan wondered. Yes, she was pretty, but London was full of beautiful women, many of whom were happy to chase after a ducal connection. She was frighteningly smart, and intriguingly mysterious. Her body drew his like a witchcraft spell. But somehow he knew, in these quiet moments when they were alone and her guard was down, that it was more than sex.

He wound a long strand of her hair around his wrist and remembered the flashing look of trust in her eyes when she agreed to let him help her. When she let him glimpse the past she kept so hidden. Never would he have thought Lily St. Claire would *trust* him. Never would he have thought he would earn her trust.

Women came to him for pleasure, but never for shelter or strength. They liked his good looks, his name, what he could do for them in bed. But Lily needed more, and he found that intoxicating.

He just couldn't let himself come to need her in return. He didn't need anyone at all anymore.

Aidan dropped his head back to stare up at the glow of light on the ceiling. He thought of Lily's tale of the St. Claire woman and the Huntington man whose passion had torn them apart. It was no wonder her brothers hated him, if they had grown up with the knowledge that his family had once done their best to destroy theirs. Aidan, of course, knew nothing of those people. A family with as much power as his crushed many in their wake, and they seldom remembered it.

It was another very good reason not to trust whatever it was he felt when Lily lay in his arms like this. Caring too much, needing too much—it destroyed people. This was just lust, or perhaps the need to feel like the white knight and not the rogue for once in his life. That was all. Soon enough it would fade, and he would go back to his old ways.

But first he would make sure Lily was safe. And the only way he could do that was to find and destroy Tom Beaumont. That he *could* do. He didn't have connections in every part of London for nothing.

Aidan heard a loud crashing noise from downstairs, a shriek of laughter, and he knew their stolen moments of peace grew short. He sat up slowly, careful not to wake Lily yet, and raked his hair back from his face. His gaze fell on her desk, and he remembered he had another task here, one he had almost forgotten in the whirlwind that had been his time with Lily.

He needed to find Freddy Bassington's letters. She had them somewhere, or else she had destroyed them. He had to find out, to set his friend's mind at ease.

Aidan studied Lily's sleeping face. He didn't know why she kept Freddy's letters. Blackmail didn't seem to be her style at all. Perhaps she, like him, couldn't trust in people's finer intentions. Most people had none. It was safer to have something tangible to hold against them, if necessary. Aidan didn't want to see Lily hurt again, but he couldn't let poor, romantic Freddy be hurt either. Slowly, so as not to wake Lily, he slid off the chaise and went to the desk.

Lily heard a soft click and sat up with a gasp as she was torn out of sleep. For an instant, she couldn't remember where she was or what was happening. She didn't know what woke her. But then she remembered she was in her office, where she had just made love with Aidan. She rubbed her hand over her eyes and looked around her darkened office, still half asleep.

To her shock, she found Aidan standing behind her desk. One of the drawers was half open, and he watched her with a startled, wary look in his eyes.

"What are you doing?" she asked. A cold feeling swept

over her, and she knew she didn't want to hear the answer. She swung her legs off the chaise and started to gather her clothes. "What are you looking for?"

She heard Aidan close the drawer and lean his hands on her desk. He didn't say anything, and when Lily looked at him, his face was a cool blank.

"What are you doing?" she said again fiercely.

Aidan shook his head. "What exactly do you want from Freddy Bassington, Lily?"

Freddy Bassington? Whatever Lily had expected and feared, it wasn't that. She hadn't even thought of Freddy in so long and had almost forgotten the packet of his silly letters she had tucked away at home.

She sat very still. "How do you know Freddy Bassington?" she said. "And what does he have to do with you going through my desk?"

"He is a friend of mine," Aidan said quietly. "He came to me not long ago full of remorse for sending you some letters."

So that was what this was about. Lily felt cold and so, so foolish. She had become fascinated with Aidan, and all he was after were his friend's letters.

"And that's why you came to me? To get Freddy's silly letters back?" Lily was so furious she couldn't look up—furious with herself and with Aidan. She wanted to throw something at him, shout at him, but all she could do was stare at the floor.

"Of course not, Lily," Aidan said. He sounded far too calm. "It's not like that at all. He merely asked if I could find out about his letters, what had happened to them. I said I would try. He is my friend, after all."

"And I am merely your lover!" Lily's anger finally

escaped in a shriek. She scooped up her slipper from the floor and tossed it at him. He easily ducked out of the way. "So he knows about us? Who else knows?"

"No one knows. Lily, stop that. Look at me." Through her haze of anger, she heard him come around the desk. His arms closed around her hard, pinning her arms to her sides. He held her against him too easily as she struggled.

He didn't even let go when she gave up and slumped in his grasp.

"I knew better than to ever trust a man, no matter how handsome and kind he might appear," she said. "That's why I kept Freddy's letters, to make sure he stayed away and ceased his silliness. But with you, Aidan Huntington, I have no excuse. You never even tried to appear harmless. I just..."

I can't stay away from you. The words she couldn't say aloud haunted her. She closed her eyes and twisted out of his arms to slump down wearily on the chaise.

"Please, Aidan, just go," she whispered. She wanted to be alone before she curled up into a ball and lost all her pride.

She sensed Aidan hesitate behind her. "I never meant you harm, Lily," he said, and she felt him press a kiss to her hair. "I wish you could believe that, trust it."

"I don't know how to trust," she said. "Go, Aidan. Just...go." She felt like she would shatter if he didn't leave.

"Fine. I will go now," he said. "Because you ask it of me. But I will be back. This is not over, Lily."

Lily kept her eyes closed until she heard the door click shut behind him. Only then did she let out a sob and fall back onto the chaise. She had been such a fool.

Chapter Sixteen

Lady Sophia Huntington carefully studied the cards in her hand. Not a bad hand, but not as good as she would like either. Her usual good luck at the card table wasn't with her tonight.

Or maybe she was distracted.

Sophia peeked over the edge of the cards to study the man across from her through the beaded eyeholes of her mask. Dominic St. Claire. She knew it was him, even though he, too, wore a mask, a swath of stark black silk over his chiseled face. No one else she had ever seen had hair quite that shade of pure, molten gold, or such fine shoulders under his perfectly tailored coat. His eyes, the deep, pure green of summer leaves, gazed back at her steadily, making something flutter nervously deep inside of her.

No wonder her parents didn't like her going to the theater, she thought wryly. One glimpse of such a godlike being onstage and she wouldn't be able to bear her pompous, pale, parentally approved suitors any longer.

And he was wrecking her concentration at cards as well. She definitely couldn't have that. Not when she had finally been able to escape her family's guard and sneak into the Devil's Fancy using her cousin Bill's invitation. It would be hard to come back again, so she would have to make the most of this evening.

But she might have tried harder to come here a little sooner if she had known Dominic was one of the owners. She had thought about him far too much ever since that glimpse in the park.

"Well, madam?" he asked, in his deep, smooth actor's voice. A small smile played over his lips, which were surprisingly full and sensual for a man.

Sophia, who was such a good card player in part because she had become adept at reading people's faces, couldn't fathom what that smile meant at all. Did he hold a good hand?

Or was he flirting with her?

Sophia looked back down at her cards. "Two more, please."

Dominic took two cards from the deck and slid them across the small, red-draped table to her. He had beautiful hands, the skin smooth and faintly bronzed and dusted with pale blond hair, and his tapering fingers were made for theatrical gestures on a stage or for wielding a sword.

Or tracing a soft touch over a woman's skin, which she had heard he was quite adept at doing.

Sophia forced down an instinctive shiver at the vision of his hand on her body and forced herself to forget he was there, so close, watching her. She had just wagered the last of her quarterly allowance, and she couldn't afford to lose her focus now. She slowly turned over the new cards and almost sighed.

Luck was really not with her tonight.

She laid out her cards on the table, hoping against hope his hand was worse. That faint hope died when he revealed his own cards, and he had her beat by several points.

"You win again, sir," she said with another sigh. "It seems Lady Luck favors a sinfully handsome scoundrel as much as the next woman."

Dominic laughed, and the emerald sparkle in his eyes almost made it worth losing.

Almost. Sophia needed that money.

"Forgive me, madam," he said. He gathered the scattered cards from across the table and lazily shuffled them back into the deck. "I take no pleasure in disobliging a lady. Shall we play again? Lady Luck is often fickle."

Sophia shook her head regretfully. She longed to play again and try to get back that money. It was what so often led her into trouble, the obsessive thought that with the next hand her luck would surely turn. Equally bitter was the thought that now she would lose Dominic's company. She had never enjoyed losing at cards so much as with him.

But she had nothing left to wager. She wore her grandmother's diamond and onyx earrings, necklace, and hair clips to go with her black satin gown, and her mother would definitely notice if they were gone.

"I'm done for the evening, sir," she said. "But I confess I've never enjoyed losing quite so much. It's no wonder your club is so successful."

His head tilted slightly as he studied her, his green eyes growing darker. "And how do you know I own this club?"

Sophia smiled and leaned closer to him, resting her arms on the table as she reached out to smooth one fingertip over a lost card. Oh, yes, he did bring out a spirit of the devil in her. "Oh, I know a great deal about you."

"That's hardly fair, is it?" he said, laughter lurking in his voice. Laughter and something darker, something she couldn't read. "I know nothing about you, except that you are a fierce opponent at the card table."

His fingers slid over her hand. It was a light touch, teasing, testing, his skin cool through her lace gloves. But Sophia felt like fire had just licked along her arm, burning and shocking. She had to force herself to stay still and not jerk away and run screaming from the salon. She had never felt anything like it. It was almost... frightening.

She touched the tip of her tongue to her dry lips as his hand slid away. "Wh-what do you want to know?"

He suddenly frowned, as if a shadow passed over his face. "Everything."

Something seemed to sizzle in the air between them. Sophia couldn't look away from him. The game, which had started out so light and fun, such a dare, had become something so much more. It had become something she didn't understand at all.

She had wanted to see Dominic St. Claire tonight. Something had driven her to seek him out after she had seen him at the park and felt so strangely drawn to him. But now... now she felt afraid of what he awoke in her.

And Sophia was never afraid.

"Come with me," Dominic said. He rose to his feet, his gilded chair scraping back over the parquet floor, and took her hand in his. His smooth, polished, charming manners suddenly took on a raw edge, and it was as if she were glimpsing the feral power under his poetical beauty. And it made her even more afraid.

Yet she couldn't pull her hand away. She couldn't turn and run as she longed to. Something in her bound her to his touch. He was so very different from everything she had ever known, every convention her parents pushed onto her, every safe suitor and narrow expectation. Something in him called out to the secret darkness within her that always brought her to places like the Devil's Fancy, to card tables and deep play.

Something in him was the same as in her. She had that terrible certainty as she looked up into his forest-green eyes. And she let him take her hand and lead her through the crowded salon.

The hour grew late, and champagne had been flowing freely, driving the laughter louder and louder. Ladies leaned on their escort's shoulders as they watched the roulette wheel spin wildly, and she could hear music from the ballroom. But it was nothing to her, a mere echo. The only real thing was Dominic's hand on hers. What was she doing?

Where had he been all those long, dull months and years of her life?

He led her down the staircase, past couples who sat against the banisters whispering together. They went to the cold marble foyer where she had talked her way past the grim-faced butler earlier that evening. The man wasn't there now, and there was only the quiet of the night after the loud party.

Dominic opened a door half hidden in the wall and tugged her in after him. When the door closed, they were closed off in darkness. The only light was a faint glow from a window high in the wall. Sophia leaned back against the door and saw they were in a tiny sitting room of sorts, crowded with the hulking shapes of furniture.

But then Dominic braced his palm flat to the door above her head, his warm, tall body close to hers, and she knew only him. He pulled off his mask and threw it to the floor. His face was lean and harsh in the light, his eyes brilliant as he stared down at her.

Sophia thought he must be a supremely intense Hamlet. It was no wonder ladies flocked to his theater.

"Who are you?" he asked, his voice low and rough.

Sophia swallowed hard. "Just a woman who enjoys a good game of cards."

"And what else do you enjoy?" He reached up and gently traced the curve of her jaw with his fingertips. Sophia shivered, and his fingers skimmed lightly over her cheek.

When she felt him touch the edge of her mask, she drew her head back. A little spark of reality came back to her. She was daring, true; something drove her to seek out places like this, to find somewhere beyond her small, restricted world. But she didn't want to be completely ruined either.

And she also remembered the dark glare Dominic gave her cousin Aidan in the park. He did not like her family. He couldn't know who she was.

His hand slid away from the mask to toy with her earring and the curl of hair over the soft shell of her ear. His mouth followed, and Sophia gasped at the feeling of his hot kiss, the sound of his breath against her. Her knees went weak beneath her, and she pressed back harder against the door.

Dominic's lips moved along her neck, pressing light, caressing nips to her skin and then soothing them with the tip of his tongue. Sophia clutched at his shoulders to keep from falling, and she felt the ripple of his powerful muscles beneath the layers of fabric. She had never felt like this before. None of the kisses her suitors pressed on her in garden groves at society balls could possibly compare. They always made her want to laugh at the ridiculousness of it all. But this…

This made her feel as if his touch had made her come completely, gloriously alive for the very first time. Not even the rush of a winning hand of cards made her feel this way.

Dominic groaned, and she felt his tall body press even closer against her. His arm came around her waist and pulled her up on her toes.

"Who are you? Where do I know you from?" he said hoarsely as he kissed the corner of her mouth. "Tell me."

Sophia frantically shook her head. Her thoughts went all hazy when he did that, so fractured and unfocused she couldn't put them together. She feared she would shout out her name for him.

"Tell me," he whispered again, and kissed the other corner of her parted lips. "I have to know."

"I'm no one at all," she answered.

The tip of his tongue traced her lower lip, and she opened to him with a gasp. His mouth covered hers in a hot, starving kiss, his tongue pressing deep to twine with hers.

Sophia's nails dug into his shoulders. This was definitely *not* like any other kiss she had ever had! Those fumbling caresses from boys who had groped at her in the dark, even as she sensed their fear of her, could never have prepared her for the force that was Dominic St. Claire. He would not be afraid of anything. He claimed what he wanted and…oh, but he was so *good* at kissing.

He drew back from her lips, his eyes a bright green in the shadows. "Tell me," he demanded again.

And Sophia wanted so much to do just that, to give him her name and hear him say it in that wondrous voice of his. But then this precious moment would be shattered. She didn't know why he hated her cousin. She only knew she never wanted him to look at her that way. She never wanted his desire to become icy with hatred.

This moment was all she could have with him.

"No," she answered, finding strength in the sure knowledge that she had to keep him from finding out she was Lady Sophia Huntington. From finding out what his kiss meant to her. "I am no one. You have to let me go."

His arm tightened around her waist. "No," he said, his voice a low growl full of dark determination. "I've just found you."

Suddenly desperate to be gone, to not give in to the power he held over her, Sophia frantically shook her head. "Please, Dominic..."

"No! I need you to tell me who you are."

"Then I'm sorry," she whispered. "So very, very sorry."

His head tilted back from her. "Sorry?"

Taking a deep breath, Sophia brought her knee up hard between his legs. Her old nanny had once told her to do that if she needed to escape from a man, and she hadn't been sure it would work. But Dominic gave an agonized shout and fell to the floor, letting her go.

Absolutely appalled at what she had done, Sophia almost knelt beside him. Until he shouted a foul name at her, a string of the dirtiest curses she had ever heard, and she knew she had to get out of there while she still could.

"I'm so, so sorry!" she cried again, and dragged open

the door. She let it slam behind her and ran for the entrance as fast as her heeled shoes would carry her. With the one stroke of luck she had had all evening, the foyer was deserted, and she found a hansom on the street outside.

Once safely in the carriage, Sophia yanked off her mask and covered her face with shaking hands.

"Oh, heavens above," she whispered, quite sure she was going to be sick. "What have I done?"

Chapter Seventeen

"If you'll wait here, sir, I'll fetch Madame Marie at once," the maidservant said with a bob of a curtsy. She deposited a tray of wine and refreshments on a table and hurried out of the room.

Aidan poured himself a glass of the excellent Burgundy and examined the chamber around him as he waited. Madame Marie's house on now-respectable Seymour Place was not the usual sort of bawdy house or cheap bagnio, but a house of discretion and exemplary service. Only those who could afford her hefty fees were allowed in.

But Marie also knew everything that went on in the shadows of London. She had spies in every quarter. She was one of Aidan's most valuable friends, and one with a connection he had not thought of before.

Which was why he was allowed to wait here, in her own sitting room, where only her most privileged clients were admitted.

Aidan studied the fine, carved furniture of dark wood, upholstered in dark red velvet that matched the wallpaper, and the heavy window draperies that kept out prying eyes. Like the rest of the house, the colors were those of night, rich and exotic but not in bad taste. It could have been any house, except for the collection of fine porcelain phalluses on the fireplace mantel and the three erotic paintings on the wall.

Aidan examined the series of three scenes. In the first, a woman clad only in stockings and a rumpled chemise was perched on a stool while a man with his breeches around his knees dove between her legs. In the second, the same man took the woman from behind as she bent over the stool. And in the third, the woman whipped the man's backside as another female masturbated him. He appeared to be enjoying himself a great deal in all three.

"Very elegant," Aidan muttered with a laugh.

The door to the sitting room opened to a rustle of fine satin and a whiff of heady lilac perfume. "Do you like 'em? They just got here last week, from France. They do the best work in Paris. I'm going to move them out to the salon next week, give everyone a peek."

Aidan turned to smile at the tall redhead. "Hello, Marie. Your artwork is exceptional, as always."

A wide grin spread over her rouged lips, and she ran across the room to throw her arms around him. "Aidan, my darlin'! We haven't seen you in an age. The girls have been so sad without you."

Aidan laughed. "They couldn't possibly have the time to miss me."

"Ah, well, I do keep 'em busy. Not that I can stop 'em asking about you every night. And I've missed you too. Have you found yourself a respectable girl, then? Mended your ways?"

Aidan thought of Lily's quiet, dark eyes, her soft, white hands—and what those hands did to him. "Not exactly. But I have been a bit occupied lately."

"Sounds interesting. Here, love, sit down. Have some more wine and tell me what brings you here today. It's a few hours yet until our busy time."

"Actually, I came to ask for your help, Marie." Aidan sat down across from her as she settled next to the fire, her feet in their high-heeled shoes up on a tapestry stool.

"Of course, Aidan love, anything for you. After what you did for my Sally last year, I can't thank you enough."

"I need to find a man named Tom Beaumont. Perhaps you know him?"

Marie's hand froze as she lifted her wineglass to her lips. "Now what would a toff like you want with a bad 'un like that?"

"He hurt a friend of mine." Just as Aidan had hurt her—and now he had to make it all up to her.

"And you're after revenge, is that it?" Marie drained her glass and shook her head. "You wouldn't be the first. Best to let that one go, I'd say."

"I can't do that, Marie," Aidan said, his voice quiet and ice-cold. "I want him gone."

"You and everyone else. Before he was transported to Australia, he was into all the usual things. Thieving, pickpocketing, forgery, prostitution, blackmail, running padding-kens. He had his dirty fingers in every pie there was."

"But you do know he's back now?"

"Aye, I know that. Everyone knows. I can't tell you how many thieves and whores have gone to ground since old Handsome Tom Beaumont showed up in London again.

We thought we were done with him for good." Marie gave him a shrewd look. "The friend you're out to protect—it's a woman?"

"Yes."

"He must have hurt her a great deal, then."

Aidan gave a brusque nod as he remembered the wariness that was always lurking in Lily's eyes, the flashes of pain she tried to hide. "I won't let him do it again. She deserves so much better." She deserved better from Aidan as well. So much better.

"Is she a lady?"

He slowly turned his empty glass in his hand as he studied the paintings on the wall. "This house was your mother's before it was yours, wasn't it, Marie?"

She nodded, not seeming to notice the sudden change in subject. "She bought a ninety-year lease on the building when she opened her 'French' house way back when this neighborhood wasn't so respectable. She was a shrewd old thing. But I had to diversify a bit, of course. Tastes these days are so much more complex."

"And her name was Madame Josephine?"

"That it was." Marie laughed. "You're all nostalgic tonight, love. What's that about, eh?"

"I think the woman I'm trying to protect had a mother who once worked here."

Marie's eyes widened. "Did she, now? Must have been when I was a child."

"Do you remember a Frenchwoman, then?" Aidan said.

"Lots of girls here like to say they're French."

"Well, she was truly French. A deft hand with a whip. She had a daughter about your age."

"Sandrine!" Marie cried. "Must be her. No one else had a kid then but Mum. Sandrine was a real beauty, such dark eyes and pale skin. And she had a rare talent with that riding crop. Gentlemen would pay a high sum for an hour with her. Too bad about the opium. It gets a lot of girls in the end. I never touch the stuff myself. And you know her daughter?"

"Lily. Beaumont has been a threat to her."

"What a rotter he is. I do remember Lily, a quiet little girl, didn't say much. She ran off after her mum died." Marie gave a dark scowl as she poured out more wine. "She was one of our own, though, no two ways about it. Can't let a bastard like Beaumont get her."

"I knew you would agree with me, Marie."

She went to her desk and quickly scrawled something across a scrap of paper. "If you go to this address and talk to a riverman named Piker, he can help you out. Just let me know what you find out. I'd like a chance at Beaumont myself."

"Thank you, Marie." Aidan tucked the paper into his pocket and kissed her powdered cheek. "I promise you—I will get him."

Marie grinned up at him. "She's a lucky lady indeed, Aidan my love. You tell her we remember her mum here. And if she ever needs work..."

Aidan thought of Lily's graceful hand wielding the crop more deftly than the woman in that painting could ever hope for, and he laughed. "She would make you a fortune here, Marie. But I intend to keep her talents to myself for a while to come..."

* * *

"Well, now, ain't you the handsome one? Down here looking for some company, are you?"

Aidan turned to see a girl leaning against the low wall that held back the muddy banks of the river. She was small and thin, her skin a pale grayish color under her paint, her hair a tangled skein of pale yellow. She wore a low-cut gown of grubby white muslin, barely covered by a threadbare shawl.

And she was much too young to be out looking for customers on the rough Wapping docks. Aidan remembered what Lily had told him about her childhood, how she ran away to avoid prostituting herself only to find herself starving and stealing on the streets. This could have been Lily, would have been her if the bastard he looked for today had any say in it.

It made him even more determined to bring Tom Beaumont down.

He gave the girl a gentle smile. "Not company, love, but some information."

She scowled and pulled her shawl closer around her. "What sort of information?"

Aidan drew out a handful of coins and held them out to her. Her scowl vanished. "I'm looking for a river dredger named Piker."

"What would you want with him, now?" she said, still staring at the coins.

"I was told he knows something I would very much like to find out."

The girl licked her lips. "He'll be at his boat right now. Too early to be out on the river. Under the bridge down that way, first one you come to."

"Thank you." Aidan handed her the money, which she

quickly tucked away in her bodice. "You wouldn't happen to know of a man named Tom Beaumont, would you?"

Her eyes widened, and she frantically shook her head. "Not me. I mind my own business, and so should you."

Aidan gave her a nod and turned to make his way along the riverbank, his old boots sucked in by the mud and muck of the low tide. As the girl had said, it was too early to be out on the river yet. All the dredgers, who made their livings hauling dead bodies and other detritus out of the Thames, were working on their small boats or mending their trawling nets. They watched him walk past without much interest. People came down to the docks seeking all sorts of things, and they had seen it all before.

A few mudlarks, children who scavenged in the sludge for whatever had washed in, were poking about with their sticks. The fishy, dirty tang of the river, blended with the old sewers that ran down to the water's edge, was strong there. Pasted along the stained brick walls were posters of people missing or descriptions of those pulled from the water.

Aidan ignored all of it, intent on what he had to do. He found the riverman named Piker just as the girl had said, under the bridge as he scraped the sludge from the hull of his small boat. He was a thin man, younger than Aidan expected, his face obscured by a bushy beard and his skin weathered by years on the river. A cap was pulled low on his brow.

"Are you Piker?" Aidan asked.

The man didn't look up from his task. "Who wants to know?"

"Marie sent me. She said you might have some information for me."

Piker laughed. "Now what would someone like you want with me?"

"I want to find Tom Beaumont, and I was told you might know where he is."

The man's eyes shot up to Aidan's face, and he dropped his scraping blade. Aidan could see it a split second before Piker ran. He took off at a flat run, but Aidan was faster. He caught Piker at the foot of the bridge steps and brought him down hard, his fist cracking on the man's jaw.

"I don't want trouble!" Piker shouted. "I don't have nothin' to do with Beaumont now. I work for myself."

"Then why did you run?" Aidan curled his fists in the man's coat and held him pinned down. "Where is he?"

"I don't know!"

Aidan drew back his fist, and Piker held up his hands in surrender. "Well?" Aidan said.

"I told him I wouldn't work for him no more," Piker said. "But he was down here the other night, trying to get a gang together."

"For what purpose?"

"To turn over a goldsmith's shop. He needs money fast, I think."

"Why?"

"I don't know, I swear! That's all I know. But my cousin Ralph went with him, the stupid tosser. You could maybe get somethin' out of him."

"Then tell me where to find this cousin of yours, and we're done," Aidan said. "But if you are lying to me, I promise you will be very sorry. I'm as bad an enemy to have as Beaumont."

Piker nodded, his face gone ashen. "I ain't lying, I swear. I don't want trouble with anyone."

Once Aidan had the information he sought from Piker, he left the docks and went in search of this Ralph in Southwark. It was time he gathered a "gang" of his own.

It was a strangely quiet night. Usually the narrow, dirty streets of that crowded neighborhood came to life in the darkness, crawling with drunks, whores, and thieves as they fought to survive for a few more hours. But people like that also seemed to have an instinct for when things were about to go very wrong, and they knew how to go to ground. Tonight only a few people scurried along in the shadows, and the cracked windows were shuttered.

Aidan slipped around a corner to a slightly wider street lined with shops that were mostly owned by Jewish proprietors who had to deal in such places. Those places were also locked up tight, but in the goldsmith's shop that Piker said Beaumont intended to "turn over," a faint light shone under the door. The silence felt thick and heavy, almost crackling in the darkness.

Aidan glanced down the street to see a ripple of movement beside the wall of another shop. It was Constable Morris and his men, waiting for the signal. Constable Morris had given Aidan some valuable information once or twice before Aidan went to the West Indies, and now Aidan had repaid those favors tenfold. Capturing Beaumont would make Morris's career—if they could carry this off and emerge unscathed themselves.

Aidan turned his attention to an upstairs window across the street, where the moonlight gleamed on a flash of steel. Nick kept watch there, pistol at the ready, but he hadn't indicated that he saw anything of Beaumont and his gang yet. Aidan drew out his own gun and held it at the ready, his whole body tense and alert as he waited.

Tom Beaumont had hurt Lily for the last time. Aidan was going to make very sure of that now.

Suddenly the night was shattered by a loud crash from the alley that ran beside the shop. A light flared in the darkness, and Aidan felt a wild excitement leap inside of him. The battle was on.

There was a startled shout and a woman's high-pitched scream. Aidan surged forward to kick down the front door of the shop, and the constables rushed into the darkened store behind him. The back door to the alley hung open, and lamplight spilled down a narrow staircase. The noise came from up there, a torrent of screams and crashes and the sound of breaking glass.

Aidan ran up the stairs to find a scene of chaos, the floor littered with coins and shards of glass and furniture overturned. Two women huddled in the corner, cowering back from two men, while a tall figure wrapped in a long, black coat fought with a skull-headed walking stick.

"Beaumont," Aidan shouted as he cocked his pistol. His blood burned hot now, ignited by the violence and by facing Beaumont at last. The man would pay for what he had done to Lily.

Tom slowly turned and let the hapless shopkeeper collapse to the floor. Dark blue eyes shone like coals in a scarred, ruined face as he looked at Aidan, and a terrible smile spread over his thin lips. Aidan was aware of the men behind him, the fighting, but this moment was between him and Tom Beaumont.

"Ah, it's Lil's fancy man," Beaumont said with a laugh. "I should have known it would be you."

"You're finished, Beaumont," Aidan said quietly. "You might as well surrender now and go peacefully."

"I did that once when they came for me," Beaumont said. "And look what happened. Won't do that again."

Beaumont stepped away from his fallen victim and tossed aside his stick. There was a sudden flash of lamplight on metal as he drew out a knife. He and Aidan circled each other warily, never taking their eyes off each other as Aidan waved the constables back. This was his fight now, and the fewer people who were hurt the better.

Suddenly Beaumont gave a terrible grin and lunged forward with his knife raised to strike, as if he cared not at all that Aidan held a weapon or that a flood of men waited to seize him. Beaumont let out a guttural shout, and Aidan slid to the right and behind him, driving him back as anger rose up in him like a crimson tide.

Aidan drove Beaumont toward the wall with a furious series of strikes and feints. He hardly noticed the vicious blows Beaumont landed, the blood that trickled down his arm from a lucky strike. Beaumont lashed out with his foot and tripped Aidan, sending him crashing to the floor.

Aidan seized Beaumont's arm as he went down and dragged him along with a violent crash. In a fight that seemed to last an hour but surely only went on for only seconds, they grappled for Aidan's gun. It went off with a deafening roar and a blinding cloud of smoke. Aidan twisted the man's arm sharply and pushed him off with one great heave as the gun clattered to the floor. Blood and sweat hung heavy in the air as Aidan became aware of the other men shouting and the women sobbing.

He scrambled to snatch the fallen gun, and just as Beaumont reached for his throat, he brought the grip of the pistol down hard on his head. Once, twice, until at last Beaumont collapsed unconscious.

Aidan leaped to his feet and stared down at the fallen man. He remembered Lily's white, frightened face, and the fury that had been ebbing away roared back. He leaned forward as if to kick Beaumont once more, but a hard hand caught his arm and dragged him back. He spun around to see it was Nick who held him as the constables swarmed around Beaumont.

"Aidan, it's done," Nick said.

Aidan scrubbed his hand over his face as exhaustion claimed him. It was done—Lily was safe now. Safe from Beaumont anyway.

She would never truly be safe from Aidan, or he from her.

Chapter Eighteen

St. Giles monster captured!

Lily ran her fingertip over the screaming black headline splashed across the newspaper. Just beneath it was a sketch of Tom Beaumont being hauled to Newgate, his weathered face twisted into a snarl. Somehow the artist made him look even uglier and more menacing than in real life, a monster in truth. She shuddered just looking at the dark gleam in his eyes.

She quickly skimmed the rest of the story, a dramatic and no doubt overblown tale of the hunt for the "notorious criminal madman" through the slums after he was blamed for the robbery and near-murder of a goldsmith in Southwark. "Informants" were of "great assistance" in the search and in the arrest which had resulted in the wounding of two constables. "Business proprietor" Nick Riley gave a statement on the great relief felt among his patrons at the apprehension of such a menace.

Informants. Lily heard Aidan's voice in her head, telling her he knew many people in many places. That she no longer had to fear Tom Beaumont. She remembered her anger the last time she was with Aidan, but this made their fight seem small and petty now.

She slowly folded up the paper and placed it next to her untouched breakfast plate. It seemed Aidan had been busy in the days since she had last seen him at the Devil's Fancy. He had sent her a few notes telling her "progress" was being made, and she was to stay safely with her family and not worry.

She had wondered so many times what he was doing, where he was. Now it appeared he had been engineering an arrest.

And she couldn't help but smile. Tom Beaumont was locked away in Newgate. No matter how he got there, he wouldn't appear in her life again. She was free of him, and her family was safe.

Oh, Aidan, she thought. *What did you do?*

"You look disgustingly happy this morning, Lily," Dominic suddenly growled from across the table.

Lily glanced up at him and smiled. Dominic had looked distinctly rough around the edges for the last few days, his golden hair rumpled, his eyes shadowed, his features sharp and almost feral. After rehearsals at the theater, he would disappear, not returning until breakfast time, if then. Now he sat slumped in his seat, his plate pushed away, nursing a cup of strong coffee. His clothes looked as if he hadn't changed them since last night, his fine coat creased and his cravat hanging loose.

He glared at her, which only made her laugh. "I am happy this morning," she said. "The sun is shining, I'm going off to buy a new hat after breakfast, and the receipts at the Majestic and the club have both been excellent lately. Why should I not be in a good mood?"

"That makes quite a change," Dominic said. "You've been all quiet and broody. Why the sudden change?" He frowned at her suspiciously. "There must be a reason."

A reason like a man? A Huntington man? Lily refused to be baited, not this morning, when she finally dared to begin to hope that things might be all right after all. She just shook her head and reached for her fork to taste her eggs.

"You are hardly in a position to complain about anyone being broody, Dominic," she said. "You've been a complete bear these last few days. What is the matter with you?"

Brendan laughed from his seat at the end of the table. Brendan hardly ever laughed, and it sounded a bit deep and rusty. Lily turned to him, startled.

"It's probably a woman," Brendan said, and calmly turned the page of his own copy of the paper. A faint smile lingered around his mouth, softening the harsh, ascetic lines of his scarred face. "I knew you would take a fall eventually, Dom. Was it the mysterious card player from the club last week?"

"A woman?" Lily said. She stared across the table at Dominic, astonished by the sudden angry flush that appeared on his unshaven cheeks. "Was it the woman in the black gown? Who was she?"

"Shut up, both of you," Dominic said, his voice full of barely leashed fury. "You know me better than to think I would 'take a fall' over a woman. Especially not a teasing witch like that one."

Lily raised her brow in question at Brendan, and he shook his head. She burned with curiosity to know what had happened between Dominic and the lady in black to make him behave like this. Dominic never lost control over a woman—they always fell right into his arms, and then he had them and moved on. But she could see very well she would learn nothing more about it today, or ever. She suspected Dominic would smash his coffee cup against the wall if she pursued the topic.

She took another bite of her eggs and said calmly, "What about the assembly at Holland House tonight? We shouldn't waste the invitation. There is sure to be some potential members for the club in attendance, and Father will want to promote the new production at the Majestic, even if he's too busy to attend himself. We need to accept whenever we receive respectable invitations like this."

William St. Claire's chair at the table was empty, as it had been ever since Katherine, Isabel, and James left for the seaside. He was deeply involved in preparing the new *Much Ado About Nothing* and dealing with new difficulties with his actors and the sets. But Katherine had written to remind Lily about the assembly and urged her to attend.

Brendan and Dominic both groaned at the mention of such a stuffy soiree.

"I know. It's sure to be deadly dull," Lily said. "But we should do our duty and go. If we attend, we will receive more invitations. I can't attend without an escort, and I want to wear my new lilac-colored gown. Dominic?"

"I'm for damned sure not going," he answered. "I have a prior engagement. Take Brendan. It's his turn to be dutiful anyway."

Lily frowned at him. She could just imagine what that "other engagement" was—at a bawdy house or gambling hell. But she could see from the hard glint in his eyes that he was not going to relent. "Very well, then. Brendan will take me."

"I don't suppose you'd believe I also have another engagement?" Brendan said.

"No, I would not. Besides, the assembly will not run very late. You can meet up with Dominic for all your debaucheries after."

There was a sudden commotion in the corridor outside the breakfast room, a burst of laughter and slamming of doors, and the butler's startled voice. Lily had just risen from her chair to see what was happening when the door flew open, and Isabel appeared there in a flurry of bonnet ribbons and red-gold curls. James trailed behind her quietly.

"I'm back!" Isabel cried. "Did you all miss me?"

"Issy, what on earth are you doing here?" Lily said as Isabel flew over to kiss her cheek before fluttering over to hug her brothers.

"You're meant to be at the seaside," Dominic growled when she threw her arms around him.

"Oh, it was so boring there," Isabel declared. "I was so happy to get Father's message saying the actress playing Hero was quite hopeless and could I come home immediately to take her place. Where is he, anyway?"

"At the theater," Brendan said, still looking bemused at his sister's sudden appearance.

"Then I should go there too," Isabel said as she reached for the teapot. "I've been studying my lines on the journey. Now, what fun things do we have planned for tonight? Dominic, you look absolutely beastly. What have you been doing to yourself while I was gone?"

* * *

"Don't scowl like that, Brendan," Lily heard Isabel say as their brother led them into the assembly. "You'll frighten everyone away. No one will want to dance with me, and I don't get to go to assemblies as often as I would like."

Brendan gave a harsh bark of laughter. "It would take much more than my frowns to keep your suitors away, more is the pity. None of these milksops hovering around here are worthy of you. Why did you make me come here anyway?" Brendan was never one for respectable society. Dominic was usually much more sociable.

"I told you," Lily said. "It's good for business to be seen in respectable places."

"Respectable," Brendan scoffed. "If you knew what half these fine people got up to when no one was looking..."

"I can well imagine," Lily said with a warning glance at Isabel, who stared at them with avid interest. "But tonight it doesn't matter. Just smile and be charming."

"Ordinarily I would say Brendan was quite the wrong brother for that sort of thing," said Isabel. "But Dominic has been such a bear all day, I wouldn't trust him within a mile of such a gathering. I've never seen him in such a temper."

Lily accepted a glass of punch from a footman's tray and sipped at the tepid brew as she thought of what Brendan had said—that Dominic was out of sorts over a woman. She had no idea what sort of female could possibly have her rakish brother so overset, but she knew all too well what it felt like to be tied up in knots by passion.

She scanned the crowds of people, half hoping—or

fearing—that Aidan might be among them. Every sort of person came to the Holland House assemblies, from the queen to well-to-do merchants, everyone vying to be seen and to meet the "right" contacts. Surely even the Huntingtons sometimes attended.

But what would she do if she did see him? She could hardly talk to him, dance with him, touch him. Demand to know what he had done to get Tom Beaumont arrested, what kind of peril he put himself in.

Or kiss him senseless.

Lily studied the people around them. It was all much more subdued than an evening at the Devil's Fancy, and a whole world away from cheap barrooms and the Lambeth night market. The young ladies, like Isabel in her pale blue organdy ruffles, wore pastels and pearls, while everyone else was a blend of dark greens and grays and purples against the men's black evening coats. The dancers, a long, orderly line moving in a quadrille, were reflected in the gilt-framed mirrors. Conversation was subdued and polite.

Lily caught a glimpse of herself in the mirrored wall, another stylish, quiet figure in her dark lilac silk gown, and was shocked at how calm she appeared.

An older couple who were frequent patrons of the Majestic stopped to ask about the new production, and Lily was soon distracted by the talk of plays. Even Brendan seemed to relax a bit from his usual tense watchfulness at social occasions. Isabel left to dance and returned as more people came by to converse. It was all a most ordinary, pleasant evening, a world away from where Lily had been lately.

But then the doors opened and a new party appeared.

The rest of the crowd seemed to part for them, and Lily heard the ripple of whispers move through the room. "The Duke of Carston..."

She stiffened, her smile fading as she looked at the new arrivals. It *was* the Duke of Carston, seated in a large wheeled chair, his duchess walking beside him. She was a plump, pretty lady with graying brown hair that had probably once been the rich chestnut of Aidan's, elegantly dressed in purple-and-blue plaid satin and diamonds. She smiled serenely around her as her fierce-faced husband scowled.

Behind them was the black-haired beauty Lily had seen Aidan with in the park. She really was quite stunning, an exotic lady clad in ruffled white silk and lace, but she seemed distracted as she looked around the room. She held on to the arm of a man who seemed entirely out of place in the staid assembly room. He was tall and very lean, his strong shoulders straining the seams of his expensive evening coat. His hair, a slightly darker brown than Aidan's and streaked with gold as if he spent lots of time outdoors, was long and tied back from the stark angles of his face. A light shadow of beard covered his jaw.

And behind them...behind them was Aidan. Smiling down at the delicate, pretty little blonde at his side.

Lily's hand tightened on her glass, and she didn't know where to look. She wanted to turn away, pretend to be indifferent, but she couldn't tear her gaze away from Aidan's face. She couldn't stop the nonsensical instinct to run to him.

Oh, she was truly a fool now.

"Look how handsome Lord Aidan is tonight," Isabel whispered in Lily's ear. "Don't you agree?"

Lily gave a choked laugh. "He always looks far too handsome for the good of us females."

"But who is that other man? He looks quite fearfully wild," Isabel said.

Lily glanced at her to see that her sister looked far too intrigued by him.

One of the ladies who stood nearby heard Isabel's question and said, "Why, that is Lord David Huntington! The heir to the Duke of Carston. It's quite strange he is here tonight. He never comes to London."

The heir, who Aidan feared would never be duke. Lily studied his stony face. He looked quite a lot like Aidan, but he did seem wild, as if he were barely confined by his fine clothes and the civilized surroundings. His golden-brown eyes were full of an almost feral caution as he scanned the gathering.

He is a hermit—he drives our father crazy, she remembered Aidan saying. The two sons of a duke, a charming rogue and a wild man. It was like something in Shakespeare.

"Lord David Huntington," Isabel murmured. "How fascinating."

"Don't get too fascinated, Issy," Brendan said roughly. "You won't ever be meeting him."

"Oh, don't be so boring, Brendan," Isabel moaned. "We are hardly the Montagues and Capulets, you know. Ouch!"

Brendan had taken Isabel's arm and was leading her out of the room. Lily hurried to keep up.

"Who is the barbarian now?" Isabel said. She tried to twist her head around to look at Lord David again, and Lily almost laughed. If Brendan wanted to discourage

Isabel's interest in David Huntington, he was going about it in entirely the wrong way.

"We've been here long enough," Brendan said. "It's time we were gone."

"Well, we can't leave without our cloaks," Lily said.

"And I have to go to the ladies' withdrawing room," Isabel huffed. She yanked her arm out of Brendan's grasp and turned toward the staircase outside the assembly room. "You just wait here and cool your temper, brother."

Lily followed her into the pink sanctuary of the withdrawing room, where ladies were having their torn hems repaired by the maids or sitting before mirrored dressing tables to see to their coiffures.

Isabel sank down onto a velvet chaise with a sigh. "Brothers. They can be such a blasted nuisance."

"He's only trying to protect you," Lily said. She automatically glanced in the mirror and smoothed her hair. She saw that her hand trembled over the brown strands. She wouldn't have expected seeing Aidan in different, respectable surroundings with his family would affect her, but somehow it had. It reminded her of the truth of who they both were. The gulf that lay between them.

"It's better than being alone in the world," she murmured.

Isabel gave her a searching glance. "Of course it is. I love my brothers, even when they make me crazy. I just don't see the need for them to behave in such a positively Borgia-like fashion whenever there's a glimpse of a Huntington."

Lily sighed and sat down next to Isabel on the chaise. "I don't either. But they *are* men, and therefore by definition unfathomable."

"Have you seen Lord Aidan since that day in the park?" Isabel whispered.

"Once or twice," Lily answered carefully. She couldn't tell Isabel the truth of her affair with Aidan, the long nights when she couldn't stay away from him. No one could know about that, ever.

Unless something had happened that night when they didn't use precautions. Then everyone would know soon enough.

No, Lily thought adamantly. She pressed her hands to her stomach, flattened by the bones of her corset. She felt ill just thinking about it. Ill and... strangely, horribly something like hopeful. But a child would mean ruin. Besides, she reminded herself, she had never conceived with her husband or anyone else, and her courses were due soon. It was nothing to fret about.

She pushed away the thought and smiled at Isabel, who was watching her thoughtfully.

"Aidan is not an evil ogre, is he?" Isabel said. "Even though he is a Huntington."

"No, he's not."

"And I am sure his brother is not either. All of that family business happened so long ago. Why can't Brendan and Dominic just forget it?"

"Because they're proud, I suppose," Lily answered. "They can't help but resent the thought that their rightful place in the world was stolen."

"Well, that doesn't mean I have to be so unreasonable," Isabel said. She had a gleam in her eyes that Lily didn't trust at all. "Do you think I could get that wild-looking Lord David to dance with me?"

Lily laughed wryly at the thought of Brendan's reaction if Isabel took to the dance floor with David Huntington. "Only if you never want to be allowed out of the house again."

"As if they could really stop me!"

"Besides, Lord David doesn't look as if he dances."

"Hmm, no, he doesn't. But you could dance with Lord Aidan," Isabel said.

Lily shook her head. "No dancing for me tonight. I think it's time we went home."

"You go ahead and wait for me outside, Lily. I have some business to attend to."

Lily noticed some of Isabel's giggly young friends beckoning to her from the corner. "No mischief, Issy."

"None at all, I promise. Not tonight anyway."

Lily nodded and made her way out of the withdrawing room. Two ladies brushed past her on their way in, and she recognized the black-haired beauty and the little blonde who had arrived with Aidan. The dark lady gave her a startled glance, as if she recognized Lily, but then the door closed behind them.

Lily turned and saw Aidan there on the landing, his palms resting lightly on the balustrade as he gazed down at the foyer below. He glanced over his shoulder at her, and he showed no surprise at seeing her there. He gave her a half-smile, and she slowly walked over to stand beside him. She knew she should turn the other way and go down the stairs, away from him, that they shouldn't be seen talking at a place like this. But something still drew her to him.

"Good evening, Lily," he said. "You look lovely, as always. That color suits you."

Lily rested her hands on the railing next to his. The white kid of her gloves glowed in the shadows. She could hear the music and chatter of the party, but it seemed so very far away. She couldn't stay there long, but for a moment it was just her and Aidan.

"I wanted to say thank you," she said quietly.

"For what?"

"You know for what. I read the account of Tom's arrest in the papers. I know you had something to do with it. Probably everything to do with it."

Aidan shrugged. "I merely acted as any of Her Majesty's concerned citizens would."

"Very few of those citizens even want to know what happens in places like Whitechapel or St. Giles. They would never know how to track down and capture someone like Tom Beaumont."

"I promised you he wouldn't bother you again, Lily."

She shook her head. "I have never known a better actor than you, Aidan."

"An actor? Not I," he said with a laugh.

"Yes, you. You want everyone to think you are so careless, only out for your own pleasure, no thought for anyone else."

"That's all very true, Lily. I am only out for my pleasure."

"No, you can't fool me. Not now. No one, not even a madman, would go chasing through the slums after someone like Tom Beaumont for a mere lark. Whatever you did, I am grateful."

He turned his head to look at her, and she was shocked by the fierce, intent light in his eyes. His hands curled into fists on the polished railing. "I don't want your gratitude, Lily."

"Then what do you want?"

"Oh, I think you know," he said in a low, quiet voice that made her shiver.

A burst of laughter floated up to them from the foyer. Lily looked down at the people there, away from Aidan, but she could still feel him watching her.

"The blond lady you came in with tonight," she said. "She is very pretty."

"Lady Henrietta Lindley."

Lady Henrietta Lindley. The young lady he was linked with in the gossip papers, the suitable bride for a duke's son. It was yet one more reminder of how far apart their worlds were, of what expectations Aidan had had placed on his shoulders by his family and by society. He might rebel against them now, but eventually everyone had to bow to duty. He could sleep with Lily, even forge a connection with her, but in the end he had to marry a Lady Henrietta. Especially if his brother failed in his duty and Aidan had to be the duke.

"Your family must be happy to see you with her," she said. "And she looked lovely on your arm."

"I don't care about her," he whispered darkly into her ear. "I want to see you."

"You are seeing me right now."

"Alone. There are things I must explain. Meet me tomorrow night? At the Carlyle Hotel?"

Lily closed her eyes. She knew she should say no, should end this now. Let him go to his Lady Henrietta while she decided what to do with her life from now on. But she nodded.

"Tomorrow night, then."

Room 303. Lily looked up at the polished brass numbers on the door and then down at the key in her hand. It had been delivered to her house that morning and all day had sat in the locked drawer of her desk like a guilty secret.

She had almost stayed away, remembering Aidan with his family and the oh-so-suitable Lady Henrietta, remembering all that lay between them. But in the end, she could no more stay away than she could cease breathing. There was something about Aidan, some terrible magic, that drew her to him.

She eased back the hood of her cloak a bit and peered back down the hallway. The Carlyle Hotel was an expensive place, full of the air of quiet discretion and secrets kept amid fresh flowers, thick carpets, and crystal chandeliers. The dark wood walls muffled any sounds, and whatever happened behind those carved doors stayed there.

She slowly slid the key into the lock and clicked it open. With a deep breath, she pushed past the door and let it close behind her.

It was dark in the chamber, the only light a beam of chalky moonlight that fell over the foot of a high, carved bed spread with satin blankets. She blinked, trying to adjust her eyes after the gaslight of the corridor.

Suddenly her wrist was caught in a hard clasp, and she was whirled around to face the wall, her cheek against the cool silk paper. She instinctively kicked back, her mouth opening to cry out, but a palm covered her mouth.

"Don't scream," Aidan whispered roughly against her ear.

In an instant, Lily went from cold fear to relief. She sagged against the wall, bracing her free hand against it. The pattern of the paper felt bumpy under her palm.

"Aidan," she murmured. "You frightened me."

"Sorry," he said, but he didn't sound repentant at all. He sounded dark and... and hungry. His hand slid slowly away from her mouth, and she caught the tip of his finger between her lips. As she sucked on it, biting lightly, he groaned.

He quickly tore away the ties of her cloak and let it drop. "I missed you, Lily," he said against her hair. He smelled of wine and his own spicy soap, and as his body pressed against her back, she realized that his shirt was open. His skin was warm and damp through her muslin gown, and she arched herself into him, wanting to feel more.

"How could you miss me?" she said, gasping when his teeth caught at her earlobe. "You just saw me last night."

"I could hardly do *this* last night, could I?" He tugged the bodice of her gown lower and cupped her breast in his palm. Two of his fingertips slid over her aching nipple, rolling it between them. "Or this." His tongue traced the curl of her ear before licking a light, hot trail down the side of her neck.

"You smell so good," he muttered. "Like violets and vanilla custard."

"Vanilla custard?" Lily's laugh broke off on a moan as he pinched at her nipple.

"Delicious," he said against her bare shoulder. "I could devour you right here."

Lily's eyes slid closed. "Then why don't you?"

He seemed to need nothing else but those words. He unfastened the back of her dress and pushed it all the way down. Then he made quick work of her corset, tearing at the lacings until it fell away along with her silk chemise and drawers. When she wore only her stockings, he pushed her to the bed, his body still at her back.

She fell down to the soft mattress on her stomach, her legs hanging down over the edge. She started to push herself up, but Aidan caught her around the hips and held her still. She felt him kneel on the floor, spreading her thighs farther apart, and with no warning, his tongue drove deep into her, his lips seeking out that one most sensitive spot.

"Aidan!" she cried as pleasure flew through her like fiery sparks. "Oh, God, Aidan." She rocked her hips back against him, her knees braced against his shoulders as he tasted her deeply. She pressed her forehead into the softness of the satin blankets and let the sensations carry her away.

His tongue swept over her slit before plunging into her again, and she felt his shoulder shift as he reached down to unfasten his trousers. His arm moved, and she sensed his hand sliding down over his erection, pumping himself. The image in her mind of him touching himself made her cry out again. She wanted to be the one touching him, feeling his hard heat under her fingers, wanting to taste him.

The thought of having Aidan in her mouth made her climax seize her, and her thighs tightened around him. "Aidan," she whispered.

He slowly let her down, pressing one last kiss to her sensitive inner thigh before he stood. She felt his hands at her waist as he slid her up onto the bed. Before she could roll over, he came down between her legs. He drew her hips up and slid his length inside her. He went in halfway, slowly, then drew back and drove forward, all the way until they were fully joined.

His hands tightened on her hips, and she felt a long shiver trembling through her body. "Lily," he said hoarsely. "You feel so good."

So did he. He felt so *right*. She pushed herself back

against him, and he started to thrust into her, hard, deep, almost punishing with need. Lily balanced her hands in front of her and curled her fingers into the blankets, feeling the slide of her nipples over the smooth satin. She turned her head to the side to watch the intent darkness on his face as he moved inside her.

His eyes were closed, his head thrown back as he kept up the fast rhythm. His face looked so austere, all taut, sculpted angles. She heard the slide of his skin over hers, the harshness of his breath, and the pleasure deep inside of her grew and grew until she was drowning in it.

"Aidan," she gasped, and his eyes flew open. Blue fire flashed down into her as he watched her hungrily.

One hand dug into her hip as his rhythm grew harder, wilder, and the other reached around her. His fingertip rubbed around the bundle of nerves at the top of her womanhood, tugging at it. She felt a scream rising up out of her throat at the rush of sensation slamming through her.

Aidan set his teeth against her shoulder and ground his hips into her bottom. "Come, Lily," he commanded harshly. "Come for me."

And she did, pressing her face into the bed to muffle her cries. His body jerked against hers, his back arching with his own climax.

Lily slowly sank down onto the bed and tried to breathe again. Her body trembled, and she felt so weak, so replete, she couldn't even sit up. She rolled onto her side and closed her eyes as languorous satisfaction washed over her.

Aidan fell onto the blankets behind her, and she could hear his breathing grow slower. He didn't touch her, but she could feel the heat of his body wrap around hers, could smell the salt of his sweat, his soap, and the starched linen of his shirt that blended with the sweetness of the flowers in the room and the musky scent of sex. After a long moment, he pressed a light kiss to her shoulder and pushed himself up off the bed.

Lily kept her eyes closed and listened as he moved around the room. She heard the rustle of cloth as he took off his clothes, and she realized they had been so lost in lust for each other that he hadn't undressed before he took her. There was the splash of water being poured into a basin.

"Lily?" he said softly, and she felt the dip of the bed as he sat down beside her. "Are you awake?"

"Mmm-hmm," she answered.

"Did I hurt you?"

Surprised by his words and the caution in his voice, she opened her eyes and looked up at him. He had lit candles on the dressing table behind him, and they cast him in a pale golden glow. His hair was damp, brushed back from his face, and his eyes looked dark as midnight in the flickering light.

"Of course you didn't hurt me," she said. She carefully sat up and slid back until she could lean on the mounds of lace-trimmed pillows. "I've never felt that way before. So...full of need. You must be some kind of magician."

A rueful smile quirked one corner of his mouth. "A sex magician?"

"The rarest and best kind," she said with a laugh. "But truly, Aidan, I don't...I never thought it could be the way it is between us in bed. My husband..." Her voice faded. She didn't want to think of Harry Nichols now, or ever again. Especially not when she was with Aidan.

"It's never been like this for me either," he said quietly.

He reached for her foot and slowly rolled her white silk stocking down her leg. He kissed each bit of skin he bared, soft, slow kisses, so tender after their rough, urgent love-making. His tongue swirled over the sensitive spot behind her knee, and Lily let her head fall back onto the pillows.

She wasn't sure she believed him when he said it had never been like that for him. He had surely been with so many women; he was so *good* in bed. He knew just where to touch, to kiss. But she liked those words nonetheless. She liked to imagine that she was special to him in some way, that these moments meant something.

Aidan removed her other stocking, leaving her naked, and she heard the soft splash of water. She opened her eyes to see he had left the basin on the bedside table. He wrung out a sponge and leaned over her to gently lather her shoulders, her arms, the curve of her breast.

"Aidan . . . ," she began.

"Let me," he said. His voice was soft, but with the unmistakable ring of command. "Let me take care of you."

She sank back down to the pillows and nodded. Slowly, she relaxed under his touch. No one had ever taken care of her like that before either, and she wasn't sure how she felt about it. Perhaps she liked it a bit too much. Perhaps she would miss it too much when he was gone.

She closed her eyes tightly and curled her fingers into the soft satin beneath her.

"Tell me about your marriage, Lily," he said as he traced the sponge over her hip.

Lily opened her eyes to stare up at the pleated canopy above her head. "Why do you want to know about him?"

"You said no one had ever made you feel this way before. Not even him?"

"Especially not him. I didn't marry Mr. Nichols for his skills in the bedchamber."

"Then why did you marry him?"

"Because it was time for me to marry, I suppose. My stage career was over before it began—I needed to do something. And he seemed suitable. Respectable. I thought he could make me that way too."

"Did your family urge you to marry him?" he asked quietly, intently.

Lily shook her head. "My brothers didn't even like him very much. He was too staid and conventional for them. And my parents wouldn't have minded if I stayed home with them forever. You see how I moved back with them when Nichols died. I just…I wanted to find my own life, I suppose. I wanted to be someone else. But it was a mistake."

"How so?" Aidan's voice hardened. "Was he cruel to you?"

"He didn't beat me or lock me in the attic, if that's what you mean. And he seemed to appreciate my help with his business. But…"

"But what?"

She shook her head again, as if to deny something to him or to her. "He wanted to make me into someone I couldn't be in the end, a placid, quiet lady to simper on his arm at parties and hostess his dinners for his business acquaintances. And he wasn't happy when I couldn't be that." She opened her eyes and smiled up at Aidan. He had dropped the sponge back into the basin and watched her closely with a frown creasing his brow. "And he didn't even have a fraction of your dexterity in the bedroom. Not that I want to increase your ego any more."

He smiled. "Impossible. I'm already the most arrogant bastard in London. Haven't you heard?"

"Who says so?"

"Almost everyone I've ever met. Including my brother."

"I must be mad, then, for I like your arrogance. You're always who you truly are. You never pretend."

"And you shouldn't either." Aidan lay down beside her on the pillows, his body stretched out so that he curled around her protectively, and he bent his head to kiss her shoulder. "You should never be anyone but *you*, Lily. Just as you are."

She twined her fingers in his hair and pulled him down to claim his lips with hers before she could do something awful, like cry. She kissed him hard, sweeping the tip of her tongue over his lower lip, but when he tried to wrap his arm around her waist and drag her closer, she drew away and pressed him down onto the bed with his arms stretched above his head.

She held his wrists there and whispered against his ear, "Stay there, Aidan."

Something blazed in his eyes as he stared up at her, and a muscle flexed along his jaw, but he didn't move. He lay perfectly still, his body hard and taut as she slid her body down over his, naked skin against naked skin. She kissed his muscled shoulder, his collarbone, and licked at the flat, dark disk of his nipple with the tip of her tongue. It puckered under her kiss, and she felt a ripple pass under his skin, but he still didn't move.

Lily traced her mouth down his ridged abdomen, trailed a kiss over his navel, both his sharp hip bones, biting lightly at one. His breath hissed in his throat, and she smiled.

She lifted her head to see that he was erect again, the vein on the underside of his penis throbbing. Moisture glistened at its tip. He *did* want her, as much as she wanted him.

She pushed herself up and straddled his hips, rubbing slowly up his hard length. His fists clenched against the bed, and she shook her head. "Don't move, Aidan."

He grinned up at her. "Whatever you wish."

Lily braced her palms against his chest and lowered herself carefully, deliberately, over his length, her wet, open womanhood taking him deep inside.

"Damn it, Lily," Aidan groaned, his head falling back onto the pillows. His eyes were closed, the muscles in his neck taut. "*Yes*. Just like that."

She reached for the carved edge of the headboard and rode him, burying him to the hilt.

Then he did touch her, his hips arching up into her so hard she cried out. He sat up and wrapped his arms around her waist, his mouth closing roughly over her breast. His teeth scraped over her nipple. She wrapped her legs around his hips and squealed as he spun her down to the bed, still inside of her.

He plunged into her, thrusting deeper, harder, his arms braced to either side of her head as their damp bodies slapped together. His teeth trailed over her arched neck, and she tightened her legs around his hips to meet him thrust for thrust.

She suddenly exploded with the force of her pleasure, crying his name over and over. "Lily," he shouted. With one more surge, he collapsed to her side, his back heaving as he tried to catch his breath.

But Lily couldn't breathe at all. She could only float free, her whole body trembling with the aftershocks. She reached out and gently stroked his shoulder, his sweat damp on her palm, his heartbeat thudding against her, into her.

Finally, when their breath had slowed and Lily's body cooled, Aidan kissed her hand lightly and rolled out of bed. She drew the sheets up around her shoulders and watched as he knelt to stir the embers in the grate back to a warming fire. He was still naked, and she couldn't help but admire the shift and movement of his lean back muscles and his long legs as he sat there. His skin glistened a pale gold.

He glanced at her over his shoulder, a half-smile on his lips. "Like what you see?"

Lily laughed. "You're the one walking around naked. If I choose to look..."

"I like the way you look at me." He pushed himself lithely to his feet and came to sit at the foot of the bed. He wrapped one of the blankets around his narrow hips. He reached for her bare foot and laid it on his thigh, his long, deft fingers massaging the arch, the ankle. His movements were gentle, as rhythmic as music, and she nearly purred with pleasure as her eyes closed.

"I'm sorry I was...rough with you tonight," he said. "I just needed you. I thought about you all day. You've completely wrecked my concentration."

Lily shook her head. "I liked it, everything about it. I think I needed you too. Too much."

His fingertips slid over the ball of her foot, easy and sensual. "Lily, why did you never marry again?"

"I told you how it was with my husband. I never want that again."

"Not every man is like that."

"Really? Well, I haven't yet met one who was different,

not one I wanted to marry." Only Aidan was truly different from other men, and they would never marry.

"You must have had admirers."

"Have I?" Puzzled by his quiet, tense tone, Lily opened her eyes and looked at him.

"Did you never think you might marry Freddy Bassington?"

Freddy Bassington. Lily found she could hardly remember him or the trouble he had once caused between her and Aidan. "Freddy didn't want to marry me. I think he only liked the pursuit. And I won't marry again."

Aidan was quiet for a long moment. Lily closed her eyes and felt him gently stroke her hair. "I am sorry, Lily," he finally said.

"Sorry?"

"Sorry for not telling you I was looking for Freddy's letters right off. Sorry for not trusting you. I wish you could believe me, trust me."

"Oh, Aidan," Lily said with a soft smile. "I do forgive you. How could I not after what you did for me? But as for trust—I have told you before. I fear I don't know how to really trust anyone."

Aidan sighed and pressed a kiss to her hair. "Oh, Lily. What a fine pair we make..."

Chapter Nineteen

" 'So you walk softly, and look sweetly, and say nothing. I am'—line. Line! Lily, are you listening?"

Lily's head snapped up at Isabel's sharp words. Isabel stood on a small stool in the dressing room backstage, running her lines as Hero while the wardrobe mistress hemmed her costume. Lily was meant to be helping Isabel as she mended a pile of other costumes, hoping that the two tasks would keep her distracted from her thoughts. The play opened tomorrow, and there was so much still to be done.

Obviously it wasn't working. Her fingers automatically slid the needle in and out of the cloth, but she couldn't quit thinking about Aidan and those damnable letters. And what had happened between them in that hotel bed.

At this point in their heedless, headlong affair, she would have thought the lust would be burned out, sputtering like the spent wick of a melted candle. Tom Beaumont was gone; Aidan had nothing else to rescue her from, and they had made love in almost every possible way. She should be furious with him about Freddy's silly letters, should be done with him and the way he turned her life so crazily upside down.

But she wasn't done. Even their quarrel over Freddy's letters showed her that Aidan cared about his friends, no matter how hard he tried to hide that. It just made her like him more, damn it all. And she did not want to *like* him.

"I'm sorry, Issy," she said. "I seem to be woolgathering today."

"You must be thinking of something very complicated indeed. You were frowning so fiercely just then." Isabel held up her arms to let the wardrobe mistress measure the tight velvet sleeves. "Was it the assembly? Or perhaps a certain gentleman you saw there?"

Lily glanced warily at the gray-haired wardrobe mistress and her scurrying assistants. They seemed to be intently focused on their tasks, but they had all worked for the St. Claires for a long time and were always interested in the family's doings. The last thing Lily needed now was for more gossip about Aidan to reach her family.

"I was merely thinking of everything that needs to be done before this play opens," Lily said briskly. "And you were the one with all the suitors at the assembly. You'll have to choose one of them someday soon."

Isabel gave her head an adamant shake but went perfectly still at a stern look from the wardrobe mistress. "Not any one of *them*. They're horribly dull, and they treat me like a stupid, breakable little china doll. There's nothing intriguing about them at all."

Intriguing. Lily stabbed her needle hard at the shirtsleeve in her hand. That was the problem with Aidan; he was much too intriguing. Every time she thought she had him figured out, he went and revealed a new facet to her. He was never really what he pretended to be—the spoiled, gorgeous, hedonistic son of an aristocrat. He was so, so much more.

"More lines, Lily?" Isabel said.

Lily nodded, glad of any distraction. "Hero says, 'I am yours for the walk, and especially when I walk away' . . ."

It was hours before she could escape from the theater to find some fresh air. James was listening to actors run lines in the wings, a task meant to keep him busy. The stage was a dizzying hive of activity, the carpenters hammering together the set of the palace at Modena, musicians tuning up in the pit, actors practicing their sword fights in the aisles. Dominic fought the fiercest, as if he were pouring out all his foul temper of the last few days into the stage blade.

"Damn it all, Dom!" his opponent shouted as Dominic knocked him hard to the floor again. "It's just a rehearsal, man. You don't actually have to wound me."

Dominic just wiped his shirtsleeve over his brow and said, "Again."

Lily thought it best to avoid him. She took Isabel's arm and led her between the red velvet seats of the stalls as they headed for the exit. They waved to their father, who was hurrying across the stage to make sure the sets were to his specifications. Sawdust covered his coat, and his dark hair stood on end from all his frantic tugging.

"We're going to find some luncheon, Father," Isabel called. "Shall we bring you back some refreshments?"

"No time for that now," William answered. "No, no! That balcony door does not go there."

"We will bring you something anyway," Isabel insisted. "Mama would be angry if she found out you weren't eating."

William just ran off again, grabbing a hammer to take care of the errant balcony door himself, and there was a sudden shout from Dominic's opponent and a crash as he went down again.

"Come on," Lily said, tugging at Isabel's arm. "Let's get out of here now."

"Good idea."

They hurried out into the bright warmth of the day and turned toward the small park near the theater for a quick turn on the pathways. The fine weather had drawn lots of people outdoors, and the park was crowded with black-clad nannies ushering their charges along with their hoops and dolls. Ladies took shelter under lacy parasols, and couples whispered in the shade of the trees.

Lily took in a deep breath. With Tom Beaumont gone, the day seemed even lovelier. She seemed to walk lighter, and she had the sudden urge to laugh at absolutely nothing.

If only Aidan was there to share it with her...

No. Lily shook her head sternly at herself. She couldn't think that way. She could share nothing with Aidan but their secret meetings, and even those would have to end soon. She would have to move on with her life again. She could never be a duchess.

"What a lovely day," Isabel said. "And so wonderfully quiet out here. I always forget how very chaotic the theater gets just before a show opens."

Lily laughed. "Do you wish you were still on holiday with Mama, then?"

"Not at all. I love the theater, even the loud parts of it. And the seaside wasn't as peaceful as everyone seems to think."

"Was it not?"

Isabel shook her head. "James kept vanishing off someplace, and Mother couldn't quit fretting about everyone.

She is quite convinced we are all making very unwise decisions lately, especially when it come to romance."

"She might not be very wrong about that," Lily murmured. She turned what Isabel said about James over in her mind. "Where did James go?" Were his days of seeking out rough neighborhoods and dangerous people not as behind him as she had thought?

"I have no idea. No one tells me anything. It's very tiresome." Isabel stopped at a cart to buy a cone of sugared almonds, and they shared the treat as they went on with their stroll. "Tell me, Lily, do you know very much about Lord Aidan's brother?"

Lily, who was still worrying about James and what he might be up to, gave Isabel a sharp, surprised glance. Did she have to worry about Isabel now as well? "Not much. Aidan says Lord David prefers to keep to himself in the countryside. I said he seldom appears in town."

"A hermit duke. How fascinating." Isabel munched thoughtfully on an almond before she added, "He was very handsome, don't you think? Almost as handsome as your Lord Aidan. Perhaps their gouty old father was good-looking in his youth and passed it on to his sons? Though I hope they won't age like him. It would be a shame to lose such gorgeousness."

Lily choked on a laugh. "Issy! They are Huntingtons."

"So that means they can't be handsome? Oh, Lily, come now. You know that the evil, tempting sorcerer is always sinfully handsome. I wonder how I could contrive to meet with Lord David. Would your Aidan help me with that?"

"No, he would not. It would be a very bad idea for you to encounter Lord David Huntington. And besides, he is not *my* Aidan. He was merely helping me with a task that is now over."

"Oh, Lily," Isabel sighed. "I would never have thought you would become as tiresome about the Huntingtons as Dominic and Brendan. Should we find some food to take back to the theater? Father will never eat if we don't make him."

"Of course," Lily said automatically, still caught up in thoughts of Aidan, James, and being "tiresome." They came out on the other side of the park, onto a busier street lined with bustling shops and cafes. It was very near where she met Aidan the second time, when he asked her to tea.

A newsboy stood on the corner, waving a broadsheet over his head as a crowd gathered around him.

"Criminal madman escapes from Newgate!" the boy cried. "Read the tale here, hot off the presses. Danger stalks London! Death around every corner!"

A bolt of ice shot through Lily as she heard the words, and she felt far away from the buzz of fear and excitement from the gathered crowd. The warm, lovely day went hazy around her, as if a freezing fog had swept in and covered the whole world in an instant. Her hand tightened on Isabel's arm, and she barely heard her sister call out her name.

It couldn't be. It could *not.* He was locked away, he would be executed soon, and he was out of her life for good. No one could escape from Newgate.

But she knew with a terrible certainty that it was true. That this was not a dream. She drifted toward the newsboy and his crowd, half aware of Isabel scurrying after her. She didn't feel as if she were in the world at all, not the world of pavements and buildings and parks.

She tossed the boy a coin and snatched up the smudged,

hastily printed sheet. ESCAPE FROM NEWGATE! the headline read, and below it was a sketch of a wild-eyed, gaunt-faced Tom Beaumont being wrenched to the ground by constables. Below it was a drawing of the prison itself with arrows pointing to the roof of one of the towers.

Lily leaned back against a shop wall and hastily read the story. It was an amazing tale. It seemed that Beaumont had seen an iron and granite cistern at one corner of the wall in the prison airing yard, one that reached up above the roof and the spiked railing along the roofline. When the guards were changing shifts, he kicked off his boots and used the traction of his bare feet to climb the cistern. He pulled himself to the rim and gripped the spiked iron railing and hung on desperately with lacerated, bleeding hands. He worked his way around the flat roof and then jumped onto a ledge below, moving from building to building until he was past the prison and onto Newgate Street, where he could disappear back into the twisted slums from whence he came.

The breath was knocked out of her lungs.

"Lily, what is it? You look so pale." Isabel leaned against her shoulder to scan the paper. "Oh, no. How horrible! Who is this man?"

Lily turned to stare at her sister's worried face. Tom had come after her family before with James, but James was out of reach now. What would Tom do now that he was free and on the run? He would be desperate, even more than he was before, as he tried to evade capture. And he would not just disappear. She knew he would never abandon revenge until it was done.

Would he come after Isabel now? Sweet, dear, beautiful Isabel?

"We have to get back to the theater," Lily said. She grabbed Isabel's hand and rushed back along the streets, not even seeing where she was going, who she raced past.

"What, right now? Lily, what's the matter? Who is that man?"

"I can't talk now, Issy," Lily answered. They came to the Majestic's stage door, and she held tightly to her sister's hand. "I must go do something, and I don't know when I'll be back. Promise me you will stay close to Father, or to Dominic or Brendan, until I return."

"Lily, what—"

"Promise me!"

Isabel nodded, her eyes bright with confused tears. "I promise, Lily. But, please, if you're in danger, don't go. Stay here with us."

Lily shook her head. "I have to take care of this, once and for all. I love you, Issy. I'll be back. Now go and find Father."

Isabel looked as if she longed to argue with Lily, to protest and cling to her. But she nodded and ducked through the door.

Once Lily was sure Isabel was inside, she spun around and hurried to the end of the lane, the newspaper crushed in her gloved hands. This time Tom Beaumont would not escape.

This time she would end it.

•

"So, David, what brings you back to the bosom of the family?" Aidan asked his brother as he poured out two generous glasses of brandy. It was still afternoon, but they needed some sort of fortification in the Huntington town house, especially after luncheon with their parents.

"Not my choice, believe me," David said. He took the glass Aidan handed him and knocked back half of it in one swallow. "Mother sent me an urgent message saying Father was ill. I dutifully hurried to town, only to find he was not quite as ill as she implied."

"Very sneaky of Mother," Aidan said. He sat down across from David and stretched out his legs as he sipped his own brandy. "How did she get you to the assembly?"

David shrugged. "She got all teary-eyed and insisted I do at least one duty before I left. Duty now done, I intend to get out of London tomorrow. Especially before she can throw any more heiresses at me."

"Very wise," Aidan said with a chuckle. They seldom saw David in town; their mother was bound to take full advantage of every moment he was here to matchmake. He wondered what those heiresses thought when they came face-to-face with David, with his long hair and rough clothes.

Not that it mattered when a ducal coronet was at stake.

"What about you?" David said. "I understand the banns will soon be called for you and Lady Henrietta."

"Then you understand wrong. I have no more desire to marry than you do." Aidan had never wanted to marry, never wanted to subject any woman to having him for a husband. But somehow now he saw Lily in his mind as he made that protest, saw her smile, heard her rare laughter.

"Indeed? I hear you have some sort of ladylove."

Aidan snorted. "Where did you hear that?"

"In the stables. Servants always know what's really going on. They say you've been hiding her away somewhere, that no one knows who she is." David finished his drink and pushed himself up from the settee to go and pour another glass. He was in his shirtsleeves and riding boots and leather breeches, his hair loose over his shoulders. "Not that I'm surprised. You always have had women flocking around you, but you don't usually go to such lengths to hide them."

"It's no one's business who I might be seeing," Aidan answered. He was used to being the subject of gossip, but somehow it made him angry that there was cheap speculation about Lily. "Especially not the grooms. There's nothing at all of interest going on in my life."

David laughed. "Ah, so there *is* a new lady. She must be quite fascinating if you want to keep her to yourself. Who is she?"

"No one you know, David. But was there no lady at the assembly who caught *your* eye? No one who tempts you to do your ducal duty?"

David shrugged, but a shadow seemed to drift over his face as he stared down into his glass. His long, scarred, sun-browned fingers tightened on the heavy crystal.

Aidan sat up in interest. "So someone did catch you eye. Who was it?"

"I don't know her name. We were not introduced," David said. He took a long drink. "I saw her when we came in. She was . . . very beautiful."

"Well, well," Aidan said with a laugh. "She must have been beautiful indeed if you noticed her. You are usually off in your own strange world. What did she look like, then?"

David shook his head, and a knock at the drawing room door interrupted the suddenly interesting conversation. The butler came in with a bow.

"If our mother is asking for us, tell her we're occupied

at the moment," Aidan said. David always teased him about his love life—it was time for a little payback.

"It's not Her Grace, Lord Aidan," the butler said, looking strangely hesitant. "There is a... a female asking for you at the servants' entrance in the kitchen. She says it is most urgent."

Aidan was intrigued. He finished his brandy in one deep swallow and put the glass down on the nearest cluttered table. "What female?"

"She wouldn't give her name, and she wears a veil. But she was quite insistent."

"That does sound intriguing, Aidan," David said. "Is this your mystery lady showing herself at last? You had best go see what this is all about."

"So I shall. But our conversation isn't over yet, David. I want to hear more about your beautiful lady at the assembly." Aidan followed the butler down the maze of staircases and through the kitchens, which were quiet at that hour between tea and dinner, the faint scent of roasting meats and sugary baking hanging on the cool air.

The woman hovered in the shadows just inside the door, her slender body held tense as if she would flee at any moment. She wore a purple walking dress and jacket, and a dark veil hung from her bonnet to conceal her face. When she eased it back, Aidan could see it was Celeste, one of Madame Marie's girls.

"He's escaped," Celeste said. "Tom Beaumont. And a lady named Lily came around looking for news. Marie sent me to fetch you and tell you that."

"What!" Aidan shouted. "Tell me what has happened. Exactly."

She held out the paper in her hand, and he quickly read

the lurid tale of Tom Beaumont's escape from prison. A cold, still fury settled over him as the words sank in.

"I went to your lodgings, but the woman downstairs said you were probably here," Celeste explained.

"Tell me what Lily was doing at Marie's house. Is she still there?"

Celeste shook her head. "She wouldn't come in, just wanted to ask the doormen some questions. Marie thinks she's going to try and catch Beaumont herself."

Hell no, she will not. "And where did she go when she left? I assume Marie had her followed."

"To a place called the Devil's Fancy in Mayfair. As far as I know, she's still there." Celeste's stare turned speculative as she studied him. "Who is this Lily? Someone special?"

Aidan nodded. Lily *was* special—and he wouldn't risk her life by letting her run around the city after Beaumont. He had to find her now.

The door behind them opened, and Aidan heard his brother say, "Tell me how I can help."

Chapter Twenty

She was really there again. Lily could hardly believe it. Her throat felt so tight she could barely get the words out. She sat rigid on the edge of a velvet chair, her hands clutching at the gilded arms.

She hadn't been in Madame Josephine's establishment for years, not since her mother's death, and she'd thought she would never see it again. That it would only live as a memory, a place that was just a dream. Something to struggle to forget. But here she was, as if no time had passed at all. Here in her mother's brothel, with Tom Beaumont lurking out there somewhere, she was just that feral street child again, fighting tooth and nail to survive.

Yet back then she was completely alone. Now Aidan was with her, and that made all the difference. He kept the wild desperation inside of her at bay.

He had found her as she paced at the Devil's Fancy, trying to decide what her next move would be since Madame Marie's fierce majordomo wouldn't let her in. She had been about to come back and break into the brothel when Aidan appeared and insisted he would help her.

Aidan prowled between the windows in the small

room where they waited, his long fingers parting the heavy red velvet draperies to study the street below. He had discarded his coat, and the fine white linen of his shirt glowed in the dim light from the candles. The lean muscles of his back and shoulders were coiled and tense, as if he were ready to attack.

"It grows dark now, and we need to rest and decide what to do next," he said. "This is a safe place, and Marie and her girls might have information that would be useful to us."

Lily forced herself to sit back on the chaise and relax. She did feel tired. But being here, in the place of her childhood, filled her with a nervous energy. As did Aidan's prowling.

"You don't seem to be resting, though," she said.

He tossed her a half-smile over his shoulder. "I'm watching to see who might be arriving."

Lily studied the small but luxurious chamber, the red velvet furnishings and tawny silk paper on the walls, the thick carpet on the floor, and the erotic paintings on gilded easels. Oil burners in the corners gave off a rich scent of roses and musk that was so much like the perfume her mother used to wear. From beyond the thick door, she could hear music and the silvery ring of feminine laughter. Yes, it was all much as she remembered. All that was lacking was the whistle of the whip, but that was sure to come later.

"I doubt Marie would let the likes of Tom Beaumont near her place," Lily said. "Not if she's like her mother. Josephine was most particular about her clientele, and she kept her doors well guarded."

"Oh, Marie is every bit as particular as her mother

was," Aidan said. "And Beaumont isn't stupid enough to show his face in this part of town. But even girls as expensive as Marie's hear things and know people. One of them is sure to have news for us. Marie will ask discreetly and be here soon."

"And Marie was the one who led you to the river dredgers," Lily said. She frowned as she studied Aidan's expressionless face. She had the terrible feeling that she had only scratched the surface of knowing this man. She knew he had a life that was hidden from his family and the aristocratic world. What did she not see about him?

Lily turned away from him, suddenly frightened by her longing to know him. She wrapped her arms tightly around herself as if to hold him away from her. But he had already crept on stealthy feet past all her careful guards.

"She must be a good friend to you indeed," she said.

"I have known Marie for some time, yes," Aidan answered. "She's helped me out on several occasions, and I loaned her a substantial sum when she wanted to expand her premises last year."

Lily heard him move to the table where a maid had left a tray of refreshments. The crystal glasses clinked as he poured out some wine. "Is she your mistress?" she said before she could stop the words. She didn't really want to know what Marie was to him.

He was silent for a long moment, and she glanced up to find that he watched her closely. One of his long fingers tapped against the wine carafe.

"No, she is not," he said quietly. "I have no mistress. I've never wanted to be that... formal."

He walked across the room, slowly and deliberately, almost as if he feared he would frighten her away. And she did want to flee. She felt all the muscles in her body coil as if to spring away, but she could only sit there, frozen, like a hapless rabbit as the predator crept closer.

He held out one of the glasses. "Drink this. You've had nothing to eat or drink all day, and it will be a long night."

"Thank you," she whispered, and sipped at the wine. It was good, of course, French, only the best in Marie's house.

Aidan sat down in the chair across from hers and stretched out his long legs in front of him. He held his glass loosely between his fingers, but he didn't drink from it, merely turned it around as the candlelight caught on the ruby-red facets.

"Is it as you remember here?" he said.

"Yes," Lily answered. "Perhaps the furnishings are a bit more luxurious. Marie must have used part of your loan to decorate. I could almost think—" She broke off and shook her head. It was a mistake to think that way. So many mistakes.

"Almost think what, Lily?" he asked softly.

She looked at him, and suddenly she was so tired. Tired of secrets and the past, tired of fighting against everything. "I could almost think my mother would walk through that door again, that I could see her and tell her all the things I've wanted to all these years. I never, ever wanted to be like her, and make her mistakes." Lily swallowed the rest of her wine, hoping the rich red liquid would give her a jolt of new courage.

"You are not like her, Lily," Aidan said. "You are much too strong to ever end up like her. You drive me to insanity sometimes. But I've never met anyone like you."

Lily had never met anyone like him either. She had never even imagined someone like Aidan Huntington could exist in the world. Things would be horribly dull once he was gone from her life.

The door opened, and Madame Marie appeared there. Lily sat up straight in her chair, a shock running through her. Marie looked so much like her mother, Josephine, with bright red hair piled atop her head and a tall, buxom figure set off perfectly by a low-cut satin gown. She had the same shrewd glint in her eyes, the same hard set to her rouged mouth. But it softened when she saw Aidan.

"So you're still after that bastard, are you, Aidan my love?" Marie said as she closed the door behind her and set a valise down on the rug. "You don't give up."

"Never, Marie. You know that. The constables can't hold him, it seems, so someone has to take care of it."

Marie shook her head. "You just have a care for yourself out there—that's all I'll say. I know I can't stop you."

"But can you help me again?" Aidan said. "Have you heard anything?"

"I might have. Jasmine has a sister who works in a tavern down by the docks. Jasmine was all worried-like because she's heard this sister had taken up with Beaumont after he got back to London. To get the opium, y'know. You can talk to Jasmine in a bit; she's with a client now." Marie suddenly turned to Lily. "And you must be Sandrine's girl."

"I...yes. I'm Sandrine's daughter," Lily answered. It felt strange to say her mother's name again, when it had only been a whisper of a thought for so long. She stiffened her shoulders under Marie's steady regard.

"It's good to see you again, and looking so well too," Marie said. "I've heard about you from Aidan. You must be somethin' special."

Lily glanced at Aidan, who gave a wry smile. "I don't know about that," she said.

Marie gave an unladylike snort. "Anyone who'll go chasing after the likes of Tom Beaumont must be special. Brave or foolish, one of those. And I ain't never heard Aidan talk about a woman like he does you. Here," she said, tossing the valise to Lily. "Something to change into. You can't go running into Whitechapel dressed all in silk like that, can you?"

"Thank you," Lily murmured. Her mind still whirled as she wondered what exactly Aidan had said about her.

"I've got to go now," Marie said. "Can't let the likes of Beaumont get in the way of business. Someone will come to take you to Jasmine soon." She hurried across the room in a cloud of sweet lilac perfume to grab Aidan by the shoulders and kiss his lips soundly. "You be careful, love. You hear me? My girls would go into weeping and wailing if anything happened to you, and that would *definitely* be bad for business."

"I will be careful, Marie," he answered.

Marie patted his cheek, smiled at Lily, and whirled back out of the room. There was a burst of laughter outside as she opened the door, and then they were closed into quiet again.

"Love?" Lily said, watching Aidan as he wiped rouge off his jaw.

"I told you," he said ruefully. "We're old friends."

"So it would seem." Lily opened the valise and dug through the clothes packed there. They weren't the fine satins Marie and her girls wore, but the garments of a dockside streetwalker. Scuffed boots, a faded red-striped skirt, a chemise with a low, gathered neckline, and a black bodice laced up the front. The theatrical side of Lily, the one that knew how to play a role, approved.

"Need some assistance?" Aidan said.

Lily slowly unfastened the jet buttons of her jacket. "You are quite good at playing ladies' maid, I remember."

"Oh, I'm good at many, many things," he murmured.

She remembered that as well. Despite the dangers they faced, and the knowledge of where they were, she felt a warm shiver of awareness slide over her skin as he watched her. She laid her jacket aside and turned to let him unfasten the back of her dress.

His fingers were deft and quick as he slid the buttons free and eased the long, tight sleeves down her arms. The gown fell to the floor in a silken whisper, and he moved to unlace her corset. As its restriction eased, she felt him trace the back of his fingers along the groove of her spine, his touch warm through the fine silk chemise he had given her.

"Lily," he whispered, and he bent his head to kiss her on the vulnerable nape of her neck. His lips were parted, hot as he tasted her. Lily trembled, and he tossed her corset to the floor. His hands slid around her waist and pulled her back against his body. She curved into him and cried out when his teeth bit down lightly on her bare shoulder.

"Do you trust me, Lily?" he said against her skin. "Do you trust me to keep you safe?"

"I trust you, Aidan," she said, and to her shock, she realized it was true. She did trust him, did feel safe with him. Even here, she no longer had any fear. "But do you trust me? Do you trust me to work with you to find Beaumont?"

"Yes," he said. "I should lock you up here and not let you out until the bastard is dead. But God help me, there is no one I want by my side in any fight more than you. My fierce warrior goddess."

Those words meant more to Lily than anything else ever could. They trusted each other; they were together in this. For just a little while longer, she was not alone.

She reached down for the hem of her chemise and drew it off, letting the thin silk drift to the chair. She took up the rougher cotton of the borrowed chemise and pulled it on before she could give in to temptation and spin around in Aidan's arms to twine her fingers in his hair and draw his mouth to her naked breast.

She handed him the black bodice and let him fit it around her waist. He drew the laces of it tight, working in silence.

By the time she was dressed in the new clothes and her hair was rearranged, released from its tight, smooth coil into loose, tangled waves, the maidservant had reappeared.

"Madame says I'm to take you to Jasmine now," she said with a curtsy, as well mannered as if she worked for the queen. She led them out of the sitting room and into a secret passage tucked behind the main corridors.

"Wait here, if you please," the maid said as she ushered them into a small room. "Jasmine will be done in just a few minutes."

Lily slid into the chamber as Aidan followed and closed the door behind them. It was even smaller than the sitting room where they had been before, a dark space lit by one wall sconce. As she blinked, letting her eyes adjust to the dimness, she saw a small, grille-covered opening midway up one wall that let in a bit more light. From beyond that opening, she could hear a man's shouts of pleasure, the whistle of a whip against bare skin.

And it seemed this room was meant to be a possible extension of the scenes in there, a place where those so inclined could watch. Lily could make out iron rings bolted to the walls, with chains hanging down from them. A table covered with a jumble of ominous-looking instruments lurked in one corner, while in the other was a velvet chaise draped with a fur throw.

She leaned against the wall and studied it all. She thought of the assembly rooms, all those respectable-looking, morally correct people who kept on the right masks to keep their places at the queen's court. Which of them would faint if they knew such a place existed? And which of them visited here in secret, paying Marie's high prices for the ultimate in secret fulfillment?

She almost laughed to imagine it all. But then she remembered Aidan's naked, gorgeous body stretched out under her, and the laugh turned into a choking cough.

Aidan went and peered through the little window into the next room, and a wry smile curved his lips. "I think Jasmine will be more than a few minutes," he said. "She appears to be quite occupied for the time being."

Lily went to his side and went up on her toes in her borrowed boots to look through the window. Jasmine's customer, a portly, red-faced gentleman, was bent over a brocade ottoman, his bare backside in the air. The skin was already a bright pink, but Jasmine, a tall brunette fully dressed in a stylish black velvet ball gown, still wielded the whip over him.

"You have been naughty indeed," she said sternly. "I don't think you are sufficiently punished yet. You don't seem truly sorry."

"I am sorry! I truly am," the man babbled.

"Not enough." And the whip flashed through the air again.

"She's very good," Lily commented wryly.

"Not as good as you, I daresay." Aidan slid his arm around her waist and spun her back to the wall. She was caught there with his hands braced to either side of her, his body pressed to hers. He bent his head to trace his lips lazily over her neck. "Whatever can we do to fill the time while we wait?"

She could think of a few things, things involving those intriguing items left so conveniently near. But then his mouth moved over the curve of her shoulder, his teeth scraping lightly over her skin, and she could hardly think at all. She knew she should push him away and concentrate on what they had to do—find Tom Beaumont. Aidan's mouth, though, his touch...He made her *want* to forget. To believe there was only him. And the danger around them only made her want him more urgently.

She caught the back of his head in her palms, twisting her fingers in his hair. His kiss slid lower, his tongue licking along the soft swell of her breast pushed high by the tight-laced bodice. Behind her closed eyes, she could feel every shifting movement he made, every soft breath. His hands closed hard on her hips and pulled her against him until she could feel his erection. She could hear the whip from the next room, and the man's screams of ecstasy.

"I fear I've also been very, very bad," Aidan whispered darkly against Lily's skin. His fist closed in the fabric of her skirt and dragged it slowly up her leg until he could trace his fingers over the soft bare skin of her thigh above her garters.

Before his touch could reach her damp, aching core, she pushed him back with a laugh. He fell away a step, staring down at her with burning eyes. Something came over her at that look of his, that hot desire that seemed to heat her skin wherever he stared at her. Something that felt powerful and needful at the same time, so wonderful after the helplessness of facing Tom again. Aidan, this handsome, sexy, powerful man, wanted *her.* She seemed to find a strength from that knowledge, a strength she didn't even know she possessed.

She slid her hands up his chest and untied his cravat as she made him walk backward to the wall. When he leaned against it, still watching her, she quickly unfastened his shirt and peeled it away from his chest. His whole body grew taut, and she sensed again that way he had of watching a woman so closely, responding to her, gauging her desires and answering them with his mouth, his hands, his penis. As if he could read what a woman needed just from looking at her.

It was no wonder so many women loved him, Lily thought as she ran her hands lightly over his naked chest. No wonder *she* needed him, when she had pushed away and denied her own needs, her own nature, for so long.

His skin was smooth and warm, slightly damp with sweat under her touch, the muscles hard. She traced her fingers over his flat stomach, then his hip bones as she nudged his trousers lower. His erection sprang free, hard and ready, and she smoothed her fingertip over the pearly drop of liquid at its tip.

Aidan groaned and reached out for her, but she caught his wrists and pressed them back to the wall. She moved his arms up and wrapped his fingers around the chains that hung there. A muscle flexed in his jaw, and for a moment, she was sure he would break away. But then his grasp tightened on the chains, and she smiled.

She leaned against him, bracing her palms on his strong shoulders. She could feel the tension in his muscles there as he held himself bound. "You *have* been very naughty," she whispered, and she caught his nipple between her teeth.

He groaned as she bit down lightly and sucked. Her touch glided down his sides, over the stretch of his ribs, his lean waist. She swept her palms over the taut curve of his buttocks, scoring him gently with her nails, pressing her fingertip over his puckered opening before she traced her caress along the top of his hair-dusted thigh.

"How should you be punished?" she mused.

"A good, hard fuck should do it," he said hoarsely.

Lily laughed. "That doesn't sound like punishment, now, does it? I suppose I could get out the whip like Jasmine, but I remember you rather like that too." She went up on her toes to whisper in his ear. "I think I know what else you like…"

The chains rattled as his fists tightened around them. "Lily," he said warningly.

"Shhh." She kissed his neck, bit at the curve just where it met his shoulder. She slid down his body until she knelt at his feet. She shook back her hair and looked up at him.

His eyes were hooded, his skin drawn taut over his jaw and his aristocratic cheekbones as he stared down at her. The veins in his arms stood out as he wrapped the chain tightly around his fists. She gave him a smile and slid her parted lips over his erection.

The chains clashed again, and his hips jerked against her. She pressed her palms to his buttocks and held him to her mouth. She traced her tongue flat over his length, tasting the faint, warm saltiness of him, inhaling the sweet musk of his desire. His desire for her.

She slid deeper, slowly wrapping one hand around his base, until he touched the back of her throat, and she swallowed.

"Oh, God, Lily," he groaned. "Suck me. Just like that."

She drew off him, until her lips touched just the sensitive tip. "So naughty," she said, and licked up his length again, harder. She slid her hand around his base to cradle his heavy testicles, and she could feel how tight they were with need. Then she drew him deep again and sucked hard.

Aidan's control snapped. With a shout that echoed the cries in the next room, his hands released the chains and closed tightly over her shoulders. He dragged her up into his arms and carried her to the chaise in the corner. As they went, she felt one of his hands reach for something, but then he laid her down on the velvet cushions and fell between her spread legs, and she didn't know anything but him.

"What do you do to me, Lily?" he muttered as he kissed her neck, openmouthed, hot, wet. His hand roughly pushed her skirts up around her waist and tugged down her underthings until he could thrust two fingers into her wet folds. He crooked them, brushing against that spot that made her cry out.

When she reached out for him, he caught her wrists in his free hand and pushed them into the cushions above her head. His other hand left her, even though she cried out in protest and writhed against his hold. Her cry turned louder when she felt the cold metal of manacles snap around her wrists.

"Aidan!" she protested.

He grinned down at her. "I'm not the only one who has been naughty, now, am I?"

"Aidan." She tried to move her bound hands, but the

chain was wrapped around something on the chaise and she was stretched out before him. Under his power. It should have made her panic, scream in protest and fear. Yet somehow as she looked up into his eyes, she felt… safe. Safe, and full of a fresh, hot surge of desire.

She arched up in silent entreaty, and his smile turned satisfied. His hand slid between her legs again, pressing her thighs wider apart. His finger slid into her again, then another and another, delightfully rough and calloused against her sensitive skin. She closed her eyes and gave herself over to the sensations of his touch. He bent his head and his lips slid over her cheekbone, the pulse that beat in her temple.

"I think they're almost done in there," he said.

Lily listened carefully and found that the man's screams had turned to whimpers. "Then you should hurry, shouldn't you?"

His lips curved in a smile against her. "Ah, so sad. I do like having you bound here at my mercy."

"Be nice and I might let you do it again."

"Aren't I always nice, Lily?" His hand eased away from her, and she felt him kneel between her legs, the tip of his manhood stretching her as he slid into her, one slow inch at a time. "Very, very nice."

Lily moaned. He slid deeper, deeper, until suddenly he drew back and plunged in to the hilt. His hips circled over hers, pulling him even closer than she would have thought possible.

"You're being very nice right now," she said. She longed to touch him, to run her hands through his hair and over the taut muscles of his naked back where the shirt fell away, but she was bound. All she could do was arch herself tighter against him, closer until she wasn't sure where he ended and she began. They were as one being.

"Take me, Aidan," she said, and his hips pistoned faster, harder. She met him thrust for thrust, the tension inside of her growing hotter and tighter until she feared she would break with it. She cried out incoherently, her hips twisting under his until the pleasure building in her shattered. She cried out his name.

His body tightened over hers, his hips suddenly still. "Lily," he whispered, just before he came with a deep shudder. He sank down onto the chaise beside her, reaching up to unfasten the manacles.

Lily sighed and turned her face away to stare blindly at the red-painted wall. She suddenly felt so vulnerable, so sad, and she didn't know why. He took her hand in his, and she felt the soft, gentle touch of his lips on the faint red marks on her wrist. She suddenly wanted to snatch her hand away, to curl into a ball and cry.

But there was no time for that, no time to decipher why she suddenly felt that way. The room next to theirs was silent now.

Aidan rolled off the chaise, and she heard him gathering his clothes and putting himself together again. She slowly sat up and shook her skirts down over her legs as she looked for her underthings. She had just found them under the gilded legs of the chaise when the door opened and Jasmine stood there.

She smiled as she studied Lily and Aidan. "Well, now. It looks like you two kept yourselves busy. Marie says you want to find my sister?"

* * *

Aidan held on to Lily's arm as they made their way down the narrow alley. Rough stone walls rose up close on either side, and the smell of rotting garbage and the tang of the nearby river were strong there, but it was strangely quiet. The doors and windows were closed up tightly.

Lily was quiet too. She had said barely a word since they left Madame Marie's, just walked with him and followed his lead as they looked for the address where Jasmine said her sister could usually be found. Her face looked very calm and still under the folds of her shawl, all her emotions hidden from him. Had it all been too much, Marie's place, the rough sex?

"Are you all right?" he asked quietly.

She nodded. "Perfectly so."

She said nothing else, and Aidan decided to leave her to her thoughts—for now. They had an errand to do. But he wouldn't let her hide much longer.

"I think this is the place," he said as he studied the building at the end of the alley. It looked just like all the others, dark and rough, the windows shuttered, but the peeling, black-painted door was marked with mysterious white Oriental symbols. A short flight of stone steps led down to another door at the basement level.

They made their way down the stairs, their boots thudding on the chipped stone, and Aidan pounded on the door. Lily pressed close to his side, still silent and watchful.

A tiny, elderly woman with a shriveled face and tangled gray hair opened the door a crack and peered outside.

"Jasmine sent us to find Ruby," Aidan said. She tried to slam the door, but he blocked it with his boot. "You don't want to turn us away," he said in a hard, unyielding tone.

The woman muttered something in a language that

sounded like Russian or Polish. She glared at him from tiny black eyes, but she pulled the door open.

"Does everyone do what you say?" Lily whispered in his ear.

"If they know what's good for them."

The old woman led them down a dark, narrow corridor and into an open room at the end. It felt almost like stepping into hell, a black, hazy space broken by red-orange circles of light from oil lamps. Sparks flared as pipes were lit and then went out. A thick, sticky-sweet cloud hung over everything.

Lily's fingers convulsed on Aidan's sleeve, and he glanced down at her in concern. She studied the room with a small frown on her brow, and he remembered what she had told him—her mother had been an opium addict.

Had Sandrine been one of those figures slumped on grubby mattresses on the floor, inhaling the smoke from their pipes and falling back with eyes closed, in a stupor? Had Lily watched this every day, breathing the cloying fumes of the drug as her mother's perfume?

The old woman gestured toward a raised couch in the corner. "Miss Ruby," she said, and vanished into the darkness.

Aidan wrapped his arm protectively around Lily's shoulders. "Do you want to wait here?" he asked in a low voice. "I can talk to her, find out what we need to know, and then we can leave."

Lily leaned against him, but she shook her head. "She won't want to talk. She's off in her own world. I know how to get information from someone when they're on opium."

"Did you have to find your mother in places like this?"

"No, she never came to the dens. She didn't smoke it. She drank it in wine, and working at Madame Josephine's had its perks—her bottles were delivered to her." She gave a bitter little smile. "She couldn't help herself."

She hurried toward the couch in the corner, her shoulders held stiff and her head high as if she were marching bravely into hell itself. Aidan caught up with her and they both knelt beside the woman stretched out on her side on the couch, the paraphernalia of opium smoking on a table beside her, the pipe and lamp and the small, sticky gray ball in a dish.

The woman looked much like Jasmine, tall and dark-haired, but she was as thin and pale as an ephemeral ghost. Her hair was tangled where it fell on her shoulders, left bare by a loose bodice. She stared up at them with dull, uninterested eyes. Her bony fingers caressed the pipe.

"Who're you?" she said.

"Your sister Jasmine sent us," Lily said. Her lips were drawn into a tight line as she studied the wasted woman in front of her. Aidan knew he wasn't the only one who could get people to listen.

"Did she now? She knows I won't leave here." Ruby gave a dry laugh that ended on a cough. "She's always trying to rescue me."

"Not this time," Aidan said. "She said you could give us information."

"About what?"

"About the whereabouts of Tom Beaumont."

Ruby's drowsiness vanished, and her eyes narrowed. She tried to sit up but couldn't. "If I knew where that piece of shit was, I would stay far away. I never want to see him again." She turned her head to show a long, thin scar along her jaw, her earlobe sliced away into a mass of scar tissue. "He did *this* to me."

"You're not the only one who would like to see the last of him," Lily said. "That's what we're trying to do. But we need your help."

Ruby gave a soft snort. "You need more than that to take down the likes of Beaumont. But good luck to you."

Aidan grabbed her arm to keep her from rolling away. "When was the last time you saw him?"

Ruby closed her eyes as if to sink back into her stupor. Her arm was limp in his grasp, and he let her go. But Lily bent down and shook her hard by the shoulders. "Where is he?" Lily demanded.

"I don't know," Ruby answered. "But I know someone who might. My friend Sarah, over in the Devil's Acre. She can't stay away from him, the stupid slut."

"Give us her address," Lily said. Once that information was secured, they left Ruby to her opium dreams again. The alleyway was just as deserted as before, but the sky was beginning to lighten and a fog was rolling in off the river. The night wouldn't last much longer.

Lily leaned against Aidan's shoulder and he looked down to see the pale, tired strain on her face. "Where is your family, Lily?" he asked.

"A new play opens tonight," she said wearily. "They won't miss me for a while."

"Then come on," he said, wrapping his arm around her waist. "We'll go back to my lodgings for a few hours."

"Shouldn't we—"

"No," he said firmly. "We'll need our rest and something to eat if we're going to find Beaumont, and you look like you're ready to faint. Come and sleep in my bed for a while."

Chapter Twenty-one

Such a pretty, pretty girl.

Lily felt a soft, fleeting touch on her hair, and she almost screamed until she realized it was only a dream. A hazy, cloudy, smoky dream, but one she couldn't free herself from.

She could smell sweet rose-musk perfume and the heavy, cloying scent of opium that was thick in the back of her throat. She twisted around to see that it was her mother who stroked her hair, who spoke to her softly in that musical French accent. Sandrine lay back on her pink satin chaise, her dark hair trailing around her in mermaid waves, her eyes slumberous from the drug. She trailed her white, soft fingers down Lily's cheek.

"So very pretty," she murmured. "Just like me, non?"

"No," Lily whispered. She was overwhelmed by the flood of so many emotions she had suppressed and denied for so long. Grief and memory, regret, love. "No, I'm not like you."

Sandrine laughed. "But of course you are, ma petite. You can't escape what you are, where you come from. I am part of you." Her smile turned teasing. "Your fine gentleman seems to appreciate that about you. My talent. The touch of the gutter..."

"No!" Lily frantically shook her head, but Sandrine just laughed. She reached for her glass of wine, but it spilled, a torrent of bright bloodred on the pink satin and her mother's white skin.

Lily tried to run from it, but a rough hand caught her and spun her around. She found herself caught by Tom Beaumont, who laughed at her struggles and her screams. The more she tried to flee, the more trapped she became.

"Please, please..."

"Please!" Lily sat up straight, and for an instant, she didn't know where she was. The remnants of the dream clung to her, like the last cold wisps of a fog, and she half feared she was a child again, huddled in the meager shelter of a stone doorway. But then she heard a breath beside her, and she twisted around to see Aidan sleeping on the bed, and she remembered they were in his lodgings.

When they stumbled in during the sunrise hour, they had fallen fully dressed amid the bedclothes and down into exhausted slumber. Aidan lay sprawled on his back, his arms flung out. His hair was rumpled over his face, and Lily sighed as she studied him.

How much he had done for her, this man. He had chased villains all over London, through slums and brothels and gutters, fought and ran and literally carried her when she needed it. She had never had a champion before. She had always been alone. But now, even with Tom Beaumont at large in the city, even with the past so close she could reach out and touch it like a bony-fingered phantom, she had somehow never felt *less* alone.

Aidan was so much more than she would have thought him to be. And he made her begin to think she could be more too.

"Oh, Aidan," she whispered. "I am so sorry I dragged you into this." She tucked the loose blankets around his shoulders and slid out of bed. She couldn't sleep any longer, but he needed to.

Lily went to the window and eased back the edge of the curtain to peer outside. It was still night, but the sky was starting to turn pale gray at the edges. Soon the streetlamps would be put out and a new day would begin, but she wanted to hold that light back and stay in this quiet, still moment, where she was with Aidan and nothing could touch them.

She glanced back at the bed where he slept, and her heart ached at the sight of his face against the rumpled sheets. When had she let her caution down enough for him to slip inside? She couldn't remember—it seemed he had always been there, always been a part of her. When he was torn out of her life again, would something inside of her rip open and bleed?

"Oh, Aidan," she whispered. She spun away from the sight of him and sat down at a desk in the corner, seeking some kind of distraction. There were haphazard stacks of books there and a pile of manuscript pages closely covered with Aidan's bold, black handwriting. Several of the words and lines were crossed out and overwritten with others.

Lily noticed the familiar cadence of stage directions

and dialogue and remembered when he told her he wanted to write plays the first night they met. So he *did* write plays, here in the quiet of his room. What did he pour out onto the page? Unable to help herself, she reached for the top page and scanned the words written there as if they would give her some clue to the enigmatic man who had come to mean too much to her.

To her surprise, it was not a tale of historical drama and heroism or a drawing room romance, which were all the rage now on the London stage. Instead it was a dark story set in places like barrooms and Madame Marie's establishment, populated by people who faced the gritty realities of life every day. As she read on, drawn deeper into the plot, she saw that Aidan had a true gift for words. He had captured the rhythm of speech perfectly, drawing pictures of the characters' inner beings through their words and their interactions with each other.

The main character, Nell, was a milliner who kept all her suitors at bay with a sharp wit. One man, a sailor named Will, was obviously meant for her, but too much stood in the way of their love—Nell's ambition to leave the millinery trade, Will's work, another handsome scoundrel who courted Nell. They were surrounded by the world of music halls and barrooms, by Nell's friends and enemies, shopgirls, servants, laborers, all of them with their own dreams. Their own joys and sorrows.

It was an entire world populated by people who felt real and whole, so true to life.

But all too soon the pages were done, the play ending in the middle of a scene of dangerous action. Lily nearly cursed when she turned a paper over and saw there was no more. The play had taken her out of herself completely and into the world Aidan created. A world populated by people she knew so well.

She laid her hand on the last page and blinked back the prickle of sudden tears from her eyes.

"Lily?" Aidan said from the bed, his voice hoarse from sleep. He sat up, his shoulders tense as he scanned the room.

"I'm over here," she answered.

"What are you doing?"

"Discovering that you, Aidan Huntington, are a terrible fraud."

Aidan swung his long legs out of the bed and moved slowly across the room to the desk. His eyes were narrowed. "Did you read that?"

"Yes. And I can't believe you go through your life pretending to be such a care-for-nothing rake when you have this rare gift. You *see* people; you capture them here in your words." Lily swallowed hard. "Why do you not reveal yourself? This would do any theater proud."

In answer, Aidan scowled and snatched the pages off the desk. They fluttered to the floor. "No one is meant to see that. What would the world say about a duke's son who dares to write about barkeeps and milliners?"

"Aidan!" Lily jumped up from her chair and knelt to gather up the papers. The precious pages had given her a glimpse of Aidan's soul. "You could produce it anonymously. No one would have to know. But if your family realized—"

He gave a bitter laugh. "Don't you think they already see me as enough of a scapegrace, Lily? This writing is for me. That is all." He knelt beside her and took the papers to put them away in a drawer.

"But it shouldn't be." She reached up and caught his

face between her hands to force him to look at her. "I know what it means to love your family and yet not to truly belong with them, Aidan. To always feel…apart. Alone. To always be watching life, pretending at it, and never being true to yourself."

"Lily." Aidan seized her hands tightly in his, and in his beautiful eyes she saw something she had never glimpsed there before. Pain. "Your parents and your siblings, they love you. You do belong with them. But I never should have been a duke's son. I write those plays to remember the world I do understand, but I don't belong there either."

Lily shook her head. "I love my family, too, but I always know I'm not a real St. Claire. I always remember how my life was before them, no matter how hard I try to forget. I remember my real mother. And since Tom Beaumont came back"—she shuddered—"I remember him too. I was almost able to convince myself those days with him were only a nightmare, but they were too real."

She knew she couldn't tell this tale if Aidan looked at her with those clear blue eyes that saw everything. She pushed herself to her feet and went to the window. She pressed her palms to the cool glass and stared down at the empty, fog-laced street below.

Aidan seemed to sense what she needed him to do and stayed where he was, just listening to her in silence.

"I told you I ran away from Madame Josephine's after my mother died," she said. "And that Tom Beaumont was the one who found me. He had me steal for him but not prostitute myself, which is what I was escaping from at Madame Josephine's. I made friends with some of the other children. I had food, a place to sleep. It didn't seem so bad. Until…"

Her voice broke, and she heard Aidan rise to his feet. She held up her hand to warn him back. She would break now if he touched her. "I have never told anyone this part of the story, Aidan. I thought I really could escape my mother's life, that as bad as mine was, it was not *that* bad. But Tom had known of my mother. She was famous in certain circles. That was why he sought me out. And he said it would be a shame to let my familial . . . talents . . . go to waste. When I protested and tried to run, he . . . he took me anyway. He raped me. He said when I was properly trained, I could go to one of his brothels or out onto the streets. But the St. Claires found me before it could happen again, and I . . . I . . ."

She did break off then, a ragged sob escaping before she could catch it. She pressed her fingers over her face. He would hate her now, turn from her in disgust, this extraordinary man who was unlike any other she had ever known. She had never told anyone what Tom really did to her, not even her parents, and for a moment she was lost again in the horror of it all.

"Now you see how . . . how filthy I really am," she said. Lily rubbed her hands hard over her aching eyes, as if she could dash away the old images.

Suddenly she felt Aidan's arms around her waist, and her eyes flew open to see that he knelt before her, staring up as he held her. The pale gray light of earliest dawn fell across the perfect angles of his face, and written there she saw the strangest mix of fury, determination, and deepest tenderness.

She had the unreal feeling of being in a poem or a fairy tale in that moment, where the knight swore fealty to his lady and vowed to be her champion. It was as if whatever was hidden inside of him reached out to her own secret heart and wrapped around it, tying her to him.

"Lily," he said roughly. "I promise you I will find him, and this time there will be no constables, no prisons. I will kill him myself, and he will never hurt you again."

Lily couldn't speak through the ache in her throat, and she shook her head. Aidan was more a threat to her than Tom Beaumont had ever been. For Aidan held her heart, and she feared she would never be able to reclaim it. All those careful years of guarding her emotions, keeping herself apart, they were all for nothing. Aidan had claimed her in one effortless smile.

She threaded her fingers through his hair and stared down at him for one endless and yet far-too-brief instant.

Suddenly there was a loud knock at the door, and Lily let him go and turned her face away. Aidan rose smoothly to his feet, and to her relief, he went to the door with just one searching look at her face. If he had pressed her, if he had kissed her, she feared she would shatter and never be able to put herself together again.

She heard him move away into the sitting room and open the door, then heard the low, harsh murmur of voices. She quickly found her shoes and smoothed her hair, managing to somewhat compose herself before he returned.

His expression was unreadable as he held up a hastily scrawled note. "It's from David," he said. "He's found something."

Chapter Twenty-two

Aidan held on to Lily's hand as they made their way through the narrow lanes of the Devil's Acre. The night was over now, dawn creeping along the dingy alleys, and all the thieves and whores had scattered to their hidey-holes. There were only laundresses and dockworkers making their way to another day's work, yawning behind their caps, to see Aidan and Lily as they hurried by.

Lily had said nothing since they left Aidan's lodgings. She let him hold on to her, but he sensed she had drawn back into herself, her eyes shuttered against him. He wouldn't drag her out, not yet, but he knew something profound had shifted between them when he put his arms around her and swore he would kill Tom Beaumont for what the man had done to her.

He didn't want to merely kill the bastard; he wanted to rip him limb from limb, slowly, painfully, for putting that terrible flash of pain in Lily's eyes. Every bit of Aidan's civilized, aristocratic veneer dropped away, and he had only instinct to go on now. If he was alone right now, Aidan knew he would hunt Beaumont down like the animal he was and tear him apart.

But he was not alone. He had Lily with him, and she had to come first.

Aidan glanced back at her. She had drawn her shawl up over her head and around her shoulders to cover her costume, and she looked back at him steadily from under the folds of black cloth. That morning, they had revealed themselves to each other in a way that was so raw and real that Aidan had felt torn open. No one else had ever done that to him.

No one else had ever been more important than himself. But now Lily was. She was not just inspiration for his writing, not just a good fuck or a distraction. She was… more. And he didn't know what to do with that new, terrible realization. It was something so completely foreign to him.

And whatever had happened between them seemed to have startled her too. She had withdrawn from him, retreated behind her protective walls. If he wanted her to come back to him—and he didn't know yet if he did—he would have to lay siege to her all over again.

But for now, they had to find Beaumont and take care of him once and for all.

"All right?" Aidan asked. "I think this is the place David described in his message."

Lily nodded, still silent. She followed him up a narrow wooden staircase that was built haphazardly against the side of an ancient, half-timbered building. Most of the windows were open, letting out the sounds of crying children and sleep-heavy arguments, along with the smells of frying onions and boiled cabbage, the tang of harsh lye soap.

At the top of the stairs, a door flapped open. The old wood was splintered, as if it had been violently bashed in, and broken pottery was scattered across the floor just inside. A thin wailing came from an inner room. Aidan held Lily behind him and peered inside.

David stood near the dingy whitewashed wall, his arms crossed over his chest as he watched something impassively. He had put on a rough wool coat but otherwise looked as he had earlier, with his collarless shirt and wild long hair. No bruises or blood.

"David," Aidan said quietly, and his brother turned to look at him.

"Ah, there you are," David said calmly, as if they were meeting in a ballroom or at a St. James club. "I see you got my message."

Aidan led Lily into the room, still holding her close at his side. "What is this?" Aidan asked David.

"I know a few people at the docks, just as you do, brother," David said. "Perhaps you remember Molly?"

Aidan nodded brusquely. Molly—one of his brother's women. David didn't indulge in romance often, but when he did, his women remained intensely attached and loyal to him even after it ended. And for a man who refused to leave the countryside often, he had a wide acquaintance.

"Well, Molly heard from one of her friends who works the streets that one of Beaumont's mistresses had rooms here, and he has been seen skulking around after his escape. It turned out to be that Sarah you sent me word of. I got here only to find that Beaumont had already left, after taking out his temper on the poor woman."

Aidan studied the doorway into the other room. The wailing had stopped, and now he could hear the murmur of women's voices, harshly accented. "She knows where he's gone?"

David shrugged. "I could get little out of her. Perhaps you'll have better luck, brother. You have a softer touch than me when it comes to the ladies." His gaze slid over Lily.

Lily stared back at him. "I think that your old nanny was quite right," she said.

David's brow arched. "I beg your pardon?"

"You two *were* changeling children, left in the duke's nursery by dark fairies," she said, and David threw back his head to laugh.

"So we were...Mrs. Nichols, is it?" David said. "We are a terrible disappointment to our father."

"But we do know how to get things done when we need to," Aidan added.

"I'm beginning to see that," Lily murmured.

"I'll go see if I can persuade this Sarah to confide in me," Aidan said. He made his way into the other chamber, David and Lily close behind him. It was a bedroom of sorts, with a narrow straw mattress pushed against one wall and a trunk spilling clothes out onto the dirty floor. A young woman huddled on the bed, her head down and the tangles of her blond hair falling over her face. Her bony shoulders, wrapped in a thin dressing gown, heaved with sobs. An older woman knelt beside her, whispering in her ear and holding out a beaker of ale.

"Hush now, girl," the woman said. "He's gone. You need to get yourself together."

"He'll be back," the girl sniffled. "He always is. Even when you think he's gone..."

"And when might that be, Sarah?" Aidan asked quietly.

The woman's head shot up, tense as a fox run to earth, and Aidan saw with a wrench that her thin face was bruised. She wiped at the smear of dried blood under her nose. "Who are you, then?"

"This is my brother," David said, using that soft, coaxing voice that always soothed his wild horses. "We were sent here by Molly, remember?"

Sarah nodded warily. "I remember. Well, I don't know when he'll be back, so you'd better go look for him somewhere else. Does he owe you money or somethin'? I told him not to mess with toffs." Her dull blue eyes slid past Aidan and widened when she glimpsed Lily at his shoulder. She went white under her livid bruises, as if she glimpsed a ghost. "You!"

"Hello, Sarah," Lily said. "It's been a while, hasn't it?"

Aidan glanced down at her to find that she watched the other woman calmly. Too calmly. It reminded him of her demeanor with Marie in the brothel. "You know her?"

Lily nodded. "She worked for Tom when I did, as a pickpocket around the theaters. I guess she never left. I should have known when Ruby told us." She slipped away from him and went to kneel beside the bed. "What happened here, Sarah?"

Sarah stared at her. "He's after you, you know, Lil. You got away from him back then, and he can't have that."

"I know. I've had a couple of run-ins with him since he got back to London," Lily said. "Where is he now?"

"Gone to find you, hasn't he? He took the last of my money and smashed up the place, ranting about you and those fancy St. Claires. Stinking drunk, he was," Sarah said. "I'd get out of town if I was you, Lil."

"It looks like you should have gone a long time ago, Sarah." Lily's voice was calm, but Aidan could see the taut line of her back and the way her fingers trembled slightly.

"We can't all be as lucky as you," Sarah said sullenly. "But your luck can't hold."

"Where has he gone?" Lily asked.

"I dunno for sure. He kept going on about the St. Claires and the theater, maybe Jimmy something."

"James? The theater?" Lily looked back at Aidan, panic flashing in her eyes. "The Majestic?"

"How should I know? I haven't worked the theaters in years. But he thinks you'll be there, wherever it is."

"Let's go," Aidan said. He took Lily's arm and drew her to her feet.

Lily untied the purse at her waist and pressed it into Sarah's hand. "Go now, Sarah, leave London," she said softly.

Sarah just nodded and turned her face away. Lily went with Aidan, but he saw the hollow despair in her eyes, felt how taut her arm was under his touch, as if she would break. He saw her thoughts in that instant—she could have been that bruised woman huddled on the bed, emaciated, old beyond her years, abused.

But she would never have those fears again, not if he could help it. Nothing would ever hurt her again.

Chapter Twenty-three

Lily heard the loud voices from the patrons as she led Aidan through the back door of the theater. There was still time before the curtain rose on that night's play, but the aristocratic audience was already gathering in the boxes, waiting for another magical night at the Majestic. The excitement was palpable in the air, and the smells of greasepaint and candle smoke hung heavy. From somewhere behind the scenery she could hear the pounding of hammers for last-minute repairs and her father's raised voice as he worried about the progress. Just like an ordinary night at the theater for the St. Claires.

But Lily's heart thudded loudly in her ears, and her skin prickled with sharp awareness. Something wasn't right here.

"I'm going to look in the dressing rooms," she told Aidan and his brother, who were close at her back.

"I will go with you," Aidan said. His firm voice brooked no arguments.

"What can I do?" David asked.

"Check the boxes," Lily suggested. She gestured to the gleaming gold and white boxes above their heads, swathed in red velvet draperies and dignified silence. But anything could lurk in their shadows. As David strode away, she took Aidan's hand and led him to the stairs that went past the orchestra pit and down into the secret world backstage.

She had never realized before just how many places there were to hide in a theater. Twisting, narrow corridors, so much like the streets of the old slums, led off in every direction, dressing rooms and storage closets and rehearsal spaces. Scenery flats and props were piled haphazardly along the walls, and she could hear the muffled sounds of voices from the stage above their heads.

But the backstage area itself was eerily deserted. Every shadow cast by a carelessly hung costume or false suit of armor seemed to move with menace. Lily shivered and held tightly to Aidan's hand.

At the foot of the stairs that led up to the family's dressing rooms, she paused to take a deep breath. She tried to listen, to hear past the familiar echoes and creaks of a theater. He was here somewhere, Tom Beaumont. She could taste it in the sour nausea at the back of her throat, feel it in the tingle of her fingertips. Every instinct she had ever had while living on the streets, every sense that kept her alive back then, was on alert.

But she wasn't alone now, as she had been back then. She had Aidan at her back.

She looked back at him, and he watched her steadily. His very calmness made her feel calm, too, and as he looked into her eyes, he seemed to see what she was thinking. He shifted on his booted feet, his coat falling back, and she saw the dagger and pistol at his waist.

Suddenly a sharp cry, abruptly cut off, shattered the

eerie calm of backstage. It seemed to float down the stairs before vanishing, leaving the quiet even more terribly fraught than before.

"Isabel!" Lily cried. She lifted her hem and ran as fast as she could up the rest of the stairs and down the corridor lined with closed doors.

Small windows set high in the wall let in the pale yellow moonlight, which illuminated one open door at the end of the row. It was Isabel's dressing room, the most easily accessible of the small rooms, and Lily paused only for an instant to draw her knife from the strap above her boot before she skidded through the doorway.

"No," she whispered. "No, no, no."

Aidan pushed her back to the wall, blocking her with his body, but over his shoulder she could see the wreck of the small room. Isabel's dressing table stool was overturned, the tray of her greasepaints scattered and smeared over the floor. Her velvet Hero costume lay in a crumpled heap, one sleeve stained with a horrible red streak that looked like blood.

But Isabel was gone.

Lily pushed at Aidan's shoulders and he let her go. She leaned her palms on the ruins of Isabel's dressing table, her heart gone still, and that was when she saw the crudely scrawled note under her sister's overturned scent bottle.

Come get me, Lily girl.

And a perfect icy stillness came over her. It was as if she could hear and smell everything so much more acutely, but her emotions and fears had vanished. She crumpled the torn scrap of paper in her fist.

"Oh, I will," she murmured. And Tom would be very, very sorry when she did.

"Lily," Aidan said, and she felt his touch on her arm. "Where did he go?"

She closed her eyes and just listened. She heard a door slam somewhere in the warren of corridors, and she knew. "The roof. He's gone to the roof."

"I don't suppose it would do any good if I ordered you to stay here, to fetch David and your brothers while I went after Beaumont alone?" he said tightly.

Lily shook her head. "You know me better than that, Aidan. It's me he's after. If I'm there, he'll let my sister go."

Aidan's studied her, and for an instant, she was sure he would grab her and tie her up and leave her here while he went after Tom alone. She turned, ready to run, but then he gave a brusque nod.

"Stay close to me, then," he commanded.

Lily brought him to the door at the end of the corridor that opened onto a winding staircase. It led up to the wings of the stage, the quickest way from the dressing rooms when it was time for an actor's entrance. Beyond that it opened into the walkways above the stage and eventually the flat roof. Lily knew that the stagehands and her brothers often went up there to sneak a smoke behind her mother's back, but otherwise it was usually deserted. The play had begun onstage, but she could hear the actors' words faltering as Hero did not make her appearance.

Then she heard another muffled scream and a dull thud, and a man's rough voice muttered a curse. Not the roof, then, but the walkways. Lily pointed at a doorway and Aidan nodded. He drew out his pistol and held it easily in one hand while the other closed around her arm.

They ran up the sloping platform that led to the first

walkway. Here they were high above the stage, among hanging scenery waiting to be lowered and the fringed swags of the curtain. It was dark up there, the lights of the stage barely reaching the railings, and between the wooden slats of the floor there was only empty space. The air was stale and dusty, and the walkway swayed as Lily and Aidan stepped out onto it. They could hardly walk next to each other on the narrow space, and the voices from the stage were only a vague echo there.

"Let go of me, you cocksucking bastard!" Lily heard Isabel cry. The crudity in her sister's sweet voice would have been laughable if not for the fear lurking there. Holding on to Aidan's shoulder, Lily peered frantically into the shadows halfway over the stage.

Isabel wore a white dressing gown over her chemise and petticoats, a gleaming beacon of light. One of the shoulders was ripped away, and Tom Beaumont held her arm in a bruising grip. She looked terrified, her eyes wide and frantic, but she was fighting him with everything she had.

Tom's fist went back and struck Isabel across the cheek. Her head snapped back, and she cried out in pain.

Fury unlike any Lily had ever known washed over her at the sight of the bruise on her sweet, innocent sister's face. Aidan rushed forward, only to be backhanded by Tom. Aidan fell hard to the walkway and lay still, and Lily screamed out at the sight.

"Tom," she called out. "Let her go. It's me you want, isn't it? Only me. She has no part in this."

Tom twisted around to look at Lily, still holding on to Isabel's arm as she sagged toward the floor. A terrible smile moved across his face. "I knew this would bring you out, Lily my girl. You always were a loyal one, except to me. And when I was the one who took care of you too. After all I did, you betrayed me."

"I'm here now," she said. "Let her go. I'll do what you want."

"Lily, no," Isabel sobbed. "No, I won't let you do this for me."

"Such devotion," Tom sneered. But he did let Isabel go, pushing her away hard so she stumbled to her knees. Isabel clung to the railing above her head.

Lily couldn't hear Aidan behind her, but she knew he was there. She could feel his presence. She could only fleetingly hope he would stay hidden in the shadows where Tom couldn't see him. Not yet. But she kept all her attention focused on Tom, on every tiny movement he made and every flicker in his eyes as she tried to predict his next move.

"Why did you come back here, Tom?" she said quietly. "There's nothing for you in London."

"You know me better than that, Lily," he answered. He leaned back against the railing and drew out his knife from inside his mended coat. He pared his nails, that gesture she remembered too well, a lazy action that preceded violence. "I never do forget a betrayal. I always repay it, even if it takes years. And I've had lots of time to think about you."

"I never betrayed you."

"So it was just coincidence I got caught and transported right after your fancy new family took you in? I don't think so, my girl. You owe me." He flipped his blade in his hand as he slowly smiled at her. "You were always my cleverest girl, Lily. Not as pretty as your mum, but you haven't done so badly for yourself. We could work together now, like we should have all along. That's why I came back here—I heard you were in a good position to help your old friends now."

Lily remembered the way she had had to "work" for him when she was a child, and she shuddered. "What do you want from me, Tom?" she asked again.

"Oh, Lil, you know what I want. I want what you gave that pretty duke's son. I want what's under your fancy skirts, like it used to be." Suddenly Tom's eyes shifted. Lily fell back a step, but he was bigger and just a bit faster. He lunged forward and grabbed her hard by the waist, dragging her up against his body, his scarred face pressing close to hers.

Lily almost gagged at his scent of smoke and stale onions, unwashed skin and greasy wool, and that acrid smell that was all his. It sent her hurtling back into the past, to that old mindless fear.

"You destroyed everything I had worked for, my fine girl," he whispered as he brushed his mouth over her temple. "Now I want it back, starting with you."

He pressed an openmouthed kiss to her lips, hot and wet, and when she cried out, he pressed his tongue deep into her throat. His hand closed over her breast, his fingers cruelly pinching her nipple. Lily felt like she was drowning, smothering in terror.

Running on instinct, she tried to drive her knee between his legs. She got in a glancing blow before he jerked back, and she bit hard at his cheek until she tasted blood.

"You filthy little whore!" he shouted. "Now I'll have to teach you *and* your bitch sister a lesson."

He backhanded her hard across the face, a blow that sent her sprawling onto the floor. Her head landed against the wood with a loud thud, and for an instant, she couldn't see anything but a shower of sparks behind her eyes. Everything went hot and dark around her.

Then she heard Isabel scream and the pounding of footsteps up the stairs from the stage. She felt her sister's hand on her shoulder and heard her sob, "Lily, no, no."

Tom growled out a string of curses, and his hand closed around Lily's ankle to drag her out of Isabel's grasp. She had never felt so dazed or weak, but she managed to twist her body onto her stomach and reach out for the railing. This could not be the end! She hadn't seen her family again. She hadn't made sure Isabel was safe. She hadn't...

She hadn't told Aidan she loved him.

"No!" she screamed, and kicked out blindly.

Tom cursed again and ripped at her skirt as she tried to fight him, tried not to slip down into unconsciousness. Suddenly, he was gone, and she sprawled back down onto the floor.

She pushed herself up on her hands and twisted around to find it was Aidan who had pulled Tom away from her and was now bashing the man's head into the floor. He held Tom's arm behind his back as he pressed his knee hard into the villain's back.

Aidan held him there effortlessly, beating him with a frightening, almost methodical efficiency. Lily could see that Tom was struggling with all his considerable strength, but he couldn't get away from Aidan. The air was filled with the sound of Tom's shouts, the thuds as he hit the floor, Isabel's sobs. She heard her brother's shouts as they reached the top of the walkway ramp, obviously having heard the fight from the stage below. She heard her own ragged breath as it tore in and out of her lungs.

But Aidan made no sound at all. And Lily had never seen such a terrifying look on anyone's face as he wore now, a calm lack of any expression as he stared down at the man he was beating to a bloody pulp.

"Aidan!" David shouted. "Enough, brother!"

Dominic pulled Lily to her feet, holding her steady as she staggered on her numb legs. She saw Brendan lifting Isabel into his arms. Lily's head pounded painfully, and her whole body ached, yet she couldn't turn away from the horrible sight of Aidan and Tom.

At David's words, Aidan finally glanced up. His eyes flickered over her for an instant, but the sight of her seemed to awaken some faint spark of life deep in their dark blue depths. He lowered Tom to the floor, at the last second flipping him over onto his back. Tom's nose was broken, his eye swollen shut, and his face covered with blood.

"Please, Aidan," Lily whispered. Everything about Aidan now showed him as a man ready to kill in an instant. But she couldn't let him do that, not for her. "Please don't."

He didn't look at her again, but something seemed to shift in his body. As Lily watched, he hauled Tom to his feet and pressed him back hard against the railing as Aidan's fists twisted in his coat.

"If you dare touch her again," he said, so calm, so elegant, "I will slice off your dick and feed it to my mother's lapdogs. In fact, I just might do that anyway."

"I will help you with that, Lord Aidan," Dominic said. Lily stared up at him, startled to find he watched Aidan with a glint of agreement and near-respect in his eyes. He still held on to Lily's arms as she swayed dizzily.

"You see," Aidan said, still in that horribly polite voice, "you are quite outnumbered here, Tom Beaumont. No one would blink if I gutted you right here like you deserve. But I hate to make such a mess in front of ladies. Would you rather I just hand you over to Her Majesty's authorities? I am quite sure there will be no chance for any escape this time. Or maybe I could just give you one little push..."

Below them the audience gasped, caught by the real-life drama enfolding before them.

"No," Lily sobbed. "No, Aidan, please."

"Aidan." David stepped forward and held up a coil of rope in his hand. "You can let him go now."

Aidan twisted his fist against Tom's throat until the man choked, and for a moment, Lily was sure he would go against his own words and kill Tom anyway. Then Aidan pushed Tom back and to the side, as if he could no longer dirty his hands, and stepped away as David and Dominic moved forward.

Lily saw only a flicker of movement from Tom's arm, and she cried out. But it was too late. Tom's blade sank deep into Aidan's shoulder, sending Aidan staggering back. David caught him before he could hit the floor.

As the blade dragged free from Aidan's body, Tom's momentum made him stumble into the railing. As Lily watched, horrified, he fell over it and vanished from sight. She could hear his shouts as he tumbled down and down onto the stage, then a loud thud and... nothing.

Tom was gone in an instant, yet all she could see was Aidan, the blood seeping onto his shirt, his face blanched of color as he went an ashen gray. His brother lowered him down to the floor, and Lily choked back a sob as she staggered to his side.

"Oh, God, Aidan, no," she whispered. She reached down and tore open his shirt to examine the raw, jagged wound that marred his perfect, smooth, golden skin. She bent down and kissed his lips. They were cold under hers, and she kissed him again, trying frantically to make him warm, make him well, to force her own life into him. She dashed away the tears prickling at her eyes and shook her head in violent denial.

Someone held a strip of white cloth in front of her, and she glanced up to see that Dominic knelt beside her, holding out the scarf from his costume. She folded it quickly into a tight pad and pressed it hard to Aidan's shoulder, trying to stop the bleeding. It was soaked through too quickly.

"I'm going for the doctor," Dominic said, and as he hurried away, David hauled Aidan up to sit propped against his chest.

"It's only a scratch," Aidan said hoarsely. "Don't cry, Lily. You know I'm not worth it."

Lily dashed the back of her hand over her cheek. She hadn't even realized she was crying until that instant, but her face was wet with tears. *So stupid.* Tears were not what would save Aidan now. And she was the one who had brought him here.

Suddenly Isabel was beside her, ripping apart her dressing gown to make fresh bandages. She helped Lily wrap them around Aidan's shoulder, all of them struggling to keep him from fading into unconsciousness.

"He's only doing this to garner attention from pretty

ladies, aren't you, Aidan?" David said teasingly, but Lily could hear the edge of fear in his voice.

"You don't need to go to such extremes for me, Aidan," Lily said. "You already have my full attention, don't you know? You already have me."

The audience was loud again as the ushers tried to herd them out of the theater, but she hardly heard it. She knew only Aidan. "I'll beat you senseless if you dare die on me now," she said as she tied off the ends of the bandage. "We aren't nearly done yet."

"I'm going to hold you to that," he said. Then his eyes closed, and his head slumped back on his brother's shoulder.

"No!" Lily cried. "No, Aidan, no..." She wrapped her arms tightly around his chest and held on to him. She couldn't lose him, her lover, her champion, the man who showed her the beauty and fun of life. She couldn't go on without him.

She was only vaguely aware of being gently lifted away from him and held in Brendan's arms as a doctor knelt beside Aidan with his black bag and stagehands brought in a stretcher. Her head felt so light, everything so hazy and cold around her. Her head pounded as if it would split open, and she shivered.

"Lily!" she heard someone shout, just before she fainted away.

Chapter Twenty-four

"Aidan, wake up. You can't lie here forever just so pretty girls can weep over you and bathe your fevered brow."

Aidan heard his brother's deep voice as if it echoed down a long, dark tunnel. He struggled up from the haze of sleep, but it felt like crawling out of that tunnel into the light again. His dreams drifted farther and farther away. He pried his gritty eyes open and found himself staring up at the ceiling of his own bedchamber.

And his whole body ached, especially his throbbing shoulder. The sunlight from the window pierced into his head, and he winced as he turned away. The pain reminded him that it wasn't just a dream; it was real. Tom Beaumont, the theater, the knife—all of it.

Aidan remembered Lily crumpled on the walkway, so still when Tom Beaumont pushed her down and she hit her head. He remembered the terrible grief and fury that overcame him in the instant when he was sure he had lost her. The feeling that everything was over and he had nothing to lose, nothing to live for.

"Lily," he growled, and pushed back the bedclothes tucked tightly around him to sit up. David held him down.

"She's fine," David said in a soothing voice Aidan had never heard his brother use on humans before, only on temperamental horses. Aidan was sure then he must have been dying if David was going easy on him now.

But Aidan shoved against his hand. "Where is she?"

"Her brother came to fetch her, to take her home so she could pack some clothes," David said, struggling to hold Aidan down. "Damn it, man, don't make me tie you down! She'll be furious if she gets back to find you out of bed when the doctor said you should rest. And I don't want to face her temper. Your woman is a veritable Valkyrie when she's angry."

"Yes, she is." Aidan slowly sank back down onto the bed and closed his eyes. "She wasn't hurt?"

"Just a few bruises. She wouldn't let the doctor look at them, though. She hasn't been away from this bed until her brother made her leave this morning." David sat back in his chair once he was sure Aidan would stay still, a flash of raw relief in his eyes. "She'll be happy to see you awake. We were afraid there for a while. You were raving with fever."

Aidan frowned. "How long have I been here?"

"Three days now. Mother sent a basketful of calves'-foot jelly, and I stole some of Father's good wine when you want it. I convinced them to stay away until you're feeling better." David paused, tapping his calloused fingertips on the chair arm. "I thought you might want to tell them about Mrs. Nichols yourself."

Aidan nodded and turned his head to stare out the window. The sun was a pale yellow in a vivid blue sky. "Beaumont is dead?"

"Quite dead. And the inquiry was a very short one.

Her Majesty's government commends you on your heroic actions."

"Heroic," Aidan snorted. "I should have killed the man in the first place, not trusted in the prison to hold him. Then Lily would never have gone through this."

"I doubt she holds it against you in any way, considering how carefully she's nursed you these last few days."

"I hold it against myself."

"Then you are too hard on yourself, Aidan. I never would have thought it of you. And you have a second chance now," David said. "What will you do with it?"

Aidan closed his eyes, and for an instant, every fear he had when he'd thought he lost Lily came back to him. "I'm going to marry Lily and take her away from here, if she'll have me. I'm not going to lose her again."

David just nodded, as if the news that his brother meant to marry a St. Claire, a greengrocer's widow, a child of the slums, was of no surprise to him at all. "Where will you go?"

"Anywhere she wants to. Italy, maybe. Paris, Zurich. But preferably somewhere warm and beautiful." Somewhere he could spend the rest of his life making her smile, making her forget.

"Good luck to you, then," David said.

"And what will *you* do?"

"Me? Go back to the country, of course. I've had enough of London life for a while, as adventurous as you've made it, Aidan."

Aidan opened his eyes and studied his brother's face. A half-smile lingered on David's lips, but his eyes were shadowed. "What of your lady from the assembly? Did you ever find her?"

David's smile widened. "I did. In a most unexpected place."

"And?"

There was a sudden knock at the door. "Come in," Aidan called, vowing to get more out of his brother later.

It was Freddy Bassington, his shock of red hair bright in the dim room. He held a hamper in his hands, no doubt more invalid's jelly. He grinned when he saw Aidan sitting up against the pillows.

"You're alive!" Freddy cried. He dumped the hamper on the dressing table and rushed over to shake Aidan's hand enthusiastically.

"Was there some doubt?" Aidan said as he extracted his hand.

"Rumors have been flying all over town," Freddy said. "You're quite the *on dit* now."

"Until a new elopement or affair," Aidan said. "Do sit down, Freddy, and quit hovering."

Freddy laughed and dropped onto the chair next to David's. "I had to see for myself you were well. And to say thank you."

"Thanks for what?"

"I received my letters back last week," Freddy said. "Burned 'em all. It's the last time I write to a lady, I promise."

Aidan doubted that. Freddy would be in love again next week. But Lily had returned the letters? What had changed her mind about trusting?

They talked for a while longer, about trivial matters of gossip and mutual friends, until Aidan heard the sitting room door open and the murmur of voices. Lily hurried into the bedchamber, her glowering blond brother behind her. A bright smile lip up her face when she saw Aidan awake, and she rushed over to the bed, ignoring everyone else in the room.

"Aidan," she said softly. "How are you feeling? Is the fever gone?"

Aidan smiled up at her. He had never seen anything as beautiful in his life as the soft curve of her lips as she smiled at him. "Perhaps you should kiss my brow and check for yourself. And then kiss other things and make them better too..."

Lily laughed. "Flirting already? You must feel better." Then she did just that, framing his face gently in her gloved hands and pressing her lips to his forehead.

"Umm-hmm," David coughed. "Perhaps that is our cue to leave you alone."

Lily twisted around to smile at him, but her smile faded when she saw Freddy sitting there staring at her. "Mr. Bassington," she murmured.

"M-Mrs. Nichols," he stammered. "I wasn't expecting to see you here."

"Nor I you. I trust you received my package?" Lily said.

"I did, yes. Th-thank you."

David drew Freddy and Dominic St. Claire out of the room, closing the door behind them. Aidan could hear the sound of their voices in the sitting room and the clatter of glasses as they drank his father's wine, but he was alone with Lily at last. There was so very much he needed to say to her, to make her understand, make her marry him.

But for once in his life, now when they were so very important, words failed him.

Lily untied the ribbons of her bonnet and slowly set it aside before she glanced in Aidan's small shaving mirror and smoothed her hair. She couldn't stop peeking at Aidan's reflection in the glass, trying to reassure herself that he was there, that he was alive and breathing and whole. That he had not been stolen from her.

Those hours of sitting by his bed, listening to his nightmares, frantically trying to get him to take the medicines, bathing his fevered skin, had been torture. She had feared the bed where they had made love would be his deathbed. *She* had brought him to that, the man she loved, the man who had dared to go to battle for her. She had never imagined such a man as Aidan existed, so brave, so intelligent. He made her laugh, he made her think... and he was wonderful in bed. And he was her champion, her knight. He couldn't be taken from her now.

But here he sat, his head propped on his good arm as he watched her. She wanted to weep with sheer joy, to fall down on her knees beside his bed and hold his hand in hers and feel the living, breathing heat of him. She wanted...

She wanted to tell him the truth, now that he was awake to hear her. That she loved him, had loved him ever since that dark, intense night at the hunting lodge. No one had ever seen her, really seen her, as he did. He understood her because they were alike, deep down in their most hidden souls. And that bound them together.

She wanted to tell him all of that. Everything she had pushed down and concealed so tightly for so long was straining to burst free. She wanted to be free at last, and she knew that only Aidan could give her that.

Yet something held her back. He was so very quiet, so watchful as he studied her with those summer-blue eyes she loved so much. She couldn't read his thoughts there; he was always damnably good at that stillness that seemed to shut out everything else. Perhaps he was trying to decipher how best to tell her good-bye.

The silence stretched out, enveloping the whole room. At last, Lily couldn't stand it any longer. She whirled around and marched over to sit down on the edge of his bed again. If he was going to say good-bye, then she would let him get it over with.

Then she could creep away and nurse her broken heart.

"You gave us all quite a fright," she said. "I know you are no stranger to brawls, Aidan, but that was quite beyond the pale."

He reached out his hand and just touched the edge of her skirt with his fingertips. His knuckles were scraped and bruised. "What if I promised to be very, very careful from now on?"

"I hope that you will. I don't think I could bear..." Her voice broke, and she squeezed her eyes shut to try and compose herself. But when she took a deep breath, all she could smell was Aidan, his spicy soap, the sweet darkness of him. "I thought you were dead, and I couldn't go on."

Suddenly she felt his warm hand seize hers, and he pressed her palm to his lips. Lily's eyes flew open to see that his own eyes were closed as he kissed her. He inhaled at the pulse point of her wrist. She laid her other hand behind his head, threading her fingers through the rough silk of his hair as she cradled him against her. *So precious.*

"Marry me," he said urgently.

"What did you say?" she gasped. Whatever she had imagined or hoped Aidan might say to her when he woke up, that was beyond her hopes.

"I said—no, I am begging you—please marry me. I don't ever want to be without you, and I know that the only way to keep you from running away from me is to make you my wife." He held her hand against his cheek, his eyes piercing into her as he looked up at her.

Lily could only stare at him in shock. "I…you can't marry me. What if you have to be the duke someday?"

"Lily. I know that everything that's happened in our time together hasn't exactly shown you that I could be a good husband. I've dragged you through barrooms and brothels. I've gotten us both wounded. Your family hates me…"

"You saved me!" Lily cried. "You killed Tom, you saved me and Isabel too. We never have to fear him again because of you. Surely even two blockheads like Dominic and Brendan can see that."

"But why would they want me for a brother-in-law? A Huntington, a lazy aristocrat?"

She shook her head and curled her fingers around his hand as if by holding him she could make him see all that he was to her. "Aidan, you are so, so much more than all of that. You are so intelligent and creative. You are the best friend anyone could have, as I'm sure Nick and Freddy and Marie and dozens of others would agree. You understand things other people can't, and you are strong and…"

"And a god in bed?" he said teasingly.

She gave a choked laugh. "Well…you are that, too, though I hesitate to feed your monstrous ego even further. And you are rich and have a title on top of everything else. You are a worthy husband to any woman. To Lady Henrietta Lindley, as your parents wish for you. You shouldn't propose to me."

"Lily St. Claire, you are the only woman I would propose to," Aidan said fiercely. "You're the only woman for me in the world, and you would make an excellent duchess. I love you. And if you say no, I warn you I will not go away. I will haunt the theater. I will send flowers to your house every hour. I will write you terrible poetry. Freddy's letters will be nothing compared to mine. I will not stop until—"

Lily suddenly leaned forward and kissed him, stopping his words with her lips. He tasted of wine and medicine, and of his own delicious self that had intoxicated her since their first kiss behind the theater so long ago. She knew now that it had been him ever since then. With him, she was truly free.

His arm closed around her waist and he fell onto his back, carrying her with him. He twisted his hand into her hair and held her still as his tongue tangled with hers, and they kissed as if it were the first time all over again.

Lily drew back at last and rested her cheek on his chest, the smooth, warm skin bare between the lacing of his nightshirt. She could hear the steady, reassuring rhythm of his heartbeat. "I can see I'll have to marry you, then, if only to keep you from becoming a public nuisance. And because I love you, too, of course."

She felt him raise his head to look down at her, his hand going still in her hair. "Do you really mean that, Lily?"

"Yes. Yes, Aidan, I love you, and I will marry you. I've never known anyone like you in all my life. If you are mad enough to propose to me, then I am mad enough to say yes."

"Lily, Lily my darling, I promise you won't be sorry," Aidan said, kissing the top of her head. "I will spend the rest of my life making you happy."

"You make me happy just by being here." She turned

her head to kiss the pulse that beat so steadily and reassuringly at the base of his throat. "Just by being you."

"Then we should have a very easygoing marriage."

"Unlike our courtship?"

He chuckled against her hair. "When will you marry me? Next week? I can get a special license."

"Not until the doctor says you can get out of bed." Lily propped her chin on his chest and smiled up at him. "I want you to be quite hale and hearty for the wedding night."

He tilted his head to one side and gave a roguish grin that made her heart beat faster. "Will you get out your riding crop again?"

"If you ask me nicely."

"Oh, I can ask very nicely indeed." He slid down on the pillows and kissed her neck lightly, making her giggle. "Very, very nicely."

"Not until your wound is healed."

"You are no fun today, Lily," Aidan groaned. He fell back to the bed as she scrambled to sit up beside him. "But soon enough you will be Lady Aidan Huntington, and we will have fun all night long."

"Lady Aidan?" she said. "That sounds so strange."

"Then we'll go to France, and you can be Madame Huntington. Or Italy, and be Signora Huntington. Wherever you want, whoever you want to be."

"I have always wanted to see Italy." Lily sat up against the carved headboard, her hands folded in her lap. "But what will your parents think of it all?"

Aidan gave an impolite snort. "I don't give a damn what they think. But I do care what your family thinks. I will call on them tomorrow."

Lily sighed as she imagined what might happen when

Aidan Huntington faced the whole St. Claire clan. "Are you sure you want to do that? Dominic has begun to come around, but Brendan and my father..."

"They are your family, Lily. You love them, and therefore I want them to love me. Or at least tolerate me and not skewer me in the street like Romeo did to Tybalt," he said stubbornly. "I will call on them properly."

"Then I think that will be the first proper thing you ever did in your life."

"You like me as improper as possible, Lady Aidan, admit it."

Lily laughed. "I do quite like it when you're naughty, Lord Aidan. But not in my family's drawing room. The St. Claires might be one of the most scandalous families in London, but they do have their limits. And you can call on them when the doctor says you can get up and not before."

"If you insist." Aidan's hand crept to the hem of her skirt and slowly drew it up until he could softly caress her stockinged ankle. "But if I must stay in bed, I'll need a diversion."

Lily shivered at the sensation of his hand sliding over her thin stocking. Oh, how she had missed this! How she had longed for his touch when they were apart. But now it would be hers—*he* would be hers—every night for the rest of her life. She thought her heart might burst with too much happiness.

She gasped as his fingertips traced over that sensitive spot just behind her knee, but she pushed his hand away and shook her skirts back into place. "Not until the wedding night."

Aidan groaned. "You are a cruel, cruel woman."

"I know." Lily leaned over him and smiled as she gently kissed his lips. "But you like it."

Epilogue

"You are quite sure this is what you want? A Huntington?" Lily heard Dominic say.

She turned to smile at him amid the chaos backstage at the Majestic. It was the second opening night of *Much Ado About Nothing*, and the sensation of the notorious criminal Tom Beaumont being killed at the theater meant they were even more crowded than usual. Every seat was sold out, and excitement buzzed through the boxes and stalls as everyone waited for the curtain to rise.

And she felt so much excitement of her own that she could hardly stand still. Tomorrow was her wedding day.

"Of course it's what I want," she said.

Dominic nodded and leaned his hand on the scenery flat behind them as he studied her. He wore his black velvet costume, his blond hair brushed back severely from his face. He looked suitably villainous to be Don John, but he finally smiled. It had taken some time, but after seeing what Aidan did to save Lily and Isabel, he had come around somewhat.

But only to Aidan. The rest of the Huntington family were still an object of deepest hatred.

Lily smoothed the braid-trimmed collar of his doublet. "He makes me happier than I ever thought it was possible to be. I'm so lucky to have him."

"Not half as lucky as he is to have you," Dominic said. "Father certainly made him work to win permission to marry you."

She laughed as she remembered. "I don't think sending Aidan to open a new theater was much of a punishment in the end. He can't wait to take on such a project." And she hoped to one day persuade him to produce his own plays there. But that was for the future.

"Even though the theater is in Edinburgh?"

"Scotland might be interesting. And it's not forever." Only until the Huntingtons came to accept their marriage. Lily didn't say that aloud, though. Dominic seemed to be in a good mood at last, and she didn't want to spoil it. "We won't go there until after the honeymoon in Italy anyway. Once I return, I expect you might be the next to hear wedding bells."

He gave a harsh laugh, and she saw something harden in his eyes. "Not me, sister dear. I'm not made for marriage."

"One day some extraordinary lady will come along, Dominic, and change your mind. I am quite sure of it," Lily said. "After all, it happened to me. And I never expected it at all."

"Five minutes, Mr. St. Claire!" the stage manager called.

Dominic nodded to him. "Lily, I think your wedding plans have addled your mind. You'll have to turn your new matchmaking urges onto Isabel and forget me."

"Isabel is young yet. And we shall see what happens

to you. Now go, you'll miss your cue." Lily gave him a quick kiss on his cheek and watched him hurry toward the wings where the other actors waited.

She could hear the orchestra launch into the prelude, muffled through the thick velvet curtains, and she tiptoed over to peek out at the audience. All the silks and jewels seemed to sparkle in the lights, excitement humming in the air. She smiled and glanced up at the box to the left where Aidan's mother sat. The duke was not there, of course. After a blazing row where he threw a vase at Aidan and tried to run him over with his wheeled chair, he hadn't been seen. But the duchess sat there in her brown velvet and diamonds, studying the gathering through her opera glasses, a silent, stalwart presence.

Next to her sat a woman Lily had never seen before, a petite lady in lilac silk and spangled net, her white-blond hair twisted atop her head. She nodded at something the duchess whispered in her ear, but otherwise she was as still and pale as a statue.

Lily heard a sound from the walkway above her head, and she nearly jumped. The fear and chaos of that terrible day had faded, pushed aside by happier days with Aidan and wedding plans, but sometimes nightmares still haunted her. She looked up to see Brendan leaning his palms on the railing, his black evening clothes and dark hair making him a part of the shadows. He stared at the duchess's box from his spot above, a hard glare in his eyes that seemed to be directed to the lady in lilac.

Then his stare shifted to Lily, and he nodded but didn't smile. Dominic and their parents had come to accept the marriage, but Brendan had not. From the way he looked at the duchess's companion, the raw fury and pain that had flickered over his face for the merest instant, she feared it would be a long time until he did.

Brendan turned and disappeared into the scenery. Lily studied the audience again and waved to Isabel as her sister took her place onstage. Isabel looked beautiful in her Hero costume, her face radiant in her happiness to be onstage again. She had left that day behind as well, throwing herself into the play and into helping Lily choose wedding clothes. But Isabel seemed older now somehow, not as girlish or exuberant as before.

An arm suddenly slid around Lily's waist and drew her farther back into the wings. For an instant, she grew tense, ready to fight, but then she smelled Aidan's wonderfully familiar scent of spicy soap and warm skin, fine wool, and starched linen, and she laughed.

"Having a good evening?" he asked as he spun her around in his arms.

"Better now," she said. She went up on her toes in her satin slippers to tangle her fingers in the soft hair at his nape. She pressed her lips to his and breathed in the scent and heat of him, marveling again that he was hers. That tomorrow he would be her husband. "What have you been doing?"

"I got my mother settled in her box with my cousin Elizabeth, and then I helped your father with a last-minute scenery adjustment," he answered. "But I have to agree—the night just got much, much better."

He bent his head to kiss her neck, his lips sliding lightly over her skin until she shivered. "Come to the dressing room with me now. No one is there."

Lily shook her head, even as she wanted nothing more than to drag him into an empty room and tear his clothes off. "Not until tomorrow night. Then it will all be proper."

Aidan groaned and bit gently at the curve of her shoulder above her satin sleeve. "You are killing me. I don't love you for your properness, you know."

"Oh, I know. You love me for my riding crop." Lily pressed a soft kiss to the corner of his mouth and smiled at him. "And because I can't do without you."

"You'll never have to. We're going to be together from now on. Life will always be one big adventure for us, Lily, I promise. Adventure and unending naughty nights."

One big adventure. Once, all Lily had wanted was quiet, stable respectability. Now adventure sounded exactly right, but only with Aidan. Always with Aidan.

"I love you, Lily," he said as the curtain soared up and the footlights flared.

And Lily had never heard sweeter words in all her life. "And I love you, Aidan. Forever."

Historical Note

Thank you so much for reading *One Naughty Night*, the first adventure of the St. Claire family. I loved spending time with these characters and learning more about their world. Ever since I was about ten years old and read *Jane Eyre*, I have loved the Victorian era, so it was fascinating to dig deeper.

The sixty years of Victoria's reign marked a huge shift in society and the way the world worked. The way people traveled, shopped, dealt with illness and childbirth—even the way people dressed and read—were very different from what had come before. Life was transformed for everyone by gaslight and then electricity, the railroads, factories, the world of the arts (literature from authors such as Dickens, Thackeray, and the Brontë sisters; the theater boom led by Irving and Terry; as well as music, painting, and the decorative arts), and exploration and the expansion of the British Empire into every corner of the globe.

But it was also a time of vast social differences, the rise of the middle classes, a new emphasis on the appearance of "respectability," and a whole hidden underworld of dark activities. I loved incorporating all these aspects of Victorian life into *One Naughty Night* and can't wait to see what happens next for the St. Claires and the Huntingtons. (Watch for Dominic and Sophia's story in *Two Sinful Secrets . . .*)

If you're interested in learning more about the Victorian era, I have historical information and background tidbits on my website, http://laurelmckee.net. Here are a few sources I especially enjoyed:

Donald Thomas, *The Victorian Underworld* (1998)
Jennifer Hall-Witt, *Fashionable Acts: Opera and Elite Culture in London 1780–1880* (2007)
Michael Mason, *The Making of Victorian Sexuality* (1994)
Suzanne Fagence Cooper, *The Victorian Woman* (2001)
Richard D. Altick, *Victorian People and Ideas* (1973)
J. J. Tobias, *Crime and Police in England, 1700–1900* (1979)
Sally Mitchell, *Daily Life in Victorian England* (2009)
F. M. L. Thompson, *The Rise of Respectable Society 1830–1900* (1988)

Enjoy a tantalizing peek at the next seductive St. Claire romance!

Please turn this page
for a preview of

Two Sinful Secrets

Chapter One

Baden-Baden, 1848

When in doubt, Sophia Huntington Westman believed, give them a glimpse of stocking. That usually did the trick.

Especially when one is dealt an unfortunate hand of cards.

Sophia carefully studied the array of cards in her hand, but the colors didn't change. She sighed and tried to keep her face calm and expressionless. She *needed* to win this game. Her stash of funds was growing astonishingly low, and she would be thrown out of her hotel if she couldn't pay soon. But luck had utterly deserted her tonight.

Not for the first time, she cursed the memory of her husband, the poor, late, not much lamented Captain Jack Westman. He had been so very handsome, so exciting, so sure Sophia was meant to be with him. That charming confidence had been what convinced her to elope with him, despite her family's dire threats to cut her off without a penny if she married someone so unsuitable for a duke's niece.

But Jack's confidence turned out to come from the bottom of a brandy bottle. And when the drink killed him, sending him stumbling drunkenly in front of a milk wagon not far from where Sophia was taking the Baden-Baden waters, she was left here a penniless widow trying to make enough money to get home.

Though what she would do once she got back to England, Sophia had no idea.

She peeked over the top of her cards at the man who sat across from her. Lord Hammond had been her opponent in card games before. He always seemed to be in the casino when she arrived, and he always kissed her hand gallantly, fetched her wine, inquired after her health. So very solicitous. Yet she had hoped for an easier mark tonight of all nights. Tonight, when she needed to win so badly. Lord Hammond was too shrewd a player.

But when he had taken her arm and invited her to a game of all fours, she somehow couldn't say no. Lord Hammond, despite his fine English-gentleman manners, was obviously a man who expected to get what he wanted. That had been clear to Sophia the first time she met him here at the casino, for she had encountered his type many times in her travels with Jack. Rich, powerful lords, much like her uncle the Duke of Carston, who had every whim indulged with a snap of their fingers.

But a card game was *all* he would get from Sophia. She hoped never to be so desperate that she had to give him anything else.

He was studying his own cards, a cool smile on his lips. He *was* handsome; she would say that for him. Older than her own twenty-three years by two decades, he was tall and well built in his expensively cut clothes.

His dark hair, gray at the temples, was cut short to frame his austere face and fathomless dark eyes. Women flocked around him, as he was that singular rarity—a handsome, rich lord. And he did seem to admire Sophia.

If she was really smart, Sophia thought as she looked at him, she would take advantage of that admiration. She would cultivate it and encourage it. Lord Hammond could make the financial worries that had plagued her for so long vanish.

But she had never claimed to be especially smart. If she was, she wouldn't have married Jack. And there was something in Lord Hammond's eyes when he looked at her that she did not like. Some icy gleam of speculation that sent a shiver down her spine. She wanted to finish the game and be done with this wearisome night.

But first she had to win his money.

He raised his eyes from his cards and his smile widened as he looked at her. He was as good a card player as she was; she could read nothing about his hand on his face. Sophia remembered her thought about a glimpse of stocking and returned his smile with a bright one of her own.

She turned slightly on her gilded chair, and her black satin skirts rustled as she moved. She glanced around the casino as she moved. Everything in the casino was gilded or painted with lavish classical scenes, the floors covered in Aubusson carpets and the walls papered in patterned silks. The colors were rich and elegant, the perfect backdrop for the fashionably dressed and bejeweled patrons who strolled between the tables and gathered around the roulette wheel. Despite her woes, Sophia liked coming to that place—its opulence made her feel calmer, more sure that everything would work out in the end. That nothing could go completely wrong in such a beautiful place.

Only one other establishment had ever been so lovely, and that was the Devil's Fancy club in London. But she had not seen it in years, not since before she met Jack. Before she lost everything, when she was a spoiled, naive girl who thought there could be no consequences for sneaking out of her parents' house to go and gamble.

The thought of the Devil's Fancy made her freeze in her chair. She closed her eyes for an instant and it was like she was there again. That long-ago night was so vivid in her memory. *He* was vivid in her memory. Dominic St. Claire.

She remembered his eyes, so intensely green as he looked at her across the card table. They would crinkle at the corners when he laughed or grow dark when he touched her with those elegant, long-fingered hands. He had made her feel as if she were the only woman in the room, the only woman in the whole world, when he focused his intent on her.

And when he kissed her...

Sophia shivered when she remembered the way his lips felt on hers. She had never wanted a man before, never felt herself turn hot and melt under a touch, as if the whole world had vanished except for him. Not even with poor Jack, who she had thought she loved.

But Dominic had too many women, and they all came so easily to him. Surely he made them all feel as he had her that night. He was like a dream to her now. A precious, lost dream she took out like a glittering little gem when life seemed too lonely and cold. It reminded her of the girl she had once been. And it reminded her of how life *could* be, in another realm, another time.

But now was not the time for such memories. Now was the time for cold, hard reality. She couldn't afford to be distracted, not when faced with a man like Lord Hammond. She had to win tonight. Whatever it took.

Sophia opened her eyes and smiled at Lord Hammond. His own smile hardened, a flicker of some cold light flashing through his dark gaze. Sophia casually crossed her legs beneath her heavy skirts and let the ruffled hem fall back to reveal her black satin heel and show a bit of white silk stocking. She swung her foot a bit as she studied the cards in her hand.

Lord Hammond's attention went right where she hoped it would, to her slim ankle, and in the mirror behind him she had a quick glimpse of his cards in his careless moment. Not so good as she had feared. She could still save this evening and come out ahead.

Her glance flickered over her own reflection. Her skin looked very pale against the stark black of her gown and the sleek, glossy coils of her black hair. She had no jewels left to soften her austere attire and make her fit in with the rich crowd. There was only the narrow black ribbon around her throat and a guilty pink blush on her cheeks.

Huntingtons never cheat! She remembered her father shouting that when her brother was caught once in a con artist's scheme and lost a great deal of money. Huntingtons were an ancient ducal family, not cheaters. Not elopers. Yet here she was, driven to be both in her desperation.

I am doing what I must to survive, she told herself sternly. She had no room for honor or sentiment now, not if she didn't want to starve. Cards were the only thing she was good at. It was either gamble or whore for the likes of Lord Hammond. And she was not that desperate—yet.

Sophia turned away from her reflection and from the memory of Dominic St. Claire's green eyes. She gently fanned herself with her cards and laughed. "My goodness, but it is warm in here tonight," she said. "I swear Baden-Baden grows more crowded by the day."

Lord Hammond's gaze slid from her ankle up over her décolletage in the low-cut gown, and his smile widened. Sophia knew that look in his eyes. It was the look of a man who believed his goal was clearly in sight now. But she had a goal too. She would win his money without surrendering more than the merest glimpse of her person. They couldn't both win.

"Perhaps we should go for a stroll in the gardens," Lord Hammond said smoothly. "It is much cooler, and quieter, there. I have been wanting the chance for private conversation with you, Mrs. Westman."

"How very flattering of you, Lord Hammond," Sophia answered. Over his shoulder, she saw a lady entering the casino, a tall, stunning redhead clad in dove-gray silk with a truly stupendous collar of diamonds around her throat. It was Lady Gifford, who was rumored to be Lord Hammond's latest mistress. She gave him a stricken, wide-eyed look before she whirled away and vanished into the crowd.

Sophia looked back down at her cards. "There are so many who wish to...converse with you, Lord Hammond," she murmured.

"Ah, but I can see only you, Mrs. Westman," he answered. "You look particularly lovely tonight. I am sure the gardens would be the perfect setting for your rare beauty."

"How sweet of you to say so," Sophia said with a smile. "But we should finish our game first, yes? It would be a shame to let the cards go to waste."

His gaze traced over her bodice again, slowly and with a clear intent. Sophia had to fight to keep her smile in place. "Of course, my dear Mrs. Westman. We certainly must finish the game."

As Lord Hammond ordered more champagne, Sophia requested two more cards and improved her hand. But beating her opponent was not quite as easy as she had hoped.

An hour had passed with neither of them pulling ahead enough to win when Lord Hammond's smile abruptly vanished. He folded his cards between his fingers and said with an exasperated note in his voice, "The night is wasting, Mrs. Westman."

Sophia peeked at him over her cards. "Is it indeed, Lord Hammond? It seems rather early to me." She really agreed with him, but not for the same reasons she was sure he had. She was tired and wanted to find her bed—alone.

If she went back to the hotel with enough money to pay for that bed, of course.

"It is too crowded here," Lord Hammond said. "So I propose we make this simple. We each draw a card, and high draw wins."

Intriguing. Sophia did like a high-stakes game—usually. "And what are the stakes?"

"I will wager a thousand pounds," he said easily, as if that vast amount was mere pocket change. For him it probably was.

But it made Sophia catch her breath. *A thousand pounds.* Enough to get her home to England and help her set up a new life, a new business. One where she wouldn't have to whore, or marry, again, or crawl back to her family and beg for forgiveness. One where she could be independent. All on the draw of one card.

But…

"I cannot wager such a sum in return," she said cautiously.

"I would not expect you to, my dear Mrs. Westman," Lord Hammond said with a smile Sophia did not like at all. "All I ask is that you walk with me in the garden, and perhaps accompany me to my suite. I have some paintings I recently acquired that might interest you."

Paintings her foot. Sophia took his meaning quite clearly, for he was not the first to propose such an arrangement. She let her skirts drop, concealing her shoes, and put on her sternest, most governessish expression. "Lord Hammond, how very shocking you are."

He laughed as he shuffled the cards. The gold signet ring on his finger gleamed. "And I fear missishness does not suit you, Mrs. Westman. I would never have thought you a lady to break down from a dare."

He was too right about that, Sophia thought wryly. She had always been too ready to run headlong into a dare. Anything her family didn't want her to do she had always wanted to do all the more. It was what had led her here. She should probably get up and march out of the casino—straight into homelessness. And it looked as if it might rain later.

Despite herself, she was very tempted by the wager Lord Hammond offered. With one turn of a card, her troubles would be over—or at least postponed. Or she could be in even more trouble than before. She shivered to think of Lord Hammond's hands on her, of those cold eyes looking at her naked body.

But there were no other promising games in the casino tonight, no other prospects. And she was down to her last farthing. That gnawing feeling of desperation deep inside had become all too familiar. It was time to leap before she looked.

"Very well, Lord Hammond," she said. She struggled to smile and keep her voice steady. "I accept your wager."

"Splendid, Mrs. Westman. You are ever intriguing. I knew you would not fail me." Lord Hammond raised his hand in an imperious gesture and a footman hurried over with a sealed pack of cards. As Sophia watched, Lord Hammond broke the seal and shuffled the cards. He laid the neat stack before her. "Ladies draw first."

Sophia stared down at the cards. They looked so innocent, mere printed pasteboard. She handled such things every night. Somehow she felt as if they would come to life and bite her when she touched them. She had truly fallen low.

She took a deep breath to steady herself and reached for the top card. Shockingly, her hand did not shake. She flipped over the card, her stomach in knots.

Queen of diamonds. Not bad. But it could be beat.

Lord Hammond nodded and reached for the next card. Sophia held her breath. It seemed as if time itself slowed down as he flipped it over. All the noise around her, the laughter, the chatter, the clatter of the roulette wheel, faded in her ears. She swallowed hard and looked down.

The six of clubs. She had won. She was a thousand pounds richer. A shocked laugh escaped her lips.

"Well," Lord Hammond said, "it appears luck favors you tonight, Mrs. Westman." His voice was low and tight and filled with a barely leashed raw fury. She had never heard such a tone from the suave, cool man before.

She glanced up to find him staring at her with burning dark eyes. A dull red flush spread over his face and his hand clenched in a fist on the table. Another shiver slid down her spine, banishing the rush of victorious relief. Lord Hammond was not a man used to being thwarted.

"It would appear so," she answered slowly.

Lord Hammond nodded and waved the footman forward again. He spoke a curt word in the liveried man's ear and sent him scurrying away. "I have sent for the key to my safe. You will understand, Mrs. Westman, that I do not carry such a sum on me."

"Of course not," Sophia murmured, still half stunned by what had happened.

"Will you have a glass of wine with me while we wait? I would consider it more than compensation for my sad loss."

Sophia did *not* want to have a drink with him, or sit here any longer than she had to. His smile had become too congenial, too charming, and those shivers along her spine had become even colder. She had the urge to leap to her feet and run from the casino. But she did have to wait for her money.

She swept a glance around the lavish room. It seemed even more crowded, and the laughter was even louder thanks to the freely flowing champagne. She surely couldn't get into too much trouble there.

"Thank you," she said. "A glass of champagne would be delightful."

Lord Hammond rose smoothly from the table and offered her his arm. Sophia had grown accustomed to acting in the last few years; the life of a gambler, traveling from one spa town to another, demanded constant deception. Yet it took everything she had to stand and slide her hand onto Lord Hammond's sleeve. She shook out her heavy skirts and gave him a smile as he led her from the main salon into the bar area.

It was no less crowded there. A throng of people, like a merry, fluttering horde of brightly clad butterflies, gathered around the gleaming white marble bar. The gold-framed mirrors on the wall reflected them back in an endless sparkling vista. The barmaids scurried to serve them all.

Lord Hammond was immediately given glasses of the finest pale golden champagne. He handed one to Sophia and held up his own in salute.

"To your great good fortune, Mrs. Westman," he said. "What shall you do now?"

Sophia shrugged and sipped at her wine. "Try another town, I suppose. This one does not suit me so well as I had hoped."

"The sad memories of Captain Westman's demise, I would imagine," he said, all smooth, polite conversation. "But this place will be dull without you."

"Dull?" Sophia laughed, and gestured with her glass at the crowded room. "I shall not be missed one jot."

"I will miss you very much." He studied her closely over the edge of his glass until she had to glance away. "I do wish you would reconsider my offer, Mrs. Westman. I could certainly give you far more than a thousand pounds."

Sophia fidgeted with her glass and studied the array of bottles behind the bar. Where on earth was that blasted safe key? She wanted to be far away from here as quickly as possible. "Your offer of a walk in the garden, Lord Hammond?" she said, trying to feign wide-eyed innocence.

"Oh, come, Mrs. Westman. I have made no secret of my admiration for you," he said, a note of impatience in his voice. "I am a wealthy man. I could give you whatever you wanted."

Sophia wondered what Lady Hammond, rumored to be an invalid back in England, thought of that. But the poor woman was probably quite used to it all. Sophia never wanted something like that for herself. She only wanted to be her own woman at long last. Free to make her own way, to see the world on her own terms...

And perhaps find another man who made her feel like Dominic St. Claire once had. A man who, unlike Dominic, would think her the only woman he wanted.

"You are so kind to flatter me like that, Lord Hammond," she answered carefully. "But I am so recently widowed. I need time to mourn properly. I couldn't possibly think of a man other than Captain Westman just yet."

His eyes narrowed. "Quite understandable, my dear. But I hope when you are ready to cast off your widow's weeds that you will think of me." Suddenly he reached out to lightly stroke a fingertip over the ribbon at her throat.

Sophia flinched and fell back a step before she could stop herself. Lord Hammond gave a humorless laugh.

"You deserve to wear diamonds and pearls," he said. "I could give you that. Just remember, my dear, one day you are going to need me even more than you do now, and I will always be waiting."

Sophia desperately hoped not. She turned to set her glass down on the bar, and to her relief she saw the footman returning at last with the safe key. Lord Hammond brushed away the man's apologies for the delay and took Sophia's elbow in his hand to lead her out of the bar.

"Come, Mrs. Westman, let us collect your winnings," Lord Hammond said as they made their way through the soaring domed foyer and down the marble steps to the lower level where the wealthier patrons kept their guarded safes. Lord Hammond was now all brisk efficiency, leading her along without another word or untoward touch, but Sophia couldn't shake away that urge to run. Especially as the noise of the casino faded behind them and there was only the whooshing echo of their footsteps on the cold stone floor.

He led her past the guards and along the row of iron safes until he found the one he sought. He turned the key in the lock and swung open the heavy door. Sophia glimpsed bags of coins, stacks of bank notes, and black velvet jewel cases. It was a veritable Aladdin's cave of riches, but she had only a glimpse before he hastily removed one of the stacks of notes, put them into a bag, and pressed it into her hands.

"There you are, Mrs. Westman, your fair winnings," he said. "Feel free to count it."

Sophia shook her head and held on to the bag tightly. It felt like such a slight thing in her hands, yet it was her salvation. "I trust you, Lord Hammond." As far as she could throw him. But yet she doubted he would cheat on a gambling debt, even one to a woman.

"Just remember my offer, my dear. I will be waiting." He reached for her free hand and raised it to his lips for a lingering kiss.

Sophia could bear his touch no longer. She snatched back her hand and spun around on her heel to hurry out of the casino. She pushed past the people in the foyer and rushed out of the doors and into the gardens to the public walkway. She didn't stop until she was in her hotel room with the door locked behind her.

She dropped the bag onto the end of her narrow bed and fell down onto the pillows with a sigh as her gown billowed around her like a black cloud. Only one more night here in this cursed place, and then she could catch the morning train for home. One more night with the likes of Lord Hammond just beyond the door, waiting to snatch her up when she stumbled. One more night not knowing where her next meal was coming from.

She was free. Almost.

Sophia rolled over and reached beneath her pillow to draw out a book. It was quite old, bound in cracked brown leather with the pages yellowing at the edges. But that book had been one of her best companions since she left home with Jack all those long months ago. Every night she read a precious entry before she went to sleep and she didn't feel so very alone.

She opened it where she had left off, carefully turning the brittle pages closely written in faded brown ink in a careful hand. But first she smoothed her fingertip over the inscription on the first page.

Mary Huntington, Her Book, Gifted in the Year 1665.

Mary Huntington, the first Duchess of Carston, and a woman completely unknown in Sophia's family. Unlike every other ancestor on the family tree, there were no portraits of her on the walls, no heirloom jewels that had once belonged to her. Sophia had never heard of her until she found this dusty book on a neglected shelf in her grandfather's library one boring, rainy Christmas. When she began to read, it was as if Mary had come back to life and began to speak to her. As if Mary were a long-lost friend, a woman just as impulsive and wild-hearted as Sophia was.

A long-lost friend with a sad tale to tell. Mary was terribly in love with her handsome husband but was miserably unhappy. He left her at their country house when he went off to Charles II's merry court, and Mary wrote of her loneliness and longing, all the storms of her emotions and the ways she kept herself busy in the country. Sophia felt as if Mary were reaching out to her over the decades. She took the diary with her wherever she went, and somehow she never felt alone.

She never wanted to be like Mary, with her whole life, all her emotions and everything she was, wrapped up in a man. Sophia had fallen prey to such fairy-tale dreams before, and she couldn't do it ever again.

Sophia traced a gentle touch over the worn leather cover. "Everything will be fine now, Mary," she whispered. "I can go home and start again. Things will be better in England."

If only she could make herself believe that. England had seemed such a distant dream ever since she made the romantic, foolish, impulsive decision to run off with Jack. Her sheltered, pampered life there hadn't seemed real. But the England she was going to now, and the life she would make for herself, would be very different.

Sophia slid the diary back under her pillow and sat up to reach for the bag of bank notes. They were all there, a thousand pounds worth. She fanned them out and looked down at them as she tried to make herself believe they were real.

The bag fell to the bed and Sophia heard a rustling noise from inside. Curious, and half hopeful there was yet more money inside, she reached for it and peered into its depths. It wasn't bank notes but a sheaf of documents sealed with official-looking red wax.

As she started to take it from the bag to examine it closer, there was a sudden noise at her door. Startled, Sophia dropped the bag and sat up straight, every fiber of her body tense and alert. The doorknob rattled as someone tried to turn it. When it held, there was a scraping noise against the old wood, as if that person attempted to pick the lock.

Hardly daring to breathe, Sophia slid off the bed and tiptoed to the door. She held her skirts tight against her to still their rustling with one hand and reached for a straight-backed chair with the other. She wedged it under the knob and stood back to listen, holding her breath.

"Hier!" she heard the hotel's stern owner cry, muffled through the door. "I don't allow people who are not paying guests to wander the hallways at all hours. This is a respectable establishment. Who are you, anyway? What do you want with Frau Westman?"

"A thousand apologies," a man said, his voice deep and echoing, indistinguishable through the door. "I was merely returning something Frau Westman left at the casino."

"Then you can leave it with me. She already owes me enough for her stay..."

Sophia listened as the stranger was bustled away from her door and their voices faded. She turned and hurried to the window to watch from the shadows as the hotel's front door opened. A tall figure clad in an elegant evening cape emerged, and Sophia felt that panic clutch at her deep inside again. It was Lord Hammond.

She had to get out of there. Quickly.

Sophia slid back from the window and pulled the valise out from under the bed. She could pack her meager belongings in fifteen minutes and be on the first train out before it was light. It was past time for her to go home.

THE DISH

Where authors give you the inside scoop!

♥ ♥ ♥ ♥ ♥ ♥ ♥ ♥ ♥ ♥ ♥ ♥ ♥ ♥ ♥

From the desk of Paula Quinn

Dear Reader,

I'm so excited to tell you about my latest in the Children of the Mist series, CONQUERED BY A HIGHLANDER. I loved introducing you to Colin MacGregor in *Ravished by a Highlander* and then meeting up with him again in *Tamed by a Highlander*, but finally the youngest, battle-hungry MacGregor gets his own story. And let me tell you all, I enjoyed every page, every word.

Colin wasn't a difficult hero to write. There were no mysteries complicating his character, no ghosts or regrets haunting him from his past. He was born with a passion to fight and to conquer. Nothing more. Nothing less. He was easy to write. He was a badass in *Ravished* and he's a hardass now. My dilemma was what kind of woman would it take to win him? The painted birds fluttering about the many courts he's visited barely held his attention. A warrior wouldn't suit him any better than a wallflower would. I knew early on that the Lady who tried to take hold of this soldier's heart had to possess the innate strength to face her fiercest foe...and the tenderness to recognize something more than a fighter in Colin's confident gaze.

I found Gillian Dearly hidden away in the turrets of a castle overlooking the sea, her fingers busy strumming melodies on her beloved lute while her thoughts carried her to places far beyond her prison walls. She wasn't waiting for a hero, deciding years ago that she would rescue herself. She was perfect for Colin. She also possessed one other thing, a weapon so powerful, even Colin found himself at the mercy of it.

A three-year-old little boy named Edmund.

Like Colin, I didn't intend for Edmund Dearly or his mother to change the path of my story, but they brought out something in the warrior—whom I thought I knew so well—something warm and wonderful and infinitely sexier than any swagger. They brought out the man.

For me, nothing I've written before this book exemplifies the essence of a true hero more than watching Colin fall in love with Gillian *and* with her child. Not many things are more valiant than a battle-hardened warrior who puts down his practice sword so he can take a kid fishing or save him from bedtime monsters... except maybe a mother who defiantly goes into battle each day in order to give her child a better life. Gillian Dearly was Edmund's hero and she quickly became mine. How could a man like Colin *not* fall in love with her?

Having to end the Children of the Mist series was bittersweet, but I'm thrilled to say there will be more MacGregors of Skye visiting the pages of future books. Camlochlin will live on for another generation at least. And not just in words but in art. Master painter James Lyman has immortalized the home of our beloved MacGregors in beautiful color and with an innate understanding of how the fortress should be represented. Visit PaulaQuinn.com to order a print of your own, signed and numbered by the artist.

Until we meet again, to you mothers and fathers, husbands and wives, sons and daughters, sisters and brothers, and friends, who put yourselves aside for someone you love, I shout Huzzah! Camlochlin was built for people like you.

Paula Quinn

Find her at Facebook

Twitter @Paula_Quinn

♥ ♥ ♥ ♥ ♥ ♥ ♥ ♥ ♥ ♥ ♥ ♥ ♥ ♥ ♥

From the desk of Jill Shalvis

Dear Reader,

From the very first moment I put Mysterious Cute Guy on the page, I fell in love. There's just something about a big, bad, sexy guy whom you know nothing about that fires the imagination. But I have to be honest: When he made a cameo in *Head Over Heels* (literally a walk-on role only; in fact I believe he only gets a mention or two), I knew nothing about him. Nothing. I never intended to, either. He was just one of life's little (okay, big, bad, and sexy) mysteries.

Then my editor called me. Said the first three Lucky Harbor books had done so well that they'd like three more, please. And maybe one of the heroes could be Mysterious Cute Guy.

It was fun coming up with a story to go with this enigmatic figure, not to mention a name: Ty Garrison. More fun still to give this ex-Navy SEAL a rough, tortured, bad-boy past and a sweet, giving, good-girl heroine

(Mallory Quinn, ER nurse). Oh, the fun I had with these two: a bad boy trying to go good, and a good girl looking for a walk on the wild side. Hope you have as much fun reading their story, LUCKY IN LOVE.

And then, stick around. Because Mallory's two Chocoholics-in-crime partners, Amy and Grace, get their own love stories in July and August with *At Last* and then *Forever and a Day*.

Happy Reading!

Jill Shalvis

http://www.jillshalvis.com

http://www.facebook.com/jillshalvis

♥ ♥ ♥ ♥ ♥ ♥ ♥ ♥ ♥ ♥ ♥ ♥ ♥ ♥ ♥

From the desk of Lori Wilde

Dear Reader,

Ah ,June! Love is in the air, and it's the time for weddings and romance. With KISS THE BRIDE, you get two romantic books in one, *There Goes the Bride* and *Once Smitten, Twice Shy*. Both stories are filled with brides, bouquets, and those devastatingly handsome grooms. But best friends Delaney and Tish go through a lot of ups and downs on their path to happily ever after.

For those of you hoping for a June wedding of your

own, how do you tell if your guy is ready for commitment? He might be ready to pop the question if...

- Instead of saying "I" when making future plans, he starts saying "we."
- He gives you his ATM pass code.
- He takes you on vacation with his family.
- Out of the blue, your best friend asks your ring size.
- He sells his sports car/motorcycle and says he's outgrown that juvenile phase of his life.
- He opens a gold card to get a higher spending limit—say, to pay for a honeymoon.
- When you get a wedding invitation in the mail, he doesn't groan but instead asks where the bride and groom got the invitations printed.
- He starts remembering to leave the toilet seat down.
- When poker night with the guys rolls around, he says he'd rather stay home and watch *The Wedding Planner* with you.
- He becomes your dad's best golfing buddy

I hope you enjoy KISS THE BRIDE.

Happy reading,

Lori Wilde

loriwilde.com

Facebook http://facebook.com/lori.wilde

Twitter @LoriWilde

♥ ♥ ♥ ♥ ♥ ♥ ♥ ♥ ♥ ♥ ♥ ♥ ♥ ♥ ♥

From the desk of Laurel McKee

Dear Reader,

When I was about eight years old, someone gave me a picture book called *Life in Victorian England*. I lost the book in a move years ago, but I still remember the gorgeous watercolor illustrations. Ladies in brightly colored hoopskirts and men in frock coats and top hats doing things like walking in the park, ice-skating at Christmas, and dancing in ballrooms. I was completely hooked on this magical world called "the Victorian Age" and couldn't get enough of it! I read stuff like *Jane Eyre, Little Women*, and *Bleak House*, watched every movie where there was the potential for bonnets, and drove my parents crazy by saying all the time, "Well, in the Victorian age it was like this..."

As I got older and started to study history in a more serious way, I found that beneath this pretty and proper facade was something far darker. Darker—and a lot more interesting. There was a flourishing underworld in Victorian England, all the more intense for being well hidden and suppressed. Prostitution, theft, and the drug trade expanded, and London was bursting at the seams thanks to changes brought about by the Industrial Revolution. The theater and the visual arts were taking on a new life. Even Queen Victoria was not exactly the prissy sourpuss everyone thinks she was. (She and Albert had nine children, after all—and enjoyed making them!)

I've always wanted to set a story in these Victorian

years, with the juxtaposition of what's seen on the surface and what is really going on underneath. But I never came up with just the right characters for this complex setting. The inspiration came (as it so often does for me, don't laugh) from clothes. I was watching my DVD of *Young Victoria* for about the fifth time, and when the coronation ball scene came on, I thought, "I really want a heroine who could wear a gown just like that..."

And Lily St. Claire popped into my head and brought along her whole family of Victorian underworld rakes. I had to run and get out my notebook to write down everything Lily had to tell me. I loved her from that first minute—a woman who created a glamorous life for herself from a childhood on the streets of the London slums. A tough, independent woman (with gorgeous clothes, of course) who thinks she doesn't need anyone—until she meets this absolutely yummy son a duke. Too bad his family is the St. Claire family's old enemy...

I hope you enjoy the adventures of Lily and Aidan as much as I have. It was so much fun to spend some time in Victorian London. Look for more St. Claire trouble to come.

In the meantime, visit my website at http://laurelmckee.net for more info on the characters and the history behind the book.

Laurel McKee

Find out more ab

V

www.hachettebookgrou

Find us

http://www.facebo

Follow

http://twitter.c

NEW AND U

Each month we

and rea

CONTESTS A

We give away galleys, autographed copies,
and all kinds of exclusive items.

AUTHOR INFO

You'll find bios, articles, and links to personal websites
for all your favorite authors—and so much more.

GET SOCIAL

Connect with your favorite authors, editors, and
other Forever fans, and share what's important to you.

THE BUZZ

Sign up for our monthly romance newsletter,
and be the first to read all about it.